TURNAROUND

IS THERE LIGHT AT THE END OF THE TUNNEL?

SANDIE TRAVELLER

authorHOUSE®

AuthorHouse™ UK
1663 Liberty Drive
Bloomington, IN 47403 USA
www.authorhouse.co.uk
Phone: 0800.197.4150

Published by AuthorHouse 11/11/2014

ISBN: 978-1-4969-9308-3 (sc)
ISBN: 978-1-4969-9307-6 (hc)
ISBN: 978-1-4969-9309-0 (e)

"To Paul and Sophie, and not forgetting Leo …
you light up my life"

"This above all; to thine own self be true"

William Shakespeare, *'Hamlet,' Act I, Scene iii*

AUTHOR'S NOTE

*The characters in this novel are purely fictional and are
not intended to portray any persons living or dead*

Preface

IN THE FINAL throes of a painful divorce, I was put forward by a well-meaning friend, to appear on a popular TV makeover show. The resultant changes to my dated look, and instant local 'stardom' once the programme was aired, meant I could no longer hide behind a mask of obscurity. I am forever grateful to the two formidable lady presenters for showing me how to embrace my single status with the confidence that stemmed from their whole new look for this 'Cinderella'. (I will never forget their hilarious reaction to my confession that my underwear was purchased, three for a pound, from a bargain shop!) They truly were Fairy Godmothers transforming this sartorial misfit into someone able to grace any ball. Whilst Prince Charming has sadly eluded me, it certainly got me thinking.... Can changing your look, change your life? I can truly say it did mine, for the better, but can the same be said for Lyndsey, the heroine of this story.................?

Sandie Traveller (aka *the 'Pound-Shop knicker' girl*), Author, September 2014

Acknowledgements

WITH SPECIAL THANKS to my sister Jan, fellow author, and invaluable help and for best friends Mieke and Claire, without whom this book would never have been written. Also for Simon who always believed in me, and for Trish, Kelly, Derek, Tina, Shirley, Jean, Loretta, Maureen, et al – the class of '06

"Can changing your look can your life.......?"

Prologue

'Lyndsey. Lyndsey Daly?'

It was a stranger's voice. One she did not recognize. Lyndsey looked up from the pile of books she was cataloguing. In the doorway to the library stood a tall woman, elegantly dressed in a trouser suit of tailored blue silk. Her hair, expertly blonded, hung in an unbroken curtain to her shoulders. The woman was not alone. Alongside her stood a fashion clone, garbed in a shift dress of the palest green linen, dark hair cut into a lustrous bob. She was shorter and infinitely more curvaceous than her sophisticated counterpart. Sexy, in an almost mannish way.

'Hello darling' said the clone.

Milling around the duo was an entourage, all, it seemed to Lyndsey, dressed in black. They were crowding around the front desk, barring the entrance with the sheer weight of their bodies. It was Friday morning and the library was quiet after the mid-week rush. The arrival of the strange women, with their cut glass accents, and band of followers, shattered the silence.

Lyndsey noticed that one of the throng was carrying a video camera, its lens pointed in her direction. The recording button blinked like the reddened eye of a Cyclops. Another held aloft a clipboard, with a pen poised meaningfully. The woman who had spoken first, moved forward to stand directly in front of the counter, acting for all the World like a member of the public waiting to get their library books issued. But there the similarity ended. How many members of the public would shove a microphone in her face, thought Lyndsey, side-stepping as the offending article was lunged forward like a fencer parrying a blow.

'You are Lyndsey Daly' It was not so much a question as a statement, delivered in the perfectly modulated voice of an aristocrat. Such a plummy accent was a rarity in this area, thought Lyndsey, wondering what the hell was going on. The microphone wavered inches from her mouth. Bewildered, she stood in mid action behind the counter, reference stamp raised in one hand, book held open in the other.

'Yes. I am'

The woman smiled at her, and Lyndsey thought it looked a conspiratorial smile, as if she was about to share some huge joke. Regarding her closely, Lyndsey realized, with a shock, that she looked familiar. In an effort to place where she had seen the woman before; where she might have known her from, Lyndsey screwed up her forehead as though it might concentrate her thoughts.

'Don't frown darling. You're on telly.' The regal voice whispered the words, then spoke more loudly, 'Have you seen Channel 7's 'Turnaround?'

Lyndsey found herself nodding dumbly.

'Congratulations. You're on the Programme.'

Chapter One

'IT WAS A pea' Lyndsey said, 'A pea broke us up'.

She knew her words sounded ridiculous, absurd even, but she let them hang in the air. She wasn't going to denounce or deny them. 'Tell the truth and shame the devil', her mother always said. Well this was one devil she was determined to shame. The devil that presided over the wasteland of her marriage.

'A pea', the solicitor's voice held a note of mild query. Lyndsey studied him across the desk, and saw that the stubby hand with bitten fingernails that only a moment ago had been rapidly making notes was now suspended in mid-air, the pen levelled like a dart. Lyndsey noticed things like fingernails. She wondered if the solicitor was any good at his job with fingernails like that. Surely it suggested someone wracked by insecurities, with a hefty dollop of low self-esteem thrown in for good measure. Not the type of person you wanted fighting your corner in a divorce court.

'I'd better explain', she said, relieved to see the pen once again make contact with the notepad, 'Ray was late home one night last week, and found a pea on the kitchen floor. I'd been defrosting the freezer...'

The sound of the pen resuming its tract along the page was a reassuring one, and Lyndsey briefly luxuriated in it. It made her feel pro-active, as though she was finally taking control of her life.

'He asked me what the pea was doing on the floor…and I said.' She was struck by the absurdity of what she was about to say, and a rogue bubble of laughter found its way up from her chest and threatened to burst forth. With difficulty she quelled it. The Partner of Messrs. Parsloes & Dean would doubtless view such an outburst with the cynicism of one who earned their living listening to depressing details of marital discord. Mr. Parsloe Senior was fat and sweaty. He mopped his brow with a grubby handkerchief, before prompting, 'so your husband pointed out something on the kitchen floor that perhaps he felt shouldn't have been there, and you said…?'

'I said, it's waiting for a bus.' There, the words were out, 'the pea I mean. I was being facetious. And then…'

It was stuffy in the cramped office. She guessed the radiator was set on high to keep out any semblance of October chill.

'And then?' His voice nudged.

Lyndsey knew the next part was going to be difficult. How to put into words Ray's interrogations that accompanied the most insignificant domestic trifle. Those interminable question and answer sessions where she began to feel she was in the dock and her husband was some particularly ferocious prosecuting Counsel.

'We talked until the early hours. About the pea. About why I was so slapdash around the kitchen. My sloppiness in general. Why, when he'd pointed it out on the floor, I hadn't immediately leapt to pick it up, y'know, dustpan in hand. It culminated in a debate about why I trivialised matters he finds important.'

'Marriage is about give and take. Could it be that you irritated your husband by not taking seriously his concerns.'

Lyndsey's wry smile barely masked the bitterness she felt, 'Oh, I irritated him all right. He always wants me to say sorry. To beg forgiveness for things I am supposed to have done that have upset him, offended him, disappointed him.'

Disappointment. That was the word that summed up their relationship, Lyndsey thought, beginning to fry inside her coat. She wanted to take it off but had lost the top button from the blouse underneath. Ray always made her feel that she had let him down. Fallen short on the wifely ideals that he clung to like a monkey on a wet tree.

Mr. Parsloe was busy writing. Without looking up from the pad, he said, 'The pea incident in itself does not seem reason enough to end a marriage that has lasted ...' he consulted his notes, 'fourteen years. I assume it was the final straw?'

'Or the final pea', said Lyndsey attempting a stab at humour. She could feel the onset of the familiar lethargy, which came from both dealing with Ray, and trying to explain his actions to others. No-body could understand the grinding day-to-day reality of living with someone who made an alpine range out of the humblest molehill. A husband whose mantra for life was *explain, justify, apologise.*

She let her eyes travel the room, taking in the filing cabinets, the shelves of legal journals, the window with its slatted blind. On the sill, a wilting spider plant was begging for water.

With an effort, she said, 'that was it exactly. The final straw.'

She realised with a shock that she wanted to sleep. To close her eyes and drift off in this cell like room with its droning clock, and pervading smell of dust.

'Did your husband lose his temper?'

'Ray's too self-controlled for that. We simply had the usual post mortem into the early hours.'

'Can you explain what you mean?'

This was going to be the difficult bit, thought Lyndsey. How did one describe the tortuous accusations that Ray continually levelled at her regarding the minutia of their domestic life? Only a fly living on the wall could describe it with any authority. You had to be there, live it, witness it, to understand it.

'He won't let a subject drop. Wrings every ounce out of an incident until it is dry, and then squeezes some more. I have to explain everything, and if he isn't satisfied with my explanation, I have to justify. If he doesn't accept my justification, I'm forced to make a grovelling apology.' Lyndsey dropped her head. It was beginning to ache.

Frantic flutterings at the window made her look up. A duo of crane flies, in the dance of death, was making a final desperate assault against the unyielding glass.

Daddy Long Legs...... Lyndsey hated them, these harbingers of dank mornings and chill twilights. She shuffled in her seat. It pivoted on a metallic frame, the coarse covering causing friction against her nylon clad knees. Glare from the unforgiving strip light burned the top of her head, and gave the solicitors balding pate a gloss.

The Partner put down the pen, and steepled sausage fingers.

'Mrs. Daly', he said, 'you are here to instigate divorce proceedings against your husband.' he checked the sheaf of papers, and Lyndsey thought 'he's forgotten Ray's name already, 'Raymond Daly, are you not?'

The ugly bitten nails, clearly on view, served only to stiffen Lyndsey's resolve that she was not about to be browbeaten by this man. She knew by his patronising tone what was coming next,

'So far you've provided no evidence that would stand up in a Divorce Court. Notwithstanding the fact that these are the days of 'no-fault' divorces, a District Judge would still need convincing that your relationship was beyond any hope of salvation.'

Lyndsey felt a trickle of sweat run down her back. Trying to inject a note of firmness in her voice, she said, 'I consider my husband's treatment of me to be unreasonable. Surely that's sufficient grounds.'

'I'll need at least one further example of what you consider to be unreasonable.' Came the dry response.

Her recall was immediate. 'There was the night of the fluorescent sheep.'

The pen came to an abrupt halt. She ignored the quizzical expression on the solicitor's greasy face, and said, Cassie, Cassandra – that's our daughter...'

The notes rustled as he consulted them, 'Ah yes, the only child. Aged eleven.'

Lyndsey nodded, 'had made fluorescent sheep at school. It was part of an I.T. project. They were moulded on plastic and painted bright green. Designed to glow in the dark. Most kids had made stars, and moons, and planets, but Cass made sheep. She thought they would help me sleep. Y'know by counting them.'

'Your daughter is aware of your marital discord?'

'Somewhat. She heard me crying the night of the pea. It woke her. I told her I was crying because I was tired and couldn't sleep. I'm not sure she believed me. Kids are more astute than we think. But she made me the sheep nonetheless.'

One of the crane flies had expired. It lay prone on the sill, legs splayed. Lyndsey watched as its partner clambered brutishly over the corpse. It made her think of herself and Ray. She had been dying inside and he'd neither noticed nor cared. Wind buffeted the glass, and Lyndsey remembered, with a maternal stab, that Cassie had gone to school that morning clad only in her uniform. She'd refused to wear her duffle coat, after classmates had nicknamed her Paddington Bear.

'Together, we stuck them on the bedroom ceiling,' she said, continuing her tale of woe concerning the sheep, 'during the night they fell off. One by one they started dropping on the bed. Ray sleeps with his mouth open, and well.... you can guess the rest.'

The solicitor raised an eyebrow but said nothing.

'Ray went mad. I suppose the shock of waking up set him off. He moaned at me till the morning. About how I shouldn't have put the sheep above the bed, how I should have stuck them properly, how they had marked the emulsion, how they should have been put in Cassie's room not ours, how her school was encouraging childish pursuits, how I should have made sure she was doing homework instead of plastering the ceiling with glow in the dark stickers, how this, how that, how the other...on and on and on.'

The solicitor finished writing and put down his pen. With an air of finality he screwed on its top.

Lyndsey had given him a pea and fluorescent sheep. She hoped it was enough.

Chapter Two

RAIN WAS FALLING as Lyndsey left the solicitor's office. Hurrying past the parade of shops, she caught sight of her reflection in the florist's window. Her hair, scrunched that morning into its customary spikes, now plastered her head like a swimmer's cap.

'God, I look awful', she thought. Even in the fading light of afternoon, the shadows underneath her eyes were all too evident, and her face was ghostly white. It was prematurely dark, and Lyndsey peeled back a sodden cuff to check the time. Almost four. If she hurried she could meet Cassie from school. She was seized by an overpowering need to see her child, as if by doing so, she could expunge the guilt of wanting to tear asunder the parental bond. Her interview with the solicitor had set in motion a process which might ultimately part Cassandra from her father.

Lyndsey opened her umbrella. A rainbow striped affair, it was the one used by Ray when he went fishing. The brolly enclosed her in a multi-coloured bubble, and the rain punching its roof was deafening. It was like sheltering underneath a waterfall, she thought, joining pedestrians waiting to cross the road. The green man on the zebra crossing seemed determined not to make an appearance, and Lyndsey lost count of the cars streaming by before his flashing red counterpart retired. She run on wet tarmac, made slippery by the rain, and headed on through the park entrance, her heels skittering on the sodden carpet of leaves. Trees rustled in a glorious technicolour display, but Lyndsey, nose peaking from the brim of the brolly, hardly noticed. Conscious that the school bell had gone, she broke into a cautious trot. A flotilla of ducks was making its way off the pond, their disappointed quacking making her resolve to bring bread next time. The children's playground looked forlornly empty, swings creaking on heavy chains, and the see-saw frozen in tip-tilted motion. Lyndsey remembered the times she had spent there with Cassandra, when her daughter was younger. During school holidays, they would bring crisps and sandwiches when it was fine, flasks of soup and crusty rolls when it was not. Cassie wouldn't play on the swings and roundabouts now, thought Lyndsey with a pang. The handle of the umbrella wavered in her grasp, and it wasn't entirely due to the gusting of the wind. Her hand shook, as she remembered the day, just a few short weeks back, when her child had started secondary school.

It was early September, and hot. The summer, which had got off to inauspicious start of cloudy drizzle, suddenly seemed to remember that it had a role to play, and kicked in the month of August with untrammelled blue skies and searing heat. As if making up for lost time, the weather held its sunny course.

On the morning of her first day at Brackendale High, Cassandra had stood in the bright kitchen seemingly swamped by her uniform of pleated grey skirt, white blouse and red tie. The matching cardigan, and blazer bearing the Brackendale crest, lay discarded on their hangers on the hall carpet, their cellophane jackets scattered like confetti. Lyndsey, aware of the cost of these items, which had taken the best part of her weeks salary, itched to retrieve them, but something in Cassie's expression kept her anchored to the breakfast table.

There was mutinous set to the child's mouth, and her grey eyes glistened with unshed tears.

Ray had looked up over the top of his paper, 'You look so grown up darling.'

Lyndsey agreed, 'a proper schoolgirl.'

Cassandra pulled a face, 'I hate it mum. The skirt is ever so scratchy, and I'm choking in this tie. I tried to do it the way you showed me dad, and its taken simply ages.'

'We should have got one of those clip-on's' Lyndsey ventured, 'it would have saved time.' whereupon Ray, stirring his coffee, had turned to her, and spoke in his customary patient tone as if explaining something to a dim-witted dolt, 'now Lyn, we've discussed this. It's time Cass learned to do things for herself, and doing up a tie is one of them.' He tapped the rim of his cup firmly with the spoon, as if signalling to his wife that her part in the conversation was terminated.

'You've done a pretty good job, princess. Just a bit crooked. Come here.'

Dutifully Cassandra obliged, standing quietly while her father adjusted the tie, and smoothed down the stiff collar of his daughter's blouse. Lyndsey had watched this tender tableau, unable to quite dispel the feeling of exclusion it engendered somewhere deep within her. There was stillness to the scene, accentuated by the heavy humid air, and the lack of even of the slightest breeze from the opened windows.

On the way to school, Cassandra had lagged behind Lyndsey, reluctance to reach their destination evident in every footfall, whilst keeping up a constant litany of complaints.

'This bag is so heavy, mum.'

'These shoes hurt.'

'This hair band is too tight.'

She was hot, she was thirsty, she was ill.

'I've got a headache mum,' She'd announced as they reached the playground. Lyndsey had steered the child onto a nearby bench, and sat beside her.

'I know you're scared, darling. Senior school is bound to feel a bit strange, but you'll soon settle in.' The pep talk had lasted five minutes, culminating in a hug of support from Lyndsey.

When she'd collected Cassandra at the end of that first day, her daughter was withdrawn. In an effort to cheer the schoolgirl, her mother had suggested a half hour in the park, and a burger bar tea. At this, Cassandra had swivelled around to see who was within earshot as if fearful of being overheard by a fellow pupil.

'Mum, playgrounds are for kids,' she'd hissed.

'But sweetheart, you're only eleven, and it used to be such fun.'

'Used to be mum,' Cassie said, and her face reddened. Seeing this, Lyndsey had not pushed the point, but her daughter's assertion that she was no longer a child hurt more than she would have thought possible.

Deep in this recollection, Lyndsey hardly noticed that she had reached the gates of Brackendale High. A knot of pupils were clogging the entrance. They were obviously Year 11's, for they sported the swaggering insouciance of fifteen year olds. Lyndsey thought the boys looked menacing with their cropped hairstyles, and hard eyes, but to her, the girls seemed worse. Language, which would not have been out of place in a working men's club, was screeched aloud, and, despite the school uniform, they managed to look like a bunch of hookers. Skirts were hoisted high, tights were black, heels were high. One girl gave Lyndsey a steely look, as she slouched past. In contrast, the first formers who were beginning to stream out Lower School block looked like miniatures; they seemed so small in comparison. Lyndsey, shivering against a concrete pillar, thought the various ages and sizes of the pupils resembled those Russian dolls that slotted one inside the other. They started off big in Year 11, but got progressively smaller, down to that academic year's new intake. Her daughter Cassandra was one. Lyndsey's heart ached for her. How hard it must be to be the smallest fish in this gigantic pond, inhabited by the barracudas of veteran pupils.

She wondered how she was going to break the news of the divorce to her daughter. The prospect of telling Ray, their marriage was finally over was scary enough. She wilted at the thought of telling Renee. Her mother and husband had always been members of the same mutually appreciative fan club. But Cassie was going to prove the hardest of all. She baulked at the revelation which she knew lay ahead.

As if on cue, Lyndsey saw Cassandra filter out of the green double doors, the last in a dawdling crocodile. She looked small and vulnerable, her oversized bag weighing down one shoulder. To keep out the chill, she had wrapped the grey blazer tightly around her middle, and seemed hunched into it, like someone in hiding. Lyndsey resolved to buy her a padded jacket over half term, even though it would mean flouting her husband's rule.

'She'll wear it, and that's an end to it,' He'd said firmly the weekend before, when the 'coat' issue had surfaced, incongruously enough over the Sunday lunch dessert. Lyndsey had made an orange suet pudding liberally steeped in marmalade, and Ray, raising the spoon to his lips, had said, 'Paddington Bear would love this, eh Pumpkin?' reaching out with his free hand to ruffle Cassandra's hair. The child froze, the rigidity of her form indicative of some secret inner torment. Lyndsey, observing this inter-action between father and daughter, wondered what had caused this imperceptible reaction from her child. Whether it was Ray's use of the childhood 'pumpkin' endearment which was now, given Cassie's age, becoming obsolete, whether it was the muffing up of a hairstyle, or whether the mention of 'Paddington Bear' was a reminder of the ribbing she had suffered at school, from the wearing of the coat. Cassandra's next words confirmed it was the latter,

'I want a different coat, Dad. Nobody wears duffels any more.'

'Only toy bears' Ray's attempt at humour was falling flat, Lyndsey thought, 'perhaps we should get you some red wellies too, Cass.'

'Dad, it's not funny.'

Lyndsey dabbed her serviette at a blob of marmalade, which had spilt onto the tablecloth, and said, keeping her voice light, 'It's true Ray. What school kids do you see wearing them, these days?'

'Can you do that with a wet cloth please Lyn.'

'What?' She'd said, momentarily nonplussed.

'The marmalade', he said, gesturing at the offending stain with his spoon, 'you're just spreading the stickiness. How many times do I need tell you that dry cloths are for cleaning dust, wet are for cleaning spills.'

Lyndsey quickly got up, and made for the kitchen, not so concerned for the fate of her tablecloth as hoping to forestall the inevitable character assassination that lay ahead if she ignored her husband. Savagely, she ran hot tap water over a J-cloth at the pristine kitchen sink, hearing the unspoken words echoing in her head 'don't you care about the state of our home, Lyn? Don't you care that the tablecloth cost good money, Lyn? Don't you care that you are ruining a perfectly good serviette Lyn? Don't you care, don't you care, don't you care...' The mantra played relentlessly somewhere deep inside her skull.

On her return to the dining room, gloomy on the overcast afternoon, she found the dispute over the coat had reached new proportions,

'I picked out that coat for you, Cass, and you are going to wear it. I've never heard such nonsense that they call you names in school just because it has toggle buttons. Tell them where to get off.'

Cassandra seemed to recoil at this suggestion, appearing to her mother to be too small for the chair, like Alice after drinking the shrinking potion in Wonderland. 'Dad, it'll make things worse. Can't I change it for something else? Like one of those ski jackets that the other girls wear.'

'And have my daughter resembling a teenage tart? Certainly not. School coats are not meant to be a fashion statement. A duffle coat is warm and practical. I wore one when I was at school, and so did your mother.'

He looked up from pouring custard, as if expecting Lyndsey to confirm this fact.

'God, that was thirty years ago Ray. Things change.'

'They only change if we allow them. Children should remain children Lyn, not mini adults. When Cassie is eighteen she can do what she likes, but until then, what we say goes.'

You mean what you say goes, thought Lyndsey, but she kept a hold on tongue. Provoking Ray further could gain nothing.

It occurred to Lyndsey now, as she was jostled aside at the school gates, that seeking legal advice to end the marriage would not only provoke her husband, but would be akin to poking him with a stick. She was sure he would react like a tethered dog. Snarling, with suppressed fury.

Cassandra, temporarily blocked from view by a minibus, emerged alone. The pupils had formed pairs, chattering intently as they headed home, but Cassie continued her dogged solitary path, eyes fixed on some distant landmark. Lyndsey felt her heart contract. She wanted to scoop the child up and hug her fiercely. It took all her self will not to start running towards her daughter with arms outstretched, the way she had often greeted her at Park Lane Juniors. But the days were gone when Cassandra would welcome a public display of affection. Without actually telling her mother so, she had managed to convey by frigid body language that to be seen hugging a parent would make her the object of derision amongst her peers.

It was only when she was yards from the gate, Lyndsey could tell, by her daughter's reddened eyes, that Cassie had been crying.

Chapter Three

'CASSANDRA DALY', THE voice harpooned Cassie at the classroom door, 'A quick word if you please.'

She felt a familiar, yet irrational dread. Mr. Butcher had a habit of shouting during lessons to restore order, and it made her jump. Despite two months of having him as her Form Tutor, she still flinched every time he bellowed at a miscreant in class. She hoped he wasn't going to bellow now. After eight hours in this noisy hellhole so different from Park Lane Primary, she didn't think her ears could stand it.

Had she given him reason to shout at her? Teachers only asked you remain behind if you had done something wrong, she remembered that from Junior School. The naughty pupils were always kept back and reprimanded about some misdemeanour in class, when the home bell rang. She searched her mind frantically for clues as to why she was being recalled. None materialised. Her homework had been handed in on time, she was polite in class, she had so far managed to keep herself out of trouble. As if sensing her internal dilemma, the boy beside her said, 'What you dun, Paddington?' His voice was silky in her ear, 'forgot to give teech a blow job.' His companion guffawed. 'Not her,' he said, giving Cassandra a vicious dig in the ribs, 'lesbo ain't she.'

Cassie felt embarrassment flood her. She could not assimilate into her understanding the sexual innuendos that crept in during every conversation with classmates. It seemed that she was daily being confronted by a World that traumatised her. A World peopled by sniggering boys who smuggled copies of the Daily Star into every lesson, passing around cuttings of topless models in suggestive poses, and girls whose main topic of conversation seemed to revolve around how many 'fellas' they'd snogged'. It was so alien to Cassandra. She still cuddled her toy panda in bed, and her collection of Barbie Dolls had pride of place on the unoccupied top bunk.

She hovered in the doorway of the form room, still unsure. Pupils streamed past her, the majority smirking at her plight, and she stood aside until the tidal wave ebbed. She felt like a salmon in the wildlife documentary she had watched with her mother on TV during the summer holidays. The poor fish, she remembered, had struggled to swim upstream to reach its spawning ground.

The stragglers departed, their feet echoing in the corridor, and Cassie was left alone. Alone with Mr. Butcher. He of the booming voice, and sarcastic jibes. She could feel him watching her, and she dropped her eyes to the floor, noticing that a scuffed mark on the boards resembled a rabbit's head. Tentatively, she began to trace the outline of the ears with her shoe.

'Cassandra, please come and sit down.' Surprised at the gentleness in his tone, Cassie looked up. He was indicating the chair in front of his desk with a ruler. She approached with the caution of someone confronting an un-caged lion, which might, at any moment, cease its benign purring and begin to roar. The chair, its seat worn thin from the application of so many different bottoms, creaked hard as she lowered herself upon it as if Cassie was the fattest girl in class. Which she patently was not. Mr. Butcher, watching her intently under his bushy brows, thought she was the smallest eleven year old he'd ever encountered in Year 7. An elf of a child, with skin so translucent you could see the veins clearly underneath, and eyes that appeared too big for her tiny heart shaped face. There was something insubstantial about her; ethereal even, and he mentally cast her as one of the fairies in Midsummer Night's Dream. Peaseblossom perhaps, or Mustardseed, the fine, flyaway hair the colour of beech leaves. All she needed was a pair of wings, and gossamer dress to complete the picture.

She sat before him, a cross-legged pixie on a toadstool, and there was such trepidation in those grey eyes, that he deliberately lowered his voice an octave so as not to overwhelm her.

'Cassandra, I've asked you to stay behind for a few minutes because I am concerned that you do not seem to have settled in class. You're very quiet, and I've noticed that you haven't made many friends. Of course, Secondary School is a big shock to many kids after the Primaries, and you might be naturally shy, but....' At this he paused, and pushed his glasses up the bridge of his nose to study a folder, 'I have your referral letter from your teacher at Park Lane Juniors. She says, and I quote, 'this pupil is a joy to teach, a bright chatterbox who is always first to put her hand up in class in answer to any question.' Cassie didn't want to hear this. Her eyes strayed to the rabbit on the floor. From her vantage point in the middle of the room she could see that cracks on the boards had given it whiskers.

She didn't look up, as Mr. Butcher continued, 'so shyness is not a problem. But where is that bright chatterbox referred to? I see no evidence of it before me. You are as quiet as a

mouse in class, and as for being eager to answer questions...'
He sighed, and Cassie mistook it as one of disappointment
rather than concern.

'Cassandra, look at me.'

With great reluctance, Cassie lifted her head. It felt
unaccountably heavy, as though someone had placed weights
on each shoulder.

'If you are experiencing problems in school, you must tell
me. I'm here to help.' She was unable to speak. The same
invisible hand that bore down on her neck was now clamped
over her mouth.

'Are you being bullied perhaps? Picked on, made fun of?'

Mutely, she shook her head. She couldn't tell Mr. Butcher
that every day she ran the gauntlet of snide comments about
her undeveloped body, her stick like legs, her Paddington
bear coat. Couldn't tell him how they laughed at the oversized
uniform that swamped her tiny frame, how they smirked
at her scant knowledge of the mechanics of sex, how they
re-buffed her hesitant attempts at friendship. Her fellow
classmates both bewildered and frightened her. They were all
so much bigger, more macho and streetwise than she. Even
the girls were loud and belligerent, as if trying to outdo the
boys. Cassie couldn't compete, and had stopped trying. She
treated every day at school as an ordeal to be got through with
the least amount of trauma, hiding herself at the back of the
classroom, and keeping her head down. During lessons, she
worked diligently, concentrating on each subject in an effort
to lose herself in the mechanics of Maths, English, or History,
and thus block out reality. Sometimes, during a lull in class,
she would listen to her own breathing, and it sounded so loud,
her heart thumping painfully against her rib cage, that she
was sure it was drawing attention.

The classroom was in its usual close of day chaotic state. It smelt of feet. Desks and chairs had been knocked haphazardly aside in the home time rush, and the wastepaper bin was overturned, spilling balled up sheets of paper onto the floor. The white board that took up the entire length of the wall behind the teacher's desk sported a map of Italy drawn with dry marker pen. Cassie fiddled with her watch strap, trying to blot out the sound of rain lashing the windows, and the vertical blinds which rattled in the draught like members of an orchestra tuning up their instruments.

'You live with both parents,' Mr. Butcher's voice was soft, and when Cassie sneaked him a look, she saw that he was stroking his beard, and studying her Pupil Record, 'and have no siblings.'

'Siblings?' It was the first word Cassie had spoken, and she was shocked at the tremulous tone of her voice. She hoped she wasn't about to cry. Tears came easily these days, and the teacher's sympathetic questioning was bringing them perilously close.

'Brothers and sisters.'

'No, there's only me.'

'I see. Any pets?'

'I'd love a dog, but my dad won't have animals in the house. He says they're unhygienic.' Someone in the next classroom was playing a radio. Cassie wondered why Mr. Butcher didn't get up and shut the door. She wasn't to know that it was against school rules for a teacher to be closeted alone with a pupil. She also wasn't to know that the man sitting in front of her was awash with pity for this lonely kid, bereft by her own admission. He knew from the address on her pupil record that she lived in one of the squat Georgian villas that bordered the park, and guessed how empty that house must seem without the clamour of other children, or the rumbustious barking of a family dog.

'What about friends?'

Cassie bit her lip. 'I had lots at the juniors, but they've mostly gone to private schools. Daddy believes in state education which is why he sent me here. Said I had to learn to stand on my own two feet without privileges.'

'Poor Cassandra. You must feel very alone.'

At these kind words, tears began to course silently down her cheeks. She was too ashamed to brush them away, so sat with head bowed, letting them drip onto her skirt. 'Here', his hand materialised in her line vision, waving something white like a flag of surrender, 'borrow my handkerchief. Wipe your nose, there's a good girl.'

Cassie sniffed obediently. The silence lengthened between teacher and pupil, the former wanting to reach out and comfort this sobbing waif. Mr. Butcher wished, not for the first time, that the constraints imposed on teachers against any physical contact with pupils could be circumvented in circumstances like this. The child needed the security of an adult's arm around her shoulder. Instead, all he could do was bear witness to her pain, and resolve to keep an especially watchful eye on Cassandra Daly.

He decided that if she still seemed remote by the end of term, he would draw it to the attention of the Head. He annotated her Pupil Record to this effect, and, to mask the inadequacy he felt in not being able to offer more concrete help, forced a note of cheer into his voice, 'Now don't you fret. Things will soon get better. Its half term next week, and when you come back there will be lots of exciting Christmas projects to look forward to. Before you go, will you to promise me something?'

Cassie dabbed at her red eyes, but said nothing.

'That you'll tell me if you have problems in school.'

'I promise', she lied.

The discovery of her mother, waiting at the school gates, was another shock for Cassie, but this time an eminently more pleasurable one. Luckily, most of her fellow pupils had long since departed the school grounds, but for once she didn't care about the inevitable jibes that might follow if any latecomers spotted the presence of Mrs. Daly dutifully awaiting her daughter.

That same daughter had endured misery when she'd first started in September being the butt of 'mother and baby' jokes, the implication being that she ought to be back in nappies if she still needed her mummy to hold her hand at home time. On Sunday evening at the end of that first week, as her mother was hanging laundered uniform in Cassie's wardrobe, she broached the subject that had been plaguing her for days.

'Mum, you don't need to meet me from school.'

'But darling, I want to. I finish at the library in plenty of time.'

'I'm not a baby anymore. I can walk home myself.'

Her mother had closed the wardrobe door, and leant against it, 'What's wrong Cass?' She'd asked. As always, when faced with a situation for which she was not emotionally equipped, Cassie sought refuge in anger. 'You're always asking me questions,' She'd stormed, 'nothing's wrong OK? I'm just fed up with you treating me like a kid. No one else in my class has their mum meet them, and lots of them have a longer journey home than me. They think I'm a wimp.' She couldn't bear to look at the hurt expression on her mother's face, or hear the quiet finality in her voice as she said, 'OK Cassandra, I get it. Guess Dad's right. It's time I let you grow up.' There followed the inevitable 'stranger danger' talk, and pledges sought that she would keep to the main roads, stay on the lighted path through the park, and not take any detours via the newsagents or chip shop. It might have surprised Cassie to know that for two whole weeks following this discourse, her mother had secretly tailed her home from school, hovering in shop doorways and behind trees like some spy on a mission, just to ensure the safety of her precious child.

All this was forgotten however, at the sight of the familiar figure at the school gates.

'Darling, I'm sorry about being here,' Lyndsey reached out a gloved finger and stroked her daughter's pale cheek, 'but the weather turned so bloody, and you've left your coat at home.'

'Mum, you know I won't wear...'

'Don't worry. We'll donate the duffle to a charity shop, and you can choose a new jacket. Daddy needn't know.'

Mother and daughter hugged, joint players in the conspiracy to deceive the man of the house. They shivered together in the rain, until Lyndsey pulled apart and clasped the cold palm in hers.

'Come on,' She said, raising the umbrella to shield them both, 'Let's get home and dry out.'

Splashing through puddles, they set off down the road, dodging vehicles that were streaming out of the school car-park, headlights making mirrored images on the wet pavement. Lyndsey noticed Mr. Butcher in a yellow Citroen, and recognised him as Cassie's Form Tutor from his impressive beard. She'd met him at Open Evening and was taken by his firm handshake, and economic use of words. Marriage to Ray had taught Lyndsey to be wary of talkative men, and she was therefore shamelessly attracted to strong silent types. It amazed her when her two best friends, Dee and Coral, complained that their husbands 'didn't talk to them', and spent inordinate amounts of time in the garden shed, or down the pub, or on the computer. They wittered on about the need for a 'soul-mate', one who understood the female psyche and could converse on the same emotional level. Lyndsey's response was Dickensian. Bah, soul mates, she would think with the same disparagement as Scrooge would say 'humbug.' What bliss to have a husband who only spoke when he was spoken to, thought Lyndsey, pulling back Cassie to let Mr. Butcher edge out onto the main road.

'Did you see who that was?'

The child answered by giving a slight nod.

'Do you like him?'

'Who?'

'Mr. Butcher, silly. Is he kind to you?'

'He was tonight. He asked me to stay behind for a chat.'

They were passing a row of bay fronted semis. In the illuminated window of one, Lyndsey saw a woman feeding a bird that occupied an ornate hanging cage, before, as if suddenly conscious of eyes upon her, pulling shut the curtains and blotting out this tableau. Almost absently she said aloud, 'wouldn't it fun to have a parrot? One that told jokes and sang little ditties.' Equally absently, Cassandra said, 'that's one of the things we talked about. He asked if we had pets at home.'

Lyndsey frowned. Why was Mr. Butcher enquiring whether they possessed a dog or a cat? Or indeed a parrot. Surely it had nothing to do with her daughter's schoolwork.

'I wondered why you were so late leaving class. You're not in any trouble, are you Cass?' Lyndsey turned her gaze from the house, and peered at her daughter in the gloom. Was this the reason behind the swollen eyes, and reddened cheeks. She desperately wanted to ask her daughter why'd she'd been kept behind and why she'd been crying, but Lyndsey knew from past experience, that it was a question best left to the right moment. Cassandra could be so unpredictable these days, flaring up at any real or imagined slight, or remaining silent at any question she considered intrusive.

'Nope.'

'Then why...?'

'Leave it Mum.'

The stubborn set to Cassandra's mouth indicated that she was not prepared to volunteer further information. Lyndsey made a note to tackle her later. After tea, when the warmth and security of home and hearth might induce in her daughter the urge to confide.

With that she had to be content.

Chapter Four

'GOOD MORNING, CINDY Kate.'

In common with many Asian shopkeepers, Mr. Roshi's greeting was effusive. Lyndsey loved the way he made her feel like visiting royalty. Even making the humblest of purchases filled her with a sense of importance. In the presence of Mr. Roshi's respectful servility, one became a Duchess surrounded by an entourage of bodyguards and butlers. Lyndsey was drawn to his cluttered corner shop with its haphazard profusion of confectionery, tinned goods, and Indian spices, like a stray cat grabbing a welcome respite on the hearth of somebody's fire. Mr. Roshi's hand was the one that stoked that blaze, throwing on extra logs of emotional comfort.

He'd already folded her favourite magazine, and was passing it across the counter to Lyndsey with the ceremony of a footman handing the Queen a letter on a silver tray.

'Terrible weather we're having, Cindy Kate. Like a monsoon.'

'Can't expect much else for late October, Mr. Roshi.' She said this with a faint smile of bemusement; a bemusement she always felt when the shopkeeper called her by this name. It had come about innocently enough. On joining the library, she had volunteered to run the National Lottery syndicate, collecting the stake money from the staff and buying a ticket for every mid-week and Saturday draw. Mr. Roshi, new to the corner shop, had mistaken her pronouncement of 'I'm the syndicate', as the offering of her name. Lyndsey, fazed by his delight over what he perceived to be an invitation to address her on first name terms, had not the heart to disabuse him. Neither then nor now. So Cindy Kate she became. Secretly she rather liked the name. It made her feel risqué, as though she were a call girl. Their advertisement cards were prolific in all the local phone boxes, and shop windows, and sported imaginative names such as Lorelei and Trixie Lee. In Mr. Roshi's humble emporium, Lyndsey became a seductress treated with old fashioned respect, quite unlike her real self. Which was why she continued to patronize his shop, enjoying the abandonment of shedding her own skin and becoming someone else, albeit only briefly. Especially now, when she didn't like herself very much. She was ditching her husband wasn't she? Didn't that make her a home-wrecker by default, and therefore someone un-deserving of common courtesy.

Lyndsey stole a glance at Cassie. Her daughter was down the aisle of video rental tapes, admiring herself in a mirrored display stand. She was wearing the new coat, proudly purchased the day before from a trendy boutique in town, and was twisting this way and that to better see her reflection. Lyndsey thought the marine blue jacket with fur lined hood and cuffs, and red appliqué chevrons on both sleeves made her daughter look like some miniature Eskimo with arms bloodied from gutting fish.

The corner store was empty. This surprised Lyndsey, since it was the Half Term holiday and Christmas was looming. She supposed the torrential rain and bitter winds were keeping people closeted indoors. She wished she, too, were home, instead of on this mission. A mission she could no longer put off. A mission to tell her mother she was getting a divorce.

Cassandra was inordinately pleased with her new coat. While her mother was busy in conversation with the nodding Mr. Roshi, she surveyed her reflection in the mirrored panel above the dvd rental rack. What pleased her most was the chevron logo, which spoke of a popular and sought after make. This garment was a high fashion statement, and would, Cassandra hoped, convey to her fellow classmates that she possessed the necessary 'Savvy' when it came to wearing street cred gear.

Was it too big? She frowned, her face becoming gnome like. Her mother had insisted on buying the biggest size "so it would last through another winter", but Cass now felt a dart of anxiety that it was swamping her small frame. She took a quick surreptitious glance around the shop, thankful that it was still empty, and bit her lips to redden them. Then she thrust out her tiny bud breasts, pulled back her shoulders, and began to patrol the aisle, with an exaggerated gait, like a mannequin on a catwalk. All the time her eyes never left the mirror. In her mind, she was trying to picture her first day back at school, forward planning as to whether she could pinch a smear of mum's lipstick, and maybe, just maybe, her stud earrings. Jewellery and make-up were forbidden at Brackendale High, but Cassandra had been confused to discover this rule routinely flouted. She had never seen such a preponderance of Kohl eyeliner and lip gloss amongst classmates before. One girl even had the temerity to bedeck her lobes with hoops that hung to her shoulder, and a brazenly crafted crucifix around her neck. She sat next at the next desk to Cassie, was called Olu, and came from Nigeria. She was big, bold and black, and Cassandra envied her immensely. Beside this ebony giantess, she felt smaller, paler, and even more insignificant than usual. Olu had a booming laugh and teeth so brilliant they looked painted. She called everyone 'man' including the teacher, and had enormous jutting out breasts, even bigger than Nana's.

Cassandra stopped her pirouetting, and glanced across at her mother. Thank goodness Mrs. Daly didn't know what was in her mind. It was bad to think of breasts, and she mentally scolded herself. 'Tits' the boys at school called them.

'Hey, get 'em out', one had yelled at her only last week as she came last in the cross country run only to find the gym door bolted. Scarlet with embarrassment she'd skirted the playground, clad in her PE kit of skimpy shorts and T-shirt, the latter painfully advertising her lack of development. The boys, a group of Year 9's had whooped and catcalled her, breaking out into jeering laughter when one shouted, 'Tits – she ain't got any'.

Her mother, pausing in conversation with the shopkeeper had turned around. Cassie felt, rather than saw, the eyes searching her face. Panicked, both by being caught thinking bad thoughts, and studying her reflection – vanity was also something bad (this her dad had told her on more than one occasion), she dropped to her knees and began sifting through the rack of dvd rentals as though she'd been meaning to choose one all along.

Cassie picked up a case which sported a particularly lurid cover. It was called 'Killer Spree'. She'd overheard Olu talking about it in the toilets. The black girl was regaling another over the plot machinations with gusto. Cassie, locked securely in one of the cubicles listened in fascinated horror to the tale of severed heads put on spikes, and virgins having their blood drunk. She wondered if her mother would allow her to take the dvd out for one night. What a triumphant return to school she could have next Monday. Not only sporting one of the trendiest coats in the playground, but also boasting to Olu that she, too, had seen the film, and no, she did not find it particularly frightening. Pretty boring actually.

Regretfully she replaced the plastic case in its allotted slot on the shelf, watching as the corpse depicted on the cover slid out of sight. Dead bodies fascinated Cassie almost as much as other girl's breasts. A gust of wind threw a handful of leaves at the shop window. It sounded like the tapping of a thousand tiny hands. Through the glass, Cassandra could see the sandwich board advertising the Evening Standard do a backwards dance along the pavement.

She straightened up, her thin calves protruding from the coat like a bonfire Guy propped up on sticks. The middle row of dvds contained the children's section; the only ones she was permitted to choose.

Remembering Mr. Butcher's probing as to whether or not she owned a pet, Cassie selected a disc entitled "Beethoven's Third". A daft looking St. Bernard, surrounded by a tumble of pups, gazed up from the cover. She'd enjoy watching that far more than a scary movie, but it wouldn't do for her peers at Brackendale High to know. Covertly, she placed it under her arm, carefully shielding the content by the padded folds of the coat.

Her dad wouldn't let her have a dog. Watching the film would be a poor substitute but one that would have to suffice. For the time being.

Lyndsey was struggling with her new telescopic umbrella. (Raymond had vetoed the use of his fishing one, after discovering it had been stored damp under the stairs). The mechanism seemed to have jammed. When Cassandra spoke to her in a stage whisper, she said, distractedly, 'Sorry darling? What did you say?'

'I said, why don't you tell him your proper name'

'Who?'

'Mr. Roshi of course.'

The umbrella sprung into life, capturing Lyndsey and her daughter in the shop doorway. A gust of wind threatened to send them toppling back into the newsagents, but Lyndsey battled gamely on. The glass on the door front rattled alarmingly, and the Open sign spun around to reveal itself as Closed. A stray crisp packet and motley collection of leaves sneaked into the shop between Lyndsey's feet, like gatecrashers at a party.

'I haven't the heart to, darling.'

'Well, that's silly,' Cassandra pulled up the hood of her coat, her fingers stroking the fur lining as if with renewed pleasure at its purchase, 'It's embarrassing Mum. Cindy Kate is a stupid name for someone so old.'

Lyndsey let out a guffaw of laughter, but the wind snatched it from her mouth. 'Goodness, I'm only thirty three. Hardly ancient.'

'Nearly thirty four' rejoined Cassie with the smugness of youth, 'and your hair is white like Nana's.'

'Nan's hair is silvery blonde,' she said firmly, determined to terminate the conversation, 'as is mine.'

Cassandra said, in a voice that held a pedantic edge, 'Don't change the subject Mummy. You should tell Mr. Roshi your proper name.'

Lyndsey sighed. The wind lobbed a handful of gritty dirt at her face. She rubbed her cheek ruefully with the edge of her scarf, before saying, 'Oh darling, perhaps I should, but it would make him feel terrible, and he'd think I was more than a bit dumb for letting the misunderstanding continue. So what's the point? He's happy to call me Cindy Kate, and so am I. I quite like the name you know. Its more fun than my own.'

Cassandra kicked aside an empty coke can that was whirling around her booted feet, 'I think you're being daft.' She said stubbornly.

Lyndsey began to walk briskly to the car, which was parked on a double yellow. All she needed, she thought grimly, was to find a ticket on the windscreen. Her daughter jog trotted in an effort to keep up.

'Go back and tell him, Mummy'.

'Cassie, leave it please.'

'But you've always told me not to tell lies, and now you're telling them to Mr. Roshi.'

'It's not a lie'.'

'It is,' Her daughter persisted.

Lyndsey had reached the car, and was fumbling in her pocket for the keys. Thankfully there was no parking ticket adorning the windscreen. Instead, someone had bent back one of her wipers. Mindless vandalism always invoked a feeling of impotent rage within her, which wasn't helped by Cassandra's whispered chant, 'Liar, liar, your pants on fire.'

Her daughter had developed the habit, and it was a tedious one, of hanging onto a subject long after it should have decently been laid to rest. Learned behaviour from what the child had witnessed in the home environment since toddlerhood. Lyndsey knew it was growing up seeing one parent subjecting the other to a verbal assault course for any perceived misdemeanor. She sighed. Her daughter was growing to be like her father in more ways than one, thought Lyndsey and a pall descended upon her which had little to do with the inclement weather.

In the street it was more like midnight than mid-day. The sky was black and sullen, the rain hammering metal rods into the pavement. Lyndsey shook the umbrella and dumped it into onto the back seat of the car. She motioned to Cassandra to get inside. She noticed that the child was clutching her dvd rental, discreetly clad in a paper bag in both hands.

'You can watch Beethoven at Nana's' she said, hanging onto the driver's handle with all her strength. 'Goodness, this wind is strong. We're going to get blown across the road.'

The ten minute drive to her mother's flat conveniently situated to the rear of Arnos Grove tube, took three times as long. Traffic cones littered the road like skittles, and rain flung itself in a flurry against Lyndsey's windscreen. With only one wiper working, she found her vision hampered by a build up of sodden leaves.

Lyndsey drew up in front of the elegant block of maisonettes. A wheelie bin, buffeted by the wind, was doing a crazed dance in front of the row of garages. She cut the engine, and sat for a moment savoring the silence. Cassie, absorbed in smoothing out a rogue crease in the new coat, was quiet too. Lyndsey felt in her own coat pocket for the letter, craning her head round to check her mother's flat. The kitchen light was on. It signified that Renee was in residence. Waste was an anathema to her mother, and she would never go out and leave a bulb burning in an empty room.

She didn't know whether she felt relief or disappointment that her mother was home.

Chapter Five

RENEE FAIRBROTHER WAS enjoying the woman's section of her daily newspaper, aided by a cup of tea and a chocolate wafer. She was reading the weekly make-over page, hosted by TV fashion guru's, Savannah Hooper-Greenhill and Thalia Emmerson. It sported photographs of a plumpish middle aged lady, in the classic 'before' and 'after' pose, under the caption, 'A bad Penny becomes a silver dollar.......'

Avidly, Renee read on.

'Penelope Cramer, 41-year old housewife from Devizes, Wiltshire, despaired with the way she looked. My kids and husband call me a 'has been' she wails. Luckily for Penny, help is on hand from our very own experts to aid this lady find style. After a day in London spent with Savannah and Thalia of Channel 7's 'Turnaround', and a stunning new wardrobe courtesy of this newspaper, a shining new Penny has emerged...'

Renee couldn't help but agree. The lady in the photographs had certainly been transformed. It was amazing what a sharp new hairstyle, professional make up, and flattering clothes could achieve, Renee thought. The fashion 'guinea pig' looked ten years younger in the 'after' picture, and at least a stone lighter.

A flake of chocolate had fallen onto the reader's smart pencil skirt. Another one had impaled itself onto the buttonhole of her cardigan. With great care she retrieved them. Melted chocolate, she knew, was the very devil for staining clothes.

Renee returned her attention to the article, noting the 'Tip of the Week' for giving oneself instant style. *'Team flesh coloured tights with matching shoes and scarf for a co-ordinated look'* it said.

She'd seen the perfect scarf gracing the neck of a dummy in the window of a High Street store earlier that week. It was a creamy voile containing minute flecks of gold. Renee thought that it would warm her complexion and pale blonde tresses. She stole a quick glance at her reflection in the microwave, and the sight cheered her.

'Not bad for an old dame..' She said aloud. Her skin was smooth and unlined; her hair thick and lustrous. Despite being mature in years, Renee felt she was wearing well. Couldn't afford to let the guard drop though, she thought. Old age was an invidious enemy, one that sneaked up when you weren't looking, and peppered you with shots. An army that attacked in the night, and re-grouped during the day. Before you knew it, Renee thought, it had fired off a salvo and you woke up one morning and discovered a wrinkle in the mirror. One that wasn't there the day before. A new scarf might be a weapon in the waning looks war, but it was a feeble one. She felt like King Canute trying to hold back the tide. The years were accumulating; gathering in wait for her, and she was powerless to stop their advance. A year short of the big Six –O, and already Renee was dreading the impending day.

Outside a car door slammed. The noise momentarily drowned the drum of rain. At the sound of footsteps on the path, Renee got to her feet.

She reached the front door just as the bell trilled. 'Lyndsey, love,' she exclaimed with genuine pleasure, 'and Cassie too. Give nana a kiss, sweetheart.'

Renee pulled the door wide, bending to receive her grand-daughters peck. 'Goodness, the pair of you look frozen.' As always she stepped seamlessly into her role of grandmotherly concern.

'Mum,' Lyndsey acknowledged with a hug, which surprised Renee by both its intensity and duration. There was something wrong. She knew it. With a mother's unerring instinct for sensing a problem with her child. She drew back from the embrace, and searched her daughter's face critically. Lyndsey was very pale, and there was a dispirited sag to her shoulders.

'Darling, what's wrong?'

Her daughter's reply was offhand, 'This and that.'

Renee stiffened. Did Lyndsey's deliberate vagueness mask a deeper problem, she wondered. To hide her own growing anxiety, she busied helping Cassandra off with her coat.

'This is posh,' she said, 'Is it new?'

'Yes Nana. Mum's bought it for school.'

'Very trendy, I'm sure.'

'It cost a fortune.' Cut in Lyndsey.

Renee resolved to pay for the coat. 'Come into the kitchen in the warm. Cup of tea?'

'Does the Pope pray?' Lyndsey said, wringing her hands together, whether to bring back circulation or as a sign of suppressed anxiety, Renee couldn't be sure. She hoped it was the former. A weariness of spirit was descending upon her. She had spent what had seemed like her entire life sorting out other people's problems... her late husband Doug, Lyndsey, Cassie, friends, neighbours... She was one of life's copers; one to whom all and sundry turned in their hour of need. It was a role she'd always been happy to occupy, but lately....just lately... Where had this worm of doubt wriggled from, she wondered. The doubt that told her the days of dealing with the problems of others were numbered. For the first time in her life, she, Renee Fairbrother was admitting defeat. She wanted someone to fuss her for a change; to have concern for her; to comfort her. It must have shown in her face, for Lyndsey said, 'You alright, mum?'

'Of course,' Renee forced a smile, as she shepherded the tall thin woman and the small thin girl along the narrow passageway. In the kitchen, Cassandra clambered onto a bar stool and sat there, matchstick legs swinging. Lyndsey settled herself on a chair. Renee refilled the kettle, letting her gaze briefly wander over the dank expanse of communal lawn outside the window.

'The garden looks a mess.'

'You should see ours,' Lyndsey said, 'fallen leaves, muddy patches. Nothing looks nice this time of year.'

Renee located a packet of scones, 'How about a cream tea? That should cheer us all up. We can pretend its summer.'

'Brill,' Cassandra said, 'Got any strawberry jam, Nan?'

'In the larder. I'll get the cream.'

The child went on a jam hunt. She put a large jar on the table, and said, with an air of reproach towards her mother, 'you've got lovely stuff in the cupboard Nana. Blackcurrant jam, and lemon curd, and that chocolate nutty spread. We never have anything like that at home.'

She emphasized the 'never'.

'Don't be silly, Cass,' Lyndsey's reply sounded unnecessarily sharp, and Renee again felt the seeds of unease sprout within her, 'We have honey and marmalade on the table at every breakfast.'

'Only 'cos dad likes them,' Came back the grumble, 'Why can't we have the chocolate stuff.'

'Don't whine darling. You know why. Daddy thinks those things are manufactured rubbish.'

'Daddy's a pig.'

Renee rushed at the defense of her son-in-law, 'Now, now, young lady,' she said warningly, 'that's no way to talk about your father.' She swirled boiling water and loose tea in a large Brown Betty, banging the spoon on the sides to emphasize her displeasure in both the tone and direction of the conversation.

'Well, he is.' Said Cassandra stubbornly.

Renee met the eyes of her daughter. Lyndsey shrugged. 'It's the pet thing again. Cass has got a bee in her bonnet about a dog. Seems something her teacher said has sparked her off. Raymond won't hear of it. You know his views on animals in the house.'

Again Renee felt a stab of unease. Her daughter never called her husband by his full name. It was 'Ray' this, or 'Ray' that. Was the stiffly formal use of 'Raymond' a further indication that all was not well within their marriage? At her last visit, to a sumptuous Sunday lunch, Renee had been aware of a frost in the atmosphere between husband and wife, which both had tried, unsuccessfully, to camouflage. Her son-in-law, with forced smiles and banter, her daughter with gay laughter verging on the hysterical.

'Daddy's so mean, Nana.' Cassandra, back on the bar stool, was swinging her black stockinged legs in agitation, 'a girl at school has just got a Dalmatian puppy for her birthday.'

Despite sharing her son-in-law's aversion to animals in the home, Renee patted her grand-daughter consolingly on the shoulder.

'Can she watch her dvd, mum?'

Pouring the tea into delicate bone china cups for herself and Lyndsey, and a mug for Cassandra, Renee nodded. She placed the mug and a plate consisting of a split scone dolloped with cream and jam onto a tray, and took her grand-daughter's arm with her free hand, 'Come with nana darling. I'll put the fire on for you'

She led the child into the chilly lounge. Renee switched on the dancing coal effect, and all three bars. Cassandra dropped to her knees in front of the dvd player, inserted the Beethoven disc with practised ease, and punched buttons on the remote control. Renee admired the way the tiny 11 year old was so in control of electronic equipment, when she herself was fazed by the Dvd's Operations Manual. Cassie could handle ipods, laptops, and mobile phones with imperturbability. The young seemed so comfortable in this brave new world, she thought, whilst those of advanced years struggled to keep up.

Renee set the tray on the coffee table, and stood for a moment looking down at her only grand-child. She looked so tiny; so vulnerable, she thought, feeling a surge of protectiveness. Dressed in purple top and skirt in cosy velour, the mousy blonde hair drawn back into a scrunchie, Cassandra reminded her of poster she'd seen advertising the West End production of "Les Miserables." The artists' impression of the wan Cosette could have been her very own grand-daughter. Huge eyes dominating a pale heart shaped face, staring beseechingly down at Renee from the top deck of the No.47 bus as it had passed her out shopping. Victor Hugo could have modelled his frail orphan on the very child that knelt by her feet, finger still tracing the glass front of the TV, thought Renee. The same fragility of being. The same beguiling delicacy. The same winsome expression that tore at one's hearts strings like a mad violinist.

'Enjoy the film, sweetheart.'

Cassandra, absorbed with the unfolding canine drama, appeared not to have heard. Renee left the room closing the door softly behind her. Lyndsey pulled the solicitor's letter from her handbag, and placed it on the table. To fortify herself for the ordeal of showing it to her mother, she took a gulp of tea. It was hot and strong. Nobody made tea quite like mum, she thought. Her hand moulded to the cup with its faded pattern of sprigged flowers, and its familiarity added to her sense of comfort. Memories of childhood flooded back. The tick of the clock on the dresser on which her father's pipe and tobacco reposed. Oh, the smell of that smoke, she remembered, closing her eyes in the luxury of it. Dad would sit at the scrubbed table, puffing reflectively. Lyndsey, as ever fascinated by this strange ritual, would watch, chin propped on hands, as the blue ribbons curled up towards the ceiling. Whereupon they vanished. She remembered, as a child, wondering where the smoke went. For a long time she thought a genie lived up among the eaves, and each pipe her father smoked, added to its size.

Her eyes were drawn back to the letter. For the past week it had been a dragging weight on her conscience like Marley's chains. Having re-read its contents every hour during the past seven days, she was now thoroughly conversant with its contents. Terrifying words, on stiff cream paper bearing the logo of a lowered portcullis underneath "Parsloes & Dean' in bold print......

> 'Dear Mr. Daly,
>
> *We are writing to inform you that your wife, Lyndsey Marie Daly, has visited this office in order to instigate Divorce Proceedings against you. We, as her appointed legal representatives, are of the opinion that she has sufficient grounds to bring about this action, and would urge you to appoint a solicitor to represent your own interests in this regard.*

Lyndsey took a bite out of the scone. She did it in effort to calm herself but the swallowing of a blob of cream had the opposite effect. She felt sick. Her stomach went into fast spin. Lyndsey clutched the table edge, as a wave of giddiness engulfed her. An indigestible lump of scone had wedged itself somewhere behind her ribs, and she groaned. The final words of the letter danced in front of her eyes,

In due course we shall be asking Mrs. Daly to return to this office in order to complete a Sworn Affidavit detailing events leading to the breakdown of the marriage, which shall be duly presented to Court.

Yours faithfully,

Oh God, God, God... Raymond was blissfully unaware of what she was seeking to do. Every morning since the appointment with Mr. Parsloe, she'd flung herself downstairs at the sound of the postman with the sole intention of secreting the letter away. Some paralyzing fear had told her that she needed to acquaint herself with its contents before returning it to the mat for Ray to find. Didn't it say somewhere in the Bible 'Know thine enemy?' Hadn't she also heard it said that "forewarned is forearmed"...

But each day that passed quadrupled her dread. It became harder and harder to let the letter leave her fevered possession. Her husband's imagined reaction began to grow out of all proportion. At first, she thought he'd be pissed off to find she'd sought legal advice behind his back. Now, a week later, his reaction had grown to frightening proportions in her mind.

Nausea overcome Lyndsey. Slumped across the table, she sensed someone enter the room. An arm went around her shoulders and she heard Renee's voice, sounding as if it were coming from a long way off, 'Lyndsey love, what's happened? Oh my darling..'

She felt her head being lifted and cradled in her mother's ample bosom. The older woman rocked her gently, stroking her hair, and muttering endearments. Clarity of mind came back to Lyndsey. She felt the nausea recede like a tide on the turn. Shakily she said, 'It's OK Mum. I think I must have fainted.'

'Fainted? You're not pregnant…?'

'No, nothing like that.'

'Oh' Renee sounded disappointed. Lyndsey felt guilty. She knew how much her mother wanted another grandchild. It was a futile dream on Renee's part, but Lyndsey could not reveal the reason behind that futility. That deep within the most private part of herself, an inter-uterine device guarded the entrance to her womb. Fitted when the realization had hit Lyndsey, that, despite her love for Cassandra, she wanted no more children. Now, when her husband claimed his conjugal rights, she could submit, triumphant in the knowledge that no pregnancy would result. Only the night before, as she lay spread-eagled on the bed, Raymond bearing down on her like a rutting stag, she knew that whilst a single eager sperm might be successful in reaching its target, no foetus could grow around the tiny plastic contraption inserted into her womb.

Lyndsey focused gray eyes, as translucent and soft as a doe's, onto her mother's face. 'Sorry mum, I know how much you'd like an addition to the Fairbrother clan.'

Renee said, 'You were an only child, so perhaps it runs in the family. Anyway, what's more at issue here is to find out why you fainted. Healthy young women don't just flake out unless there is something physically wrong. Goodness, when I was your age I had the strength and stamina of an ox.'

Lyndsey flinched. She guessed what was coming next. Once her mother had embarked on such a tirade, nothing would deter her. From the lounge came the distant bark of a dog, and a child's laughter. Cass was obviously enjoying the film, she thought. Good old Beethoven. The dvd St. Bernard had saved the day, just as his working contemporaries did on the Swiss slopes with their barrels of brandy to revive fallen skiers.

'You've let yourself go too, darling, and I admit to being perplexed. Even as a little girl, you were always insistent on wearing the prettiest dresses, and spent hours in your teens experimenting with the latest hairstyle and make-up. For some reason you've lost interest in the way you look, and I wish you'd tell me why.'

Lyndsey opened her mouth to protest, and promptly shut it like a goldfish. Her mother was in full throttle, and nothing would stop her having her say, except maybe an asteroid hitting the earth, and their area of North London in particular.

'No good you looking defensive Lyn. It has to be said, and I wish I'd raised the subject before now. There's obviously a problem with your self-image, and the best short term remedy is some retail therapy. Let me treat you to a day at the beauty salon. We'll have the full works together. Hair, skin, nails. I'll buy you a super new outfit to round it off.'

Her mother pushed the newspaper across the table and tapped at the opened page, 'Read this. The lady in the article had lost the will to look nice. Those clever style guru's from the telly took her in hand, and worked their usual magic. You have to admit she looks a million dollars after the fashion revamp, and you'd look a billion darling with that beautiful face of yours.'

Exasperated beyond measure, Lyndsey flung the newspaper aside, 'for fuck's sake Mum, it's not a makeover I need.'

'What then?'

'Here goes' thought Lyndsey. Taking the deepest of breaths, she spoke the two words that had seemed glued to her tongue, 'A divorce.'

Chapter Six

RENEE BUSTLED UP the pathway. After a sleepless night, she was not in the best of moods and it showed by her forceful rat-tatting on the door.

Lyndsey opened it a crack and peered through. Renee grimaced at the sliver view of her daughter. Mascara smudged eyes and hair that evidently hadn't seen a comb that morning.

'Oh mum, it's you,' Her daughter sounded nonplussed. 'You'd better come in.'

Renee marched into the hall, and deposited her handbag on the telephone table. Catching sight of herself in the mirror above, she adjusted the gold flecked scarf around her neck. On her way to Lyndsey's house to tackle her daughter regarding the bombshell of the previous day, she'd detoured via the High Street and treated herself not only to the scarf, but a new lipstick. She'd bought one for Lyndsey too. She felt that by making these simple purchases she was somehow arming herself for what was to come.

'Where's Cassandra?'

'In her bedroom listening to 'One Direction' on her iPod.'

'What direction...?'

'It's a boy band mum. All the kids are crazy about them.'

'Ah.. well don't let her know I'm here just yet. I want a private word first.'

Lyndsey led the way into the conservatory. Renee frowned at her back view. The girl was wearing a baggy man's sweater over a crumpled skirt, whose material was the colour and texture of porridge. On her feet were flip flops, better suited to a beach.

In contrast, she herself was dressed in a smart suede skirt and matching jacket, and her cloud of silver hair had been artfully tamed into its usual sleek bob.

It was cold in the conservatory. The black floor tiles matched the clouds outside. On the wicker sofa, a batch of photographs had been fanned out, as though a dealer were setting a gaming table for cards. Each one bore a yellow post-it note sticker. Renee glanced down at the nearest. It read, 'Iron this' in bold handwriting, heavily underlined as if to add emphasis to the words. Puzzled, Renee bent to pick it up. The photograph was a facial shot of her son-in-law Raymond, which showed all too clearly the wrinkles developing around his eyes.

Evidently reading the questioning look on her mother's face, Lyndsey shrugged. She said, 'Just a bit of fun mum. At Ray's expense.'

'A bit of fun..' Echoed Renee. She picked up another photograph. A holiday snap. Raymond Daly stretched out on a lounger by a pool, surrounded by the detritus of a man at leisure. Newspapers, sunglasses, an empty glass, discarded shoes. The post it note read, 'Needs tidying up. See to it.' A third photograph showed an aerial view of the top of her son-in-law's head, obviously taken from a hotel balcony. His thinning hair on the crown was evident. 'Bald patch needs seeding. Attend please Lyn.' Ordered the handwriting on the yellow note.

'What on earth..?' Renee began, allowing the photos to slip from her fingers like confetti.

'Petty, I know.' Came the reply. Lyndsey began to pile the photographs together. There was something defensive in her demeanor, thought Renee, awaiting an explanation.

'Post-it notes are one of Raymond's favourite means of communication. He dots them around the house to draw my attention to chores that he considers urgent. What you see here is merely today's offerings. I counted them this morning after he'd left for work. There are eleven. A bumper batch. He always leaves more during school holidays to make sure I can't 'swan off out all day' as he puts it. Eleven tasks I have to ensure are done before he gets home otherwise my neck'll be in the noose. So forgive my joke with the photographs. It's my pathetic private attempt to get my own back…'

Renee had listened in impassive silence. She said, 'I can't help but agree it's an outrageous way to treat a wife. As though you were nothing more than a secretary.'

Facing her daughter, she continued, 'but darling, surely throwing in the towel isn't the answer. Maybe you and Raymond could benefit from some professional counselling before you act with such finality, and I'd be happy to tackle him on any contentious issues on your behalf. Such as this post-it note fiasco.' In the murky light of the conservatory Renee studied Lyndsey's face to see if her words were making any impact, 'ending a union is such an irrevocable step, especially where a child is involved. All I ask is that you consider the consequences. Have you any idea of the upheaval such an action will entail, not only to your life darling, but those around you. The sale of property, the assignment of pension rights, the issue of custody over Cassandra. A nightmare in the making.'

'So you won't support me,' said Lyndsey, and Renee heard the stubborn note to her voice. She sat on one of the Lloyd Loom chairs, careful to ensure that the cane did not snag her nylons. She gestured to her daughter to sit on the other one, but the girl remained resolutely on her feet.

The garden beyond the glass was shrouded in gloom. It was that time of year when daylight struggled to gain a foothold, thought Renee. Somehow the premature closing down of the day drew a parallel with the closing down of her daughter's marriage. A marriage, which she'd had no idea was in such terminal trouble.

'It's not a question of whether or not I'll support you, Lyndsey. I'm just knocked for six by the news.'

'Don't pretend mum. It can't be that much of a surprise.'

Renee shivered, and it wasn't entirely due to the chill, 'What makes you think I wouldn't find it so? I honestly had no idea things between you and Raymond had reached this...' She sought for the right word, but her vocabulary seemed to have imploded - it was as though her brain were an upturned Scrabble board with all the letters scattered. '..Impasse.' That was it. Impasse. The right word. The perfect word.

Her daughter retorted, 'There's none so blind as those that refuse to see.'

Renee looked up at her, 'So make me see. What has gone so wrong with your marriage that warrants hot footing off to a solicitor without discussing it with your mother first. Is there another woman? Raymond is a good looking man, with a low boredom threshold and high libido. You've admitted as much to me in the past. Have you caught him straying?'

'No.'

'What then? Is he neglecting you? Spending too much time at the office?'

'No.'

'Then surely you're making a terrible mistake.'

'Exactly what I knew you'd say. Now you can see why I didn't let on about my appointment at Parsloes.'

'Don't you think you should have.'

'I know you Mum. You'd have tried to talk me out of it.'

'That's true up to a point,' said Renee choosing her words carefully, 'No observer, either impartial, or involved, can ever really get to grips with the dynamics that make up a relationship. The most unlikely pairings make the most wonderful couples, I find.'

'But Raymond is basically a good man, Lyn. Look around you – at this house. He works hard to provide for his family. Of course he has his annoying ways – doesn't everyone? He can be pedantic and bull headed. I can see that but what man isn't? The fault can't only be one sided love. It takes two make a marriage as it takes two to break it. You're not the easiest person to live with Lyndsey, as I can testify. I'm your mother remember. You have a tendency to daydream your life away.' She smiled at the younger women, who was picking disconsolately at the leaf of a potted palm.

Lyndsey said, 'I might have guessed.'

'Guessed what?'

'That you'd take his part. You always were a fully paid up member of Ray's fan club weren't you mother dearest.'

'Oh love,' Renee plucked at the baggy sleeve of her daughter's jumper in anguish, 'you know I didn't mean..'

'Didn't mean what, mum? Didn't mean that you are so blinkered by Ray's Mr. Nice Guy impersonation that you can't see what he's really like underneath. Didn't mean that just because he doesn't beat me, or gamble, or muck about with other women, that that makes him the perfect husband. Have you any idea what it's like to be married to someone so bloody perfect. Someone who insists that you've got to be bloody perfect too, not just some of the time, but all of the time. I have to be the most accomplished cook, the most adventurous love maker, the most earth-like of earth mothers, the most seasoned hostess when he invites business colleagues over... The minute I let slip mum,' Lyndsey's voice was rising to fever pitch now, and Renee looked at her in alarm, 'the fucking minute I let slip, he's on my case. Do you realize now why I've let myself go as you term it? It's the only way I can rebel short of going on the bottle to drown my woes' Lyndsey was shouting now, her doe eyes awash with tears. She was razoring both hands through her hair, making the urchin crop stand up like an unmown lawn.

Renee stood up in alarm. She'd never seen her daughter so distraught. 'Calm yourself.'

'That's exactly what my dearly beloved is going to say. I can hear him now. 'You're suffering from your nerves Lyn, you're having an early menopause Lyn, it's the time of the month Lyn, you're having a mid-life crisis Lyn.'

'He'll come up with every reason in the book to lay the blame at my door. Of course, he'll deny any responsibility for our marriage falling apart. After all, he's Mr. Rationality. Mister Let's Sit Down and Talk This Through Calmly. Me seeking to engineer a split between us, will just be symptomatic to him of a totally irrational female driven by her hormones into acting foolishly.'

'He'll make me out to be mad. Paint a picture of some crazy Mrs. Rochester weaving a path across the attic floor...'

Renee felt it was time to stop these rantings. 'Get a grip. Nothing's going be achieved by losing control like this.'

'You're right. I've got to keep my cool when I break the news.'

'You mean he doesn't know you're planning to divorce him?' Renee was stunned, 'but the letter...'

'He's not seen it mum. I hid it from him. I was scared you see. That's why I came round to see you yesterday. Hoping you'd give me courage and a bit of moral support. But you needn't worry any longer. I'm telling Raymond everything. Tonight.'

Neither of them heard the sound of footsteps running down the stairs.

'Why are you both shouting?' came a tremulous voice.

Renee and Lyndsey both spun around, to be confronted by the figure of Cassandra standing in the doorway. Her small pale face was stricken.

'Tell Daddy what tonight, Mummy?'

Chapter Seven

RAYMOND DALY WAS a breast man. He always had been. He was not particularly proud of the fact, but had learnt to live with it. His earliest memory was of being nestled between the blue veined orbs of his mother, sucking contentedly on a nipple. Gazing up into his mother's face, he'd basked in the golden glow of her adoration. Weaning had been an anathema to her. He'd been breastfed until he was three years old, a fact of which his mother was immensely proud. She took it as proof of her mastery of all things maternal. Growing up, Raymond continued to touch his mother's breasts, until his father, chancing upon mother and son nude from the waist up one day, flew into a rage, and forbade any future physical contact. Ray had been ten years old. He recalled, with a shudder, his father calling him "a filthy little ejit", and his mother "a whore". His mother never again allowed him to touch her, and Ray never forgave his father for the curtailment of this pleasure.

Ever since those halcyon days of childhood he was on a quest to latch his mouth around a rubbery nipple. Breasts spelt his mother. Breasts spelt warm milk. Breasts spelt security. And to Ray, now in the thick of a mid-life crisis which was robbing his sang-froid, security was everything.

Not for the first time he wondered why he had married Lyndsey.

Why he'd even been attracted to her in the first place.

Lyndsey with her washboard chest, and non-existent hips. He thought of the luscious curves of his mother, the copious breasts into which his tiny fingers were once permitted to knead, and groaned. He groaned again as someone elbowed past him on the platform, noticing that the throng of commuters was swelled by the inclusion of tired, fractious children. There seemed legions of them. Half Term, he remembered, feeling an unaccustomed pang of guilt that he hadn't taken at least one day's leave to do something fun with Cassandra. A trip to Alton Towers perhaps, or a visit to the Madame Tussauds, or even a ride on the London Eye. He was suddenly consumed with the awareness that his little girl was growing up fast, and there would soon become a time when she wouldn't want to do things with her dear old dad. When teenage boys would become her raison d'etre and banishment of her father into the emotional hinterlands would swiftly fellow. He inwardly cursed himself for not making more of her Autumn term break, and the guilt he felt made him despise even more the children around him coming home on the Tube after a fun day out. One, a scruffy tyke of about five barged into his leg. Ray staggered, almost losing balance. He just managed to prevent his copy of the Daily Sport, cunningly concealed inside the more respectable Standard, from slipping out onto the floor.

A draught of air swept along the cavern of the underground station, signalling the imminent arrival of the train. The platform smelt of decaying fast food. Gritty dust peppered Ray's face. He scowled. He hated the daily grind of commuting, almost as much as he hated other people's kids. The only child he could tolerate was his own daughter, and it was a constant sore that Lyndsey had so far only managed to provide him with one child. Ray wanted a son to carry on the Daly name. Making love to his wife was a burden that he was determined to shoulder in the quest for another offspring, and he made a silent pact with himself as the train whooshed past his face, that tonight he would once again clamber aboard her bony hips in an effort to plant his seed. She could resist all she liked. Ray didn't mind a bit of a fight. In fact, her resistance was often the only thing that gave him enjoyment of the procedure.

The train slewed to a halt.

A big man, tall and broad shouldered, Ray was able to muscle his way on board, holding back the pressing weight of humanity behind him, by the sheer bulk of his frame. Unusually, for this time of night, there were two vacant seats in the carriage. Ray pounced on one. The other, across the aisle, was taken by an elderly man, accompanied by a youth, whose awkward body language and pimple encrusted forehead spoke of one suffering the agonies of adolescence. A grandfather and grandson, Ray surmised. Probably the old boy had taken the youngster on a round of London museums in attempt to educate the lad during his half term holiday.

At the next station, St. Paul's, a Chinese girl alighted. She was stunning. A curtain of blue black hair hung to her waist, and she possessed a petite but perfectly honed figure. Moving along the crowded aisle, she paused in front of Ray, and lifted a delicate hand to clasp the overhead hanger. After a swift appraisal, he paid her scant attention. Her tits weren't big enough.

The spotty youth gaped. He was standing next to the Chinese girl, and Ray saw a glob of saliva fall from the open mouth. He wondered, idly, whether it was the boy's first evidence of sexual awakening.

A memory came to Ray. His own first sexual encounter. He'd been thirteen years old, and, unlike the stunning Oriental, he'd dribbled over the plump 15 year old daughter of one of his mother's acquaintances. What was her name? He frowned in an effort to remember. Beverley something... Beverley Kavanagh. Yes, that was it. Fat, frizzy haired Beverley, who possessed a pair of breasts of truly gargantuan proportions. Milk white footballs with nipples that resembled bulls-eyes on a dartboard. He stretched back on the uncomfortable passenger seat, and luxuriated in their memory.

The train hurtled through the black tunnel. Through a gap in the strap hanging body bodies swaying in front on him, he caught a glimpse of his reflection in the window. It pleased him. He was 47, but felt he had aged rather well. Better than most he thought. The years had broadened his shoulders and added a rugged squareness to his chin. Even in the glass of the tube train window, he could see that his jaw was shadowed, and a quick check with his hand confirmed a tell-tale prickliness of the skin. He would need to shave before he confronted his wife tonight. Ray briefly contemplated growing another beard. As a naturally hirsute man, it was easy. In only a few days he would see a luxuriant reddish growth spreading across his face and neck. He contemplated whether to grow one merely to annoy Lyndsey. She hated beards, only marginally more than she disliked moustaches, and whenever he'd had the temerity in the past to grow facial hair, the frost in their relationship had taken on artic conditions.

Someone had once told him he resembled the actor Charles Dance. Ray couldn't see it then, but he could now. He smiled pleasedly at his reflection, before sweeping a hand to his thatch of sandy blonde hair.

'Is your mam in?' Beverley Kavanagh had called on an errand to collect a knitting pattern loaned to Mrs. Daly by her own mother. Raymond opened the front door in response to petulant trilling. Interrupted halfway through his tea, he was munching through a mouthful of Cornish pasty, but that couldn't prevent him from gaping. On the doorstep stood a broad beamed girl, hair scraped off her face into an untidy bun. She was dressed in the navy uniform of his own school, but that wasn't the reason for Ray's stuttering reaction to this unexpected visit. Crumbs of pasty spewed from his mouth, and decorated the front of his jersey, as he gazed fixedly at the ample chest straining against the confines of the girl's blouse. It was a warm evening in early spring he remembered, and Beverley was coatless, the top two buttons of her blouse undone, revealing a cleavage of mountain range proportions.

'Well, is she?'

'Er, No.' He'd stumbled over the words, his eyes never leaving that inviting white expanse of flesh which spread underneath the girl's neck like a spilled bottle of milk. The skin was dotted, he noticed, with a dusting of freckles. The girl caught him looking, and hiked up her bra straps suggestively. Ray felt his face scorch.

'You're a second year, ain't ya?' Her voice was as thick and toneless as the moo-ing of a cow, thought Raymond, before another thought struck that this girl did indeed look like a cow. A huge, lumbering red and white one, like those that often grazed the fields in the family's annual holiday to Wales.

'What's up? Cat got yer tongue?'

She had a disconcerting way of firing questions at him, without waiting for an answer.

'You on your own?'

'Yeah' the word came out in a shower of pastry crumbs.

'I'll come in then. Wait for your mum.'

'She'll be ages. It's Bingo night.'

'I'll come in anyway. I need a pee.'

Ray could never remember quite how it happened, but after directing this wholly unexpected visitor up to the bathroom, they'd ended up together on the sofa in his mum's front room. The room was fetid and sticky from the heat of the day. A vase of chrysanthemums wilted on the table, the sweet smell of their decay perfuming the air. A trapped bluebottle droned against the swathes of net curtain.

Beverley's attention was taken with an ornament of a street urchin boy leaning against a Dickensian lamp-post, occupying pride of place on the windowsill. She swivelled round to pick it up. Her legs spread. Ray's mouth had gone dry. He knew what girls' looked like "down below", had sniggered over the clinical illustration in the biology textbook along with the rest of the class. Privately, he thought female genitalia looked ugly. Like a gaping mouth. He had no desire to finger the fanny of any girl in his class, like most of the boys did, hanging around the bike sheds after school in hopeful anticipation. The girls used the contents of their knickers as a useful bartering tool, it seemed to him, to gain money and cigarettes from their gibbering acolytes. He thought it quite clever. Secretly admired them for doing so. But he just wasn't interested.

Breasts though were a different matter. He'd have given anything for a feel of a warm malleable pair.

Beverley noticed him staring fixedly in the region of her nipples.

'What's your name Daly boy?'

'Raymond'.

'Do you like these Raymond.'

She took his hand, and placed it over the wide expanse of her left breast. Then she began to circle it around, until Ray, his eyes never leaving the tantalizing glimpse of flesh between his splayed fingers, began to feel dizzy. Something strange was happening in his pants, he realized. Everything seemed to be expanding. It was as though his willy was a balloon that someone was blowing up. The sensation was thrilling. He felt his breath coming in short gasps, like the time his father took him on the 'Whip' at an amusement park at Southend on Sea.

'Tell you what,' Beverley said, in what he thought was a weirdly matter of fact voice. How could she not be affected by the delicious giddiness what was overtaking him. Did she not feel the same excitement. Evidently not, Ray decided, after hearing what she said next,

'I'll show you my tits if I can take this bit of china. I collect ornaments.'

He nodded dumbly. His mother's reaction to finding her prized piece missing when she got home later hardly registered. At that moment, he'd have given the contents of Mrs. Daly's jewellery box for the merest glimpse of those naked breasts.

Ray climaxed. It was his first time. As Beverley unbuttoned her blouse and pulled down her brassiere, freeing the twin mounds, a tidal wave of pleasure engulfed him. He felt detached from his body. Feeling as though he were nothing more than a giant penis spreading its sticky wetness over his mother's prized Marquette settee. At that moment Raymond Daly was no longer a thirteen year old schoolboy living with his parents on a suburban housing estate. He was instead a composite sum of tingling nerve endings and uncontrollable tremors.

The train juddering to a halt curtailed his ramble down memory lane. Holborn. Time to change onto the Piccadilly for the final leg of his journey home. Ray shook his head in an effort to clear it. The last vestiges of a topless Beverley Kavanagh faded away.

He stood to disembark feeling faintly disorientated, and suddenly angry. He knew where the anger came from. Lyndsey.

She was the source of it, he realized. Everything could be traced back to the shadowy spectre of his wife.

It was all her fault. This frustration. He'd married her in the hope that she could cure him of his obsession. By deliberately choosing a flat chested specimen as a partner in matrimony, he'd assumed he would get his cravings under control. By the mere dint of his choice, didn't that show his subconscious that big tits were no longer a big deal where Raymond Daly was concerned.

Now he knew he was wrong. Had always known it really if he were honest with himself. He'd married Lyndsey to cure him, and she'd proved an ineffectual antidote. She'd let him down. He wasn't cured at all. And as long as their marriage lasted, he would punish her for this fact.

Unbidden, his mind went back to the first time he'd been introduced to her. A gauche 18 year old, like a leggy bambi with her huge grey eyes and soft fawn hair. At thirty two, he'd just landed a plum job with a City investment bank and found, to his dismay, that there was a staffing crisis with the clerical help.

'Ray', his boss had said, 'meet Miss Fairbrother. She's the new temp in this department. Fresh from a local employment bureau to help us out while we're so short staffed. Lyndsey will be responsible for all the secretarial duties.'

At first he hadn't thought much of her. She was too skittish, too flighty. He found her attitude to work lacked the seriousness which he felt it demanded, and her appeasing manner irritated him. Ray liked ballsy, feisty women, and Lyndsey Fairbrother certainly was not one of those. When a permanent P.A. was appointed three months later, and Miss Fairbrother assigned by her agency elsewhere, Raymond Daly hardly noticed. Until that was, he'd happened to walk past a

Bishopsgate pub one evening, and saw a recognisable figure sitting at a table outside, checking and re-checking her watch.

'Stood you up has he?' He found himself saying to his own surprise, wondering where the words had come from. Lyndsey had glanced up, evidently startled. Ray had to admit she was prettier than remembered. Her hair had grown longer, and she was wearing it loose to her shoulders. The tight buttercup yellow dress helped to accentuate what little curves she had. It was a warm evening, early in spring, and to his astonishment, Ray felt the sap rising. Lyndsey had smiled and he realized, for the first time, quite how beguiling she could be. 'Nothing like that. I'm waiting for a friend. She said she'd meet me here at eight, but I'm beginning to wonder if I've got the wrong day.'

'I could murder a cold beer. Mind if I join you?'

She'd assented with a slight nod of the head, and Ray had joined her at the table. He bought her a glass of wine, and they chatted easily while the flow of commuters thinned on the pavement to be replaced by the early dining crowds. The friend never showed. At a quarter to nine a text message bleeped to say she had been inadvertently held up and could they re-schedule for another time.

'Her loss is my gain', Ray had said, 'How about something to eat. My favourite restaurant is just around the corner.'

'I know Mr. Daly. Veriggio's isn't it? You forget that I booked you many a business lunch there.'

'Call me Ray. Dinner with a lovely young lady beats talking office with stuffed shirt colleagues any day of the week.....'

It had been the start of a whirlwind romance. Six months later, to the day, they exchanged vows in Lyndsey's local parish church with her widowed mother, Renee, beaming happily from the aisles. Mrs Fairbrother had made no secret of the fact that she viewed this urbane professional a great catch for her daughter. A mature man to take the place perhaps, of the father the girl had lost at such an impressionable age.

The marriage had not proved a success. He wanted a wife who was not afraid to cross swords with him, not one afraid of her own shadow. After the initial excitement at landing a woman much younger than himself, a pretty ethereal creature that made him the envy of golf-course, Ray realized that the fun of moulding her into composite of a perfect wife had worn off. Like the picture of Dorian Gray, he wanted to hide her away in an attic so that he wouldn't be faced with the unhappy reflection of his own creation.

When Cassandra was born, a girl, not the longed for son, the honeymoon was well and truly over.

The tube doors sliding open bought him back to the present. Ray grimaced both from proximity of sweaty fellow commuters, and the thought of his wife. The only good thing to have come out of his marriage was Cassie. Of course he'd wanted a boy, to carry on the Daly name, and had blamed Lyndsey for not providing him with one. Indeed, it wasn't until the little girl's third birthday when she had flung her arms around her daddy and kissed him with whoops of joy at the unwrapped doll's house, that Ray's heart had finally softened. So while his daughter hadn't proved a disappointment, the same could not be said for Lyndsey. She'd been a constant source of displeasure. Especially between the sheets.

Well, she was in for it, tonight, he thought with grim satisfaction, pushing aside a commuter barring the way. He'd get home, eat supper, shave, shower, and spend some time in the company of "Bouncy Babes" his favourite porn website. That would psyche him up sufficiently to scale the unrelenting rock face of his wife's body.

He shouldered his way through the strap hangers, noticing to his surprise that the Chinese girl had gone. She must have got off at Chancery Lane he realized. Ray frowned. He guessed he'd been too deep in his Beverley Kavanagh reverie to have noticed.

One thing he did notice. As he jumped off onto the platform he glanced back at the spotty youth, who was still standing next to his grandfather in the recently vacated carriage.

A tell-tale damp patch was darkening the front of the boy's jeans.

Lyndsey had a choice of two cereals. A bumper bag of porridge oats sat on the kitchen table. Alongside it was a box of ubiquitous bran. Neither was really suited to her purpose, she thought, frowning slightly at the dilemma presented. The best type would be something sticky. Honey coated puffs of wheat, or cornflakes steeped in syrup. But there were no such concessions to a sweet tooth in the Daly household. Her husband was adamant that everything they ate should be organically produced and free from harmful additives. On this point, Lyndsey concurred with him. She too, believed in eating healthily. However, there were times, and this was one, when she wished their store cupboards held provisions that were a little more sinful.

She was wishing it not for the purpose of eating.

She had another, altogether more devious purpose in mind for the procurement of something sticky.

Lyndsey decided on the porridge oats. They had an annoying floating consistency she felt, rather more than the compact shreds of bran. She took the packet, and with deliberation, began to sprinkle them liberally around the kitchen floor. Then she went out into the hallway, shaking the packet as she went. Oat flakes settled like snow. Like Hansel and Gretel laying a trail of breadcrumbs to lead their way back to the Gingerbread House, she took a circular path around the downstairs rooms of her house. A spiral path of flakes made a figure of eight shape on the polished wood floor of the lounge. Packet almost empty, she tipped the remainder on the mat by the front door. Raymond always took his shoes off on entering the house, and Lyndsey planned that the porridge would adhere to his socks.

Satisfied with her handiwork, Lyndsey returned to the kitchen and began to liberally slop puddles of cold tea around the countertops. She sprinkled a topping of toast crumbs shaken from the tray of the toaster. Finally, she took the butter knife and added a few strategically placed smears on the kitchen table. A garnish of coffee grounds completed the desecration of her erstwhile pristine kitchen.

Was it enough? She wondered. Lyndsey leant against the sink, trying to still the anxious beat of her heart. A quick check of her watch confirmed the awful truth. Seven thirty. Any minute now she would hear Ray's key turn in the lock. Just time to go around the house turning on every light. Nothing enraged him more than finding No 19 Shenlagh Gardens lit up like a belisha beacon as he came up the garden path.

She raced around flicking switches. Turning on a lamp here, an overhead light there. For good measure she put a CD in the stereo and turned the volume up full. It was one of her secret purchases. Gregorian chants. She loved them. Ray hated them.

Almost unable to breath as the bewitching hour approached, Lyndsey returned to the kitchen and took the letter from her pocket. The letter that only a few short hours before had caused her mother such distress. She thought briefly of Cassandra. The child had not wanted to go back with Nana, but both Lyndsey and Renee had been adamant. She knew that her mother would handle Cassie's inevitable questions with the diplomatic touch for which she was renowned. The youngster had become hysterical when Lyndsey finally admitted that "what she was going to tell daddy that night" was that their marriage was over. There was to be no more mummy and daddy.

She surveyed the kitchen with a critical air. The stage was set. It looked like a carefully arranged scene in a provincial theatre. Amidst the clutter and confusion, sat the letter, carefully propped against the salt pot on the table. Lyndsey thought it so glaringly white, that her eyes hurt to look at it.

If everything went according to plan, Ray's attention would be so distracted by the mess in the house, and the wasteful use of electricity that his reaction to its contents would be muted. With any luck, thought Lyndsey, he would be in mid-lecture before he even noticed or read it. Knowing Ray, as she did, he would want to wring the very last drop out of the sodden cloth of her housewifely failings, before he would allow himself to turn to other matters. Hopefully, by the time he got around to the letter he would have worn out his powers of confrontation.

Did she have time to take a shower? Despite the cold, her armpits and groin felt clammy with sweat. If she were clean and powdered she would be more able, she thought, to deal with the inevitable eruption ahead.

Lyndsey sprinted upstairs, scattering a cloud of porridge oats. She'd reached the landing when she heard the sound she'd been dreading. A key turning in a lock, followed by the squeal of protest. Too late she remembered that one of the eleven post-it notes had asked her to apply a squirt of lubricating oil to the hinges. A smile curved her lips. There was a bitterness to it. By ignoring this command, she'd given herself another potential shield to deflect the arrows of his attack over the letter.

He would moan about the squeaky hinges for at least the time it would take for her to brew tea. She often thought that Ray's modus operandi was finding fault. He'd even chosen a profession where this inherent need to pick holes was satisfied. As I.T. Manager of the London branch of an international Bank, he was responsible for trouble shooting the computer system, finding out why monitors suddenly went bank, and disc drives became corrupted. Her spouse was trained to search for what might be wrong, instead of to appreciate what might be right.

The door slammed. Lyndsey jumped. She knew that slam. It was one of frustration and discontent. Raymond, she thought, had a way of shutting doors that spoke volumes. The door, a willing foot soldier, seemed anxious to do his bidding for it made a noise worthy of an explosive device. It rattled Lyndsey how her husband had the knack of using inanimate objects in his war of attrition against her so that at times she could almost believe they were real.

'Lyndsey,' Ray was shouting, 'Lyn, what the hell...'

She didn't hear the rest. The CD of Gregorian Chants had reached the heights of divine incantation and drowned other noise. From the lounge the sound of monks in spiritual worship echoed. Lyndsey thought that if she tried really hard she could transport herself in her imaginings to some far oft Monastery, staring out at the moon through a Gothic Arch. How wonderful to be kneeling on a cold flagstone floor, joining Monks in their nightly devotions instead of skulking here at the top of the stairs in her suburban prison. She was about to face her warder. A husband whom she was preparing to divorce. With a sinking feeling of resignation she backed into the bedroom and sat on the four poster awaiting her fate.

Soon he would know about the letter. Soon he would read it. How soon..... ? Lyndsey gulped as the monks were cut off mid flow. She couldn't see Ray's hairy, white knuckled fingers, but knew one of them had pressed the off switch on the state of the art stereo system. Silence filled the house. It was a heavy oppressive silence. A silence you got, she thought, just before a thunderstorm.

Lyndsey felt her heart race.

'This is crazy,' she told herself, 'keep calm. He's not going to hurt you. What is the worse that can happen?'

She often played this game. Ever since childhood, her mother had used the homily as a means of comforting her daughter, 'Don't fret pet. What is the worse that can happen?'

She heard her husband's footsteps on the floor below. He was in the lounge. Careful, measured footsteps, that circled the room. What was he doing? She grasped a bedpost for support and leaned forward, straining to hear.

'What the fuck?' She heard him say, 'Porridge oats... All over the fucking floor.'

He was muttering to himself, but the mutterings were loud. Evidently he suspected she was in the kitchen and wanted her to hear. This shocked Lyndsey almost as much as his use of the F-word. Ray hardly ever swore. He was not a man to express himself with profanity, he once told his mother in law. Lyndsey recalled how gratified Renee had been to receive this snippet of information. It meant another nomination for Ray to receive the "Son in Law of the Year" award. She heard him go into the kitchen. Could picture him staring aghast at the staged chaos. Then she heard him take the stairs. Two at a time.

'Have you lost the fucking plot, or what?'

He stood in the bedroom doorway, one foot raised, pointing. Lyndsey, unable to meet the hard mockery in his eyes, followed the direction of his finger, towards a left foot encased in brown sock speckled with oatmeal.

She sat transfixed.

Her husband put his foot slowly and deliberately to the floor. He leant against the doorjamb, and folded his arms.

'Am I missing something here? Tell me the point of decorating my home with breakfast cereals. The latest fad in interior design perhaps? Or have Coral, and Dee, that deadly duo of the coffee morning, persuaded you that the chattering classes leave a trail of porridge throughout their living quarters as a mark of high intellect. Organic porridge oats, I presume? Anything less would be sacrilege.'

As always, Ray was beginning to lose her. His voice held that familiar jeering note which signalled the start of a lengthy post mortem. As though he found both his wife, and her actions, slightly amusing. But not amusing enough to let it go.

She wondered whether to say a word in defense of her friends. Ray hated both Coral and Dee with a passion. Simply because, she, Lyndsey, liked them. He called Coral, with her propensity for multi layered clothing 'Oxfam Queen' and Dee, a flamboyant personality in dress and manner, an 'arse licker.' She'd never discovered where the latter jibe emanated from. Feisty Dee, with her strong opinions on everything from nuclear disarmament to the dieting industry, certainly had never licked anyone's arse, as far as Lyndsey could tell.

The bedside clock ticked remorselessly. Lyndsey tried to steady her breathing. She knew Ray wasn't finished with her yet. Knew he hadn't even reached first base.

He slapped his forehead in a parody of someone having a brainwave. The sound was like the first warning clap of thunder. The storm was about to break, she thought.

'Of course, that's it. How stupid of me. Halloween is coming up, so this must be your idea of a trick or treat.'

Halloween? Lyndsey struggled to keep track of the conversation.

'Pray tell me Lyn, which one is it?'

Lyndsey thought how large he looked framed in the doorway. He'd taken off his jacket, and stood with shirtsleeves rolled up and tie slightly awry. His arms which had once impressed her with their muscle bound strength, now looked faintly obscene. Like the legs of a butchered pig hanging from a hook in an abattoir.

With difficulty she met his eyes. Ray could out-stare an owl she thought. His cold green gaze was unblinking.

'Husband arrives home from work after a hard day's graft at the office. Ten hours to be exact. There he is on the train, crushed in amongst the hoi polloi, looking forward to wiping his feet on the welcome mat. Home Sweet Home. Perhaps wifey will greet him at the front door. Offering a kiss and cuppa. Maybe there's a smell of roast beef wafting from the kitchen, and favourite Yorkshires. Pretty picture isn't it Lyn?'

She didn't react. She felt cold and stiff. The edge of the bed dug into her thighs.

'I said, isn't it Lyn?'

Dumbly, she nodded.

'So he comes up the garden path and what does he find? His house lit up like Blackpool Tower, and monks praising the Lord.'

'Perhaps he's prepared to overlook that. After all, his wife might have forgotten to turn the lights off downstairs when she came up. Maybe she's going slightly deaf and has to have the music turned top volume. Who knows...'

Lyndsey wanted to escape the bedroom. But knew he would bar the doorway. Her only exit route. She had to let Ray get his lecture out of his system first. After all, that was what she'd planned, wasn't it? Her head was beginning to pound. The tell-tale signs of her body protesting in advance at the emotional onslaught which it knew was about to follow.

Hopefully if she stayed silent, he'd wear himself out with talking. Especially as he'd had a hard day.

Momentarily she felt a pang of guilt followed by concern for her husband. Part of her still loved him. A part that was buried deep. Once they would have laughed together at the sheer idiocracy of finding porridge sprinkled around the floor. Maybe shared a joke about Goldilocks and the Three Bears. Or was her memory playing tricks. Lyndsey furrowed her brow trying to remember. Had Ray ever found such things funny?

'I'm sorry about the porridge,' She offered lamely. 'The bag must have leaked. Let me go and make you a cup of tea. Then I'll clear the mess.'

She made to get off the bed.

'Stay where you are.' Ray's voice was sharp. 'I haven't finished yet. Not by a long chalk.'

'Explain to me this Lyndsey. Why is there a trail in the lounge? What on earth were you doing walking around in circles with a holed bag of cereal. Call me dense, but I can't see the connection. If it was over the kitchen floor, I might begin to understand.'

'I was in the middle of clearing the breakfast things,' she lied, 'Been out all day and didn't have a chance to do it earlier. Then I heard a noise, and went to investigate.'

'I see. Leaving your little trail behind you. So what was so pressing today that stopped you cleaning the place before you went out? It's half term isn't it? No school for Cassie. No stints at the library for you. Explain please.'

Lyndsey couldn't. 'Explain, please. Explain please,' the words echoed through her head. Whenever Ray said them, her mind emptied. It was though her memory banks were wiped clean. She had no concept of who she was, or why she was, or where she was. There was just the steady rise and fall of her breathing.

'I'm waiting.'

Sweat trickled down her nose. She wished she could shower. Just stand under a pelt of hot water alone and naked. She wanted to be alone more than anything else. She had long ago lost the energy to resist Ray. Long ago lost the will to fight her corner. Now she just wanted to curl up into a ball and sleep.

'Well?'

Lyndsey licked dry lips, 'Mum came round.'

'It's just not good enough is it Lyn. Surely your first duty is to your husband. To provide a well-run home. How many of those chores I set you this morning have you actually accomplished? There were a pile of shirts to be ironed, the bureau drawers to be tidied, and I expected you to get some grass seed for the lawn. What about cooking? I don't suppose you've even thought about preparing an evening meal.'

This time she shook her head. The motion set off needles of pain in her temple.

'What about poor little Cass? Has she eaten tonight? Or has the kid gone to bed early on an empty stomach.'

'Cass is with Renee.'

The hall light behind her husband threw his shadow across the bedroom floor. Lyndsey thought how monstrous it looked like some crouching giant. He stood immobile in the doorway, face rigid, lips pursed.

Those lips opened now to say, 'Oh terrific. I've looked forward all day to seeing my daughter, and now you tell me she's not here.'

'Me and mum thought it best she go. You and I have to talk.'

'About Cassandra?'

'No.'

'Then, what?'

This is it, thought Lyndsey.

'About us,' she closed her eyes, seeing black shapes dance before them. 'I want out.'

Chapter Eight

AT TWO THIRTY in the morning, Coral Simpson was woken by a ring at the door. She stumbled out of bed, rubbing sleep from her eyes. Her husband, a shapeless blob under the duvet, was oblivious to the frantic trill of the bell.

Coral looked out of the window. Angry clouds were scudding the sky. Illuminated by the porch light stood a figure shivering with cold. It was Lyndsey. What was her friend doing out alone in the middle of the night? Pausing only to wonder at this question, Coral shoved her feet into a pair of fluffy mules, grabbed the spare duvet from the ottoman and hurried downstairs.

'Hang on, Lyn'.

It took her several seconds to undo the system of security locks that protected the door to the house. She yanked it open. Lyndsey stood on the step, seemingly frozen to the spot. Coral pulled her inside.

'Into the lounge.' Coral gave her friend a shove. 'God, your hands are like ice! Time for a brandy and hot water bottle.'

In the sitting room she switched on lamps, drew curtains and checked for draughts. Satisfied, she disappeared into the kitchen. Minutes passed accompanied by sound of glassware clinking. Then Coral was back, bearing a decanter on a tray and two brandy glasses. In the other hand she held a filled hot water bottle. With the brisk precision of a nurse, she tucked it in beside the immobile girl, adjusting the duvet so that it reached Lyndsey's neck. She then poured two generous measures of Martell and handed one across.

Coral watched the figure on the settee opposite under lowered lids. So thin was her friend, that her form barely dented the cushions. She thought of the day they had met. Three years ago, when Lyndsey had joined the staff at the library. Coral, Assistant Librarian had immediately taken to porcelain fragile Lyndsey Daly with her huge gray eyes and punkish spiked hair in its extraordinary shade of silver. There was something about her quiet diligence of manner that impressed Coral, unlike her other friend Dee who did the morning shifts and could be relied upon to upset the clientele with her forthright remarks. Not so this new recruit. She learned the complexities of the library's computer system with the minimum of fuss, and never complained when asked to re-shelf the returns, a job that generally provoked a wail of protest from other members of staff. She was popular with the public too. Coral applauded the way Lyndsey took time out to help pensioners choose suitable novels, and assisted students in their search for study material. This thought made her smile. She moved her chair closer to the fire, and noticed how the roll of castors made the pale girl flinch.

'Something awful must have happened for you to come round in the middle of the night. Should I ring Ray? Let him know you're here?'

The answering shake of the head was vigorous.

'Are you warm enough? Do you want another cushion?'

Coral was firing questions in an effort to get Lyndsey to speak, but it seemed hopeless until she asked, 'Can you top up my glass please? Dutch courage is needed for what I am going to say next.'

Picking up the decanter, Coral duly obliged. Her friend took several large gulps, as though she were trying to steady herself.

'I've told Ray we're through.'

'Oh, love.' Coral was out of her chair in the flash, losing a slipper in the process. She threw her arms around the trembling blonde girl, and hugged her fiercely.

'Cassie wants a dog.' Lyndsey said somewhat pointlessly.

'Yeah, you told me.'

'Raymond would go mad if I got her one.'

'Did he go mad tonight? When you said you wanted out of the marriage?'

The nod was imperceptible. Coral joined Lyndsey on the sofa. Both she and Dee had known the troubled state of the third girl's relationship. Known that Raymond Daly was not the easiest of men. Known too that Lyndsey was finding it increasingly difficult to reconcile her dual roles of wife and mother.

What they hadn't known was that Lyndsey had actually consulted a solicitor. Actually started proceedings. Now she confessed everything.

Coral listened without comment. If she were shocked, she gave no sign. The gas fire continued to heat the room, until they were sitting in a balmy, almost tropical temperature.

'So, let me get this right. After five hours of continuous talking, you could take no more and fled the house.'

Lyndsey nodded her confirmation. 'I told Ray I needed a glass of water. My throat was so dry. We'd already undressed for bed by that stage. I'd cleaned up the mess downstairs, and he'd ordered, and consumed, a mountainous Indian take away while reading the letter. Burping and belching, and making the most disgusting smells while he dissected it word for word. I thought he was ready to let it go. Till the morning anyway.'

'But he wasn't?' Coral ventured.

'No. He followed me downstairs. Into the kitchen. I was standing at the sink, running the cold tap and he started again, and I thought, God no, I can't take anymore, I simply can't....'

'What happened?'

'Ray turned to get milk out of the fridge, and I slipped out the back door. Didn't even know where I was going. Oh shit, Coral, I was just so distraught. I had to get away from that house. Away from all those endless questions and explanations. So I came here.'

'And all I've done is ask you more.'

Lyndsey didn't reply to this. It seemed that tiredness was sweeping over her, for she yawned and closed her eyes.

Coral yawned too. Diplomatically she slid off the sofa, and placed a kiss on her friends' cheek. 'You get some rest love.'

She mounted the stairs to her bedroom, feeling troubled and helpless in equal measure. Dee and herself would have to rally around their friend over the days and weeks ahead. Find some way of deflecting Lyndsey's thoughts from the spectre of divorce, and bringing some much needed light relief into her life. At least she was getting respite from the fraught atmosphere at Shenlagh Gardens.

Coral wasn't to know that there was no rest for her friend. Wasn't to know that the moment she'd left the room, the other girl opened both eyes and stared up at the ceiling until the gray light of dawn crept into the room.

Renee Fairbrother was woken from a fitful sleep at the same time as Coral. This time it wasn't by way of a ring at the front door, but a frantic banging on her bedroom window. She leapt out of bed as if scalded. Though the filmy nets, she could see, silhouetted against the street lamps, the figure of a man. A big man, tall, broad shouldered. She knew instinctively who it was. Her son-in-law, Raymond Daly.

'I've been half expecting you.' She opened the front door, hastily pulling tight the belt on her dressing gown. Her lavish breasts, encased in a soft comfortable sleep bra, stretched the material of her robe. He said nothing. Pushed her aside and stood in the hallway, clasping and unclasping his hands.

'Is she here?' He hissed, and his voice sounded hoarse.

'Cass – yes, she's..'

'Not Cassandra', he interrupted savagely, 'Lyndsey. Where is she?'

A needle of fear pricked Renee. 'She's not with you?'

'No.'

The reply was short. Curt. Angry.

Renee gestured towards the kitchen. Once inside, she closed the door and sank heavily into a chair, gazing up at her son in law in concern, 'Please sit down Ray, and take off your wet coat. You'll catch a chill.'

He remained resolutely on his feet. 'Don't pretend you fucking care if I catch a chill or not. I bet you and your bitch of a daughter would quite like to see me dead.'

'Language please, Raymond' Renee was shocked to hear her son in law use profanities, 'I can see you're upset, but there's no need.'

'Yes, there is a bloody need. Do you know she did to me tonight? Do you know what she said? Your darling daughter? She's divorcing me, that's what. Even been to see a solicitor. Without consulting me first. But of course you know, don't you Renee. I can see it in your face. Yea Gods and little fishes, tell me what the hell I've done to merit this sort of treatment.'

'Did you row?'

He began to circle the kitchen table. She thought he resembled a lion, with his red gold mane and opaque green eyes. A lion exploring the cramped parameters of its cage. 'No, we didn't row. We were having what I thought was a measured discussion. I was trying to discover what had motivated her to do such a crazy thing. I mean rushing off to some legal johnny and starting proceedings. It's hardly rational behaviour, wouldn't you agree? If you ask me Reen, she's lost the plot.

'You make it sound as though she's losing her mind.'

Abruptly he stopped the frantic pacing and pulled out a chair. He slumped into it. 'Yes, that's it exactly. Tonight when I got home from work she was playing mad monk music on the stereo at full volume. There was a trail of porridge all over the house, and the breakfast things hadn't been touched. She said she'd been with you and didn't have time to clean.'

His voice sounded muffled, as though he were about to cry. Renee put out a hand and stroked his arm gently. She couldn't bear to see anyone in such evident distress. 'That's true, Raymond. I did visit Shenlagh Gardens today.'

'I bet the second you stepped inside the front door, she couldn't wait to show you that bastard letter. Did you have a good laugh at my expense?'

'No, my love. I was as shocked as you to read it.'

His large shoulders heaved, under the hastily attired pullover. From its V neck poked the striped collar of a pyjama top. Renee felt a tide of sympathy for her son-her-law well up from the depths of her being. It was dreadful to see such a strong powerful man reduced to this shambling wreck. She said, 'If it helps, I feel the pain of this situation as much as you.'

Renee went to the fridge. She took out a can of Guinness, which she occasionally drunk to supplement her iron intake. Without asking, she pushed it across the table to her son-in-law.

'Drink this. You'd better stay the night. No point in going home now. I'll make you up a bed on the settee. We'll talk more in the morning. Decide what's to be done.'

Dumbly he took the can, buckled it open, and took a swig. Renee saw that the pupils of his eyes were dilated.

'First, I shall ring Coral. Then Dee. Check if Lyndsey is safe. They won't thank me for ringing in the middle of the night, but we have to know.'

Renee left her son in law hunched morosely over the beer. The phone was in the hallway, and with the heaviest of hearts, she picked up the receiver.

When she returned a few minutes later, it was to be greeted by the heart rending sight of the big man staring morosely into space. The can had been crushed double in one meaty hand.

'Dearest Raymond' Renee put her arms around him, at a loss to know how to offer more comfort, 'Lyndsey's at Coral's'

The next thing she knew, he was breaking down completely, and burying his head amongst the soft fold of her cleavage.

Chapter Nine

DEE AND CORAL were sharing lunchtime sandwiches in the staff room of the library. Through the opened door, they could see Lyndsey busy at work on the returns desk.

'We've got to do something to help that poor mare.' Dee said, through a mouthful of cheese and pickle, 'just look at the state of her.'

'She's been crying again. Came in this morning red eyed, with that haunted look you see on the jackets of horror novels.' Coral wiped away of blob of prawn mayonnaise on her chin with a serviette, 'things at Shenlagh Gardens must be pretty hellish.'

'I asked her to decorate the library for Halloween,' observed Dee, 'thought it might take her mind off things, but she's even managed to balls that up.'

Coral nodded. The pumpkins on the front desk were tilting drunkenly to one side, and the papier mache witch suspended from the ceiling was hanging precariously from a broomstick, wig askew.

As if aware that she was being talked about, Lyndsey turned and gave a halfhearted nod to her fellow librarians. Dee pretended to smile back, saying to Coral through clenched teeth, 'what on earth is she wearing? Spotted tights simply do not go with a striped woollen dress. And those shoes..'

Both friends stared across the library floor at the offending brogues Dee continued, 'Even her mother would have more sense than to don a pair like that. They're positively grannyish.'

'Which Mrs. Fairbrother is not.' Coral put in, 'A sexy dame if ever there was one. She could knock spots off Lyndsey in the fashion and glamour stakes, and she must be pushing sixty. A delicious amalgamation of Honor Blackman, Gloria Hunniford, and Joanna Lumley. If I didn't know better, I'd say Renee was the daughter and Lyn the mum.'

Dee unwrapped a blueberry muffin, and took a reflective bite. 'She called in yesterday to change her borrowings. Lyndsey was busy helping that blind chappie choose a book on tape, so I saw to Mrs. F. 'Course she wouldn't divulge any info about our dear Lyn re the situation with Ray'

'Honestly the pair of them can be so infuriating.' said Coral with feeling, 'keeping stum like a couple of clams.'

'Anyway, I thought what a truly handsome woman she is. Not a hair out of place, beautifully made up, and although her clothes are a mite sensible, they are always so, so....'

'tailored.' Supplied Coral helpfully.

'I was going to say flattering. Pity that Lyndsey can't take a leaf out of dear old mum's book. It's getting so that I'm embarrassed to be seen out with her.' Dee scrabbled in her bag for a banana, and began to unpeel it, 'we went down the market the other day and the bloke on the stall thought she was sleeping rough. He said, 'buy yourself a hot meal love', and actually tried to give her money.'

'No', Coral choked on the remains of her sandwich.

'As true as I'm sat here,' Dee waved the banana skin as if to emphasise her next words, 'we simply must get that poor little cat out of the mire.'

They both watched as the object of their scrutiny bent down to help a small boy struggling with a picture book almost as large as himself. The tights, patterned with pink polka dots, had gathered in unsightly rolls around her skinny ankles.

Coral wiped the crumbs off her hands in an attitude of determination, 'You and I Dee,' she said importantly, 'are going to become unofficial fairy Godmothers.'

'What are you getting at?'

'Cinderella is going to the Ball. With our help'

Chapter Ten

'RAYMOND, LYNDSEY AND I have been talking.'

It was a freezing Sunday in early November. In an effort to provide Cassandra with a semblance of family life normality, Renee had been invited for lunch to Shenlagh Gardens.

'Talking. What about?'

'Please don't be obtuse. You know full well the only subject on all our minds at the moment. The state of play of your marriage.'

'Ah'.

Lunch had been eaten, dessert served, the kitchen cleared. At a pre-arranged signal, Lyndsey had suggested a walk in the park to the protesting Cassie.

Left alone in the house with her son-in-law, Renee had made a cafetiere of coffee and taken it into the lounge where Ray sat moodily staring at the flames of the fire.

'We think it might be a good idea if you moved out for a while. Give you both a breathing space. Lyndsey has pledged to put any further legal proceedings on hold if you agree.'

He'd picked up the poker, and poked testily at a log, 'Well, you have been having a cosy chat haven't you, mother-in-law dearest. Tell me, who has cooked up this little scheme?'

'I have. I put it to Lyndsey in the week. She saw the sense in what I was proposing. That a temporary separation might be all that is needed to put your relationship back on track.'

'You're a conniving bitch, aren't you Reen? Still, why should I be surprised. Must be where Lyn gets it from. Like mother like daughter.'

'I'm trying to save your marriage.'

'By driving a wedge between us?'

Renee tried not to be diverted by the anger in his voice. She busied herself pouring coffee, as the silence in the room lengthened broken only by the crackling of the fire. 'Raymond dear, the wedge is of your own making. Lyndsey has bared her soul to me about why she finds the marriage no longer tenable. It seems you are always 'on her case' as she puts it. You are a forceful personality my dear, and perhaps that is the root of the problem. Lyndsey feels crushed by you. Suffocated. Perhaps she should have made you aware of this sooner. You could have thrashed it out together, maybe moderated your behaviour. Reached an understanding, before things deteriorated to this impasse. But Lyndsey is passive, and, like all passive people, has slowly come to the boil. I know my daughter. Better than anyone else does. Better than you do, I think. She cannot sustain boiling point for long. Passives soon weary of having to take charge of their lives, and make difficult decisions. Divorcing you is the hardest one she has ever had to take. She wants to be able to throw in the towel.'

Ray had stood and was pacing the room, `So what's stopping her telling that leech of a solicitor to go fuck himself?'

Renee handed him the coffee cup, 'Language dear please. Why don't you sit down. You're making me nervous.' He ignored her and continued to pace.

Renee continued, 'In one word, pride. She is too proud to admit defeat. Engaging a solicitor has been an act of rebellion on her part. Rebelling not only against you, but also against the constraints marriage imposes. If she can instruct the lawyer to put proceedings on hold she is saving face. Not only with him, but with herself. That's why I came up with the idea of you staying at my place for a while, and put it to her.'

'You think it will work?'

'Yes. I think you and Lyndsey would benefit from time apart. You are both feeling raw. Wounds need time to heal, not constantly raked over so that the blood never clots. I'm banking on Lyndsey seeing sense. After all, you never appreciate anything until you no longer have it. With her husband gone, she could start to see the institution of marriage in a new light. A much more flattering light.'

Her son-in-law was leaning against the mantelpiece, his huge body blocking the fire. He drank some coffee, before saying, 'I see your point, but I'm not wholly convinced. Moving out seems defeatist.'

Renee pressed home her advantage, 'Consider Cassie. The atmosphere in this house is dreadful. You could cut it with the bluntest of knives. I am worried about the effect this is having on her. Caught between warring parents, even though you both try to conceal your antipathy from her. Children are extremely perceptive you know. If you love your kid, one of you should leave.'

'That sounds like emotional blackmail.'

'It is.'

'You said 'one' of us. So why me? Why doesn't Lyndsey leave. Move in with you?'

'Logistics.'

`Explain please.'

'My second bedroom is small. Not big enough for Cassie too. She has to stay with her mother, surely you can see that. You work long hours Ray, and the child would be spending too much time alone if left here with you. Lyndsey gets her to school on time, makes her packed lunch, washes her uniform, is there when she gets home. Besides which, it would be too unsettling for her to leave her bedroom, with all her nick knacks.'

`What about me? Having to leave MY bedroom. My nick knacks?' There was heavy irony in his tone.

'You're a grown up Raymond. You can deal with it. Cassandra is a child. She cannot be expected to deal with both the temporary loss of a parent and the temporary loss of her own home. None of this is her fault'

`Nor mine! Lyn bloody started it.'

Privately, Renee agreed with him. She was disappointed in her daughter for seeking to splinter their cosy family unit. She forbade herself comment however.

`Seems like I'm boxed into a corner. You've presented me with fait accompli, haven't you mother in law dearest?'

Again, Renee forbade comment. They finished their coffee in silence. She regarded her son-in-law with sadness and compassion. He was staring into the distance as if seeing something that wasn't there. She looked at his head, reflected in the ornate mantel mirror. His thick rusty coloured hair was tousled, where moments earlier he had raked hands through it in a gesture of despair. He raked it again, but now the gesture spoke of capitulation.

'You win,' he said, speaking the words slowly as though they hurt him to voice them, 'I'll move in tonight.'

That same evening, Dee rang Coral at home.

'Can't talk long,' she said, by way of introduction, 'old man's treating me to a meal out. He's letting the engine run on the car.'

Coral frowned. Her own old man was slumped in front of the TV, the remains of his dinner on a tray. She closed the lounge door, cutting off the hysterical sound of a game show.

'Re Cinderella. I think I've found the answer.'

At this, Coral perked up. The two friends had been toying with ways in which they could help Lyndsey since their discussion in the library, but had dismissed all suggestions as being either impractical or unworkable.

'So come on. Don't keep me in suspenders.'

'Suspenders might be very apt. With stockings and lingerie. Some chic outfits to go on top, and the crowning glory – a sassy new hairstyle.'

'Dee Hapgood, you've lost me.' Coral said, beginning to feel exasperated. It was bad enough her partner in crime being taken out to dinner by an adoring spouse when her own was belching on the sofa, without compounding the felony by being obtuse.

'Look up Page 97 of this week's TV guide. Underneath the programme listings there's an advertisement. I reckon we should apply on behalf of a certain person. If you agree, take the next step...'

When Dee rang off, Coral went into the lounge, and removed the magazine from her husband's lap. She flicked through the pages. At first she almost missed the ad referred to, tucked away in a box in the corner of the page.

> 'Do you know a lady who might benefit from a makeover.' It read, 'Have you a friend, relative, or partner who has no sense of style. Someone who might benefit from £5,000 to spend on a new wardrobe. If so the makers of Channel 7's "Turnaround" would like to hear from you.'

Coral walked thoughtfully to the corner of the room. She switched on the computer, and waited, with growing impatience, as it whirred into life. Typing in the website address given, she waited for the 'Turnaround' page to load. She knew the programme well. Both she and Dee were avid watchers, and often compared the performance of the two fashion gurus, Savannah Hooper-Greenhill and Thalia Emmerson, who presented the show. They loved the contributors. Ordinary women like themselves who were transformed from dowdy dowagers into stunning stars by the mere application of the right clothes, make-up and hairstyle. Lyndsey confessed she had never been a regular watcher of 'Turnaround'. Coral and Dee privately thought it was because she wasn't allowed to. Raymond Daly was renowned for his labelling of everything that wasn't highbrow political debate as 'junk TV'.

Following the on-screen prompts, she clicked the mouse on the relevant icon, and began to fill in Lyndsey's details. Name, address, date of birth, height, weight.

In the background her husband snored, oblivious to the fact that his wife had transmuted into a new persona.

No longer Coral Simpson.

She was now Fairy Godmother.

Chapter Eleven

CASSANDRA DALY HAD gone missing. Mr. Butcher had seen her only half an hour before, a forlorn figure kicking up scuds of turf on the edge of the school playing field. She'd looked very small; very alone. Pupils had gathered in desultory groups around the perimeter like knots in a length of string. Their conversation was punctuated by swear words and guffaws of laughter. In this human herd, there was one animal denied access. One animal who was ostracized from the group. Cassandra Daly.

He'd recognized her by her Eskimo coat. The child seemed to live in it he thought, even though this Monday was unseasonably warm. The sun shone, and birds sang in the skeletal branches of trees that bordered the entrance gates. Pupils had seized the opportunity to disrobe outer garments, the boys rolling up sleeves of shirts to better display burgeoning muscles, the girls hiking their skirts up an inch shorter. In the bright light, the child in the padded coat was an incongruous sight. She must be sweating within its folds, thought Mr. Butcher.

On lunchtime playground duty, his attention had then become diverted by a tussle between two Year 11's over possession of an i-pad and cigarettes. He'd confiscated the latter, and hauled the miscreants off to the Head Teacher's study for some appropriate punishment to be meted out. Mr. Butcher had no high hopes of this however. The Head Teacher was no stickler for discipline, and preferred to let the kids make their own rules. In this Inner City Comprehensive, with its sprawling building blocks, anarchy was rife. After this dispiriting exercise, Mr. Butcher chose not to return to the playground, but instead mounted the worn concrete stairs to his third floor classroom and settled down with a sausage roll and the Racing Post.

He realized there was an empty desk during afternoon registration.

'Has anyone seen Cass Daly?'

There was some sniggering from the back row. He clearly heard someone say, 'Mama Cass.'

'Stand up whoever said that.'

Chairs shuffled at the rear of the room, before lanky form of a boy arose.

'Me sir.'

'OK Collinson, since Mama Cass was a member of a 70's group known as the Mamas and Papas, and was famous for being an extra-large lady, I fail to see the connection with the Daly girl who is unquestionably the smallest pupil here. Explain please.'

The teacher was angry and trying not to show it. A champion of the weak and vulnerable, he felt an uncharacteristic rage towards the oafish baboons who sullied his class.

All eyes were on Collinson, awaiting his next words. An air of excitement filled the room. The smell of blood was in the air. Savages thought Mr. Butcher, in despair.

The boy, evidently enjoyed his moment in the limelight, took time before replying, 'Well, its like this sir. She cries. Like a baby. Mammma, Mammma..' He aped the wail of an infant. A ripple of laughter greeted this remark.

'That's enough.' Mr. Butcher's tone was sharp. He signaled Collinson to sit down with a curt flick of the hand. 'I'd like a volunteer to check the ladies please. See if Cassandra is in there.'

The back row of boys all put up their hands at this, and one called out 'Me please Mr. Butcher, Sir. I'll check the tarts toilets for you,' a comment which engendered another wave of jeering laughter.

He chose to ignore this. 'Olu, would you oblige, please.'

The black girl rose leisurely from her seat, and made for the door, hooped ear-rings glinting in the sun-light which coursed through the dusty windows. The teacher loosened his tie. He felt both hot and cold at the same time. Hot with the unexpected heat of the day, and the anger he felt directed at the uncaring mob before him. Yet cold with a feeling of dread that he couldn't quite source about the whereabouts of Cassandra Daly.

'She ain't there.' Olu was back in the class, her lips expertly re-glossed during the trip to the girl's toilets, a fact which added to Mr. Butcher's despair. How can I educate these kids he thought, when they are so uncaring about each other. How can I instill the value of human life, when they are more concerned with touching up their make-up than the fate of a fellow pupil.

'Open your textbooks to the middle section,' he intoned, coming to an instant decision, 'answer the questions in the left hand column. No conferring with each other. I'll be back shortly.'

He checked the sick room, and then the school office. The Head Teacher's secretary confirmed that neither Mr. nor Mrs. Daly had come to collect their daughter. No absences for dental appointments had been requested from school.

Mr Butcher pushed open the glass swing doors into the glare of the playground. The sharp sunlight bounced off the tarmac, making his eyes hurt. He paused to polish his glasses, before making his way to the entrance gates and scanning the roadway outside in both directions. A woman was pushing a buggy to his left. To his right, a man cleaned his car with a bucket of soapy water, rap music blaring from its rolled down window. There was no sign of the solitary figure in the blue coat.

He turned, and walked to the edge of the playing field. This where he had last seen her, how long ago? He checked his watch. Forty minutes. He raised a hand to above his eyes to shield himself from the harsh blue of the sky. The field stretched out before him, a vast slab in a concrete jungle. Away to the left, the white goalposts of the football pitch threw a network of spider shadows. To the right, the tennis courts, with their sagging wire netting surround looked faintly sinister to Mr. Butcher. Like some kind of prisoner of war camp he thought, where the inmates had all been executed. He was just about to return to the school office and ring Mrs. Daly to see if her daughter had come home, when he caught sight of a telltale flash of blue. It was Cassie Daly all right, he thought with a sense of relief. This was immediately followed by a surge of panic. She was crouching by the furthermost loop of the sports track, and even from this distance, her teacher could see she was not alone.

Mr. Butcher began to run.

'Sit', commanded Cassie. She made her voice sound deliberately solemn. Animals needed to know who was boss, that much she knew. And this dog definitely needed a firm hand. A shaggy German Shepherd with a coat the colour of wet earth, and paws the size of saucers. He was a collarless giant of a dog, with a lolling tongue. Cassie acknowledged to herself that she already loved him with the devotion of a long standing owner.

He sat obediently, facing her crouching form. They were almost nose to nose. Cassie smiled. She fumbled in her coat pocket for another wine gum. The dog took it in one gulp. A glutinous strand of saliva dripped from its jaws, and pooled on the ground.

'Ugh, messy boy.' She wiped away the spittle with a tissue. It stuck to the black muzzle, shredding as she pulled it free so that the alsatian resembled her dad when he'd cut himself shaving.

Her dad....

For a brief second, Cassie allowed herself the pain of thinking of her father. He'd been gone since Bonfire Night, and without him, she found her home an alien environment equal to that of school. Her mother, distant and distracted, had been no help. Whenever Cass had tried to talk to her, she'd been left with the disquieting feeling that although she made the right noises, her mother hadn't actually heard a word she'd said. Feeling bereft, the schoolgirl had retreated into herself, finding a quiet place within where no-one could reach her. Not her father, or gran, or kids in her class, nor her mother. Least of all her mother.

The dog waited patiently for another wine gum, his round yellow eyes fixed unwaveringly on hers. Cassie obliged. This time it was one of her favourites, bearing the inscription "Sherry" in raised jelly letters. Her legs were beginning to ache from being bent unnaturally under her body. She shifted her weight, kneeling on the ground, oblivious to the threat of grass stains on the knees of her tights. Mum would moan. She didn't care. Cassie had stopped caring about a lot of things, she thought. Including the fact that she had now fed the dog her entire tube of wine gums, a daily treat which somehow made the long afternoon stuck in lessons bearable. But she wasn't stuck in lessons now. She knew the rest of her class would be ten minutes into double geography, and it mattered not one jot to her. All that mattered was the wolf-like dog and his rapt attention.

'What's your name?' She asked him, for the fifth time. He cocked his head on one side, ears erect like cheese triangles.

'I shall call you Mozart,' She decided aloud. 'A composer like Beethoven. He's a St. Bernard you know. In films. Only a pretend one though. Not real.'

The dog began to pant, tongue the texture of orange peel hanging lop-sidedly from his mouth.

'Poor boy. Are you hot?'

She was hot too. Cassie could feel her school uniform sticking uncomfortably to her back. But she wouldn't take the coat off. Not even if it were a heatwave, she thought. The coat was her protection. In it she felt safe. Although it's designer label had not had the desired effect of making her acceptable to her peers, she nevertheless drew comfort from wearing it. She could disappear within its folds. Become anonymous. Walking home from school with the hood shielding her face, she felt herself invisible from those around. Invisible, and, strangely enough, invincible. Wearing it, she became like Joseph in his coat of many colours, facing up to might of Egypt. Somehow, it was as though the thick material deflected the ghostly blows of daily life. Arrows of malice, shot at her from fellow pupils, just bounced off, their pointed barbs unable to penetrate the quilted padding. Her coat was her shield and defender, and she resolutely refused to take it off. Especially now her dad had gone.

Cassie didn't hear the sound of running feet, but the dog did. She could sense him stiffen. He stopped panting. Then he let out a growl. A low throaty sound full of menace. Then she heard the laboured breathing of someone approaching her from behind. Mozart bared his teeth. He looked more like a wolf than ever, the girl decided, as his lip curled back in a snarl.

She glanced over her shoulder. Mr. Butcher, red faced and sweating, tie askew, stood a little way off. Cassie could see beads of perspiration nestled in his beard, miniature bird's eggs in a nest. Chest heaving, he bent over and rested both hands on his knees. His breath came in laboured gasps as he said,

'Cassandra, come away from that dog. Slowly now. Back towards me.'

She could detect the note of panic in his voice.

'It's OK sir, he won't hurt me. He's my friend. Aren't you boy?' To demonstrate the truth of this statement, Cassie reached out and stroked the alsatian's head. He allowed her to do so, whilst continuing to keep up the stentorian grumble in his throat.

'Cassandra Daly, do as I say. Can't you hear it growling? Come here. This minute!'

She wanted to disobey him. Wanted to remain knees down in the mud of the school playing field with her new found friend. A devil voice somewhere in the back of her head was urging her to ignore the teacher. This devil voice wasn't new to Cassie. She'd been hearing it more and more lately. Hearing it whenever her mother spoke to her.

She was sick of adults trying to control her life. Trying to impinge their will on hers. Trying, in their clumsy way to make things right, but only succeeding in making things more horribly wrong.

Mozart was becoming agitated. It was though he could sense the tension in the air between child and adult. Hackles rose on his back, and the top lip curled even wider showing a glint of razor sharp teeth.

'There, there, Mozart.' Her voice was calm and steady unlike that of the shrieking demon in her ear, 'steady good dog.'

She could hear Mr. Butcher give a snort of exasperation. 'Cassandra I order you to get away from that animal and return to the school building immediately.'

'Shan't.'

There was another gasp, this time louder.

'You insolent child. I'm trying to help you. That beast looks and sounds dangerous to me. Like he's ready to attack. For your own safety I want you come over here.'

'No' She was openly defiant now, and it felt good. She was powerful, in control, not only of the German Shepherd, but of her teacher. Dominion over an animal and adult gave her a delicious fillip. For too long, she had felt powerless. Had felt at the mercy of other people, swirled about like a discarded can tossed into a flooded gutter. Her mother was divorcing her dad, and hadn't sought her opinion. Her dad had left home and hadn't even told her he was going. Her gran knew everything, yet told Cassandra nothing. It was as though no-one trusted her ability to accept the truth. She wasn't a baby anymore, she thought with a sudden flare of rebellion. Wasn't a child to be protected from the vagaries of the world.

Mr. Butcher was speaking. It took a moment or two for his words to penetrate her consciousness.

'...I shall have no alternative but to telephone your mother,' He was saying, 'get her to come to the school as a matter of urgency.'

Reluctantly Cassie got to her feet. The hood of her coat was pulled well down over her face, concealing her expression from view. Mr. Butcher would have been shocked if he'd have seen it, for there was no sweetness in her smile. It was one of secret triumph.

Chapter Twelve

'I'M BEING FOLLOWED.'

Lyndsey, Dee and Coral were sitting in the Coffee Lounge of the Pomegranate Health Suite. The two older women looked up in surprise at this statement. Dee dropped her spoon with a clatter in the cup of lemon tea that she was nursing in her lap,

'Followed Lyn. Surely not?'

Lyndsey didn't miss the curious glance that flitted between her friends. It was though they were telegraphing some unspoken message. Ever attuned to the body language of others, she said, 'What is it? Do you know something?'

'Know something,' echoed Coral with what Lyndsey felt was annoying complacency. 'Whatever do you mean?'

'Oh come on. I saw the look you just gave each other. Either you think I'm right about being followed, or....' Her voice tailed off. She took a sip of the Café Latte. It had cooled slightly, and left a moustache of foam around her mouth. She dabbed it with a serviette, her eyes never leaving Coral's face.

'Or what?' Dee took up the reins of the conversation. She was toying with the slice of lemon in her cup keeping her face and voice lowered.

'Or you both think I'm going mad. Imagining things.'

'It seems a likely conclusion Lyn. You have been under a lot of stress lately.'

'Don't be so damm patronizing.' Lyndsey was amazed herself at the strident ring in her voice. God, is it all beginning to get to me, she thought.

'Hey, Lyn, chill.' Coral sounded surprised, 'I'm sure Dee didn't mean..'

'No, sorry. I'm jumping at shadows. You'd think I'd be relaxed after that work out we've just had in the gym instead of being so bloody uptight.'

A Health Suite employee, in the familiar green overall emblazoned with a pomegranate logo, came over with a menu. He was a young man, obviously gay, with black hair pulled back in a ponytail.

'Are you lunching ladies?' He proffered the bar snack menu.

'You betcha.' Coral began the customary hunt in her hold-all for her customary missing spectacles. Dee took the menu, and began to give it an all absorbing glance. 'Give us a minute.' She said to the young man. He moved across to the next table.

Lyndsey let her gaze idly follow him.

Diagonally across the bar counter, a plate glass window separated the swimming pool from diners. A small girl stood at the water's edge, holding the hand of a tall woman wearing a towelling bikini. The child wore a swimming costume of livid green, and reminded Lyndsey of a miniature lime lolly. Even from this distance, the little girl resembled Cassandra at a similar age, and Lyndsey let out an involuntary sigh. Harking back to her daughter's uncomplicated early childhood was becoming a habit lately she thought.

Lyndsey had tried everything she knew to get Cass to open up to her, but the eleven year remained remote. Bribery with toys and games were no longer an option. The once trusted palliatives of a new Barbie or Disney film complete with popcorn and cola had lost their power. Her mother had took another tack. Offering instead girlie expeditions to Boots to buy sparkly eyeshadows in the miserable acceptance that her daughter was no longer a child to be mollified with toys.

'How about a trip to Brent Cross tonight darling?' She'd suggested, only that morning over the silent breakfast table, 'We could go in 'Teeny Girl' and buy you a trendy new outfit.'

Cassandra had not paused in her steady consumption of muesli, 'no thanks mummy.'

'Why not, sweetheart. It'll be fun. We can..'

'I said no,' Her daughter cut in with such a note of steely determination in her youthful voice that Lyndsey was brow beaten into submission. She tried to temporize, 'How about Roller Ball instead? We can have a burger after.'

This time Cassie hadn't even deigned to answer. Just continued to eat, head bowed, shoulders hunched. Lyndsey's heart ached at the sight of her dejected little form. She looked so young, so vulnerable somehow.

'Cass, we need to talk. About me and daddy and what's happening. It must be scary for you, this topsy turvy life we're living.'

At this the cereal bowl was pushed aside with such force that milk fountained across the table. Her daughter stood up, thin body enveloped by the over large school uniform.

'Mummy, leave it. I'm Ok, honestly I am.' She dragged her bag, bulging with books and stationery, along the hallway, donning the Eskimo coat as she went. Lyndsey trailed after her to the front door.

On the step the youngster hesitated, 'Are you going to the shops?'

'Yes, you need new vests. It's my day off so I'm meeting Dee and Coral at the gym first.'

'Can you get me something?'

Lyndsey's heart leapt with joy at this request. At last Cass was relying on her. At last she wanted her mother's input. 'What is it darling? Tights? Hair spray? A teen mag?'

'Dog food.'

'Dog food..but why.....?' Lyndsey found herself echoing (did Cass need it for some sort of school project...perhaps a donation to charity....?) but her daughter was already scuttling down the path, weighed down by her shoulder bag and quilted coat. She looked, thought Lyndsey, like a miniature explorer off to conquer the frozen wastes of Brackendale High.

In the swimming pool, the little girl in the green costume had finally gathered enough courage to jump in. Lyndsey watched as the two heads bobbed in the water – the turbaned one of the mother, and the smaller one of the child. They looked like seals, she thought. Mummy seal and baby seal.

On the table to her right sat a solitary young man. He was hugging a sports-bag to his chest as though it contained his worldly possessions instead of sweaty trainers and socks. He sensed Lyndsey looking and caught her eye. For a brief moment their gazes held. She felt an unwelcome stab of recognition. He looked familiar, but she couldn't place where she'd seen him before. Good looking, with a mop of golden brown hair cut into a shaggy style. The gay waiter was hovering beside him with a notebook at the ready, almost dribbling with lust, but the boy was unembarrassed by such slavish attention. He seemed totally preoccupied with the holdall, thought Lyndsey, wondering why he kept adjusting its position across his knees.

Dee tapped her with the menu, 'Come on Lyn, you were miles away. Hurry up and order. We're starving.'

'Eat a bloody horse.' Confirmed Coral.

Lyndsey gave the menu a cursory glance. She didn't feel like eating, but knew a supreme effort to shovel something down was needed. Both her friends had been alarmed at her loss of weight when they'd donned their leotards in the changing room. To avoid further censure, a lunch must be ordered, and more importantly, consumed.

'Jacket potato please. With cheese, and salad.' She told the waiter. He was not listening, attention still directed at the young man at the next table. Lyndsey noticed that the sports bag was still being lovely cradled across their fellow diner's knees.

Dee, ever forceful, clicked her fingers in front of the waiter's glazed expression.

'Hey sonny Jim, did you get that.?'

'Eer, sorry, no.' His voice, heavily accented with Italian, didn't sound sorry at all. Patiently, Lyndsey repeated her order. He headed off towards the kitchen doors, giving his pony tail a petulant flick as he went.

'I've ordered some wine to go with lunch.' Coral said, 'the non-alcoholic stuff. To celebrate that we've managed to get you out at last from that self-imposed exile.'

'Is that all you're celebrating,' said Lyndsey with a smile.

'Whatever do you mean?' Dee took a last swig of lemon tea, and placed the empty cup with careful deliberation on the table. Lyndsey wasn't fooled. She knew they were keeping something from her.

'You both took an inordinate amount of care and time blow drying your hair and applying make-up after our showers. Usually it's a quick rub down with a towel, and just look at those togs. Tailored trousers and blouses. What happened to the tracksuits you both arrived in.'

Lyndsey's smile broadened. Her friends, she thought, were trying hard to assume expressions of blank innocence at her words. 'So I wondered,' she said, adding an innocent tone herself and stirring the last of her Café Latte with practised indifference, 'Whether you planned to meet someone here. Someone of the male persuasion.'

Dee's answering snort of laughter sounded forced to Lyndsey, 'Honestly Lyn, the very idea.'

'Us after men?' said Coral with a note of incredulity, 'Let me tell you my dear girl, from a married woman of twenty years standing, that I need another man like Rod Stewart needs another blonde.'

'Hear, hear,' Dee nodded her agreement, 'at my time of life it's not a new man I need, but a new dishwasher.'

'So why the primping and preening?'

'A girl needs to make an effort.' Dee answered, 'a piece of advice you would do well to follow Lyn. Coral and I have meaning to broach the subject with you for ages.'

'What subject?'

'Well since it has been raised, the subject of you letting yourself go. Looks-wise we mean. You seem to have lost interest in yourself Lyn. Your hair, clothes, make up. As your best friends, we can't help but be concerned.'

Lyndsey gave a smile of self-deprecation. 'Have you been talking to my mother? She's got the self same bee in her bonnet about my dress sense. I know I look a mess at the moment, but everything seems so much effort. Somehow I can't be bothered to make it.'

'A sign of depression,' said Dee firmly, 'Hubbie was exactly the same when he was made redundant three years ago. He slunk into a well of apathy, and if you're not careful Lyn, you will too.'

'Why not go to the docs?' suggested Coral, 'get some Prozac.'

'Or a lover.' Said Dee.

Lyndsey laughed at this. 'I'll be a zombie on the former, and a psycho with the latter. No thanks girls. I'll deal with it. In my own time.'

They were good friends she thought. She was lucky to have them. Determined to maximize their listening ears, she returned to the subject that was so troubling her.

'You know what I said about me being followed,' she stirred the remains of her Café Latte, which had sank to a blob of froth in the bottom of the cup, 'please don't pooh, pooh it, because I sure I am. Being spied on I mean.'

Again she noticed the wary glance that passed between her two friends. Keeping her voice casual, Lyndsey said, 'You two know something. I'm sure of it.'

When they didn't immediately answer, she went on, 'It's Ray isn't it? He's hired a private detective to trail me, find out stuff. Incriminating stuff. Trying to catch me with a lover I suppose, or drunk in some pub, or gambling away the housekeeping in the bookies.'

'That's a ridiculous notion,' said Dee.

Coral nodded her agreement, 'Crazy. There would be no point. You told us yourself that divorce law has changed since the old days of wives trying to catch the old man shacked up with his secretary, or vice versa. Didn't your solicitor say it was now a 'no fault/no blame' set up.'

Dee took up the cudgel, 'Coral's right. Ray would gain nothing from trying to have you followed.'

'Except if he wanted to fight for full custody of Cass.'

'Oh Lyn, why would he? He works full time for God's sake. How could he look after her. Anyway, you're a fantastic mother. Everybody can see that.'

'So don't worry about it.' Coral said, in accord with her friend, 'even if he were having you tailed by some private dick like Colombo in a grubby mac, what would he find out? That you go shopping. That you work in library? That you occasionally, very occasionally, come to the gym. Hardly evidence of an unfit parent.'

Lyndsey felt troubled. She knew it showed in her face. 'I guess you're right. But I still can't shake off this feeling, that, for the past week or two, someone is watching me. Dogging my every footstep.'

The waiter had arrived with their food. He balanced the tray expertly in the crook of his arm, and lobbed plates at the table as though he were throwing a Frisbee. Lyndsey noted that his eyes never left the handsome young man on the next table. That same young man, Lyndsey also noted, was lingering over the consumption of a coffee and bagel, as though he were waiting for someone. The waiter detoured around his table on the way back to the kitchen.

Lyndsey picked up a fork and began to jab half-heartedly at the jacket potato that steamed in front of her.

'Don't you think you're being a bit paranoid, Lyn?' asked Dee gently, 'Imagining you're being followed by private 'tecs. You've been watching too many Hollywood movies.'

Lyndsey swallowed a mouthful of potato. She shifted uncomfortably in her track suit. She was sitting directly below the glass canopied roof, in full glare of the low noon-day sun. Unzipping the top, she hung it over the back of chair thinking that Dee and Coral seemed watchful, as if waiting for her to speak.

'I guess you're right,' she said at last, keeping her gaze lowered and addressing the cucumber slices on her plate, 'Perhaps I'm jumping at shadows.' Lyndsey decided to drop the subject, disappointed with her friends. They simply hadn't taken her concerns seriously.

The conversation moved on, became more desultory. They finished their lunch and ordered more coffee. Dee had her customary lemon tea.

Coral paid the bill. She'd been insistent that it was her treat. Dee was brusque, Lyndsey blushingly grateful.

All three hoiked up sports bags and made their way to the revolving exit doors of the Sports Centre. Lyndsey noticed that the young man had gone. A half-eaten bagel lay on his plate. He'd obviously been stood up, she thought, wondering what girl would be stupid enough to toy with the emotions of such a dishy specimen.

Outside it was grim and grey. Typical of capricious December weather, the sun had vanished behind a bank of sullen cloud. It seemed to have sprung up from nowhere. Spots of rain were beginning to fall. Lyndsey pulled on her track suit top, pausing on the top step to zip it up.

A knot of people were gathered at the foot of the disabled ramp. She heard them talking to Dee and Coral. An earnest looking girl holding a clipboard, and two men, one holding a microphone, the other a camera.

'Market research,' called out Dee, gesturing to Lyndsey to join them, 'they want to know where we shop for sports-wear.'

'Clothes in general, really,' said the girl with the clipboard. She had wild red hair escaping from pins all over her head, and was wearing a mac the colour of horse dung.

Coral said, 'chain stores have some great swimming cossies. Very trendy. Bought a leopard skin print one with suede fringing only last week ready for next summer.'

Dee said, 'gym wear too. You can get some snazzy leotards in the High Street.'

'What about you?' asked the red haired girl, 'Where do you buy your clothes?'

Lyndsey had joined the group at the foot of the steps, standing tentatively on the edge of their circle. She felt all eyes upon her.

'Oh Gosh, I haven't bought anything new for ages.' She felt embarrassed to confess to such a female failing,

'Could I ask you why?'

'No time I guess.' Or no inclination she thought, but wisely kept this to herself.

'You work then?'

'Yes.'

'Could you tell me where?'

Notes were being made on the clipboard.

'She works in a library.' Cut in Coral, 'with me and Dee here.'

'Full time?' probed the Market Researcher.

'Are you filming us?' asked Lyndsey suddenly aware of the intrusion.

'only for private viewing at our PR Company. We have to put together customer profiles you see. You don't object do you?'

About to open her mouth to object, Dee forestalled her, 'Course we don't mind. Make sure you get my best side though.'

This provoked laughter among the film crew threesome. The redhead turned back to Lyndsey, 'Can you remember the last item of clothing you bought.'

'This tracksuit, I think,' Lyndsey screwed up her face in an effort to remember. She had definitely let herself go, she thought in dismay. Outdated clothes, a grown out hairstyle. A barrage of questions were asked, but her replies became automatic. She was getting wet and anxious to get her shopping done and get home. Dee and Coral, however, seemed in no hurry to move. Lyndsey suspected they were enjoying their brief foray into the limelight.

Lyndsey made her apologies and extricated herself from the group. 'Sorry, I have to go,' she said, 'Cass needs some new vests.'

'OK,' said Dee, 'ring me.'

'See you in the library.' said Coral, 'tomorrow.'

'Thanks for your time,' finished the girl with the clipboard, 'Appreciate it.'

It occurred to Lyndsey as she hurried to her car, that Dee and Coral had known about the presence of the market researchers. Was that why they had been so concerned to get their hair and make-up right after their work out showers? But for what reason? And how could they have known?

She puzzled on this, as she hunted for her keys in the sports bag. The car park was situated at the rear of the Gym Hall, alongside a row of bald flowerbeds. A squally wind had blown up, and was beating a line of hedging conifers about the head. As she settled herself behind the steering wheel, apprehension seized Lyndsey. It was a feeling she had begun to recognize. Someone was watching her.

Swivelling in the driver's seat, she caught sight of a tall figure. disappearing behind the wall of the gymnasium. It was the young man from the café. She was sure of it.

Chapter Thirteen

'A ROMANTIC DINNER for two?'

Renee felt a blush flame her face, but it was a pleasing one. She shrugged in answer to the check-out girl's comment. The conveyor belt continued its leisurely pace, displaying her purchases. A duo of Norfolk Duck breasts, Caesar salad, game chips, double cream, black grapes. She added a box of table candles to the pile, and wheeled her empty trolley through the gap between tills.

'Someone is going to be eating well tonight. Lucky man.' The cashier took Renee's money and handed her the till receipt with a knowing wink. This innocent insinuation that there was a romantic element to the meal, made the shopper answer with unnecessary curtness.

'It's simply dinner for my lodger.'

Renee wondered what the till girl would think if she knew the lodger in question was her son in law, Raymond Daly, and that he was sharing her roof in the hope that it might mend his marriage. Would she still be implying that the meal was a romantic one?

Frankly thought Renee, echoing the words of Rhett Butler, 'I don't give a damm what you think, you silly girl' Her concern was for Ray. He was so depressed. She hoped that making the effort to cook him an extra special meal would cheer him.

She hurried from the supermarket, glad to leave behind tinsel bedecked aisles and piped Christmas melodies. Renee's ears, unaccustomed to exposure, felt cold in the bitter air. The previous week she'd had her hair cut in a more youthful style, trying, and failing, to persuade Lyndsey to join her. Gone was the soft bob favoured by those of mature years. Now she sported a geometric style that made her look as though she were wearing a silver skull cap. Pushing the trolley across the car park, she caught sight of a familiar figure sitting on the bonnet of her car.

'Hi Mum'.

'Darling, what a surprise.' Renee gave Lyndsey a hug. A raw wind funnelled through the row of vehicles and stung Renee's eyes. Her daughter shivered, and glanced nervously around.

'Darling you're cold. Sit in the car while I unload the shopping.'

'If I'm trembling with anything, its fear not cold.'

'Fear? Of what?'

'I'm being followed, and before you say anything, it is not my imagination. There's a man tailing me. It started with just a feeling that there was someone dogging my footsteps when I was just going about my daily business. Then this morning I went to the gym with Dee and Coral. There was this young guy sitting at the next table, and I got the feeling that he had me under some sort of surveillance.'

'Why didn't you confront him' said Renee, feeling a spurt of irritation at her daughter's complacency, 'if you thought he was up to no good.'

'I didn't realize that he might be person on my tail. I'd not actually seen anyone, just had this sixth sense that I was being shadowed. It was only as I was leaving Pomegranates, that I caught sight of this bloke watching my car.'

'I see.' Renee said, but she didn't. Not entirely. Yet she was filled with a sense of unease. The wind was rustling the carrier bags packed in her trolley. It sounded sinister, like trees in a forest. Her daugher's fears seemed to be transmitting themselves to Renee, for she began to feel unaccountably threatened. Lyndsey seemed to read her expression, for she said, 'don't worry, I'm pretty sure he's not around at this moment in time. The feeling has gone.'

'What feeling?'

'A prickle on the neck sensation. Difficult to explain. An intuitive hang over from our cave man ancestry I guess, when they had to be on constant guard from predators.'

'the thing is Mum, it occurred to me that he, whoever, he is, is being paid to watch me. By someone who wants to know what I'm up to every minute of the day.'

'But darling, who would want to do that? For what purpose?'

'Ray. If a hired private detective reported me up to no good it would strengthen his position if we ultimately decide to divorce. He could counter-claim against me, and negotiate a less generous financial settlement.'

Whilst Renee saw that this was an obvious conclusion for her daughter to reach, she couldn't believe it herself. Her son-in-law might be many things, but devious and underhand he was not.

'That's why I decided to come and find you doing your weekly supermarket shop. I want you to ask Ray when he gets home from work tonight. He won't tell me, but he might open up to you.'

Her son in law was in for surprise, thought Renee, with a modicum of dismay. Candlelight and confrontation.

Ray paused at his office door to give the brass name plate a quick polish with his handkerchief.

'Raymond E Daly'
Information Technology Manager

There was the definite outline of a thumbprint tarnishing its surface, and he rubbed it with off with vigour. Standing back, he gave it a quick, critical appraisal, before pushing open the teak door and entering the cool inner sanctum. He slid the lock as a safety measure, kicked back the swivel executive chair upholstered in its smart black leather, and placed his briefcase and carrier bag on the table.

Loosening his tie, he sat down and spun around to face the window. The office block was mechanically ventilated, and the hum of traffic was muted by triple glazed sealed units. Several floors below him the main thoroughfare of Leadenhall Street thronged with City workers, tourists, and Christmas shoppers. Ants, thought Ray. Millions of 'em. Human ants teeming the walkways and subways of London, all hurrying to service the needs of the Queen. Except this Queen was not a regal one, rather a symbol of mortgages, school fees, bank loans, and credit cards. Like all capital cities, he thought, his home and workplace had become a vast colony of ant people all caught on a treadmill. He was sick of London. Sick of the dirty tubes, belligerent cabbies, bearded louts thrusting copies of the 'Big Issue' at every passer by... But most of all, he was sick of his wife. Her single act of rebellion in their thirteen years of marriage in seeking to divorce him, was, in Ray's view, a major and unforgivable one. It hurt his male pride to think that he lacked the requisite qualities to make an acceptable husband, and after much soul searching had come to the conclusion that the fault was Lyndsey's not his. If he didn't measure up as a husband, then she certainly didn't measure up as a wife. She was no domestic goddess, and as for her feminine allure.. Ray spat in disgust. A globule hit the window and slid down it, leaving a frothy residue. He'd seen bigger tits running London Underground, than those on his spouse. If it weren't for Cassandra, he thought, he would leave. Up sticks and go abroad. Somewhere hot and spacious, where the women were big breasted and uninhibited. South Africa or Australia, or maybe even L.A. The thought was provocative enough to give him the burgeoning of an erection. Through the material of his beige suit trousers, he could feel his cock begin to expand and stiffen, and instinctively dropped a hand to the bulge between his legs. He rubbed himself, massaging the hardening area with a groan of pleasure at the sensation.

In the carrier bag on the desk was an awl and a door viewfinder he'd bought in the hardware store on the way to work. In the bathroom at his mother-in-laws he'd chanced upon a redundant hole drilled in one of the tiles high up on the wall, which maybe once housed a towel ring. It directly faced the shower. Closer investigation revealed only a thin skim of plaster dividing it from the guest room that run alongside. Renee, perhaps in an effort to make him feel at home in her humble maisonette, had hung up an enlarged family photograph she'd taken the previous Summer, of himself, Lyndsey and Cassandra during a day trip to a theme park. It was put above his bed. It wouldn't be difficult, he decided to drill through from the other side using the awl, and thereby give himself a secret spyhole into the shower, which would remain hidden by the picture. Inserting a spyhole of the type put in front doors, would magnify his vision. His mother in law was a stickler for hygiene, and showered twice a day, and the thought of watching at her work soaping those luscious breasts made his breath come in ragged gasps.

He was reaching climax. Ray scrabbled to release the zip of his flies, fearful that semen would stain his trousers. Released from its confines, his cock sprung red and swollen into view. He leaned back in the chair, threw back his head, and with thumb and forefinger holding the engorged rim, splayed his legs ready for orgasm.

Renee – tits – soap – hot water... The vision was all he needed. Ray was talking now, feverishly to himself, 'Oh God, oh fuck, mummy, mummy...' His voice rose in a crescendo. Draping the handkerchief over his member so that it resembled a parachutist preparing to land, he came with a whoosh of hot semen. The handkerchief ballooned upwards in a sticky bubble.

Chapter Fourteen

FLICKERING CANDLES GRACED the table. Delicious aromas of cooking filled the air, mingling with Renee's perfume. It was hot in the kitchen from the heat of the oven and her hair clung to her head like a bathing cap. She washed her hands in the sink, uncorked the wine to let it breathe, and surveyed the scene. It met with her satisfaction. Just time to change, she thought, before Raymond arrived home. Pausing to wonder what outfit to wear and deciding upon a light jersey two piece in the palest shade of lilac, she moved out into the hallway, untying her apron as she went.

The front door swung open, and she jumped, momentarily startled. She still wasn't used to the fact that Ray had insisted on having his own key so that he could come and go as pleased. Nevertheless, she felt a surge of happiness at the sight of him, and a wide smile creased her face.

'Hello you,' She said, coming forward to plant a light kiss on his cheek, 'how was your day?'

'Bloody', came the gruff reply.

Her son in law looked crumpled, thought Renee, as though he had somehow folded up on the journey home like a concertina devoid of air. Nevertheless, she could tell by the studied indifference of his expression that he welcomed her solicitude. She might be old fashioned thought Renee, but in her day women were taught to greet the man of the house on his arrival home from work with the delight and gratitude accorded to a soldier returning from war.

'Cup of tea? Or perhaps a glass of wine. There's a decent bottle of Beaujolais breathing in the kitchen.'

'Wine would be good, thanks.' He deposited his briefcase in the hall, together with a carrier bag taped up at the edges. Renee wondered what was inside it, but did not ask. Her son-in-law had laid down a set of rules before agreeing to move in, and a high degree of privacy was top of the list. To this end, she kept out of the spare bedroom which had become his temporary domain, leaving his clean laundry neatly folded on a chair by the door. Every weekend he stripped the bed of sheets himself for her to wash and tumble dry in one session.

Nevertheless, despite its obvious drawbacks to both parties, the arrangement seemed to be working well. Renee enjoyed having a man around, and looking after him gave purpose to her days. It meant more visits from Cassandra whom she adored, and rather less from Lyndsey, whom she found rather wearing these days. Even though she tried to take an objective view concerning the current impasse within her daughter's marriage, Renee heartily disapproved of Lyndsey's action in consulting Messrs. Parsloes and Dean. She thought it smacked of betrayal towards Raymond, not to mention herself and Cassie. She believed that marriage was for life, and problems within it needed to be worked at and solved, not run away from. Her marriage to Lyndsey's father had been no picnic for goodness sake, but only death could have separated them. Renee would have no more chosen to end her marriage, than fly to the moon.

Of course Raymond could be difficult. Sharing her roof with him had shown her that. Sometimes the frustrations of his situation, caused him to talk sharply to her, or even worse, to go into brooding silences that she could not penetrate. But Renee was made of stern stuff. If he answered her back, she would say mildly, 'really Raymond, that was quite uncalled for...', and his periods of quiet she would simply ignore. When he left her post-it notes of the type endured by Lyndsey, she merely ignored their instruction, screwed them up and left them pointedly on top of the fridge. He could be pedantic and critical in equal measure, but Renee had a lifetime's experience of dealing with petulance in others, and carried on in her usual calm manner. They had learnt to jog along together, and there were times when they nursed a nightcap into the early hours, putting the World to rights in desultory conversation, when she felt quite giggly, like a teenager again.

During those shared confidences, he would often let slip something about Lyndsey, and whilst Renee felt beholden to leap to her daughter's defence, she often felt that Raymond had a point. One of his complaints was that she did not appreciate how hard his job was, and how he expected a harmonious and tranquil house to come home to after a gruelling ten hour day. His recounting of Lyndsey's slapdash ways and her propensity to lose herself in daydreams, when floors needed washing, and clothes needed ironing, struck a chord within Renee. She knew her daughter better than anyone, and could identify with Raymond's irritations. She too, had felt similar annoyances when Lyndsey was young and had lived at home. The dawdling home from school, the doodling on exercise books instead of algebraic equations, the dithering over choice of uniform. Even her late father, bless his heart, had coined an affectionate nickname for their child. 'Daffy Duck' he called her.

But these thoughts Renee kept firmly to herself. It would not do to let Raymond know that she held the modicum of sympathy for him in his plight. She hoped that the glitch in her daughter's marriage was a temporary one, and knew that the only way to steer the estranged pair towards mending the rift would be to take the line of least resistance. Once Raymond had returned to Shenlagh Gardens, she would pull out all stops to get the relationship back on course. If it took giving her daughter a few stern lectures about the need to be a more responsive and pro-active wife, then so be it.

'Where are you going?' Raymond was now asking her, as she moved towards her bedroom door.

'To change out of these clothes. It's been like a Turkish bath in the kitchen.'

'No Renee,' he said, taking her by the arm, 'come and drink some of that wine with me. You can have a nice cooling shower later.'

'You're very persuasive.'

'Its part of my charm.' He smiled down at her, his chin dimpling, and Renee was struck afresh by the good looks of her son in law. He was an attractive man, she thought, with his mane of swept back red gold hair, and pale green, almost translucent eyes. Powerfully built too, like a man should be, with broad shoulders, and a muscular physique. She felt safe with him around, and it was a good feeling to be so protected.

She allowed herself to be led back into the kitchen.

'Sit down,' Ray commanded, pushing her into the chair. Meekly Renee obeyed. She liked it when he came over all forceful. He took two wine glasses out of the cupboard (she was pleased to note he knew by now which cupboard housed them) and poured out a rich red slosh for them both.

'Something smells good.' He said, sniffing the air appreciatively, 'You know how to look after a man, Renee.'

The unspoken words hung in the air, were 'unlike your daughter...' but both elected to remain silent. Renee sipped reflectively. The wine tasted of blackcurrants and wood smoke.

'I'm cooking duck, with an orange brandy sauce, and game chips. Followed by fresh fruit salad and clotted cream'

'You spoil me mother in law.'

Renee made light of it. She didn't want him to think she was making a special effort. 'Goodness don't be silly. Thought it would make a nice change from pasta that's all.'

He smiled at her again over the rim of his wine glass. It was a devilish smile, and the dimple on his chin deepened. He sees right through me, thought Renee. He knows I've made a gourmet supper just to please him.'

Darkness slanted through the window, smudging the wall above the kitchen table. She'd lit the candles for atmospheric effect rather than to aid with the lighting. Her son in law's head of hair flared red in the flame, 'He looks more like a lion, than ever', thought Renee. A musky smell was emanating from his body, a strong male odour that was not quite perspiration, but something else. She found it faintly intoxicating, and berated herself severely. Must be my hormones she thought. The HRT patches prescribed by the doctor had kick started dormant sexual desires, and she was unequal to the task of controlling them.

The duck was cooked to perfection; meat falling off the bone in succulent shreds. Ray consumed his supper in appreciative silence. He was pleased with his handiwork in the spare bedroom, managing to chisel out a hole in the plaster and insert the viewfinder with consummate ease. The magnified lens gave a panoramic view of the shower cubicle on the other side of the wall, and, knowing that he was shortly going to spy on his mother-in-law's ablutions, he was prepared to be more than unusually magnanimous towards her. As they finished dessert, he said in a deceptively casual voice,

'Put your feet up Reen, while I clear the dinner things and make coffee. No protests – I insist. The meal was sublime and the cook deserves her leisure.'

He shooed her from the kitchen, and poured himself another steadying wine. Ray accomplished the clearing up at top speed, loading the sink with frenzied haste. He couldn't get out of his mind the treat that was awaiting him. The juiciest tidbit of all juiciest tidbits – his mother in laws' bare melons, glistening with soapsuds, being sponged down by her manicured hand. Just the imagined picture of a huge blue veined breast being rinsed by those red painted nails was enough to make his cock bigger than Nelson's Column.

He brewed coffee in record time, loaded the tray with cups, cream, and the dregs of the Beaujolais, and hurried into the lounge.

Renee was sitting primly upright in the winged corner chair, flicking through the TV guide.

'Nothing good on the box,' she said without looking up, 'unless you fancy a documentary on European monetary policy.'

Ray grimaced, and said, 'let's just relax with brandy and Classic FM'

His mother in law got up and switched on the radio component of her corner hi fi system, which was default tuned to her favourite station. The fluting melodies of Debussy filled the air. She'd bought the candles in from the kitchen, and they glowed transparently atop the coffee table.

Ray settled down. He could hardly control his mounting excitement. He'd been looking forward to her nightly shower all day, pleasuring himself twice more in the course of the afternoon before he could concentrate on work.

'This gaff is so beautifully warm.' He said, moving a hand to undo another button on his shirt. 'Nice to be cossetted inside on such a freezing night. Reckon we might be in for a white Christmas.'

'Ah, sledges and snowmen.'

'How do you plan to spend it?'

'With you, Lyndsey, and Cassie of course.' Renee sounded shocked at the question. 'If Lyn doesn't want to cook lunch at Shenlagh Gardens, I'll do it here.'

She was a good looking woman he thought, regarding his mother in law under his sandy lashes. Maybe running to seed a little, but with a remarkable figure for her age, and a creamy complexion on her wide cheek boned face.

'So we're all going to play happy families around the bloody tree,'

He could not mask the brittleness in his voice. Renee sipped some coffee and said, in her calm, even voice, 'Be patient a while longer Ray. I'm sure Lyndsey will start to see sense. I know she is missing you.'

'Missing ain't kissing.' He said acidly, before adding, 'my darling wife might find she pushes the separation issue too far. I could well decide to give her the boot, not the other way around.'

At this remark, Ray thought his mother in law looked suddenly weary beneath the pert cap of hair. She was dressed in a fluted skirt teamed with a red blouse with a ruched front which rippled like a blood stained sea over her impressive chest. Her smart court shoes had been discarded in favour of a pair of slippers.

'Are you having her followed.'

The question caught Ray momentarily off guard. He dropped the spoon with a clatter on the saucer.

'Lyndsey thinks you are. To try and gather evidence against her to use in the divorce court'

'She's off her trolley.' He said darkly, and saw Renee wince imperceptibly. 'I'm sorry Reen, I know you don't like to hear ill of your daughter, but she must be seriously twisted if she thinks I'd resort to such underhand tactics.'

'Will you give me your word?'

'I tell you what I will give you.' He said leaning back on her worn velvet sofa, 'a bit of advice. Go and get yourself in the shower and ready for bed. You've had enough for one day, and so, mother in law, have I. Lyndsey needn't worry that I will throw good money after bad paying some private dick to traipse the High Street after her. I refuse to even seek legal advice in order to defend myself against her totally irrational midlife crisis.'

'My dear Raymond, I believe you. Whoever Lyndsey believes is following her, I don't think it has anything to do with you. I told her as much. But I had to ask. You do see that, don't you.?'

She was imploring him, so he said grudgingly, 'Yes.'

'I think Lyndsey is imaging things. She has been under a lot of strain lately. We all have.'

His mother in law went on, 'Perhaps you're right. I could do with an early night. A piping hot shower sounds good.'

'Off you go then,' he said, building a nest of cushions around himself and turning up the volume of Debussy with the remote control.

Renee stepped out of the shower and gave her body a vigorous rub with a towel. Her skin tingled. The water had massaged her skin with hot needles, and she felt wonderful. Invigorated and aglow. As was her custom, she took her bottle of baby lotion out of the vanity cupboard and began to smooth the pink liquid into her breasts. Her nipples were erect from the force of the water, and she gave them an extra generous squirt of lotion. Caressing her heavy breasts thus was almost soporific and she closed her eyes in the steamy confines of the bathroom, and got into the hypnotic rhythm of rubbing. Her skin began to feel silky, as the moisturiser seeped into the pores and she delighted in the touch of her own body. Beneath her spreading palms, her bosom felt like twin gigantic balls of clay; warm and malleable. She could almost mould them to any shape. Renee began to hum gently to herself, swaying to the beat of her own song.

For ten minutes she stood in front of the shower cubicle, until her body felt nicely softened. Slipping on her towelling robe that resided on hook by the door, she slid the lock, and stepped out into the hallway. It was blissfully cool after the hothouse warmth of the bathroom, and she reached back and switched off the light. As she moved towards her bedroom, the door to the guest room opened, and her son in law stood framed against the jamb. His eyes were glittering, and she noticed a film of sweat on his face, which gave him an almost immobile look, as though he were carved out of marble.

'Goodness Raymond, you startled me.'

'Sorry.'

Renee thought his speech sounded slightly slurred, and wondered just how much wine he'd consumed whilst she'd been showering.

'Goodnight then dear. 'She said, but before she could pass, he had stepped out into the hallway blocking her path. Renee felt no alarm, just a sense of puzzlement. Obviously her son in law had something on his mind, and he wasn't going to let her get to bed until he'd said his piece.

She opened her mouth to speak, but no words came out for in that moment he pulled open the top of her robe, exposing her left breast. Renee was so shocked, she was struck dumb. Worse was to follow. A large male hand, with a smattering of red hair along the knuckles, reached out and touched her nipple. The touch was exploratory, almost loving, and sent a hot shiver up her spine.

A tumbled confusion of thoughts and emotions went through her mind. Anger, swiftly followed by outrage at this affront to her decency. By touching her thus, her son in law had breached some invisible moral code that Renee held dear. Had circumvented the boundary line of acceptable behaviour. Not only had he invaded a private part of body, but his family relationship to her compounded the crime. He was her son in law for god sake, married to her daughter... She raised a hand to slap his face, a natural reflex action to defend her modesty and to punish him for this unwarranted molestation, but suddenly all thoughts of retaliation vanished.

Raymond was crying. Tears coursed down his face, as he continued to stroke her breast. The bathrobe gaped open across Renee's shoulders exposing the upper half of her body to his questing gaze. He was touching her with both hands now, but gently in an almost childlike way of wonderment.

All always, the sight of tears in others, tugged at Renee's heart. She felt acute compassion for her son in law, and acute distress at his actions in equal measure. And his touch.... Oh his touch... In all their years of marriage, her late husband Douglas had never touched her breasts in this deliciously sensual and intimate way. A way that was sending hot sparks up her spine, and giving her a curious ache in her abdomen which was not quite pleasure yet not quite pain.

Renee looked down and saw that her nipples had hardened beneath his fingers, and realized, with a faint sense of inevitability that her treacherous body had become a cohort with the man before her, siding with him in this monstrous act.

He was weeping openly now.

'Raymond', Renee said, trying but failing to sound stern, 'Raymond, you must stop...'

But his next words silenced her.

'Mama', he said, 'Oh Mama.....'

Chapter Fifteen

THE PLUMMY VOICE said, 'Have you seen Channel 7's 'Turnaround?'

Lyndsey found herself nodding dumbly. The gesture was a fraudulent one. Caught so off guard, she could hardly recall the show and was desperately trying to rack her brains as to its content.

'Congratulations. You're on the programme.'

Dumbstruck, Lyndsey dropped the date stamp. It landed with a clatter on the library desk.

'What programme? What are you talking about?' Her mouth felt dry. The woman moved forward and touched her lightly on the arm.'

'Darling, I'm Savannah Hooper-Greenhill, and this is Thalia Emmerson. We present Turnaround, a life changing show for women whom, we consider have lost their sense of style.'

Lyndsey felt her mouth drop open. Now she remembered. Remembered where she'd seen the tall woman with the blonde hair. And her equally elegant partner. She'd read about these women in her favourite magazine. Seen photos of them. The tabloids had dubbed them 'the makeover monsters'. On a rare occasion she had caught their TV show, where female victims were subjected to trial by fashion jury; a show which regularly topped the TV ratings.

Lyndsey closed her eyes. She felt physically sick. In her mind she could hear the countless times Dee and Coral had discussed the programme during lulls in the library.

One of the presenters was speaking, 'Don't take our word for it,' It was the one with the dark bob, 'even your friends think you are in need of a drastic re-vamp. In fact, it was them who put you forward for this programme.'

'My friends...'

Yes darling. Two people that care about you very much submitted your name to us. Look behind you.'

Lyndsey turned. The staff room door was being pushed open by a man wearing headphones. A sense of shock flooded her as she recognized him. The thatch of streaky hair, framing eyes of the deepest blue. He was the man on the next table at the Health Club. The man whom she was convinced had been following her, with some nefarious purpose in mind. The same man that she suspected had been hired by Ray to build up a dossier on her movements. She watched as he beckoned with an outstretched finger. Coral and Dee emerged looking sheepish as flashbulbs burst around them. They blinked, reminding Lyndsey of moles coming up from underground.

'But its Friday,' she said, stating the obvious, the bewilderment evident in her voice, 'Coral's day off. What is she doing here? And Dee too... Dee was supposed to be at the dentists...'

'Sweetie they're here for you.' Thalia Emmerson held up an expertly manicured hand to forestall the approach of the two friends, 'We'll be interviewing them later. But first we have something for you.'

Savannah Hooper-Greenhill, at a signal from her cohort, pulled a slim envelope from the inside of her jacket. 'In here is a cheque for five thousand pounds. Made out to you darling.'

'To me' Lyndsey parroted.

'For you to spend on a whole new wardrobe. New shoes, new clothes, new make-up, new hairstyle. We intend to turn you around Lyndsey Daly.'

'We've been secretly filming you,' Chipped in Thalia, 'Do you remember going to the gym with your two pals over there?'

Lyndsey recalled the day in Pomegranate's all too clearly.

'What was that you were wearing on the running machine, darling? Savannah's voice was deceptively sweet, 'Thalia and I thought it looked like a pair of baggy PE knickers, the type we all used to wear in school, and that T-shirt might have been better suited as a rag for a spot of car cleaning.'

Lyndsey felt her cheeks flush. How embarrassing. She remembered delving in the bottom drawer of her dressing table for some suitable gym attire, and alighting on the first thing that came to hand. The bedtime knickers that she wore on the first night of her period, when the flow was particularly heavy, and the stretched white T-shirt that had seen better days. Yet it was symptomatic of her attitude just lately, she was forced to admit to herself. She didn't care what she wore. How she looked. She didn't even care much about going out. Her social life had gone into an enforced state of hibernation. She hadn't wanted to go to the gym. Hadn't wanted to go anywhere. She was in 'hermit' mode, to the chagrin of those around her.

'What about the shopping trip to Brent Cross?' Savannah was saying, 'We were there Lyndsey. Following you with concealed cameras.'

Lyndsey felt sweat spread in a patch under her arms. It was hot in the library, the radiators sizzling to cocoon the public from the icy conditions outside. She cursed her choice of wear, not just because she was perspiring like a pig in her knitted two piece suit, but because she knew, with a sinking heart, that the dragon ladies would be bound to pass comment on it.

Which they now did.

'Can we talk about what you are wearing today?' Said Thalia in a deceptively chummy voice, 'this cable knit sweater and matching skirt, in a shade of vomit green.'

Lyndsey wished they hadn't mentioned vomit. She was feeling sick with apprehension.

Lyndsey slept badly. She awoke twice in the night. The first time, at 3am, she thought the events of the previous day were a dream. She lay for several minutes staring up at the ceiling, feeling dazed and slightly incredulous. For the first time since Ray had left, she mourned the loss of his comforting presence. It was horrible sleeping alone she decided, when night terrors assailed. The vast expanse of the King sized bed seemed somehow slightly alien. As though the unoccupied side resented her presence. She found herself thinking of her husband, examining every nuance of their married life together, until mental exhaustion set in, and she fell back into fitful sleep. An hour later, she awoke again. Her throat was dry, and she badly needed a drink. Catapulted into wakefulness by physical demands, Lyndsey tossed back the sheets and felt under the bed with her bare feet for slippers, like a blind person searching with their hands. Pulling on a dressing gown to counter the early morning chill, she padded downstairs, and headed, in a trance like state for the kitchen. She reached for the light switch, blinking in the glare, eyes unaccustomed to such burning brightness. As was her habit, she let the tap run until the water gushed icy from the pipes. Lyndsey filled a beaker and drunk gustily, with the rapt attention of an alcoholic presented with their favourite tipple. The water tasted wonderful. She wondered, momentarily, why she was so thirsty. Thirsty enough to have woken from a deep slumber.

She had been dreaming. That much Lyndsey knew. Something momentous had happened to her, and she couldn't quite bring it to mind. It remained tantalisingly out of reach, just like those machines at fairgrounds she thought. The ones where a hand operated miniature crane was entombed in a glass cabinet filled with rainbow trinkets, like the treasure chest of a pirate. As a child, during the family's annual beano to Clacton-on-Sea, she would be drawn to the tawdry excitement of the amusement arcades, and the crane apparatus in particular. With its claw attachment, she endeavoured to pick up a cuddly toy or paste jewel. To no avail. Even those with manual dexterity were foiled by the machinery's apparent inability to move as directed. To her childhood self, the frustration of locating the favoured trinket only for the claw to release it at the last minute, was an enduring gall.

It was cold in the kitchen. Outside the window, the streetlamp was diluting the dark. Lyndsey went into the lounge and flicked the light switch. She started at the sight that greeted her. A video camera had been set up in the corner, artfully angled and plugged into the mains ready for use. This was no ordinary camera either. Not an instamatic for holiday snaps. This was a professional piece of gadgetry, standing on a tripod, and sporting an impressive number of dials and settings.

So it was real. It had happened. The camera crew gate-crashing the library, where she Lyndsey Daly worked. The TV programme, 'Turnaround', on which she, Lyndsey Daly was going to feature. The two presenters, Savannah Hooper-Greenhill, and Thalia Emmerson lambasting she, Lyndsey Daly, for her sartorial faux pas.

The tumbler fell from her grasp. It shattered on the floor, sending shards of glass in all directions. Lyndsey stood in stupefied silence. She didn't know what to do next. Sweep up the splinters, mop up the water, scream, break into a dance, or cover up that offending camera with the nearest cushion cover as though covering up a birdcage for the night. She remembered with startling clarity the events of the previous day, but it was still difficult to believe. Difficult to believe that for the past weeks her every foray in public had been secretly filmed by the traitorous Robbie, and that, Coral and Dee, had managed to organise such a scam, and keep it a secret. It beggared belief.

Lyndsey skirted the broken glass, and stood nose to camera. Robbie had showed her how to operate it for the purpose of filming her own video diary. Such a diary, was needed he said, to flesh out the programme content. The punters he told her, liked the cosy informality of Joe Public barring his collective soul into a camera in the privacy of his own home for the edification of the great British viewing public.

She was ready to speak. With a determined set to the chin, she wrapped the dressing gown more firmly around her waist, and switched the camera into action. It's red eye blinked at her. She settled cross legged on the Chinese rug, in the position Robbie had set up for her. He'd marked out a square in tailor's chalk, which delineated a boundary out of which she must not move. It was on this outline that the lens was focussed.

Pulling the robe over bare knees to protect her modesty, she took a deep breath and began.

'It's the morning after the day before,' she intoned, 'and I can't believe my friends have done this to me. Set me up like this. I don't know whether I'm excited at the prospect of this TV programme, or dreading it. Yeah, I feel a wreck. Look a wreck. That much is true, but do I really want to be hauled over the coals by Savannah and Thalia over my choice of dress. People are going to be watching this – people I don't know, am never likely to know. Yet these same people, strangers all, will be a party to the most private areas of my life. Living in a goldfish bowl of the media spotlight is fine if you are a celebrity –if you deliberately seek the limelight. But me.... Well this has been foisted upon me without my knowledge.'

Her friends had betrayed her, that much she knew. On the pretext of helping her, they had instead thrown her into the TV spotlight when she was at her most vulnerable.

Lyndsey cleared her throat and shifted her bottom slightly on the rug, 'I could kill Dee and Coral,' and she sounded as though she meant it, 'String up the pair of them. What slime balls to go planning and plotting this behind my back. With friends like that, who need enemies. So I'm not a happy bunny. But I shall play ball. Go along with this and even ensure I enjoy it. After all, everyone is supposed to want their five minutes of fame and this will be mine.' Lyndsey smiled in spite of herself. The irony of the situation was not lost on her. Or its comediac value. Here she was in the middle of a black January night, barring her soul on camera, and developing pressure sores on her bum as a result. Not to mention the likelihood of catching her death from sitting on the draughty floor. Still, she thought, being on telly might prove fun, and the experience was one to savoured, and learned from. Plucking at the tassel of her dressing gown cord, she spoke, slowly, almost to herself, momentarily forgetful of the camera that continued to record, 'I guess I'll come out of it a different person, not just in the way I look. It will change me in some way. Make me look at things in my life afresh.'

Lyndsey leaned back against the fireplace and closed her eyes. She felt suddenly at peace with both the situation and herself. Her life up to this point she thought, had been a winding journey, where she had ended up in places she didn't want to be with people she didn't want to know, never quite being sure how she'd got there. For too long she'd allowed herself to be tossed about like a twig in the stream of someone else's consciousness. Ray's consciousness. She would surrender herself to the ministrations of Savannah and Thalia with good grace, but it would be last time. Never again, she vowed, would she succumb to the whims of others.

The miserable Christmas which had just passed was a case in point. At Renee's insistence she had been forced to play happy families with Ray needling her and making sarcastic comments at every opportunity. The enforced gaiety over the turkey lunch had stuck in Lyndsey's claw, and Cassandra had been sulky over her choice of presents. The tree moulted, the fairy lights fused, it had rained steadily all day, and at six o'clock in the evening there'd been a power cut. Boxing day hadn't been much better. Cue, thought Lyndsey, for the end of another disastrous festive season in the Daly household.

Now she sat absent mindedly twiddling with her hair, which had grown long to her shoulders. Having worn it short since her wedding day, the length took a bit of getting used to. Urchin styles had always served her well in the past. Taking inspiration from the Glam Rock and New Romantics of the seventies and eighties she had curled it softly around her face, mirroring the punk era she had then gelled it into spikes, and the age of Power Dressing had seen her wearing it plastered flat to her head. Idly, she wondered how it had become so unkempt, and realized she'd been blind to what those around her had seen. That during the breakdown of her relationship with Ray, she had sunk into apathy. It took a superhuman effort of will just to get out of bed in the morning, when all she wanted was to bury her head and go into suspended hibernation, from which she hoped to awake, sometime in the future, with the decree nisi granted, and the financial settlement rubber stamped. It was like wanting to go on holiday to an exotic location, but not wanting to make the journey to get there. Even a sojourn to the hairdressers, had, it seemed, become a trip too far.

Lyndsey yawned. The sofa looked inviting. She curled up in an igloo of cushions and fell once more into a restless sleep. She was awoken by the grey light of dawn. Outside the window, a particularly strident sparrow was serenading the bleak day with gusto. It's happy warbling made Lyndsey smile. If a bird could greet the New Year with such enthusiasm, then she jolly well ought too, she thought. Making a conscious effort to feel positive, she got to her feet, putting a hand to the small of her back to ease the ache. The camera winked at her. She winked back, and cut the power. In the kitchen Lyndsey rummaged in the broom cupboard for the dustpan. She needed to sweep the broken glass before Cassie got up. Her daughter had a penchant, she knew, for running around the house bare footed in the mornings. She would be doubly drawn into the front room to verify the presence of the camera which would elevate her mother to TV stardom. The day before Cassie had got home from school to find the house invaded by strangers sporting Channel 7 sweatshirts, which had sent her into paroxysms of delight. Lyndsey, gearing herself up for the worse, had expected a disparaging reaction from her daughter. To any self-respecting eleven year old, surely the appearance of one's mother on a TV show with such a derisory theme, was something to be abhorred. Bracing herself for some door slamming, Lyndsey was pleasantly surprised to find Cassie whooping around the house in delight. Her normally taciturn daughter came alive with the recording crew, chatting animatedly to them as they set up the video camera and checked lighting angles. It had taken all Lyndsey's powers of persuasion to convince Cass that this was a secret best kept from her father until Lyndsey deemed the time to be right to tell him.

'You know what daddy thinks of Channel 7,' she said trying to get her daughter's attention away from camera crew, 'he won't be happy to find out mummy's going to appear on one of their flagship programmes.'

'Ok, Ok....' Cassie had said, eyes shining, 'my own mum on telly ....how cool is that'.

Dustpan in hand, Lyndsey smiled at the recollection of Cassandra's untrammeled joy. The filming schedule, left by the Channel 7 team, lay on the table. Pages detailing a tightly packed itinerary, which would strangulate her own calendar for the next few weeks. Somehow she would have to juggle library shifts, caring for Cassie, visiting Renee, housework, and all the other minutiae of domestic life within the constraints that the TV programme was about to impose on her time. Not to mention finding the right moment to tell Ray that his wife would soon be baring all on national television.

Lyndsey dealt briskly with the broken glass, mopped the floor of residue water spills, and opened the lounge window to let the sharp morning air dispel the fugue in the room. The sparrow took fright, and flew up onto the eaves. Lyndsey bent her head over the cill and looked up at him. He stared down at her from his vantage point on the gable, and resumed his lusty singing.

'A cocky little character,' she said aloud, but with genuine warmth for the bird. The sparrows had a hard time of it these days, she thought. Not only were they stalked by the domestic moggy, but a new and more nefarious predator had upset the natural balance. Magpies were taking over the suburban landscape. Like an invading army, these clacking soldiers put the smaller birds to flight. Lyndsey disliked them, as she disliked anyone who pushed their weight around. The proliferation of the black and white bully boys were a modern day phenomenon that she abhorred. They always hunted in pairs, which added to Lyndsey's disapproval. Like muggers, she thought, ganging up to pick on some innocent bystander. A pair of them sat on the telegraph wire outside her window, drowning out the sparrow with their jarring song, the sound making Lyndsey think of machine gun fire.

'Two for joy,' she murmured, hoping that they wouldn't turn their murderous attention to the tiny brown bird who was now hopping along the guttering directly above the window. The magpies had their heads together, chattering in unison, as though making derisory comments about the rest of the feathered population. It occurred to her that she was like the sparrow, and Savannah and Thalia were like the magpies, ready to pounce on her choice of plumage.

'Look at the state of her,' She could almost hear them clacking, 'Honestly dahling, fancy wearing brown. It's SO last season.'

Lyndsey flapped the curtains at them. 'Shoo', she said. The magpies swung on the wire with a defiant air. 'You don't scare us,' they seemed to be saying. Silhouetted against the backdrop of rapidly lightening sky, the piebald pair threw a wavering shadow across the lounge window. Lyndsey looped the curtains into their wrought iron tie-backs, and took one last glance outside. The sun had risen, she saw. Weak lemon rays were streaking the sky, making the frost on the roofs sparkle.

The phone rang.

'Hi, is that you, Lyndsey Daly?'

She recognized the voice immediately. It's light Scottish lilt hummed over wires, 'Hope I didn't wake you, but you did say you were an early riser.'

'Robbie.'

'Aye the same. Your friendly stalker.'

'Are any stalkers friendly?' She asked.

'This one is. How you doing, hen? Still getting over the shock of yesterday?'

Lyndsey stood in the hallway, the receiver clasped to her ear. In preparation for getting dressed, she undid the tie of her dressing gown and let it slide to the floor. 'Why the wakeup call?'

'Just checking if you're OK. Answer any questions you might have about 'Turnaround' now you've had a chance to sleep on it. My job as your secret filmer is finished. Now we've done the hit, I get to wear my second hat. That of your mentor. Any concerns you might have about the filming schedule, or appearing on television bring them to me.'

Lyndsey said, 'That's the bit I can't quite believe. Me being on the box.'

She could hear his kind laughter, 'You'll be great. We were all saying what terrific camera presence you have already.'

'We?' Lyndsey queried.

Robbie's voice, so measured and gentle in her ear, said, 'Aye, the camera crew.'

'What about Savannah and Thalia?'

'They think you'll be a challenge. Savannah reckons that beneath that deceptively fragile exterior lurks a backbone of pure steel.'

It was Lyndsey's turn to laugh, 'Hardly. In fact I feel pretty wimpy lately.'

'How so?'

She found herself telling him. About the trauma of the last few months. About Ray moving out. He had the air of a kindly relative about him, that encouraged one to confide. An agony uncle. Lyndsey almost confessed to having painful periods, until common sense stopped her. 'Oh God, sorry Robbie.' She said inadequately.

'What for?'

'Rambling on like this. I'm sure you didn't ring up to find out my life story.'

'You're wrong Lyndsey. Your life story is important to us. It makes good programming to find out what makes our contributor's tick.'

'Goodness, is that what you call me? A contributor?'

There was a silence, and Lyndsey let her hand slide down her body, naked beneath the nightdress. This man invoked a feeling within her that was akin to taking a sensual bath in aromatic oils. She sank down on the stairs, her legs slightly spread, and waited.

Eventually he answered, and his tone sounded measured, as if, thought Lyndsey, he was choosing his words carefully. 'No, hen. I would call you a star.'

'Savannah and Thalia are the stars. I'm just an ordinary member of the public.'

'Don't put yourself down Lyndsey. There's nothing ordinary about you. Otherwise you wouldn't have got picked for the programme. We have hundreds of submissions you know, from people putting forward friends and relatives. Only ten are chosen for every series. You have to be pretty special to pass our vetting process.'

'You mean I wasn't a random choice?' Lyndsey was glad her phone wasn't the type where the caller could view the recipient. She wouldn't want Robbie to see her now, crouched on the bottom stair in her nightie, with mouth agape, and body clamoring for sexual release.

'Far from it. When Dee first E-mailed the research team, we asked her to send us some photos of you. Standard procedure. From the pics we can tell if someone could benefit from a fashion make over. So you passed the first hurdle. The second one was to do a screen test, to see if the camera loved you. It did.'

Puzzled Lyndsey echoed, 'A screen test? But when .....?'

She could hear Robbie shuffling some papers on the other end of the line, and wondered if he was checking her filming schedule as she had done herself just a few moments before. 'The mock market research interview with Gaynor outside the Health Club. We'd primed Dee and Coral to make sure you'd be there at the appointed time.'

Lyndsey found that her free hand had lifted her nightie and sought out the parted lips of her vagina. Almost hypnotically she began to gently knead the soft bead of her clitoris, feeling it swell and engorge beneath the probing fingertips. Shivers of delight began to emanate from her lower body as Robbie's voice, low and lilting, caressed her ear,

'you were a big hit,' he was now saying, 'we watched re-runs on the studio monitors. Everyone agreed that you would enrol the viewing public in your story. That of a woman, of a certain age, in the throes of a divorce, who had forgotten how to take care of herself. Not just looks wise, but spiritually and emotionally too.'

She was feeling wetter and wetter down below, and found herself arching her back against the stair as a tidal wave of feeling, so long suppressed, began to gush through her body. Rubbing herself frantically now as the sensations of pleasure mounted to a delicious crescendo.

As she climaxed, Lyndsey let out an involuntary gasp.

'Are you still there, hen? Everything OK....?'

She suddenly felt weak and light headed, as though she had just stumbled off a funfair roller-coaster. She took several gulps of air to steady herself before she spoke.

'What you were just saying,' she said, surprised at the tremor still in her voice, 'it sounds like Psycho-babble' to me,' She felt the need to defend herself yet was unsure why, 'how could you tell all that from someone answering a few off the cuff questions.'

'Your voice, hen. The look in your eyes when you faced the camera. Body language is a good indicator. There was a sadness about you. An air of vulnerability, not to mention a face that could launch more ships than Helen of Troy, with the right hairstyle and make up. And a body to match.' Embarrassed by this, Lyndsey could think of nothing to say. Robbie, perhaps guessing the reason for her silence, tactfully continued, 'Savannah and Thalia were unanimous in their opinion that here was the perfect clothes horse. Someone tall, slender, on whom the latest styles are going to look sensational. Someone too with whom other women can easily identify. It'll make great television. We can almost smell the BAFTA's.'

Lyndsey felt more than beguiled by Robbie. Just the sound of his voice had made her feel hornier, than Ray in his most naked virile state had ever done. No wonder the softly spoken Scot was chosen as front man for the programme, she thought. He had a way about him of inviting confidences. A gentleness of manner and lyrical voice which made you want to sit upon his knee and be rocked to sleep. After being made love to of course. She tried to picture him, wondering what he was wearing, where he was calling from. Or was he, like her, tousled haired from a night's sleep, his blue eyes dreamy? Her unspoken question was answered. In the background, she could hear a phone ringing, and an urgent female voice.

'Sorry for the noise.' He apologized after a pause, 'I'm in the office, and the lines are going crazy.'

'You work on a Saturday?'

'Aye. That's the way the cookie crumbles. We graft for nine months of the year, then take it easy for three.'

'Sounds like a pregnancy.'

'Getting the programme finally on screen is a bit like giving birth I guess. Except with a bairn, there is no such thing as taking it easy once it enters the World.'

'Spoken like one who knows. You have children yourself?'

'No, hen. Nor a lady in my life either. It's the old cliché. I'm married to my job.'

Above her head, Lyndsey could hear Cassie stirring. The creak of bedsprings from the front bedroom signaled the onslaught of her daughter.

'Robbie, I have to go. Get Cass breakfast.'

'Aye. Say hello to her from me. I'll call later with arrangements for your first shopping day. You've got the weekend to recover from the shock, then Monday morning its up in the West End for some retail therapy. Courtesy of Channel 7.'

'The cheque's burning a hole in my pocket.' She lied.

'No, it's not Lyndsey. Not yet. But it will soon. Believe me.'

He hung up. She remained on the stair, the receiver clutched to her chest, as she waited for the residue tingling between her legs to abate. Already she was missing the sound of his soft Scottish lilt. Eventually Lyndsey stood up. She picked up her discarded dressing gown and mounted the stairs, humming as she went.

There were worse things in life than having Robbie McCrae as one's mentor.

Chapter Sixteen

'YOU SHOULD HAVE seen your face,' Dee crowed, 'talk about gob smacked.' It was the following day, and they were lounging on Lyndsey's bed amongst a sea of clothes. Her friend's surprise visit had interrupted a tentative inventory of her wardrobe. Savannah and Thalia, she knew, would soon be casting their critical eye over the contents, and she wanted to dispose of the worst offenders in advance.

'If you've come here to gloat, you needn't bother.' Lyndsey removed a coat hanger that was sticking into her calves.

'Sorry, if I sounded glib. Guess me and Coral are trying to make light of our shared guilt. Putting you forward for 'Turnaround' seemed a good idea at the time, but once the project was up and running, with secret filming et al, we had second thoughts. It seemed bloody sneaky, but we were sworn to secrecy by Channel 7. They said if you got wind you were going to appear on telly, they would have to abort the whole mission and use someone else.'

'You make it sound like a NASA rocket launch.'

'Well, it was a bit like that. Everything had to be hush, hush. We were terrified you were going to suss something was up.'

Lyndsey stared up at the ceiling, where a residue mark from a fluorescent sheep remained, despite her best efforts with a scrubbing brush. 'I suppose I should have guessed. Especially when you both sat in Pomegranates in full make up, with hair tweaked. With hindsight, I know now that the guy at the next table was Robert McCrae with a concealed camera in his bag, but you knew it at the time. So whilst you and Coral were happy for me to be filmed looking like a particularly mangy dog's dinner, in contrast, you were projecting your most glam images.'

They laughed, but whilst Dee's smacked of glee, Lyndsey's was rueful. Her friend bunched up a pile of T-shirts to bolster the pillow on which her head rested, 'That's the whole point of the programme darling…. You have to look like a dog's dinner, otherwise there would be need to change you. Even you must admit Lyndsey that you need changing, and badly!'

'You're just trying to absolve your guilt', Lyndsey said and her mild tone belied the inner turmoil that was churning her stomach to mush. Me, on telly – the thought kept replaying itself in her mind.

'Seriously though, it was a hoot in Pomegranate's. At one stage, Robbie winked at Coral and gave her the thumbs up. We were convinced you might have seen, or noticed the chalk marks on the floor where the crew had positioned our table.'

'The Sports Centre was in on it too?' said Lyndsey, trying to stretch her mind around this new possibility.

'Sweetie, you are so naive. That's what we love about you. Course, they were. We had to clear the filming with the management. They took a vow of silence along with everybody else. Dead chuffed though, that their restaurant was going to feature on telly.'

'God, what a bloody conspiracy,' said Lyndsey, swiping her friend good naturedly with a coat hanger. Dee's impromptu visit had gladdened her. Raymond had taken Cass on a fishing trip, and the silence in the house weighed heavily on Lyndsey. When calling to collect the child earlier, Ray had been at his nit picking worst, and Lyndsey had endured a barrage of complaints before he'd gone. Her friend's exuberant presence was helping to dispel the gloom that her husband's tetchiness had left behind. Dee cycled legs in the air, in an off the cuff exercise session, 'You're worth it Lyn. Me and Coral have been worrying about you for quite some time. We knew a shot in the arm was badly needed but you can be bloody minded sometimes. You'd accuse us of being a pair of interfering old bags.'

'If the cap fits...'

'Ok, ok, mea culpa. But honestly we did it with your best interests at heart. We knew that if anyone could shake you out of this apathy, Channel 7's dragon ladies could.'

'Apparently a TV reviewer dubbed them Savager and Talons instead of Savannah and Thalia.'

Dee guffawed, 'Who told you that?'

'Robbie. He's been ringing me. My officially designated mentor.'

'Hmm. Cute guy.'

'Isn't he just.'

The thought of gentle Scotsman was a cheering one, and Lyndsey wallowed in it. Guilt swiftly followed. It was morally wrong to fantasise about another man, she decided, especially whilst still married to Raymond. Morally wrong also, she guessed, to let the mere thought of Robbie McCrae bring her to orgasm. A brisk walk was what was needed to clear her head, and set her mind on other things. She decided to suggest a ramble round the playing fields to her friend, and a shared pot of tea in the park café afterwards. Such a sojourn would also present the perfect excuse to curtail the clearance of her wardrobe, and let Savannah and Thalia do their worst.

Beside her Dee had dispensed with the exercises. She lay back with an exaggerated sigh of fatigue, and said, 'So Lyn, are we forgiven?'

'For what?'

'Catapulting you into TV super-stardom.'

Lyndsey picked up one of her belts, a patchwork survivor from her 'gypsy look' phrase, and toyed with the suede fringes. She never could stay cross for long, she decided, and bore no malice to Coral and Dee, though it wouldn't hurt to keep them on tenterhooks just a little longer.

'Ask me again when filming's finished.' She said.

Chapter Seventeen

A LIMO, COURTESY of Channel 7, picked Lyndsey up on Monday at the ungodly hour of 6.30am. Rising so early in the chill of the morning brought her out in goose bumps, and she lost no time in getting dressed. When ready, she pulled back the curtains, and scanned the dark for the carriage that would turn her into Cinderella. Beyond the bedroom window a gusting wind was battening the rooftops and, illuminated by the street lights, she saw a car cruise to a halt by the kerb. It was a glossy saloon, with a man in uniform and cap behind the wheel. From the passenger door stepped the familiar figure of Gaynor and, concealed by the drapes, Lyndsey watched her progress up the path.

Insistent ringing on the doorbell advertised the caller's impatience. Lyndsey opened it, and was almost blown off her feet by the gale. Hurriedly, she beckoned the researcher inside, before shutting out the wintry dawn. The girl stood in the hallway snugly zipped into a floor length coat, holding the customary clipboard and pen. Lyndsey wondered if Gaynor actually slept with them by her side.

'Hiya, Lyn,' She said chummily. Her frizzy hair was partially tamed by an orange scrunchie, and on top of her head sat a pair of tinted glasses which doubled as an Alice band. Stray tendrils of hair escaped and coiled around her face, reminding Lyndsey of the many headed snakes of the gorgon.

'Ready for your debut studio day?'

Without waiting for an answer, Gaynor said, 'A quick checklist before we leave. Have you banked the cheque?'

Lyndsey patted her jacket pocket, 'On Friday. I've got the deposit slip here.'

'I'll need to see proof.'

Dutifully, Lyndsey took out the counterfoil and showed the researcher. She scrutinised it rapidly, 'that seems to be in order. Have you read and understood the contract?

'Even the small print.'

'Any questions?'

The reply was in the negative, so Gaynor moved briskly on, 'I need to check you aren't wearing make-up.'

One look at the other's face, scrubbed bare, was enough to satisfy her on that point. 'Brill. The clothes you are wearing are a good choice too. Jeans and plain sweater is perfect non-statement garb. An anonymous casual uniform that will provide the ideal blank canvas for Thalia and Savannah to work with.'

Lyndsey was beginning to feel a spurt of irritation. She took exception at being treated like a child. The list of instructions she'd been given along with the itinerary had been followed to the letter. Despite reservations about the camera crew wanting her to appear a frightful mess for the first day of filming, she understood the reasoning behind it. Make-over programmes were far more effective when the 'after' shots were in dramatic contrast to the 'before', whether it be people, houses, or gardens. But Gaynor's attitude, she felt, verged on the patronising.

Still, she supposed the girl had a job to do. The role of researcher on a TV programme such as 'Turnaround' seemed to be a multi-task occupation. An amalgamation of interviewer, dogsbody, gopher, and fact finder, as well as being a personal assistant to the two presenters. Lyndsey thought it a fun job, so wondered why Gaynor acted with such tortured martyrdom.

As if in answer to her thoughts, the researcher gave a long suffering sigh, 'final item on my checklist is your wardrobe. Or rather its contents. Have you got your clothes packed ready?'

Lyndsey stood back, to reveal a row of bin bags lining the hall. The instructions in this respect, had been specific. She was to bag up every item of her clothing the night before, keeping back only those which she had chosen to wear the following day.

'Let me take a look' Without further ado, the girl joined Lyndsey by the banisters. She totted up the number of bags,

'Only five?'

'I don't have much gear.'

'A tramp could fill more bags than this. Time to check if you're telling porkies. The acid test will be empty hanging rails. Lead the way upstairs.'

'Oh come on,' Lyndsey protested, 'you're surely not going to root through my cupboards to see if I've kept something back.'

'That's exactly what I'm going to do. This is the second series of this programme, and every single contributor on the first did just that. In fact one lady hid most of her clothes in the bath! Sorry, Lyndsey, but the whole point of the programme is that we bin your entire clothing stock and start again. You'd only start slipping back, wearing all your old stuff again if we didn't, which would negate all Savannah and Thalia's hard work. Imagine the publicity. 'TV girls fail to make a long term impact on their makeover subjects, blah, blah, blah...' Don't look so stricken. You'll thank us in the end. The whole process will be cathartic. All the contributors of the last series agreed that getting rid of their old duds was like a spring clean of the soul. Now scoot. Make like Mother Hubbard and show me a cupboard that's bare.'

With a shrug of capitulation, Lyndsey led the way upstairs.

'Charming décor,' said Gaynor approvingly, as they entered the private sanctum of the master bedroom. Lyndsey said nothing. The other woman's presence was an invasive one, and she silently urged a quick and painless inspection of the wardrobes. The row of denuded hangers bore witness to her honesty.

Gaynor checked her watch, 'No time to do a search of the other rooms, so I'll have to take you on trust.'

'Hadn't you better check the bath?' Lyndsey couldn't resist the jibe.

The researcher ignored it. They hurried past the door to Cassandra's bedroom. Lyndsey was glad her daughter had elected to stay the previous night with her dad and grandma. Never at her best on Monday mornings, the added sting of her mother spending the day in a TV studio while she slogged away at school would have provoked a mini rebellion.

Whilst Gaynor tottered down the path with the five bin sacks, Lyndsey turned off the lights and double bolted the front door. The chauffeur opened the boot, and her bags of clothing were unceremoniously dumped inside. He instructed both passengers to put on seat belts, turned the heater up high, and fired the engine.

The car purred down the road.

Settling back on the cream leather upholstery, Lyndsey hoped to grab some shut-eye during the journey across London, but Gaynor immediately set to with a further list of instructions, 'As soon as we arrive, Robbie is going to film you taking your bags of clothes up the stairs to the apartment.'

'An apartment?' queried Lyndsey, as the limo negotiated the stream of commuter traffic heading into Southgate town, 'but I thought we were going to the Channel 7 studios.'

'No darling. For the filming of 'Turnaround' the crew rent a luxury Docklands flat.'

Savannah and Thalia's apartment was in a converted warehouse. From the outside, the building looked unprepossessing. Dull brick, and iron grilled windows. Yet the penthouse flat boasted a balcony with red painted railings, and gothic arched doorway leading onto it. The perfect des res for the archetypical City whiz kid on a six figure salary, Lyndsey decided, with a price tag to match. She stared as a man came out to stand on the balcony. He waved. She saw it was Robert McCrae and the sight of him was a joyous one. He would be on her side, she thought. Batting for her team. Whatever sartorial torture Savannah and Thalia were about to put her through, Robbie's presence would be a comfort. She returned his wave through the lowered car window.

The chauffeur had parked in a reserved bay. Lyndsey got out and stood buffeted by the gale on the pseudo cobbled pavement, whilst Gaynor manhandled her clothes from the boot. Robbie had disappeared back inside the building. A sign proclaimed it as 'Jamaica Wharf'. Lyndsey guessed that the warehouse had once been a repository for rum shipped from the West Indies. There were even a line of stanchions along the forecourt, where the steamers that contained this precious cargo, had dropped anchor. London's past and present entwined before her in dirty grey splendour.

Lyndsey rubbed her hands to keep the circulation going, checking her watch as she did so. Just gone eight o'clock. The journey hadn't taken long to carve a trail through the centre of the City from North to South. With the introduction of the congestion charge, driving in the Capital was once more an acceptable option if you needed to get from A to B quickly. Or A to Z thought Lyndsey with a smile, as a picture of the distinctive City guide came to mind.

Now the moment had arrived for her first official day of filming, she felt slightly sick. To divert herself, she studied the surroundings. The warehouse was built on the edge of the river. Father Thames, a ribbon of charcoal beneath a matching sky, made her think of a grubby quilt resting on an even grubbier mattress. A jetty, reaching out into the water, was painted the same red as the balcony rails. Old fashioned gas type lanterns ringed the quayside. All that was needed was swirling fog coming off the water, and the clip clop of a hansom cab, and the picture of Dickensian charm would be complete, thought Lyndsey. She marvelled at how the developers had managed to transform a derelict area of mud flats and gap toothed buildings, into one of such metropolitan chic.

A flock of birds had landed on the wharfside. Their cries were deafening. Gaynor had piled the plastic sacks beside the car. She came to stand beside Lyndsey. Together they surveyed the birds.

'Brent geese,' Gaynor informed, 'they feed on the eel grass which grow on the tide-fed banks. If you follow the Thames down river to the Essex estuary, you'll see thousands of them. Curlews and gulls too.'

'They sound sad,' Lyndsey commented, 'like children crying for their mothers.'

'Nothing sad about them. They're vicious little blighters. Try to feed them a crust of bread and they're likely to take your finger off.'

Gaynor picked up one of the sacks, and the wind flapped the black plastic. With a squawk of protest the birds took off, flying against the cauldron of clouds, wings outstretched. They reminded Lyndsey of a squadron of fighter pilots.

'Here here comes Rob with the camera.'

Lyndsey turned her attention from the Brent geese, and saw that it was indeed Robbie coming towards them down the paved entrance to Jamaica Wharf. Dressed casually in a jacket, cords, and workmanlike boots, he looked out of place as one employed on a TV show on which the emphasis was on high fashion. It struck her again, forcibly, how much he resembled the music star, Sting. A younger, taller, darker haired version of Gordon Sumner. He was weighed down on his left shoulder by the camera. Gaynor explained, 'We film you entering the building with bags of togs for the opening credits.'

'Hi Robski,' the researcher leant forward and let him plant a kiss on her cheek. 'How ya doing.'

'Fine Gaynor. How was the journey. Any problems?'

'Surprisingly painless, considering the rush hour. What's it like in the room at the top?'

She nodded towards the balconied apartment.

'Och, they're in the usual flap. Sidonie is spitting like a scalded cat because she's mislaid the latest mascara, and Gregor was late as per usual.'

Lyndsey was standing in the background. She felt a little like a patient lying on a hospital bed whilst the consultant and surgeon planned the operation over her inert body. As if sensing her awkwardness, Gaynor clarified, 'Our make-up artiste and resident hairdresser.'

'Oh' Lyndsey couldn't think what else to say. She scuffed her trainered feet on the cobbles, trying to bring frozen toes back to life, wishing Gaynor and Robbie would hurry up.

There was a time and place for a cosy chat, she thought, and standing on this bleak riverside wasn't it. She couldn't even join in the conversation, not being part of the production crew elite. She was an outsider. On the fringe.

'Hello hen,' Robbie seemed aware of her feelings of exclusion, for he draped an arm around her shoulders. At his touch Lyndsey felt herself relax. He was so calm, so unhurried. His voice too, held a soft easy going timbre. 'How is our star turn for the day?'

Icy gusts were foaming the surface of the Thames. Coatless, Lyndsey shivered, and Robbie imperceptibly drew her close. Almost as quickly, he dropped his arm, as if suddenly conscious of the close proximity of their bodies. Did she imagine the electricity in his touch, thought Lyndsey in confusion.

'Right, let's get moving people,' interrupted Gaynor in an imperious voice, 'Filming is scheduled to start at 9 prompt, and time costs money. If we're not careful the whole series will be running over budget.'

At this, Robbie immediately became business-like. He repositioned the camera on this shoulder, and polished the lens with a frayed square of tartan. The consummate professional, thought Lyndsey, with a flicker of admiration.

'OK, Lyndsey, let's have a shot of you getting out of the car,' he said, beckoning her to follow him to the parked limo. The chauffeur was snoozing behind the wheel, engine running to keep warm. Robbie rapped on the window. 'Can you open the door for the lady?' As the driver got out to oblige, Robbie guided Lyndsey onto the back seat. Gaynor fluffed around in the background, making notes on her clipboard, and mouthing into a mobile phone. She terminated the call, and joined Robbie by the passenger door. 'Muss your hair Lyn - we want you looking a wreck,' she instructed, 'and when you get out of the car, don't look directly at the camera. Act natural. For God's sake don't ham it up just cos you know you're on telly. This is not a Shakespearean drama we're shooting.'

Miaow, miaow, thought Lyndsey, but she dutifully ruffled her already windswept hair. She caught sight of herself in the Chauffeurs rear view mirror. Her pallid complexion bore witness to the sleepless night.

Robbie took the edge of his colleague's hectoring tone by saying gently, 'Give me a few minutes to position the camera, hen. I'll hold up one hand when ready, and count down on my fingers. When I reach five, the Chauffeur will open the door. I want you to get out, pick up the black plastic sacks, two in each hand, walk up the pathway to Jamaica Wharf and through the entrance of the building. Make the pace as natural as you can. Don't rush it, but don't dawdle either. Try and look directly ahead, and keep your expression neutral. Once inside the swing doors, wait there, as I will need to film you from the top of the stairway.'

It was roasting in the car, where the driver had let the heater blast. Lyndsey felt sweat prickle her skin, and hoped she wouldn't smell of body odour. That would be distinctly terrible. She had thoroughly showered earlier, shaved her underarms, and applied a good spray of anti-perspirant in the hope that it would keep her fresh during the ordeal of the day. Her underwear had been carefully chosen too. Plain white sports bra and matching knickers. No fancy frills or lace, and certainly nothing tarty or matronly. Thalia and Savannah, she'd remembered from the reading of a 'Turnaround' TV review, had a penchant for stripping their victims down to underwear for the delectation of the viewing public.

Robbie was doing the countdown. Her palms felt sticky. God, this was it, she thought. No turning back now. Then the gloved hand of the chauffeur grasped the door handle, and swung it open with. Lyndsey attempted to exit the vehicle in the dignified way she'd seen the Queen step out of the Royal Rolls on state occasions. Instead of climbing out in one graceful movement however, she caught her heel in the foot well and stumbled onto the cobbles. Somehow she managed to right herself, narrowly avoiding a collision with one of the fake Dickensian lamp-posts. Her cheeks went pink with mortification. After this imitation of the Keystone Cops, Lyndsey expected to hear Robbie call 'cut' but he winked instead, and motioned her to start walking. Eyes firmly fixed on the pathway, she picked up the black plastic sacks, and moved forward.

It was the longest twenty yards she'd ever travelled. Conscious of the camera trained upon her, Lyndsey wished for the ground to open up. She'd never really understood that expression but did now. A chasm ready to swallow her would have been a welcome sight, especially since the swing doors of Jamaica House refused to open. After several flustered seconds, during which the bin liners tried to take flight like balloons in the wind, she was forced to use her shoulder as a battering ram. Once inside the lobby, she dumped the bags and leaned, cross legged against a pillar. She urgently needed to pee. Whether for physical relief, or as a reaction to stress, Lyndsey couldn't be sure. All she knew was that her bladder was full to bursting point. If Robbie and Gaynor didn't appear soon, she would wet herself.

As if on cue, the latter flung back the doors to the building. The researcher was talking yet again on the mobile, 'Just finished the opening filming, on our way up the stairs now. Oh, she's perfect. Run up the path like a frightened mouse. It'll make for great television.'

'A mouse' Lyndsey could think of a more apt analogy for her grand entrance, one that included the words fairy and elephant, but Robbie was elbowing his way into the lobby, using both hands to steady the camera. He beamed at Lyndsey, 'You were brill, hen. A natural.'

More filming followed. This time there were several re-takes. Eventually, Lyndsey's ascent to the top floor was caught on camera to everyone's satisfaction.

The door to the apartment was wedged open with a wastepaper bin. Inside the hallway, chaos reigned. Speaker cabinets lined the walls, and trailing leads on the floor made Lyndsey think of Harrison Ford negotiating the pit of snakes in his incarnation as Indiana Jones. Spotlights on tripods were strategically positioned. They were so bright Lyndsey had to shield her eyes from the glare. She saw that the apartment was painted entirely white, like a hospital ward. Furnishings seemed to consist of a combination of glass, chrome, and leather. There was a hubbub of voices emanating from the open plan lounge. Sandwiched between Robbie and Gaynor, Lyndsey was led inside.

It was a spectacular room, separated by the breakfast bar of a space age kitchen. The units wouldn't have looked out of place on a rocket heading for the moon, Lyndsey thought. Everything was stainless steel, with mirrored cabinet fronts and handles. Low Japanese style coffee tables graced the seating area, sporting vases of white lilies. An impressive hi fi system in one corner was playing a collection of rock classics. The floor, polished wooden boards, was stained translucent green, and spanning the length of one wall was an arched gothic window of gargantuan proportions. The view was equally spectacular. Stretching in a vista betwixt land and sky was the Thames, its choppy surface bearing witness to the inclement weather. A cruiser making its way down river, sounded a klaxon horn. The eerie echo hardly penetrated the plate glass.

Lyndsey was jostled. It was like being at a party, where you knew no-one, she thought. The bodies seemed intent on some private agenda, and Lyndsey had never seen so many faces bearing a look of such concentration. There were a mixture of races too. A Japanese girl, wearing headphones, a muscular black guy with impressive dreadlocks wheeling a camera across the floor, and three older men of Asian descent busy arranging lighting equipment. In the middle of this melee, sat the two presenters of 'Turnaround' either end of the low slung sofa.

At least Lyndsey thought it was them. At first she couldn't be sure, and had to take a step closer before letting out a gasp.

A terrible change had been wrought in Thalia and Savannah. Gone were the glossy clothes horses that had accosted her in the library only a week earlier. Instead they looked like drab housewives planning a grocery shop. Thalia, dressed in a towelling robe, hair scraped back with an Alice band, her face sporting a thick layer of vanishing cream, was engrossed in a magazine. In one hand she held a mobile phone, in the other a polystyrene cup. She took a contented sip, before looking up to see Lyndsey staring. Through a haze of hairspray, she gave a wave. Savannah, wore a robe, which bore the embroidered insignia of Channel 7. Hair was coiled into jumbo rollers, and a mousy girl in overalls was plucking her eyebrows and tut tutting. Lyndsey guessed that this must be Sidonie, of the lost mascara fame.

'Ouch, that bloody hurt. Do be careful darling,' Savannah admonished of the hapless make-up artiste, before noticing Lyndsey.

'Good morning, Lesley' she cooed.

'Read the script,' said Thalia from the other end of the sofa, 'It's Lyndsey, not Lesley. For God Sake, don't go getting it wrong on camera.'

'Who has rattled your cage today, sweetie? You've been foul since you arrived.'

'My period has started, and I've got the most horrendous pimple on my chin. You'd better hurry up and get started on me Siddie. I'm going to need plenty of slap to disguise it.'

'I'm so behind schedule,' wailed the make-up girl, beginning to apply foundation to Savannah's forehead and cheeks with a tiny sponge which made Lyndsey think of a cube of Emmental cheese. 'Spent ages looking for that blasted mascara. Sure I put it in the beauty box last night when I got everything ready before bed.'

Thalia let out a guffaw, and dragged on her cigarette, 'blame your gay flat mate, Julian. British Airways foremost cabin cruiser. You know how much he likes pinching your make up. He must have thought he'd died and gone to heaven when a cosmetics expert wanted to rent the spare room. Bet he's mincing up the flight deck of the 737 as we speak, fluttering his blackened lashes at the captain.'

'I'll effing kill him.' Said Sidonie with feeling.

'He'd probably find it a pleasurable way to die,' said Thalia with a peal of laughter. She noticed Lyndsey once more. 'Gaynor, go and get Lyn a coffee, and get her ready for filming. We should be through with make up in about ten minutes.'

Robbie had left the trio, and was standing in the corner talking to the black guy. There seemed to be a problem with the camera. Robbie had set it on a tripod, and both men were scrutinising the lens. A flop of hair had fallen over the young Scot's forehead, and Lyndsey thought he looked vulnerable; almost school-boyish. She had a sudden longing to push the hair away from his eyes.

Gaynor caught the glance, said, 'boys and their toys, eh?' and without waiting for an answer, steered Lyndsey to the breakfast bar. A percolator was bubbling on its surface. She found two mugs and poured them coffee, adding a slosh of milk from jumbo sized carton. She slid one across to Lyndsey, with the aplomb of a bartender in a Western.

It was dark and bitter. Lyndsey gulped it down, and her nerves steadied. Glancing around the room, with its heaving mass of people and equipment, she felt a quiver of excitement. There was an air of purposeful anticipation which telegraphed to her brain, so that she too felt intoxicated. This was going to fun, she decided, and couldn't prevent a wide grin from splitting her face.

Sunlight was slicing through a gap in the cloud, throwing a cartwheel of light through the gothic arched window. Steel kitchen cabinets sparkled, and water spilt on the counter top glittered like diamonds. A bearded man with dark saturnine features joined Lyndsey and Gaynor, and helped himself to coffee. He was dressed in black, and wore an ornate cross around his neck. Lyndsey thought he wouldn't have looked out of place in a remake of Dr. Zhivago.

'Ah, Gregor, the very man,' said Gaynor, 'meet Mrs. Lyndsey Daly, our MOP for today's show. Do you want her now?'

Gregor threw Lyndsey an appraising stare. His eyes were hooded like a bird of prey. She quailed.

'darlink', he said, 'you are perfect. Bleached white hair is so Essex.'

'I'm from London.' Lyndsey bristled, 'and what's an MOP when its at home?'

'Oh those estuary vowels' The hairdresser enthused.

Gaynor said, 'It's TV speak for Member of the Public.'

Lyndsey turned her back on Gregor. He ignored this and pulled a wide toothed comb from the pocket of his flowing cloak. Jabbing it at her scalp, he said, 'black roots – simply divine.'

'What's the prognosis?' Gaynor had taken out her pen and was poised to make notes on the clipboard.

'Flatten the hair down, grease the roots so it looks like she hasn't washed it for weeks. Sprinkle with talc to make it whiter and dryer. Make sure Sidonie leaves off the blusher when she does the make-up. I want this girl to look pale as a corpse on the programme. A ghostly spectre on the sofa between our two jewelled birds.' He nodded over to where the two Turnaround presenters were having a final dusting of face powder by Sidonie.

'Finish that coffee, and follow me, darlink'. He motioned theatrically to Lyndsey. She mutely obeyed, and trailed after him into one of the bedrooms. It had undergone a transformation into a makeshift hairdressing salon and dressing room. Boxes of shoes, and handbags were piled in one corner, alongside a hanging rail draped with clothing. Seating her at the dressing table, he squirted a tube of hair grease into both palms and began to smarm down the top of her head.

Lyndsey felt like a lamb being prepared for slaughter. Basted in oil ready for the oven.

Filming started at 9.45am, three quarters of an hour late. The entire production team had gone into over-drive at the delayed start. Tempers were frayed. Lyndsey, standing self-consciously in the wings, thought it didn't bode well for the day ahead. If everyone was frazzled at this juncture, how would they be by the afternoon? Running around like headless chickens, she decided.

She had been made up to look wan and tired. Even more wan and tired than she actually felt. Her hair felt stiff with grease.

'Winsome' the programme director had pronounced when she'd finally emerged from the bedroom. He was the muscular black guy see earlier talking to Robbie. She'd been asked to parade in front of him like a contestant at a beauty pageant while he'd surveyed her appearance. When he gave a nod of approval, Lyndsey could sense the relief of the crew.

'You look perfect Mrs. Daly. I'm Vince Levene, the producer of 'Turnaround'. Any questions before we begin?' His handshake was warm and firm. 'Are you OK? Feeling nervous?' Beguiled by his wide smile, Lyndsey found herself demurring.

'Good. Then let's get started. Thalia and Savannah are ready on the sofa. You will sit between them, while they kick off with some general chit chat about you, and your life. On the monitor we'll be showing footage of your secret filming. This will be subject to their scrutiny. Nothing to worry about – they've already seen the preview and have rehearsed their comments. They'll be hard hitting about the way you look on camera, but I know you'll take it on the chin Lyndsey. It's what the programme is all about. The Americans call it tough love. Bringing you down to rock bottom so we can then build you right back up.'

The seating area of the room had been miraculously cleared. Sitting either end of the Japanese futon, like carved bookends, were the two presenters. Exquisitely coiffured, and dressed, they once again resembled the sleek racehorses that had pounced upon her in the library.

Savannah wore a plain shift dress of fine cream wool, set off by a low slung leather belt. Her hair hung in a smooth silk curtain, parted on one side. She was lounging back in a casual manner, legs crossed. Her alter ego, sat more rigidly. Thalia, face framed by bouncy curls, was wearing a white linen trouser suit with ethnic accessories. Hooped bamboo earrings, and a necklace of shark teeth which would not looked out of place on an African tribesman. Both women were beautifully made up. A man wearing headphones materialised at Lyndsey's side.

'I'm Dessie, Chief Sound Technician. Just stand still for me, there's a good girl, while I mike you up.'

He produced a miniature microphone on a clip. 'Here, feed this lead up the front of your sweater, and I'll fix it to the collar like so....'

When she had been wired up to his satisfaction, Dessie asked her to repeat the alphabet whilst he undertook a voice check.

'All through here,' he mouthed to the Producer. Vince Levene nodded, and directed the camera crew into position. Thalia gestured Lyndsey over, and patted the sofa beside her.

'Perch your butt here darling.'

A last minute adjustment to the lighting, then there was a call for hush.

'Places everyone. Ten seconds to filming. Nine, eight, seven...'The countdown began. Lyndsey shifted nervously as silence descended upon the studio. A camera moved noiselessly forward on oiled wheels. Savannah smiled into the lens, and said, 'Welcome to 'Turnaround', the programme where we take someone's life and turn it right around. I'm Savannah Hooper-Greenhill.'

'and I'm Thalia Emmerson,' said her co-host. 'We're the bad dressers worst enemy.'

'But the good dressers best friend.' Savannah said, 'As fashion gurus we know that every woman, regardless of shape, size, or age, can be made to look stylish. Not to mention sensational. Think of today's celebrities, such as Cheryl Fernandez-Versini, Katie Price, and what about the grand dame of them all, Helen Mirren? Ladies of gloss and glamour. Imagine what they looked like as their former selves. Here we have some pictures of all three ladies before fame came knocking.' Lyndsey stared as, on the large monitor in front of them came a split screen image of three undoubtedly pretty but also ordinary looking women.

Thalia took up the introductory baton, 'Today we're joined on the sofa by 33 year old Lyndsey Daly, from North London. She has bravely agreed to take up our challenge to change her from femme fatal into femme fatale. We hope to do for Lyndsey, what their personal stylists have done for Cheryl, Katie, and Helen.'

'So how are you feeling Lyndsey at this very moment?'

The camera honed in on Lyndsey's face. She could feel a flush creeping up from her neck. Thank goodness the programme wasn't going out live, was her first thought. At least any faux pas she might make could be edited before the public at large got to see her performance.

'I'm having kittens,' she said truthfully. 'A whole litter of them. This has got to be the most nerve wracking experience of my life.'

'We're here to put you at ease,' Savannah patted her arm, and with a toss of spun gold hair, continued, 'Lyndsey works as a library assistant, and is married with a daughter aged eleven. Her husband has a demanding job in the IT industry, so running the household has been left to his wife. This busy lifestyle means she has little time to focus on who she sees in the mirror, with the result, that she has let herself go.'

'It's not just us who think so,' put in Thalia, 'Lyndsey's best friends admit that they despair with the way she looks. Let's hear what they have to say.' Picking up a remote control, a red taloned nail pressed play. The TV monitor sprung into life. On the widescreen, Dee and Coral came into view. Lyndsey recognised the background. It was Dee's sitting room. They were being interviewed by Gaynor. Although the researcher had her back to the camera, Lyndsey could easily identify the voice and frizzy mane. Dee was saying, 'She's a good looking girl, but the last few months, she's completely lost the plot. Her hair needs a good cut, and her outfits seem thrown together.'

Coral agreed, 'Sometimes its embarrassing to be seen with her. We reckon she's developed colour blindness. She's started to teem things like yellow leggings with purple sweatshirts.'

'Only last week she came to work wearing a polka dot dress two sizes too big. It hung on her like washing on a line.'

Dee couldn't resist adding, 'That's one of the problems. She has lost so much weight everything swamps her.'

The researcher said, 'has she been consciously dieting?'

'Heavens no,' Coral and Dee said in unison. The latter took up the reins of conversation, 'Lyndsey has always possessed the enviable figure. Curvy, without an ounce of excess fat. Unlike most of us, she's never had to worry about dieting.'

'So why the loss of weight, do you think? Has she been ill?'

In response to Gaynor's question, Coral explained, 'Not ill no, but stressed certainly. Her private life has hit a bit of a crisis, and Lyndsey is suffering from anxiety as a result. She's admitted as much.'

'I see. Is that why you put her forward to appear on 'Turnaround'?

'Yes,' Dee nodded, 'It was Coral's idea at first, but she sold me on it. At the end of the last series, we E-mailed the programme with a photo of Lyndsey taken on one of our rare nights out with a covering letter. For six months afterwards we were corresponding regularly with the research team, whilst they built up a profile. After seeing Lyndsey in the flesh, they agreed with us. Here was a basically stunning woman who had let herself go. Had totally lost interest in her looks. Coral and I want our friend to re-discover her beautiful side.'

'Get her confidence back.' Coral affirmed.

'Not to mention also getting five grand's worth of designer clothes.' Said Dee, once more hogging the microphone.

The screen went blank. Lyndsey squirmed. It made for uncomfortable viewing to witness a character assassination against oneself, she thought, especially when carried out by close friends. Thank goodness though that they hadn't been more specific and mentioned that her marriage was the 'crisis' alluded to. Raymond's reaction on hearing such a thing on national TV did not bear thinking about.

Out of the corner of her eye, she could see Robbie. He was standing off camera, watching the proceedings. His arms were folded, and he seemed to be coolly appraising her performance. Next to him, Dessie was fiddling with the knobs on a noise box, adjusting sound levels. She couldn't see Vince but knew he was in the room somewhere, over-seeing the filming.

Gulls were wheeling against the thick plate glass of the window. The room was cool and dim in the shadows, yet bright and hot under the spotlights. One was trained on her. She shifted uncomfortably on the futon. It was leather, the kind that squeaked. Not a good choice for television, Lyndsey thought, trying to keep as still as possible.

'So Lyndsey,' said Thalia brightly, 'after those revelations, what do you think of your friends?'

'They're a pair of cows.'

'Do those cows have a point?' probed Savannah.

Lyndsey said cautiously, 'If you mean in relation to how I dress, I guess so. Clothes and make up have never made it to the top ten in my list of priorities, except maybe when I was a teenager. What you wore mattered then. It doesn't now.'

'I'm afraid we can't agree with that, sweetie. Thalia and I happen to believe that whilst manners are supposed to maketh man, stylish dressing maketh women. But tell us more about your garb in the teens and twenties. What look did you go for then?'

'A mixture of punk and gothic. Panda eyes and spiked hair. Plenty of black. Trousers, T-shirts, jackets, knee high boots. Eveything had to have a rip in it secured with a safety pin.'

'As in La Hurley's infamous BAFTA dress?'

'Kind of. Except that my versions came from flea markets and charity shops.'

Savannah moved in. Lyndsey thought that both she and Thalia were like birds of prey circling in for the kill. 'How would you describe this look?' She said in a deceptively sweet voice, pointing first at Lyndsey's baggy jeans, then at her cable knit sweater.

'Street casual?' offered their victim.

'Fraid not, darling. It's not even street walker. It's street dosser if you ask me.'

'I couldn't agree more with Savvy,' said Thalia, 'where's your dirty sleeping bag, mongrel on a bit of string, and carrier bag full of worldly goods. You look like you should be selling copies of the Big Issue outside a London tube.'

Lyndsey bristled. 'You're being rude.'

'That's our job darling. We're here to shock you out of your apathy.'

'We're the worst dressed woman's secret weapon.'

'I'm glad you mentioned that word Savannah.' Thalia faced the cameras, and said, as if reading from some rehearsed script, 'our subject for tonight's programme might find the next section uncomfortable viewing. It's secret footage taken whilst filming her over the past few weeks.' She reached across and patted Lyndsey chummily on the knee, 'fasten your safety belt Mrs. Daly, and prepare for take off.'

Again, the same manicured paw flicked on the remote control. The TV monitor swam into focus.

Lyndsey gaped. On screen she could see herself hurrying along the High Street. She looked dreadful, she had to concede that. Preoccupied and tight lipped. Hurrying with head down, trying to avoid eye contact with fellow shoppers. Her whole body language screamed 'leave me alone', and her choice of dress merged with the anonymity of her surroundings. The trousers were a dull faded black, her top ditto. Had it been intentional, she wondered? A sub-conscious uniform of protection.

'Darling, if you're going to wear trews, let's have them hipsters in a drain pipe style. That bulky high waist makes me think of a baby's nappy.'

'The colour's dreadful,' Thalia took up the gauntlet, 'Grey makes you look washed out. Savannah's right about the bottoms. The style is totally wrong for your figure.'

'What's happened to your tits?'

Lyndsey didn't think she was hearing right. 'I beg your pardon.'

'Oh don't be so bloody prudish' Savannah admonished with a wag of her finger, 'You have got tits, haven't you darling? Only it's difficult to tell in that jumper.'

'Do you have a problem with your sexuality?'

Again, Lyndsey wondered if her ears were playing her false.

'Only judging by your look' Thalia continued, waving the remote controller at the TV, 'one would doubt you enjoyed being a woman. Every feminine attribute you possess is camouflaged by shapeless clothes. You've got a good body Lyndsey. One many women would envy. So why are you trying so hard to hide it?'

Lyndsey was dumbfounded. She knew the ladies had a reputation for being uncompromising with their subjects, something upon which the national press had seized. Lyndsey recalled one TV reviewer writing, 'The fashion rottweilers savage another victim'. So she'd expected them to run true to form with some forceful ribbing, but their remarks were borderline offensive.

Lyndsey spluttered as she answered, 'I'm not trying to hide anything. Certainly not the fact that I'm a woman. On that secret footage, I was shopping for some kitchen cupboard staples. Who dresses up when they have got twenty minutes to do a quick haul around the supermarket. On that particular day I needed to get back to cook for my daughter as she was going to visit her dad......'

Lyndsey clapped a hand over her mouth in horror, hoping that Savannah and Thalia would let the slip pass. She was mistaken.

'You have separated from your husband. Temporarily?'

Mutely, she nodded.

'How does Mr. Daly view you appearing on this programme?'

Deciding there was nothing to be gained from hedging, Lyndsey said, 'He is not happy about it Savannah. His worry is for me, and ultimately our daughter. He doesn't want her to become the butt of jokes in the classroom, because her mother has appeared on TV on a programme set up to ridicule her dress sense.'

'We're not ridiculing you, darling,' said Savannah, and for the first time there was a hint of gentleness to her voice. 'We want to help you get back your self-esteem. Recover your identity and sense of worth. Underneath the baggy haphazard clothes your wear, both Thalia and I can see there is a stunningly beautiful and feminine creature struggling to get out. At the end of this programme, when we have transformed your look, you might find your husband falling in love with you all over again. We will be giving him back the woman he married. Too many let themselves go once they get that ring on their finger and start a family.'

Lyndsey thought, 'if only you knew the truth. That it is not Ray divorcing me but the other way around. It is not a question of him wanting me to be the wife I was once, but me not wanting the husband he has become.' But she stayed wisely silent.

Thalia echoed her co-presenter, 'Lyndsey Daly, we are going to peel back the layers and reveal the real you. At the end of it, you'll thank us. Past contributors have been unanimous that the final outcome was worthwhile.'

More secret filming followed. Lyndsey squirmed some more, oblivious now to the squeaky futon, as she was shown footage of herself hurrying through the park in an old mac, coming out of the dentists surgery in paint splattered cords (worn while re-touching the ceiling in Cassie's bedroom), and lastly lunching in the Health Club with Dee and Coral in threadbare joggers.

Thalia and Savannah had kept up a constant diatribe. Lyndsey's clothes were branded tacky, dull, cheap, shapeless, baggy, old fashioned, and a host of similar depressing adjectives.

Now they came to the end.

The TV monitor was switched off, and the presenters spoke directly into the camera, addressing their invisible audience.

'We think you'll agree that this lady is in dire need of help to prevent disappearance down a hole labelled fashion disaster.'

Savannah took her cue from her partner, 'Lyndsey has bought her entire wardrobe into the studio so we can see if there are any items we can successfully 'Turnaround.'

At the mention of the programme title, the producer called out 'Cut' in a loud voice, 'half hour recess everyone.'

Lyndsey slumped back on the cushions with relief. He had thrown her a temporary lifeline. She could have kissed him.

Chapter Eighteen

'LYNDSEY DALY YOU win the prize for the most entertaining wardrobe.'

It was 11am. Filming had re-commenced after a brunch of bagels, and was focussed on the second stage of the schedule. On a white board pinned to the wall the words 'Wardrobe Assessment' had been written in marker pen. It was an aide memoire for everyone in the studio, and updated with fierce precision by Gaynor.

Lyndsey's clothes had been removed from their temporary sanctuary of the black bin liners and transferred to a series of hanging rails. Sandwiched between Savannah and Thalia, she watched warily as they inspected her clothes.

Savannah continued to speak, 'Entertaining in the way a circus might be. Bizarre and slightly surreal.'

'Surreal' Agreed Thalia, with a nod.

Both women had been subjected to further ministrations by Gregor. Savannah's hair had been stiffened in place by styling spray, and Thalia's glossed with serum. In comparison, Lyndsey had been left to go 'au-naturelle'. The heat from the arc lamps had given her face a film of sweat, and further deadened her hair. She looked and felt as limp as the wrist of the hairdresser.

Outside the panoramic window, the clouds had dispersed into greyish lumps. Lyndsey thought it looked like congealed porridge. The rails had been positioned by the Gothic Arch, silhouetting her clothes against the Docklands skyline.

'We move on to your Romantic era,' the hand jangling with bracelets swished along the coat hangers. It belonged to Thalia. She selected a high-necked white-laced Victoriana blouse and pulled it free. Both she and Savannah pored over the garment, reminding Lyndsey of forensic scientists looking for clues.

'Truly amazing.' Said the former.

'Truly awful.' Echoed the latter.

'Are you a member of an amateur dramatics society?'

Lyndsey shook her head.

'We thought you might have auditioned for a role in 'The Importance of Being Ernest'.'

'As the Great Aunt.' Savannah gave a hoot of laughter, seemingly at her own wit.

Lyndsey found her voice.' What's wrong with that blouse? I happen to think its very pretty.'

'Darling, we don't do pretty. We DO fashionable.' Her tormentor said, before adding, 'besides which the style is wrong for your body shape. Too tailored and severe.'

'Someone as slim as you should wear floaty fabrics to disguise the thinness of their frame.' Thalia said.

The next item of her clothing put under the microscope was a pair of suede-fringed trousers.

'Yee Haa' said Thalia, aping someone riding a horse, 'again, wrong style, wrong shape.'

'Home, home on the range,' sang Savannah, 'where the deer and antelopes roam....'

'Where's the Stetson?'

Lyndsey felt in the throes of an awful dream from which she was struggling to wake. Such was the forceful blast of their joint presence, it was easy to believe there was no-one else in the room but herself and two presenters. She remembered what she'd read about the 'Turnaround' programme. How Savannah and Thalia often reduced their ''victims' to tears. Ordinary members of the public, working mothers and housewives like herself, were set up like Aunt Sally's at a fairground to have wet sponges thrown at them by two woman from aristocratic backgrounds who'd probably been born wearing designer spoons in their mouths. This wasn't death by chocolate. It was death by TV.

'So what have we next?' Thalia said moving along the rail, 'what specimens of fashion abominations are you about to dredge up for us Lyndsey Daly.'

They were remorseless in their attack. Savannah now took up the gauntlet thrown down by her colleague.

'We're entering your gothic phase,' the slender hand with its immaculate painted talons parted the garments with a theatrical touch worthy of Moses parting the Red Sea, 'indicative by the sheer mediocrity of shade. What was it Henry Ford said? 'You can have any colour as long as it is black.'

'But black is so easy to wear.' Mumbled Lyndsey, feeling she ought to say something in her own defence.

The two TV presenters immediately jumped into ping-pong dialogue mode. Lyndsey's eyes went from one to the other until her head began to spin. It was like being the spectator at a tennis match.

'You mean because it doesn't show the dirt?'

'So doesn't need so much washing?'

'A good colour for lazy people'.

'Or if you're going to a funeral.'

'Of course, every woman should have a little black dress.'

'For the occasional cocktail party.'

'The only time black is acceptable.'

'On pale blondes, the look can be too severe.'

'Ghostly even.'

'On someone slim it can make them appear skinny.'

'Positively skeletal.'

Lyndsey wished they would pause to draw breath, but Channel 7's dreadful duo were in full spate.

Thalia said, 'Moving on, we have your casual wear' the camera moved noiselessly in for close up. Joggers, jeans, and jumpers were filmed in their figure swamping glory. 'Talk me through this choice of colour for instance.' She selected a lurid pair of green leggings and thrust them under Lyndsey's nose.

'I was given them,' was the shame faced response.

'Given them,' repeated Savannah with a tone of incredulity in her voice, 'by whom may I ask? A munchkin? A mad leprechaun. A little green man?'

'Or perhaps one of Ken Dodd's Diddy men?' suggested Thalia. Lyndsey could see a muscle twitching in her cheek, and guessed the woman was fighting back laughter. Coat hangers clanged together, as the pair moved inexorably along the rail. Lyndsey groaned as they approached her polka dot culottes.

'Coco the Clown pants.' Pronounced Savannah, 'team it with a pom pom hat and fake red nose and you'd be a star turn under the Big Top.'

'Baggy trousers and shorts are OK for someone slim, but the pattern is ludicrous. They might work with a delicate flower print for instance. But the spots are too loud, too big.'

'And the orange background is simply awful.'

'What did you buy them for darling? A trip to the circus?'

Lyndsey was beginning to feel hot. It wasn't just the temperature in the penthouse flat was rising. Her temper was also.

'Don't you think you're coming on too strong.' She countered, a bead of sweat running down her nose and balancing on the end. Quickly she wiped it away. A dewdrop on national television would do nothing for her image.

'Nonsense,' snorted Thalia, and the ethnic beads around her neck clanged, 'we're just speaking plain.'

Savannah had reached the end of the rail, 'Finally we have the country casual look. Tell us Lyndsey, what were you thinking of when you bought these?'

She unhooked two of the hangers from the rail, and held up a pair of tweed skirts for the edification of the camera. They were calf length, thickly pleated, the colour and texture of damp sacking. Lyndsey stared at them in abject horror. They were completely hideous. Even her mother, who possessed the haute couture glamour of a mature Hollywood movie star, would look shapeless and dowdy in such attire. Acutely embarrassed, Lyndsey could only stare down at her feet, feeling like a school kid caught cheating at exams. The examiners themselves, Thalia and Savannah stood with arms folded awaiting her explanation for such a sartorial clanger.

'They were in an end of season sale.' It was a pathetic line of defence, but the only one Lyndsey could come up with. It was true. She'd seen them in the window of an old fashioned shop in her local High Street. Rashly, Lyndsey thought the offending skirts would see her through the winter in the library. Teamed with a polo necked sweater and flat shoes, the whole ensemble would shriek of a sensible librarian. Which was exactly the kind of persona she had been trying to adopt at the time.

'I'm a chameleon' she thought, 'with no personality of my own. I try to blend in with my surroundings, make myself unnoticed.' This revelation depressed her. Had she always been like this, Lyndsey wondered. Or was it marriage to Ray that had seen her morph from a risk taker into someone who kept their head firmly below the parapet. If no-one noticed you, you couldn't get shot at, was her reasoning, for Ray could always find an excuse to get out his gun. For years she had tried to escape the line of fire, but he would manage to ambush her. It was like fleeing from an assassin in the dark unaware that the pursuer was wearing night vision goggles and could track your every move.

'Bang, Bang, you're dead'

Thalia had put a hand on her shoulder. Lyndsey jumped. 'Why, darling, you're crying.' She said and her voice had lost its strident edge. Savannah turned to the producer, and made a slicing movement with her hands.

'Cut!' shouted Vince Levene. Lyndsey saw the blinking eye on the camera go blank. Glare from the arc lights was muted, as somebody dimmed them. She found herself being led, unprotestingly to the sofa. Around her the production team tactfully withdrew into the kitchen area.

Through a blur of tears, Lyndsey felt Robbie at her side.

'Come with me, hen'

To her, his voice was as comforting as a plate of warmed oatcakes dripping with butter; he took Lyndsey's hand and led her through the maze of cameras and tripod lights, out into the hallway of the apartment. The door to the second bedroom, which doubled as a hairdressing salon, was ajar. Lyndsey could see Gregor spinning around on the swivel chair smoking a cheroot. At his feet, sat the cross-legged figure of Sidonie the make-up artiste. She'd emptied the contents of her cosmetics case over the floor and was frantically sifting through the items. Still hunting for the infamous missing mascara, thought Lyndsey.

Robbie hesitated, before opening an adjacent door. He motioned her inside. It was evidently the master bedroom of the apartment. The only one, judged Lyndsey, that hadn't been bastardised by the production department into a make shift studio. An estate agent's dream, she thought. A floor to ceiling window gave a view of the Capital's skyline. In the distance she could see the icy pinnacle of the Shard and the revolving wheel of the London Eye.

The room itself was carpeted in cream, and dominated by a vast bed made up ready for occupancy with crisp white duvet and sheets. Matching bedside tables sported reading lamps with shades like upturned beehives. Behind the headboard, was a set of speakers cunningly built into the wall. Robbie settled her on the bed, and went around the room throwing switches. The lamps sprung into soft apricot life. Soothing classical music began to issue from the wall.

On the dressing table stood a box of tissues. He pulled several free, and handed them to Lyndsey.

'Wipe your eyes lassie.'

She complied.

'They mean no harm you know,' he sat beside her, denting the duvet with the weight of his body. Lyndsey knew to whom he was referring.

'They're hateful. A pair of Queen bitches.'

'Och, you've got them all wrong hen. It's just hamming up for the cameras. Makes good television to come across all brutal like. In real life, Savvy and Thals are as harmless as toothless tigers. They're lovely ladies both. Kind and caring. You'll see once you get to know them better. What you're seeing is the faces they present for the camera.'

At that moment, the toothless tigers themselves roared into the room. Savannah came first, waving a tin of luxury chocolate biscuits with a wicked glint in her eye. Thalia brought up the rear, bearing a tray of steaming mugs.

'Strong coffee is what you need, Lyn my love.' She said cheerfully, and Lyndsey looked up in surprise. Gone was that mocking edge to her voice. She sounded friendly and open.

Savannah kicked off her shoes and joined Robbie and Lyndsey on the bed. 'God, those heels were bloody killing me,' she said with feeling.

'But they're fashionable aren't they?' Lyndsey couldn't resist the quip. Both women broke into peals of good-natured laughter.

'Touché' said Savannah, then, on a more serious note, added, 'are you OK Lyndsey? We're sorry we made you cry.'

'No you're not. Reducing Joe Public to waterworks makes for good Television right?'

'Who told you that?'

'Robbie'

A pair of immaculately coiffured heads swivelled to confront the culprit. Robbie raised both hands in the air, as a gesture of surrender, 'guilty as charged.' He said, before adding, with a wink at Lyndsey, 'I've given away trade secrets.'

'Naughty boy,' said Savannah. 'But we love you dearly, don't we Thals?'

Thalia nodded. 'You're 'Turnaround's' lucky mascot, Rob.' She placed the tray of cups on the bedside cabinet, 'Careful, they're hot.'

'Has he also told you we're actually rather nice. Not at all the termagants we present on screen.' Savannah had taken the lid of the biscuit tin and was offering them to Lyndsey.

She selected a wafer and said, 'yes, but as Mandy Rice Davies said, 'he would say that wouldn't he.' Personally I think you're a pair of complete bitches.'

'As opposed to incomplete ones,' said Thalia with a roar of laughter. Her laugh was so infectious that Lyndsey found herself smiling through the residue of tears. The atmosphere in the room lightened. For the first time that day, Lyndsey found herself beginning to relax a little. Away from the camera, the two women seemed almost human.

Thalia sipped her coffee in the reflective silence that followed. Then she said, 'we obviously hit a nerve with you out there, Lyndsey. Could you tell us why?'

'It went deeper than our criticism of your clothes.' Agreed Savannah. She put an arm gently around Lyndsey's shoulders and drew her close, 'which incidentally we don't mean. All that sniping and sparring is purely for the benefit of the viewers. So what brought on the upset lovey? Is it the marital problems?'

'Your husband has walked out on you hasn't he? Moved back with his old mum'

Savannah's voice was gentle. Lyndsey looked into her eyes and saw genuine concern, 'that's not strictly true. Ray left by mutual agreement. I guess he hoped that if left to my own devices, I would come to my senses and give our marriage another go. And he's not with his old mum. He's living with his mum-in-law.'

'Your mother?'

'Why so surprised? She's always thought the world of him.'

Thalia said, 'Would you let us ask you about it? On camera.'

Savannah added, 'we promise not to be too intrusive. But our viewers will see you cry when the programme is aired. They'd like to know why.'

Lyndsey gulped down a scalding mouthful of coffee, hoping it would give her strength, 'I don't know,' she said doubtfully.

Robbie patted her knee, 'nothing to worry about hen. It's an intrinsic part of the programme. 'Turnaround' is not just about changing someone's life; it's about finding why they have managed to get themselves into a rut. Savannah and Thalia always do their armchair psychiatrists bit on the couch early on in the show. Every contributor to the programme has their life dissected before they get to sit on our sofa. We need to make sure they have a story to tell. A story the viewers can relate to and identify with.'

'What's my story?'

Robbie looked at Thalia to supply the answer. She told Lyndsey, 'yours is the typical approaching middle age crisis tale. Librarian who needs liberating. Take this scenario. Woman approaching her forties finds life no longer making sense. Her children are growing older and no longer need her. Work is providing scant fulfilment. Hubbie is distant, often absorbed in his work. Their marriage is getting stale, and one or both of them wants out. Maybe he has an affair. Wife starts to lose interest. In her looks and in herself. That's what makes someone a terrific candidate for 'Turnaround'. We take this woman and give her back her sense of self. Put into the hands of professionals. Get her hair cut by a celebrity stylist. Buy her a wardrobe of sharp sassy clothes. Send her back out into the World with attitude.'

'Fighting spirit.' Put in Robbie, munching happily on a biscuit.

'Into battle with a new set of armour.' Confirmed Thalia, swigging her coffee.

Lyndsey said, with some asperity, 'what makes you think you're qualified to turn someone's life upside down like this. Make them a laughing stock for the sake of TV ratings.'

'for the sake of a BAFTA actually,'

'I think its reprehensible.' Lyndsey tried to inject a tone of self-righteousness into her voice and failed. Miserably.

'Atta girl,' Savannah sounded approving, 'I guessed that underneath that fragile delicate exterior lurked a core of steel.'

'Oh piss off.'

Thalia clapped her hands at this ribald remark, 'Lyndsey Daly,' she said, rallying Robbie and Savannah to applause, 'I'm beginning to like you.'

'I'll second that.' Agreed Savannah.

Robbie held his coffee mug aloft in a parody of someone raising a toast at a party, 'hear, hear.'

Reluctantly Lyndsey had to admit something to herself. She was beginning to like them too. Robbie's description of the duo as toothless tigers was apt. Showing their claws in front of the cameras was just an act.

Robbie.

She liked him the best.

Chapter Nineteen

'YOU'VE GOT A terrific arse.'

Lyndsey was standing in a modern day torture chamber. A hexagonal cubicle lined with mirrors that she'd earlier mistook for a cupboard in the corner of the room. Reflecting back at her from every angle was her thin form, naked except for bra and panties. It wasn't cold, but the sheer embarrassment of standing in her underwear for the salivation of the viewing public made her shiver. The mirrors were two-way, and Lyndsey knew that on the other side a bank of cameras were recording every inch of her goose pimpled flesh. It was mid-afternoon, and filming was well underway for the third segment of the show. During lunch (take away Chinese provided by the production team) the TV presenters had facilitated a change of outfit, emerging, chameleon like from the make shift dressing room. Savannah a plum vision in palazzo pants, and silk blouse, Thalia in floaty dress studded with tiny stars. New hairstyles complimented the change. The blonde had hers piled high and secured by tortoiseshell combs; the brunette a 50's style pony tail.

'Sensational legs,' added Savannah, 'without an ounce of cellulite.'

They stood in the doorway, looking Lyndsey up and down like farmers leaning over a sheep pen on market day. They were being unusually complimentary but the subject wasn't fooled. She knew they were building up for an onslaught.

'Shapely ankles,' Thalia oozed, 'curvy calves.'

'Your arms are good,' Savannah said, 'lift them up Lyndsey, there's a love. See, no flab. No hint yet of the dreaded bingo wings.'

'Small tits, but nice and rounded and even size. Do you think she needs chicken fillets, Savvy?'

'Chicken fillets!' exclaimed Lyndsey. She had visions of them force feeding her pieces of slimy poultry.

'Not to eat darling,' said Thalia, who seemed to have the uncanny knack of correctly guessing her mind, 'as padding for your bra. They're not made of chicken, obviously, but the feel and texture make the name apt. We happen to have a set handy.' She produced, seemingly from nowhere, a box small enough to contain the shoes of a toddler. Not only is the woman a mind reader, thought Lyndsey wryly, but she's a magician as well.

Before she could voice a protest at their presence, both women joined her in the chamber of horrors. They set about inserting rubber slices into each of Lyndsey's bra cups, Savannah lifting one breast, Thalia the other. Lyndsey was so startled by their intimate manhandling of her body that she was unable to speak.

'You have to admit that looks a whole heap better.' The brunette had stood back and was surveying the duo's handiwork. The elegant blonde nodded enthusiastically, 'Or should we say breaster.'

Lyndsey gazed in awe at her many faceted reflections. Her bust had inflated into Page three girl proportions, and her cleavage spilled from the brassiere like pink blancmange from a mould.

Ray would love me like this, thought Lyndsey. He'd never made any secret of the fact that her small chest disappointed him. Early on in their marriage, she'd found a stack of pornographic magazines hidden behind the bed. The women featured possessed mammary glands of unnatural size. In one issue, the centre pages had stuck together, and prising them apart, Lyndsey had been sickened by what she saw. A plump blonde lay legs akimbo on a rug being masturbated over by several men. Semen had iced each mammoth sized breast in a white glaze and the model's mouth was an open yowl of ecstasy. But her eyes were dead.

Lyndsey shuddered at the memory.

Thalia had momentarily disappeared. Left alone, Savannah cooed at Lyndsey, 'substantial tits have given your figure hour glass proportions. And what a sexy figure it is. Concave stomach, and legs that start under your armpits.'

'But I'm so skinny. My ribs are sticking out, and just look at these bony shoulders.'

'Think positive honey. Most women would give up a year's supply of anti-wrinkle cream to be that slim. You're a perfect clotheshorse. An enviable size ten and one of the few women who look better clothed than nude, yet you dress to conceal rather than flaunt that body.'

Savannah Hooper Greenhill turned to the camera, and said, 'We're now going to show Lyndsey what she should be wearing. Show her how to 'turnaround' that dated, unflattering look, for an altogether classier one. A chic, glamorous, and self-assured woman is going to emerge from her shell by the end of this programme. Dowdy librarian Mrs Daly will be a chrysalis transmuting into the most flamboyant of butterflies.'

She turned back to Lyndsey, 'but first, I need to find out more about those dreadful knickers our lady guinea pig is wearing. Where did you buy them Lyn, and why?'

'A local pound shop.' Came the mortified reply. Unable to ignore the look of mock horror on Savannah's face, Lyndsey attempted to explain, 'it's a store where everything on display costs one pound only. You get three pairs of drawers in a pack, so it works out at brilliant value. Thirty three pence per knicker.'

'Mmm, and how long do they last, darling?'

'Roughly about five washes,'

'Before they disintegrate?'

Lyndsey nodded. Her shame was complete. 'Or they get too laddered to wear..' she finished lamely.

'Well, I think those pants are pants!" Savannah said, 'I shall make it my personal quest to get you out of those Pound Shop Passion Killers into proper lingerie. Or should I say, improper lingerie.'

This pun provoked a ripple of laughter from the camera crew.

Thalia was back. 'Try this on, Lyn. Now don't pull a face. We want to see what you look like wearing something stylish.'

A cellophane bag was shoved inside the mirrored cubicle. Lyndsey opened it. Inside was a plain white T-shirt in a stretchy cotton mix, bearing an expensive label. Hardly the cutting edge of style, she thought, but dutifully pulled it over her head. The two presenters crowed in triumph at the result.

'See how fabulous you look in something with a high neck and cutaway sleeves.'

'Now the eye is drawn away from a skinny torso towards your elegant swan neck and lithe limbs. The chicken fillets give your bust line added definition, so that a staple garment now has the "wow" factor. With the addition of funky jewellery and a pair of tailored trousers you'd have an outfit that could see you through the day and into the evening.'

'With the top half of you looking right, we're going to demonstrate just how ridiculous that dreadful pleated skirt looks.' Savannah smirked, and tossed Lyndsey her wardrobe stalwart which had been removed from the hanging rail. The resulting sight made both women cackle.

'God, they're like the witches in Macbeth,' thought Lyndsey, 'I could just picture them stirring the cauldron...hubble, bubble, toil and trouble...' She felt as though she were in the cooking pot, being boiled alive by the demonic duo. A TV dinner, she thought, mollified by her own private joke, and the knowledge that underneath their brash exteriors, Savannah and Thalia were really rather nice. Pussy cats wearing the coats of beasts. This had been proved by the kindness they'd shown her earlier after she'd broken down on film.

They instructed her to twirl for the benefit of the cameras. Lyndsey gasped. The skirt looked truly ghastly. Seen in the many angled mirrors, her rear end resembled the creased hide of an elephant. The sleek fitted lines of the T-shirt highlighted the bulky pleats.

'Miss Marple as I stand and breath.' Said Thalia.

'Solved any good cases lately?' hooted Savannah, then added, 'where are your lace-up brogues and shooting stick my dear?'

'You're not showing me on TV like this?' Lyndsey faltered.

'darling, why not? If you were misguided enough to buy that pleated monstrosity with a view to wearing it in public, why confine such an apparition to the locals. Don't the Great British public deserve that treat?'

The women were relentless. Instructing Lyndsey to undress, and remove the breast enhancers, they selected a velvet corset top from her wardrobe. She'd bought it on impulse the previous autumn, thinking it's sophisticated material might see her through the Christmas period when teemed with black trousers.

The TV presenters were in for the kill for they selected canary yellow leggings to team with it.

'Let's talk about the top first,' said Savannah, leaning on the mirrored door jamb. 'The colour is too strong and dramatic for someone with pale skin and hair. It makes you even paler, and gives your complexion a green tinge.'

'The shape is a disaster on you,' continued her cohort, 'corset tops are designed to push up ample breasts so that they peep over the top like ripe peaches. On someone like you with no tit, there is nothing to bolster. An empty pocket of material in front which is a bloody disaster to the eye of the female beholder, and a bloody big disappointment to the male.'

Lyndsey said primly, 'I don't dress to please men.'

'Liar,' scoffed Savannah, 'every woman from teens to great grannies dress to please men. Clothes are not merely to protect our modesty and keep us warm. They are also designed to send appropriate signals to the opposite sex.'

'Mother Nature has got it right. Why do you think male peacocks display their tail feathers, and monkeys show their bums?'

'Talking of bums, let's take a look at yours in those yellow leggings. Reminds me of pear halves swamped with lumpy custard. You've got a pert arse Lyndsey Daly, yet in those trews it looks bloody enormous.'

Looking at her rear view reflected in the hexagon, Lindsey had to admit Savannah had a point. Her bottom looked massive. 'Maybe it was a trick of the light, or the stretchy material, or the headachy yellow' she thought, gazing at a rear end that wouldn't look out of place on a builders site.

'An ass like a camel's' said Thalia, 'without the humps. And a flat chest makes a jutting out bum look like the prow of a ship.'

'What a tailor would term a HPS' said the blonde, nodding in agreement with her brunette counterpart.

Lyndsey's head was beginning to spin once more. The glare from the spotlight, the mirrors, and stultifying heat was making her giddy. With an effort she tried to concentrate her attention, 'HPS?'

'High Prominent Seat, sweetie.'

'Had enough of the cubicle?'

Lyndsey nodded, grateful for Savannah's suggestion.

Thalia turned to the camera, 'our subject for tonight's show, has bravely submitted her body and clothes for our inspection.'

'It is now time for us to work the 'Turnaround' magic upon this rag doll. We're going to show Lyndsey the type of clothes she should be wearing to make the maximum impact in every area of her life. Outfits in which she can work, rest, and play, in the knowledge that she looks ace.'

Savannah finished off, 'And as all the ladies out there know, once you look good on the outside, you feel confident within.'

Inside the confines of her illuminated prison, Lyndsey heard the camera crew call for a break in filming. The two presenters were beckoned away by Vince Levene, the producer, leaving Lyndsey to compose herself. Gaynor appeared, holding a Japanese kimono, 'Slip this on,' she instructed, frizzy hair waving wildly about her head in the static air, 'We've a thirty minute recess before filming the final two segways.'

'Which are?'

'It was in the schedule sent to you with the contract, Lyn.' Gaynor sounded peeved that Lyndsey hadn't memorised the document, 'first off is 'the shrink on the sofa' - the part of the programme where Savvy and Thals delve into your past to discover what has caused the lack of confidence in the way you dress. Followed by them giving you a shopping list on air. Outlining the style of clothes to buy on your retail expedition for the programme, which, as you should know (if you'd bothered to read the schedule) is set up for tomorrow in London's Oxford Street.'

The researcher's mobile phone trilled, and she wandered off, making it clear she didn't want any eavesdropping. Lyndsey ventured awkwardly into the lounge area of the apartment. Her TV inquisitors were nowhere to be seen, and she guessed they were back having makeup and hair re-touched. She wondered fleetingly if the cosmetics artiste, Sidonie, had yet managed to find the missing mascara. Lyndsey checked her watch. She wasn't surprised to see it was already four thirty. Filming for the small screen, she'd discovered, was fraught with delays and re-takes. It was a shock to realise the extent of work that went into the making of a programme for primetime TV; the reels of video tape that had to be spliced in order to distil the essence of the programme into an airtime slot. Only a small proportion of what was filmed would be screened, the wasted footage ending up gathering dust in the editing room.

At the breakfast bar in the kitchen, the production team were taking coffee. The percolator hissed and someone was buttering toast. Lyndsey was amazed at how much food was consumed by the crew. Someone mentioned 'nipping out for doughnuts', and there was a ripple of approbation at this suggestion. The microwave pinged, and the Sound Technician removed a steaming plate of noodles and chicken – re-heated left overs from the lunch.

Robbie materialised at her side.

'Lyndsey, how goes it?' he asked. She luxuriated in his voice. Soft and lilting like that of a childhood storyteller. Marriage to Ray had made her used to a voice that could freeze steam, and had inured her to gentleness of speech. Being addressed by Robert McCrae was an almost physical pleasure; a man whose voice held no harsh undertones. Listening to him was a comforting as a mug of cocoa on a cold night.

'It goes fine.'

'I've been watching stills of the show, and you're coming across great. The Producer is pleased how you are bearing up to Thals and Savvy.'

'As you told me yourself, their bark is worse than their bite.'

'Och, even their barks start wearing thin towards the end of the day. Bit like guard dogs grown tired warning of imaginary burglars.'

Lyndsey grinned. Robbie grinned back. His blue eyes twinkled. She noticed the fine creases across his forehead under the mop of hair, and the lines around his mouth. Somehow it added to his charm.

'Coffee?' he asked her, reaching for the percolator jug.

She shook her head and said, 'is there a phone here. I'd like to ring my daughter.'

'Sure. There's a landline in the master bedroom. You'll probably find a queue of people waiting to use it though. Mobiles are banned on set except for specific times.'

Robbie was wrong. Weaving her way through the throng of technicians, sound recordists and camera crew, Lyndsey made her way to the master suite, and found the room empty. She slid the lock on the door, and sat on the same bed that she'd cried on a short timer earlier. She picked up the receiver and dialled Renee's number.

Her mother answered almost immediately.

'Mum, Hi.'

'Hello darling.' Renee sounded distracted. In the background Lyndsey could hear the whirr of a food mixer.

'Is this a bad time?'

'No, silly. I'm mixing batter for Cassie's tea. A special request for pancakes, with lemon and sugar.'

'Can you put her on.'

'Actually, she'll be late from school tonight. Cass asked this morning if she could stay behind for netball practise, so I've booked her a taxi home. Hope I've done the right thing Lyn, only she seemed so keen.'

Lyndsey was disturbed by Renee's answer. To her knowledge, Cassandra had never shown any interest in sport, and surely the child would have wanted to rush home and hear all about her mother's 'Turnaround' day.

Renee was asking something. Lyndsey asked her to repeat it, then said,

'Horrible to begin with, but I'm beginning to enjoy it now. The TV team are nice people, and they're looking after me well.'

'What about our very own Savannah and Thalia. Have they been hauling you over the coals?'

'Actually Mum, they're not half as bad as the media present them. A lot of it is put on for the cameras. They're actually a couple of sweeties, and were very supportive when I had my mini breakdown.'

'Breakdown?' Renee sounded perturbed.

'It was nothing really. Just me blubbing about Ray'.

'darling please be careful.' There was no mistaking the note of caution that had crept into her mother's voice, 'Don't let them lure you into saying anything you might regret on camera. Raymond is intrinsically a good man and does not deserve trial by television. Think of Cassie. Imagine the embarrassment of having to go to school when your mum has been on prime time TV slagging off your dad.'

Lyndsey could hardly believe what she was hearing. Surely her own mother knew her better than that, 'I'm not stupid. You know I won't say or do anything to embarrass my family.'

'Or yourself darling. Remember that too much information can be a bad thing.'

They exchanged a few more words, but conversation had become stilted. Renee pleaded a return to the pancake making, and hung up.

Lyndsey stared at the silent receiver, face blank with astonishment. There had been a hectoring tone to her mother's voice that had never been encountered before. She had the uncomfortable feeling that Renee's allegiance was showing signs of cracking. That her erstwhile unswerving support for Lyndsey over the marital separation was crumbling. Was someone else the recipient of her empathy?

Was it Ray? Was Renee slowly but surely going over to his side?

The traitor!

Chapter Twenty

RENEE HUNG UP the phone, and busied herself in the kitchen. A casual observer would have noticed a frenetic edge to her actions; the cloth dragged across the counter top was flattened aggressively to the surface, the whisking blades of the food mixer plunged in and out of the washing up bowl. Renee felt driven. She was not sure what was driving her. Disparate emotions were bubbling under the surface of her cool exterior and she couldn't put a label to any. Anger and guilt swirled with ecstasy and joy in an emotional mixing bowl, where other feelings added their own ingredient. A dash of despair here, a soupcon of delight there. When the kitchen was cleared of pancake making detritus, and restored to its former order, Renee placed a tea towel over the bowl of batter for the flour mix to settle. She wished someone would place a blanket over her own head, so that she too could settle. Quell the maelstrom of emotions within

After a day of high winds and rain, the weather had calmed into a dusk of orange sky. Renee was suffocated by the four walls, and felt a powerful need to swallow some wintry air. Picking up a chair, she lugged it down the hallway, and opened her front door. The step was bathed in chill lemon light, and she positioned the chair so it faced the setting sun. Renee crossed her knees elegantly, and unzipped her smart boots. They were ginger suede with a subtle Western fringe which matched her skirt. Her V necked sweater, in fine lambs wool clung to breasts firmly encased in an uplift bra. Everything she wore was a recent purchase. On hearing the news that her daughter had been 'caught' to appear on TV, Renee had bought the book that accompanied the series, entitled 'Turnaround Tips'. Reading it had been a revelation. She realised that her own style of dress could only be termed as sensible. Under the section entitled, 'Dressing for Mature Lady' was a list of Do's and Don'ts, compiled by the ubiquitous Savannah and Thalia. Pearls and pleats were considered ageing, lace up brogues only permissible for fell walkers, and crimplene a complete non-starter. The 'Funky Fifties' were advised to go for a sexy glam look, in plain fabrics and clean lines.

After reading the book, Renee had reviewed herself critically in the bedroom mirror. What she saw was an elegant woman who needed a fresh take on fashion.

On a mission that particular day to free up space for the influx of her son-in-law's clothes, Renee had turned it into an assault on her wardrobe. The new look had been well received. Lyndsey had commented, 'Wow Mum, you look ten years younger.' Cassie had enveloped her grand-mother in a hug before yelling, 'Gran, you look ace.'

Ray had showed his appreciation in other ways.

Renee shuffled uncomfortably in her chair. Her son in law filled her thoughts often, but not, she knew, in the way he should.

The sun streaked low across the pathway, its weak warmth bathing her face. Renee put a hand tentatively up to her chin, and stroked the slender contours of her neck. Her fingers moved downward, luxuriating in the touch on her skin. She hovered by the cleft in her breastbone, and then began fine circular movement with her fingertips around the apex of her cleavage. Other hands had oh so recently made this journey. Strong hands, with chiselled stubby nails, and hair curling on the backs of knuckles.

Renee shuddered violently. It wasn't entirely a reaction to guilt, but more of an involuntary reaction to the memory of Ray's hands caressing her naked breasts. Their liaison was madness, that she knew. But it was a delicious kind of madness. A crazy heady madness, that sometimes overtook one in life. She felt like a boat without a rudder, at the mercy of wind and sea. Except now she was at the emotional mercy of the man married to her daughter.

Renee squeezed her eyes shut, wishing she could expunge the spectre of her only child from her mind. She knew convention dictated that she ought don a hair shirt and bewail her guilt. Crawl along the ground on her belly in shame. She'd acted like the trailer park trash that regularly appeared on American daytime chat shows. For a horrible moment she could picture herself appearing on one. 'And here is Renee Fairbrother', smarmed the imaginary presenter, 'who has indulged in sex-play with her son-in-law.' The audience were boo-ing and hissing in her ear. Catcalls accompanied her walk to the hot seat.

The presenter said, 'You've acted like a cheap tramp. Your daughter is backstage. We're going to bring her on. What are you going to say to her, Renee?'

Her behaviour was reprehensible, that she knew. Allowing Raymond to fondle her breasts until he brought himself to orgasm, and herself to the brink. It hadn't been an isolated incident either. Since the evening of their gourmet dinner, Ray had not been dissuaded against removing her brassiere whenever he felt the urge. Which was often. She tried to convince herself that because their liaison had not consisted of penetrative sex, no lasting damage had been done. But as each day passed, it was getting harder to do so. How could one excuse or even begin to justify such behaviour, she kept asking herself. There were no easy answers.

Renee began to hum "Greensleeves" in an effort to release some of the tension she was feeling.

> 'Alas my love, you do me wrong,
> to cast me off discourteously,
> for I have loved you so long,
> delighting in your constancy....'

Constancy. She baulked at the word. She had not been constant with the one person in the whole World who should have been assured of it by birthright. Her only child. Yet inviting her son in law to move in had seemed a sensible idea at the time. Renee looked up at the darkening sky. It was streaked with colour, reminding her of orange juice in a tinted glass. Winter had always been her husband's favourite season, and Renee found herself remembering marriage to that quiet, diffident man, from whom she'd been widowed so young.

The late Mr. Fairbrother had never rubbed her nipples between fingers so hot that it burnt her skin. Never massaged her tender breasts to the point of rapture. Not even trod the foothills, she thought recalling his inexpert fumblings. She'd loved Douglas, and he'd loved her, but neither had kindled any fire between the sheets, and both had been seemingly content to accept this blemish on an otherwise perfect marriage. But there had been odd times she could remember, when a powerful urge had simmered between her legs, demanding release. On those occasions, she had looked at Doug with rare longing, but those lustful glances had never been acknowledged, still less returned.

That old longing was back. At a time in her life, when Renee had firmly locked her sexual self away in a trunk and padlocked it with the purchase of sensible corsets, a man had aroused those long dead passions. Not just any man either. The father of her grandchild.

Cassie. Guilt jabbed a red hot stiletto into the depths of Renee's stomach.

It was colder. The sun had sunk below the rooftops, and Renee found herself sitting in shadow. Time to toss the pancakes for her grand-daughter's tea. Toss, toss…. She could almost taste the word in her mouth. Remembering Raymond's words as he whispered in her ear, 'only your tits can toss me off so quickly – so completely – so, oh so – blissfully ….Renee – remember that…..'

She forced herself to think of Cassandra. She knew the moment the child arrived home from netball practise she would be agog for news of her mother's day in the 'Turnaround' studio.

Renee stirred. Picking up the chair, she went back inside, closing the door of her maisonette on a purple twilight. The phone trilled into life. Lyndsey again, she thought with a smile.

Instead it was Ray's voice. 'I'm on my way home.'

Home. Already her son in law viewed it as such. She found her hand clutching the receiver in eager anticipation of his arrival. A knock on the kitchen window made her look up. Renee saw the top of Cassie's head bobbing by the sill.

Her grand-daughter was home too.

Chapter Twenty One

LYNDSEY PRESSED THE button on the ansaphone,

'You have four messages' intoned the computerised voice. 'Message One, received at 15.35 hours...'

'Hi, am I speaking to Lyndsey Daly...' there was a pause, before the voice continued. The speaker sounded slightly breathless, Lyndsey thought, 'this is Sally-Ann Kent of the local Gazette. We've had a tip off that you are appearing on the TV make over programme 'Turnaround' when it kicks off for its new series shortly. Any chance of an interview? Local celeb kind of thing? Call me for a chat, as soon as you get this message....'

Lyndsey grimaced. She guessed where the reporter had got the insider information. Cassie had confessed to bragging about her mother's television appearance to her class. Word had obviously got round, but Lyndsey couldn't be cross with her daughter. She knew how much Cassandra needed to shore herself up in front of her peers, and if her own five minutes of fame helped the child construct a buttress against the jibes of fellow pupils then so be it, but give an interview for the local press she dare not. Raymond would be aghast. The ansaphone bleeped. She listened to the second message.

'Hi Lyn, its Coral. Dee is here. Ring the minute you get in, we don't care how late it is. We're sinking a bottle of wine, and simply dying to know all about your day in the studio.'

She smiled, picturing them avidly waiting by the phone. No doubt getting steadily pissed. A quick glance at her watch told Lyndsey that, at ten to midnight, despite her friend's entreaties, it was too late to ring. Dee would surely have wended her way home, leaving Coral snoring on the sofa in a drunken stupor. The front door clicked quietly shut, and Robbie came into the lounge and stood behind her. He'd had problems finding a parking space for the Channel 7 pool car in which he'd driven her home. As always, his quiet presence needed no comment; no acknowledgement. She listened to the penultimate message.

It was from Ray. His voice was gruff, no-nonsense. 'Lyn, I'm ringing to check that you followed my instructions about how to conduct yourself in the studio. Don't forget that I have job and a well-respected position to uphold, which pays for the food you eat and the roof over your head. I trust you haven't compromised either me or our daughter today by blurting anything about our marriage on camera.'

As if I could forget she thought with a sigh. Ray had lambasted her on one of his pit stop visits to collect mail, about how she must maintain a front of marital bliss. About how she must not embarrass Cassie with detrimental comments about her father. About how she must act with ladylike deportment. His anger, at discovering Dee and Coral had set his wife up to appear on a programme which he deemed 'junk food for the brain', had not abated. Since Cassie had let slip that her mummy was going to be 'on the telly', Raymond had repeatedly lectured Lyndsey about how to behave in front of the great British viewing public. When he'd first found out that she was scheduled to appear on 'Turnaround', he'd ranted and raged at

Lyndsey for two hours in Renee's kitchen while grandmother and granddaughter were out at the cinema. He'd demanded that she pull out of the programme and when Lyndsey told him this was not possible as she'd signed a contract to appear, he'd spat venom. 'In that case you'd better keep this under wraps,' he'd warned, theatrically drawing a finger across her lips, 'keep it zipped.'

Unlike their daughter, Lyndsey thought wryly, Ray had not told his peers.

'You must want your head read,' he'd said, when she'd tentatively asked if anyone in his office knew, 'as if I'm likely to advertise the fact that my wife is a brainless dolt who needs a pair of toffee nosed tarts to tell her what to wear. The secretaries were talking the other day about the programme. I hung around by the photocopier listening, and it wasn't very edifying, Lyn, believe me. Members of Joe Public stupid enough to appear have their entire lifestyle dissected in front of the cameras, and the two presenters are lethal. A pair of aristocratic fillies who think it fun to mock the afflicted. They'll make mincemeat of you Lyn, and you are gullible enough to let them. Not that I particularly care what scrapes you get yourself in, now you've decided to strut your stuff on the divorce catwalk, and the misery that entails. But I do care about the effect on Cassie of her mother being paraded on prime time television for the great unwashed to gawp at. Not to mention myself. Thank goodness Daly is a fairly common surname. Hopefully, no-one will put two and two together and assume I'm your significant other.'

The message finished with a bleep.

Lyndsey felt Robbie's hand rest gently on her shoulder. He let out a low whistle, 'Phew, he doesn't pull his punches does he? Talk about giving it to you straight.'

'That's Ray all over. He could win prizes for bursting someone's bubble.'

'Someone's? Or just yours?'

'Mine is his speciality,' She felt deflated. The adrenaline rush that had carried her through the long, tiring day in the studio dissipated with her husband's phone call. As always, he had the ability to undermine her fragile self-esteem. The wave of depression that his voice invoked made her shoulders sag. Lyndsey felt the familiar blanket of apathy fall. She sank down on the sofa, feeling her knees buckle.

Robbie sat beside her. He draped an arm loosely around her shoulders and drew her close. 'Poor hen,' he soothed, patting her in the way a parent would comfort a child. After a reflective pause, he said, 'the man is a fool to treat you this way. You're quite special Lyndsey Daly, which is why we picked you for the show. All our contributors have that indefinable 'something'. Some have got forceful personalities who clash swords with Thals and Savvy, whilst others possess the 'I'm happy with the way I am, and ain't gonna change for no-one' type attitude.'

'Which category do I fall into?'

'Neither. You possess a translucent quality which shines through. A quiet dignity which lights up the screen and sends the nerve endings of the viewer into a tingle.'

'Now you're flattering me.'

'Och, I'm a down to earth Scot. We're not a race of bull shitters, who trouble to pay false compliments. Do you know what one of the camera crew said to me earlier? He said, 'that girl reminds me of Lesley Hornby in her heyday. Those huge doe like eyes, and heart shaped face'

'Lesley Hornby?'

'Better known as the famous 60s model, Twiggy. He used to work freelance on Vogue magazine apparently, and went on many of her photo shoots. The camera guy I mean.'

'Oh'.

'So I'm not the only one who thinks you're something out of the ordinary. Star quality. You've got it in spades.'

'Now stop. You're making me blush!'

In the tree outside the window, an owl hooted. An incongruous sound in the suburban night, and Lyndsey jumped. Robbie drew her closer. 'Do you think you'll patch things up? With your husband?'

She shrugged. 'I honestly don't know. Probably not. I still love the Ray I walked up the aisle with, and he will always be the father of my child, but living with him has become a pretty joyless existence. Whether or not he still loves me is open to question, but I'm sure of one thing. I irritate the hell out of him, and he never fails to let me know it.'

'I'm the wrong woman for him, and sadly, it has taken us both this long to realise it. He needs one of those forceful bolshie types you mentioned earlier.'

'Like Hester from the first series. She was a larger than life red-head, with a bark like a sergeant major, and a bite like a rottweiler. The joint efforts of Savvy and Thals failed to dent this woman's armour, and when they attempted to throw out her wardrobe, she threatened them with a coat hanger.'

Lyndsey laughed at this. It conjured up such a comical picture.

'It was assault with a deadly weapon,' said Robbie, his eyes twinkling with good humour. He stroked her cheek. It was a gesture of intimacy which Lyndsey knew she ought to rebuff, but couldn't muster up the energy to do so. Besides, it felt nice. To be gently caressed by a man was a novel experience after

Ray's rough handling, and she allowed herself to luxuriate in it.

'You seem to understand women,' she said, amazed at his sensitivity.

'Growing up the only boy amongst six sisters, I guess I canna help reading the female mind.'

A motorbike roared down the road, its headlight flaring a path across the ceiling. The sound of its engine punctured the stillness of the night. As the noise died away, Robbie said, 'was there anyone else involved?'

'Sorry?'

'In your marriage break-up?'

It was a personal question, and one she considered intrusive, but Lyndsey replied, 'No. Not on my part anyway. Neither on Ray's as far as I am aware.'

'Has he ever played around?'

'Robbie!' This time she let out a cry of protest.

'Sorry, hen. Call me a nosey bastard if you like. It's just that I care about you. We all do. Savvy, and Thals, and the production team. You're like a piece of bone china on the shelf of someone who seems better suited to an earthenware jug.'

At this show of empathy, Lyndsey said, 'What about you Robbie? Are you in a relationship, or playing the field?'

'Neither. I was with a lassie for seven years. Lived together for the last two. She was right bonnie, and soft at first, but things changed.'

'What things?'

'Och, difficult to say what exactly went wrong. Morag developed a hard edge over the years. Became very ambitious and self-seeking. A real tough cookie. In the end she became someone I couldn't recognise, and someone I didn't like very much. It was a mutual decision to part, but it caused us both sadness.'

'I'm sorry. How long ago was this?'

'We split last Summer. I moved out. Since then there's been nobody else so I've concentrated on work, and getting my new flat shipshape.'

'Are you lonely?' Lyndsey couldn't help herself asking.

'Aye, at times. Less so than when I was in the relationship though. I found it harder being with the wrong person than I do being on my own.'

She found herself nodding at his reply. 'I've never thought of it like that, but I can see what you mean. I'm achingly lonely with Raymond. Up here I mean.' Lyndsey tapped her forehead.

Robbie said, 'don't let his phone call upset you. You did nothing on the programme to be ashamed of. If it helps, I can arrange to send you a pre-view tape so he can watch it before it is aired. That should calm any fears he might have that you have been shooting your mouth off.'

Lyndsey closed her eyes and nestled in the crook of his arm. Dear Robbie she thought. He was so kind. She tried to remember verbatim the conversation with Savannah and Thalia on the 'Turnaround' sofa, when they turned their attention to her private life.

'Welcome back from Savannah and myself,' the latter had said to the camera, addressing the viewing public, 'before the break we met up with 33 year old Lyndsey Daly a librarian from North London.'

Savannah continued the précis, 'Lyndsey's two friends Dee and Coral have nominated her for our help as someone who has lost her way in her choice of dress.'

She turned to Lyndsey, who sat self-consciously in the middle of them both, 'So Lyndsey, have you enjoyed being on the programme so far?'

She nodded, as Thalia said, 'Earlier we binned the entire wardrobe of this walking fashion disaster, before concentrating on the type of styles she should be wearing to best enhance her physical assets, and disguise physical faults. Now it is time to move on to the next stage of the programme. The part where Savannah and I put Lyndsey Daly on the psychiatrist's couch and find out why she has let herself go.'

'Poor dressing is often a symptom of low self esteem,' said her co-presenter in a 'chummy' 'I'm everybody's friend' type of voice, 'so we're here to help free this particular clothes horse from the confines of her emotional stable.'

Lyndsey had taken a deep breath at this point. This was the moment she dreaded. However her resolve was strong. She was determined not to reveal too much about her private life.

'You said earlier that you and your husband are having a temporary separation. His idea or yours?'

'Both. It was a joint decision.'

'Can we ask why your marriage has reached this sorry state?'

'You can ask all you like,' Lyndsey said resolutely, 'but I prefer not to comment.'

Thalia, who had been quietly listening now broke into the conversation with a rattle of ethnic bracelets, 'Oh come now, let's not have any of this shrinking violet nonsense. Thousands of women watching this programme are likely to be in crisis relationships with their partner – it will help them to identify their own situation with yours. And help you too. A problem shared is a problem halved, so they say. In this case, Lyndsey, your marital problems shared with so many viewers, will be much more than halved. It will be a cathartic experience for you unburdening yourself on television...'

'the ladies who appeared on the first series of 'Turnaround' all found it beneficial to reveal their private traumas on camera. So, are you going to tell us what has gone wrong within your marriage?'

Lyndsey remained unconvinced and said so. Quite forcibly, she thought. Now curled up on her own sofa at the fag end of this impossibly long day, with Robbie at her side, she was glad she hadn't succumbed to the presenters' probes. She had acted, as Ray had determined she should, 'with ladylike deportment.' And monk-like silence.

Lyndsey extricated herself from Robbie's encircling arms and went to the phone. Pressing the button, the ansaphone machine whirred to the final message. Cassie's excited voice filled the room, 'Mummy, where are you? Why aren't you home yet? Surely you can't still be in the studio?' In the background, Lyndsey could hear Renee saying something to her grand-daughter, but she couldn't make out what, '..oh, and tea was lovely. Nana made some scrummy pancakes with lemon and sugar, and I had one with golden syrup too. Why can't we have syrup in our house, mummy?' A plaintive edge had crept into her daughter's voice. Lyndsey found herself smiling through the tears, 'got to go now, cos Nana says its way past my bedtime. I'll ring in the morning before I leave for school. Oh, and did you remember to get an autographed pic of Savannah and Thalia, so that I can show it to my class. Some of them don't believe you are really going to be on telly.'

Silence filled the room at the cessation of the messages. A midnight hush had descended on the road outside the bay window. Lyndsey hadn't the energy to get up and draw the curtains, so the lounge was bathed in silvery moonlight. She stole a look at Robbie sprawled on the sofa. He was staring at the ceiling, as if deep in thought. Lines of fatigue were etched around his eyes, and she thought again how much he looked a curious mixture of old and young. A little boy's face shadowed with the exhaustion of a middle-aged man. Seeing him at work all day on the set, made her realise just how tiring the TV profession could be. Robbie hadn't stopped for a single minute – liaising with the camera crew and ancillary staff, and carrying out makeshift repairs to the equipment. Then he'd been given the job of driving Lyndsey home. To his credit, he hadn't protested, she thought, with a surge of warmth for the gentle Scot. Instead, he'd given her that easy smile and said, 'my pleasure hen.'

Lyndsey too, felt exhausted. She returned to the sofa and sank back into the crook of Robbie's arm, content to remain where she was, head on his shoulder, smelling that heady masculine aroma of aftershave and sweat. Neither of them seemed able to move; to stir themselves from the torpor of tiredness. Lyndsey's limbs were as heavy as concrete, and her mind was closing in; losing track of time and place.

When Robbie spoke his voice seemed to come from a long way off, surprising Lyndsey because she had forgotten he was there. She realised, with a start, that she'd actually fallen asleep on his shoulder, and guessed that he, too, had dozed off.

'Time I was going,' he said, with a yawn, 'we've got another early start tomorrow.'

'Today' Lyndsey corrected, just managing to make out the time on her watch in the navy blue light of the waning moon, 'it's one thirty am.'

'Aw shit. I'm supposed to be meeting up with the camera crew at Bond Street tube in precisely seven hours.'

'so am I. 'It was Lyndsey's first scheduled shopping day. She was to be let loose in the West End with a cheque courtesy of Channel 7 for five grand in one pocket and a list of Savannah and Thalia's 'rules' in the other. Her every foray into fashion emporiums was to be filmed and spliced into the 'Turnaround' programme. It was an intrinsic part of the show, she was told by the Producer, and one that viewers eagerly anticipated. An exam of sorts, to test whether each contributor on the show had taken on board the two presenters advice on what they should wear in terms of colour and styles. Lyndsey knew her own 'do and don'ts' pretty well.

The second shopping day, set for the following week, was scheduled for the Lakewater Complex on the Essex/ Kent borders. On this occasion, the producer informed her, Savannah and Thalia would 'be in attendance'. She ventured to ask him what he meant by this. In response he'd given her a knowing smile, and said, 'they'll be watching you in secret.'

Lyndsey gave Robbie a nudge, 'I know pretty well what is expected of me today. I'm to spend at least half the allocated money on new togs, as well as a fitting for some made to measure upholstery....'

At this Robbie gave her a wink, 'I'd like to be a fly on the wall of the fitting room.'

'Behave,' She admonished, wagging a finger at him in a jokey fashion, 'seriously though, what can I expect to happen on the Lakewater day?'

'Och, more of the same. Spending the rest of the clothing budget. Filling in the gaps with some well-chosen accessories. Scarves, costume jewellery, bags, that sort of thing.'

'That's not what I meant.'

'Ah.'

'What I really want to know is, why are Savannah and Thalia coming along.'

'To check that you're following their rules. Buying the styles and shades on their list.'

'and if I don't...?

'If you don't, they'll jump out on you like this...' He hooked his fingers like claws, hissing in the parody of a vampire.

Lyndsey shrunk back into the sofa in mock alarm, 'Spitting venom at me like a pair of puff adders?'

'You got it in one, hen.'

'How am I supposed to shop with them at my heels?'

'They won't be. Not at first anyway. You'll be filmed by the crew, and S & T will be watching on video link at a secret location nearby. If they see you taking an item of clothing off the rail that they don't agree with, they confront you in the shop. You then have two choices. Either to front them and stick to your guns, or capitulate.'

'It makes better television if you stand and fight' Robbie said, sounding as though it was an afterthought, 'a bit of argy bargy on the box always goes down a treat with the viewing public.'

Lyndsey considered this. The prospect of being cornered in a shop with no escape route was an alarming one. She could just imagine the scenario. Herself, clutching a rogue garment to her bosom, whilst Savannah and Thalia attempted to snatch it away. She had no doubt that a tussle would follow in the form of an undignified tug of war, which would see her forced into submission by the unfair advantage of two against one.

Still, she thought, it was a week away. No point in premature worrying. She yawned. Her watch told her it was one thirty am.

'You might as well get your head down on the sofa,' she told Robbie, 'too late to go home now.

Chapter Twenty Two

'YOU ARE HANGING on to your breasts by your shoulders.'

Lyndsey stared at herself in the gilt framed mirror. A pair of hands was hoisting up her brassiere by the straps. They belonged to the proprietoress of an exclusive lingerie store situated in London's Bond Street.

'See how much better they look when lifted.'

Lyndsey nodded. She had to concede a point to the woman who now emerged from behind her back. An elegant redhead, dressed in an emerald cashmere suit which consisted of knee length skirt and tunic top. Lyndsey found herself giving the woman's choice of clothing a silent seal of approval, and this thought surprised her. Already, she thought, the close proximity of Savvy and Thalia was making her look anew at the apparel of her sisterhood. In the past, she wouldn't have given the clothes worn by a shop assistant, a second glance. Nor anyone else for that matter. The entire population of London could have walked around in bin liners, for all the notice Lyndsey would have taken.

Now it was different. Now she was beginning to develop, albeit belatedly, a taste for style. And expensive clothes. She judged that the cashmere suit must have set its wearer back several hundred pounds.

The wearer was speaking now, 'You have pretty breasts, my dear, if on the small side. A correctly fitting bra will do wonders to enhance the curves you already possess. The one you are wearing is, I'm afraid, only fit for the bin.'

'You want me to chuck it?'

'Most definitely.'

'but its one of my better ones. Almost brand new.'

The sales lady clucked in disapproval. She threw up her hands in a parody of mock horror, and said, 'then you need to dispose of your bras as soon as you get home. They are giving you no support, and what is worse, are putting added strain on your shoulders. If you are not careful my dear, you will end up with a widow's hump well before your time. How many ladies do you see walking bent double their posture is so bad? Curvature of the spine is an extremely distressing and debilitating condition, and it is my contention that many of these physical problems are worsened by women wearing badly fitting brassieres.'

Lyndsey frowned. She wasn't entirely convinced by this argument, and surmised that scepticism was written clearly on her face, for the proprietoress said, 'let me put it to you like this. Would you buy a pair of shoes without trying them on, and having your feet properly measured? Fallen arches, bunions, and in growing toenails are symptomatic of ill-fitting footwear, just as rounded shoulders, stiff necks, and back ache are symptomatic of ill-fitting bras.'

Lyndsey saw the truth in this statement, and felt that the case against poor underwear had been irrefutably put. The red-headed lady beamed, 'Do I take it I now have a convert to my cause?' She asked, and without waiting for Lyndsey's response, continued, 'let us now dispose of the bra from hell, so I can properly measure your cup-size.'

Lyndsey was conscious of the camera poking through the plush velvet curtains of the changing room. Vince Levene, the producer of 'Turnaround' had been keen to film this scene. She'd agreed, with the proviso that she wouldn't bare her naked breasts, and she now deemed it the moment to put out a warning hand, and cover the lens.

Vince took the hint. From beyond the curtain, she heard him call a halt to filming. Lyndsey slipped off her old bra, and stood with as much dignity as she could muster, whilst the proprietoress of Roscoe & Cantor took out a tape measure and placed the cold metal tip against her left nipple. She tried not to look too critically at her reflection in the floor length mirror. Shoeless, dressed in ubiquitous jeans, her top half naked, Lyndsey thought she presented a less than edifying spectacle. She decided to focus her mind on the plush surroundings. The carpet felt soft beneath her stockinged feet, and the marbled walls and hanging chandelier of the changing cubicle added a dimension of luxury that a High Street chain store could not match. Lyndsey thought of her previous forays into the World of lingerie purchasing, and couldn't resist a wry smile. Herded into in communal changing rooms where the smell of sweat was pervasive and mirrors smeared with handprints, or in cramped cubicles where, more often than not, curtains hung limp from missing rings, and door catches had been vandalised. She'd always found buying bras and knickers a dispiriting experience in the past, which might account for her recent patronage of pound shops.

Not so now. This exclusive lingerie emporium, a magnet for the well-heeled tourist, and passing celebrity, offered a level of pampered indulgence that made shopping an experience to be savoured. There were dishes of Belgian chocolates arrayed on glass topped tables in case any customer got peckish, together with jugs of iced water. Soft music played tantalisingly in the background, in contrast to the annoying thumping beats favoured by the so many High Street boutiques, which made buying clothes of any description an assault on one's eardrums which had often deafened Lyndsey. She had never understood the propensity for shops and coffee lounges to play distractingly loud music, and always harboured the thought that the staff turned it up high for their benefit not the customers. Her friends all felt the same. Many a time she or they had been forced to flee a shop midway through a purchase, or a coffee lounge halfway through a latte, because a disco beat was thumping in her ear. Not so this upmarket lingerie store. The well-heeled customer, she decided, just would not tolerate the aural misery inflicted on the high street. Now she revelled in the seductive melody of Gershwin, volume turned pleasingly low, together with the air conditioned interior of the changing room, and its lavish furnishings. It was like being in the lobby of a five star hotel rather than a retail establishment. Or a private museum. She'd been amazed to find, on entering, glass fronted display cabinets featuring exquisite boned basques edged with frou frous of French lace, which had been worn by a famous movie star in a Hollywood blockbuster which had taken almost every award at the Oscars. The plaques on each cabinet proudly proclaimed that they had been 'hand crafted by expert Roscoe & Cantor Seamstresses.' The Company itself held a Royal Warrant for providing lingerie to the Queen, and the Windsor crest was etched into the smoked glass windows. Lyndsey knew the environs of the shop were designed to impress its customers with its connections to high ranking society. She found herself duly muttering words of approbation to the manageress who had finished her measuring of Lyndsey's naked breasts, and was jotting down figures in a small leather bound book.

'I'm glad you like our humble emporium,' she said in answer to Lyndsey's praise, 'we aim to please.'

The jotter was placed in the breast pocket of the cashmere suit, which bore a gilt framed name badge. Mdme Collard, it said. Lyndsey wondered if the elegant lady really was French, or whether the continental moniker was given to add an air of Parisian haute couture to the proceedings. 'Where are you from Madame Collard?' she asked conversationally. It was embarrassing to be standing naked from the waist up in front of a virtual stranger, and Lyndsey felt an overwhelming need to fill the silence. The sales lady smiled in a benign fashion and said, 'originally Austria. But I have lived in London for the past thirty years. My grandfather, Henri Roscoe, started this business with his partner Karl Cantor back in 1908, supplying lingerie to the gentry. The original premises were in Regent Street, but we moved to this shop in the early sixties. I now run it virtually single handed with a team of eight lady seamstresses and five sales staff.' Lyndsey wondered how the shop managed to pay exorbitant rates on such a prestigious London address since she was the only customer, but Mdme Collard's next words answered this, 'our business has expanded considerably since the advent of the Internet, and we now get orders from all corners of the globe.'

'Our clients include the crème de la crème of British and American society. Nicole Kidman is one of our customers, as is the Countess of Wessex.'

'Wow' said Lyndsey, sounding dutifully impressed. Her nipples were standing erect in the air conditioned cool of the changing room, and a blush crept up from her neck. The Proprietoress must have noticed for she said, 'Oh my poor dear, you are getting cold. Let me hurry to the stock room and get you a selection of lingerie in your size.' With that she discreetly drew aside the curtain, and vanished into the confines of the shop. Lyndsey could hear her exchange muted pleasantries with the camera crew. Then Gaynor's voice was clearly heard saying, 'we're falling behind schedule. House of Fraser are expecting us at 11 am – they are cordoning off a section of the sales floor while Lyndsey shops.'

The gruff tones of Vince Levene responded, 'We'll ask them to wait. I want to get the filming of this underwear segment right, and if it takes another half hour, so be it.'

Lyndsey couldn't help a secret smile. Gaynor, the pushy researcher had met her match in the show's producer. The towering black guy who was in charge of the 'Turnaround' team was obviously a force to be reckoned with. No matter how Gaynor might fret about her precious time schedule, thought Lyndsey, Vince would remain unmoved until he considered the filming 'in the can' as he put it.

The curtain wafted aside. Mdme Collard was back, with a box. She took off the lid. Nestled inside on a bed of tissue, was an exquisite brasserie of white lace edged in lilac satin.

Lyndsey couldn't help herself blurting out, 'Oh, that is so beautiful.'

'Beautiful and functional. This particular style is underwired to lift and separate the breasts and give them proper support, but the boning is concealed in a foam lining in the lace.'

'Now lift up your arms, so I can fasten it correctly.'

Lyndsey did as she was told. In the mirror her face looked tinged pink, and her eyes held a glint of excitement. She was beginning to feel intoxicated by the whole 'Turnaround' experience. Her hair, newly washed that morning, clouded her face and shoulders in a pale blonde veil. She wanted to laugh aloud with sheer exuberance for it was a long time since she'd felt so womanly. So long since she had felt so pampered.

The bra fitted like a dream. Her breasts, in the mirror, seemed to have grown in size and stature. They stood proud and firm, and in wonderment Lyndsey stroked the soft cleft of her cleavage.

'My boobs look simply.....' Lyndsey struggled to find the apposite word, 'amazing...' she finished inadequately.

'Time for the T-shirt test,' said the Proprietoress, smiling broadly. She took out a folded square of material from the side pocket of her tunic, and held it up. Lyndsey saw that it was a plain black vest.

'Put this on, my dear. Don't worry – it is newly laundered.'

Lyndsey slipped it on over her head, and stood dumbstruck. In the mirror was a curvy blonde goddess that she almost didn't recognise as herself. The top clung to the contours of her upper torso, giving her boyish figure the hour glass proportions of a Page Three model. Suddenly she had breasts to be reckoned with. The expertly fitted bra and simple vest gave the illusion of a lush figure guaranteed to turn the head of any passing male.

Madame Collard stood back, arms folded, her expression in the mirror one of smug triumph.

'There, do you see?' she said, addressing Lyndsey's reflection 'how sensational you look in an inexpensive T-shirt. If only ladies would understand that even designer clothes will not hang right if underwear is badly fitting and the wrong size. Would you put silk cushions on a sagging sofa my dear?'

Lyndsey, following the analogy, shook her head fervently.

'Get the corsetry right, and any woman could look fabulous dressed in rags!'

As if to demonstrate, she tapped a framed poster that decorated the un-mirrored wall of the changing cubicle with a manicured nail. It depicted Marilyn Monroe, in her glamour heyday, garbed in a dress fashioned from a sack. The movie icon looked sensational. Lyndsey nodded, struck dumb by both her own transformation and the allure of Norma Jean in the poster.

Half an hour later she stepped out of the smoked glass door into the brittle sunshine of the morning, clutching a midnight blue carrier bag emblazoned with 'Roscoe & Cantor' in gold lettering. It contained two matching brassieres; one in cream lace, and one in black. The third in the set was not in the bag. Lyndsey was wearing it.

Tailed by the camera crew, Lyndsey made her way down Conduit Street, in the heart of London's fashionable West End. It was bright and cold. The pavement sparkled, and everything looked freshly washed after the torrential rain that had fallen in the night.

The sound of it on the roof had kept her awake in the early hours. She'd heard Robbie padding to the bathroom. Ensconced on the sofa, he'd been grateful to accept her offer of a bed for the night. He'd even come prepared with a change of clothing, and toiletries in a holdall.

'The first rule of being on a TV production crew,' he'd told her with a grin, 'always makes sure you have a set of clean clothes and a toothbrush. You wouldn't believe the number of times we crash down on the studio set when filming over-runs.' It was nice having a man in the house again, Lyndsey, thought when she'd woken in the morning after a fitful night's sleep. Since Ray had moved out, she'd found herself missing his masculine presence. It was nerve-wracking being a woman alone in an old house whose floorboards creaked and heating pipes gurgled continuously. Often she was jolted awake by what sounded like footsteps on the stairs, only to realise it was the joists settling for the night.

Robbie had risen with the proverbial lark, and was showered and dressed by the time Lyndsey had emerged, bleary eyed from lack of sleep.

'Cup of tea, hen?'

She'd nodded gratefully. He'd already brewed a pot, and it was just how she liked it. Hot and strong.

'I've had a recce in your fridge, and found bacon, eggs, and mushrooms. Dab hand at a fry up, me, so I'll do us a cooked brekkie. You look like you need a heavy dose of protein, Lyndsey. Very wan this morning, if you don't mind me saying so.'

'Say away. Truth is, I do feel a bit washed out.'

'A Robbie special will do you a power of good, lassie. Bread fried to a crisp in lard, eggs sunny side up, and bacon nicely curled at the edges. Sit yourself down and drink your tea, while I get cracking.'

Dutifully Lyndsey sat. She was naked under the towelling robe, but felt no threat to her modesty with Robbie. He exuded an air of protective gallantry that she found to be charmingly old fashioned. Lyndsey supposed it was his Scottish upbringing. He'd already told her that he was raised in a household of staunch Protestants occupying a remote corner of the Highlands. She'd marvelled at how he had upped sticks at the age of nineteen and made his way to London to seek his fortune. Like Dick Whittington, he'd said with a dry laugh, he hadn't found the streets paved with gold, but had worked himself up through a series of jobs until they were paved with something approaching silver. Joining Channel 7 as a mere 'runner' on set, he'd graduated from graveyard shift programmes onto the prime time ratings winner, 'Turnaround' as Production Assistant.

The breakfast was delicious. Lyndsey found herself eating ravenously. The food she thought, was almost as mouth-watering as Robbie looked that morning. Dressed in black drainpipe jeans and an orange T-shirt emblazoned with a picture of a hamster running around a wheel, and the logo 'My other job is in television.' When he'd placed the plate in front of her, Lyndsey had smelt toothpaste and soap. They ate in appreciative silence. She was conscious of a complete lack of tension. There was a mark on the tablecloth and a tannin stain on Robbie's cup, but she felt no need to apologise or explain. Not simply because he was a guest, and so not expected by the rules of etiquette to voice disapproval, Lyndsey thought, but because he was so easy going and calm. She knew if Ray had been seated at the breakfast table with her, he would have already spoilt the joyful brightness of the morning with a list of complaints. The tablecloth in particular would have irked him. Ray would not deign to sit down for his breakfast until a freshly starched white one was put on the table.

When they'd finished, Robert McCrae had poured her a second cup of tea, and said, 'scoot upstairs and get ready while I clear up.'

'No, I'll do it. You cooked. It's only fair.'

'away with you, lassie, that's an order. It's my job to look after you, and besides which I'm a bachelor, which means I'm used to washing up.' He'd given her a wink, and patted her gently on her towelling backside.

'Good looking, educated, and domesticated too. How come another woman hasn't snapped you up since Morag, Robbie?'

'The right one hasn't come along, I guess.'

'She will'

'Maybe she has already.'

Lyndsey saw he was regarding her with a curious intensity. Embarrassed she turned away. As she made her way up the stairs, she heard the tap filling the washing up bowl, and her guest singing 'Mull of Kintyre' in a surprisingly melodious voice.

Lyndsey reached the imposing entrance of flagship House of Fraser store in London's West End at twelve noon. Gaynor was flapping about their late arrival, and was promptly shouted down by both Robbie and Vince. Tempers were beginning to fray. It had been a long haul from the lingerie store, and the camera crew were flagging from the weight of their equipment. The Security Guard ushered them inside, and directed the entourage to the escalators. Lyndsey was greeted on the sales floor by a posse of assistants headed by the Departmental Manager. A section had been cordoned off from the rest of shoppers by rope barriers. She made a mental note of the amount she had to spend. Her budget for this first shopping day was three thousand pounds. The three brasseries had already blasted a sizeable hole in her purse. Lyndsey could see rows of tops arrayed on hanging rails. Quietly she began to repeat the mantra learnt from Savannah & Thalia's list of rules for someone with small breasts and a slim figure, 'high neck-lines, halter style, no scoop necks, capped sleeves work, definitely no slash necks, or three quarter length sleeves....'

Her shopping was about to begin in earnest.

Several wearisome hours later, Lyndsey was sitting on a damp wall alongside the Thames. Behind her an ancient brick tunnel run underneath a bridge carrying overground trains across the river. It had grown chilly, and she wrapped the scarf tighter around a neck that was now aching. Along with a back that felt as though it had been trampled by marauding elephants. She would never have believed that shopping with a camera crew in tow could have been quite so exhausting. Surrounding her were a veritable mountain of shopping bags from her West End retail mission. She was drained and footsore. The camera crew had regrouped into the purple dusk, and were engaged in animated discussion.

'Final part of the day, Lyndsey,' said Gaynor coming to sit beside her on the wall, and ticking off the last box on her checklist, 'we need a publicity shot to accompany the programme. It will go out to all the newspapers, TV guides, and our syndicators, and....' she broke off alarmed by the look of pure terror on Lyndsey's face, 'don't look so petrified. It's standard procedure for most of our prime time shows. We've done the same thing for every contributor that has appeared in the last two series.'

'Your syndicators...?'

'Of course. A show like 'Turnaround' is not just limited to Channel 7 you know. How do you think we make our money? Other TV stations, around the world, can buy into our syndication rights if they wish. We're very popular in the Far East for instance. Those oriental ladies are very fashion conscious and love to see what the well dressed Western woman is wearing.'

Lyndsey flinched at this news. It was a piece of information she'd rather not have known. Bad enough, she thought, to be paraded on national TV, but international TV.....! She shuddered at the unedifying prospect of people all around the world, of different cultures and customs, getting to see her stripped to bra and knickers in 'Turnarounds' infamous room of mirrors. Strangers each and every one.

The series photographer joined them, waving an aerial map of London.

'This is going to make a great shot, Lyndsey. I pinpointed this as a possible location with the pre-requisite tunnel, and its lived up to expectation. The Dickensian feel is just what I want to convey.'

'Why?' Lyndsey asked.

'Because it suits you, darling. You look like a Little Nell or perhaps Dora from David Copperfield. Winsome and waif-like. There's also an inherent sadness about you that I want to capture, which will highlight the contrast between the 'before' and 'after' image you are going to show the world once Savannah and Thalia have transformed you.'

He began to set up the camera, fussing with the position of the tripod, until he got the angles right.

Another minion from the crew set up a portable arc light.

'Put the diffuser on,' instructed the photographer, 'I want doomy colours. The colour of the sky is perfect. Purplish grey. It's all adding to the atmosphere I want to create.'

'Now Lyndsey, I want you to look up a little, so I can get the tunnel in the shot. The tag line to this photograph has already been decided on '.....is there light at the end of the tunnel'.

He motioned Gaynor away with a flick of his hand, and lined up several of the shopping bags in a pleasing tableau alongside Lyndsey on the wall. She shivered and drew her old black coat closer to her body. A gust of wind caught the top of her hair and flicked it upwards as the camera clicked.

She didn't need to try to look sad. Suddenly, she unfathomably, felt it.

Chapter Twenty Three

ON THURSDAY OF the following week, Lyndsey had a disquieting experience. It was the day before her scheduled shopping trip to the Lakewater Centre and, unlike the sojourn in London, Savannah and Thalia were booked to accompany their stooge to ensure she adhered rigidly to their fashion guidelines. The phone rang as Lyndsey was leaving for a library shift, and, thinking it was Robbie, she lifted the receiver with a sense of delicious anticipation. He was calling her daily now, and their conversations were seldom short. Neither did they revolve solely around her forthcoming appearance on 'Turnaround'. Their relationship over the past weeks had evolved, and, from merely being her mentor on the programme, Robbie had become a friend, engaging her in lively chat about a diversity of subjects. He always rung first thing every morning, to check how she'd slept and wish her a happy day. This would be followed by a further 'touch base' call during the day, and culminated in a languid hour long session in the evening. He made her laugh with his dry wit, and easy take on life, yet could be serious when she needed him to be. He also managed to compliment and calm her in equal measure. It was a heady concoction.

'Hello', she said, picturing him in the Channel 7 studios, his cornstalk hair newly washed, long legs encased in jeans. A frisson of excitement ran through Lyndsey at the vision. She knew her attraction to Robbie went beyond the bounds of what might be considered permissible, and wondered if he felt the same way. A gruff voice, not immediately recognisable, said, 'Mrs. Daly?'

'Speaking.' Not Robbie then. The surge of disappointment she felt was palpable. Lyndsey waited.

'Ah good, I'm glad I caught you home. Have tried several times before but always get the infernal answering machine, so never bother to leave a message. Don't like talking to a piece of computerised equipment.' Lyndsey felt a stab of irritation. Whoever the caller was, he was taking up valuable time. 'sorry – who is this?'

It wasn't the solicitor ringing for an update on her marital position. Nor was it anyone from Channel 7. It wasn't Dee's husband, nor Coral's. Lyndsey frowned. She didn't know any other men, but the voice sounded familiar.

'Mr. Butcher. Cassandra's form teacher at Brackendale High.'

'Oh I see. Good Morning.' Lyndsey felt the stirrings of panic, 'what's wrong? Is Cass OK?'

'That is why I'm ringing, Mrs. Daly. You know the answer to that question better than I'

'What do you mean?'

There was a sigh at the other end of the line. Lyndsey's hand tightened around the receiver.

'What I mean my dear lady, is that we have no way of knowing since your daughter is hardly ever in school.' Lyndsey slid down the wall, and landed with a thud on the telephone seat. She gazed at her reflection in the hall mirror opposite. Her hair was brushed back from her face and secured in a ponytail. Savannah and Thalia had booked her an appointment with a top London stylist for a cut and colour before the final filming day, and Lyndsey was glad of it. Her hair had grown out of any recognisable shape, and only looked tidy when tied back. Even now wispy tendrils were escaping from the elastic band, and plastering damply to her forehead in the heat of the hallway. She was taking more notice of her wardrobe, and had dressed carefully that morning in a lightweight lemon sweater and cool linen trousers. A glance out of her bedroom window when she'd got up, had told her it was going to be another crisp day, and she knew the library, with its wall of South facing plate glass windows would soon resemble the interior of an oven. She'd taken care over her make up too. Sidonie, the cosmetics artist on 'Turnaround' had shown her how to smudge Kohl liner into the corner of each eye, and how peach tinted lip-gloss and blusher helped bring warmth to her pale complexion. Her eyes looked huge in the mirror, she thought, the pupils dilated with shock at this unwelcome phone call, and the skin of her face paper white.

'God, I look like the dog in the Tinderbox.' She mouthed to herself, 'the one with eyes as big as dinner plates.' Her throat was dry as she said, 'Mr. Butcher, I'm afraid you've lost me. Cassandra goes to school every day, and hasn't been absent since joining'

'I am duty bound to agree with you there, Mrs. Daly. Young Cassandra turns up at school regular as clockwork, and gets her attendance mark in the register. Then she disappears.'

'Disappears?'

'Misses classes. The kids call it 'bunking off' but I'm afraid the School takes a rather more serious view. We call it truanting.'

Lyndsey quailed. Her throat felt suddenly painful as though she'd swallowed a hot drink too quickly.

'How long has this been going on?' She asked, aware that her voice sounded small and tremulous.

'Long enough to ring alarm bells.'

'What do you think she's been doing?

'That is the million pound question, Mrs. Daly. Some kids hang around the shopping centres all day, whilst others congregate in parks. Some sneak back home if both parents are out at work, and they know the house to be empty. It really depends on how much ready cash they have in their pocket.'

'She has been asking for extra dinner money lately. Told me the costs for lunch have gone up.'

'There has been no rise in the canteen prices Mrs. Daly.'

'Then what is she spending it on?'

'Ah, there you have it. Fruit machines in Amusement Arcades, cigarettes, maybe something more sinister.'

'You mean drugs?' Lyndsey could hardly bring herself to say the word.

'There is that possibility. Of course we can't rule out playground extortion. Bullying goes on in all schools, and although here at Brackendale we pride ourselves on keeping a lid on such behaviour, kids do fall through the net. It may be that Cassandra is being forced to hand over money, in which case fear might be the motivational factor in keeping her from class.'

'Fear... But I thought that, after her shaky start, she'd started to settle.'

'I thought so too. I confess that your daughter has caused me more than a little concern from day one, Mrs. Daly. Children like Cassandra who are small for their age, and with sensitive natures are often targeted. I've been teaching for twenty years, and every new intake can pick out the child who is going to bear the brunt of name calling. Certain kids in the class, who've been giving your daughter a hard time, have had me come down on them like a ton of bricks. I recall a lot of ribbing about her coat but I put a stop to that the moment it came to my attention. By Half Term it seemed the message had rammed home and 'mouthy crew' began to leave her alone, with the happy result I saw a distinct improvement in your youngster's confidence. All went well until Christmas.'

'Christmas? Can you elaborate?'

'She seemed to withdraw?'

'In what way?'

'Stopped participating in lessons, and sat morosely silent as when she first joined. Then started missing the odd class, prompting a steady stream of teachers to approach me with their concerns. Mr. Foster said she missed three double Geography periods in a row, and Mr. Angelo the Maths master seconded this. It has been a similar picture with IT, History, and Religious Studies.'

'This is a mystery to me, Mr. Butcher,' said Lyndsey, rubbing her forehead in puzzlement. Her temple was started to throb. 'She's been fine at home. Maybe a little quiet, but no more than usual. I thought how perky she was when she heard I was going to be on the programme... Couldn't wait to get to school and tell 'all her mates' as she put it.'

'Ah yes, your television debut.' Mr. Butcher's voice sounded disapproving thought Lyndsey, or was it her imagination. Certainly she was beginning to feel a deal of shame and remorse about her own role in this sorry saga. Things had obviously been troubling her only child, and she'd been too self-absorbed in her own pathetic bid for TV stardom to notice.

'She's been vocal about it during registration. Telling the whole class that her mum is going to be a famous TV star. However, when they found out the nature of the programme in question, the poor child became subject to some derision.'

Lyndsey leaned her aching head back against the wall. Sunlight streamed through the panelled front door, illuminating the mirror. The glare made her eyes hurt. In the kitchen, the freezer sprung into life, making a sound similar to mating crickets. From the lounge, the clock chimed the hour. She glanced at her watch. Almost nine. She would be late for work, and for once she didn't care.

'What do you mean, derision?' Lyndsey asked, painfully picking up the threads of conversation.

'There was a modicum of leg pulling Mrs. Daly, over the fact that Cassie's mother needed help in knowing what to wear. The girls in particular were quite vocal about it. Style and fashion is a subject very dear to the hearts of the majority of teenagers in our school, I'm afraid to say. If they put as much effort into learning as they do in perfecting the right 'look' then Brackendale would be at the top of the League tables.'

Lyndsey heard Mr. Butcher break off, and speak to someone who had come into the room. The voice sounded adult, and she surmised he was calling from the extension in the Staff Lounge.

'Sorry, Mrs. Daly, that was the Head. It was her suggestion that I contact you. She feels as I do - that something needs to be done urgently about your daughter.'

'Oh God.' Lyndsey said. She felt sick with apprehension for her child. What a crap mother I am, she thought bitterly. I've been so wrapped up in the programme and the marriage breakdown, that Cassie has been receiving scant attention. All I've done is to shove her onto the back burner. Except that by taking the coward's way out, and hoping that Cassandra's remoteness towards me would resolve itself, I've just made the distance between us all the greater.'

As if reading her mind, Mr. Butcher said, 'Don't upset yourself Mrs. Daly. I'm sure you've done your best, but sometimes a parent gets bogged down by the demands on their time. By joining forces with the school, you'll be able to iron out any problems brewing between yourself and your daughter. I have tried to talk to young Cassandra, but she has become somewhat truculent. This could be a defence mechanism. A barrier she has erected around herself for protection, for I understand things at home have not been going well.'

'She told you?'

'That her father had walked out, yes.'

'Cassie's dad and I are having a temporary separation. We have both tried to minimise the effect on her.'

'Naturally so, but the fact is something is troubling your daughter to such an extent that she has been missing chunks of her education. I'm very fond of young Cassandra, and do not want to see her end up like so many other teenagers. Disaffected and disillusioned with authority and the entire learning process. We must nip this in the bud.'

'I agree. Should I come and see you?'

'Exactly what I was going to suggest. The sooner the better I feel. Shall we say this afternoon at 3pm?'

Lyndsey made a quick calculation. The 'Turnaround' schedule had already used up all her holiday leave at the library, but maybe if she worked through lunch, Coral would let her knock off early. She could then make up any shortfall by working overtime. Cassie was a different matter. How would she ever make up the missing hours at school.

'I'll be there, Mr. Butcher.'

Robbie came with her. He'd been insistent. She'd rung him as soon as she put the phone down on the teacher.

'I'll come over, hen.'

'No Rob, really – there's no need.'

'Aye, there is. We've a quiet day in the studio. No filming, just catching up on admin. Any excuse to be able to leave it. You'll be doing me a favour.'

Lyndsey guessed that he was trying to lighten her worry by being flippant, but it only served to make her feel worse. It was as though she had suffered a bereavement, she thought, remembering when her father had died how her own laughter and that of others felt an affront to his memory. 'Daddy's gone,' she remembered thinking, 'how mean of me to be happy when he is rotting underneath that cold earth...' She had a sudden vision of her ten year old self standing bereft in the school playground, wanting to scream at her classmates above the hubbub of their noise 'Shut up having fun, can't you! Don't any of you realise that my dad is dead.'

'Does Ray know?' Robbie was asking.

With difficulty, Lyndsey dragged her attention back to the phone call, 'No. He's been called away on Company business to deal with a computer virus infecting the European office, so it'll give me the opportunity to find out what is going on with Cass first and get it sorted. I know Ray. He'll freak out which will make the situation worse, and make no attempt to disguise his disappointment in the little madam. The poor chap has had to cope with a barrel load of upset lately and it would be unfair to dump more on him. He sets great store by his daughter, and I don't want him to feel that yet another person he loves is letting him down.' She was referring to herself, and wondered if Robbie knew it.

'So you think he'd take it personally? As though the kid were bunking school just to spite him?'

'I know that's how he'd see it. Ray views everything in black or white. There are no shades of grey in his Universe.'

Robbie was silent for a moment. Then he said, 'I'm still coming over. I'll pick you up from the library at two, and take you straight to the school. Don't worry – I'll wait outside in the car, but I want to be there. In case you need some moral support.'

There was no arguing with him, so Lyndsey gave in. Now she was waiting in the school reception area, Robbie beside her on the hard plastic seating. It was too churlish to expect him to wait in the car, she'd decided, so when he'd parked on the road opposite Brackendale High she'd indicated he follow, and led him through the imposing pilloried entrance. Alerted to Lyndsey's arrival by a call from the School Secretary, Mr. Butcher strode across the worn parquet flooring at half past two precisely.

'Mrs. Daly, how nice.' He reached out and shook her hand warmly. 'The Head has said we can use her study. This way...'

Mouthing 'see you later' to Robbie, Lyndsey got to her feet and followed the form tutor through a swing door marked 'Private Staff Only.' And down a narrow corridor lined with prints of former Head Teachers' of the school since its inception in the year 1955.

The study was sparsely furnished. On the desk was an inflated globe the size of a beach ball. Mr. Butcher reached out a tentative finger and spun it on its axis as if giving himself some extra seconds to get his opening remark right. Lyndsey settled in the visitor's chair, and waited. The teacher stroked his beard, before taking up position behind the Head's desk. Sunlight streamed through the slatted blinds, illuminating the bald patch on the man's head, and giving his body tiger stripes. Lyndsey saw that the lapel of his shabby suit was dotted with crumbs, no doubt a legacy from a hurried sandwich lunch. He began by pushing across the desk a buff folder for her perusal. Lyndsey saw that it was the classroom register, gratified to note the ticks against Cassie's name every day for attendance. Then he showed her a batch of timetables supplied by subject tutors, where the preponderance of blanks demonstrated the absences of Lyndsey's daughter.

'Where is she now?'

Mr. Butcher said, 'Supposedly in Room B15, having Double Geography. I've checked. She's not there.'

'Shit', said Lyndsey, then immediately clapped a hand over her mouth, 'sorry – I didn't mean to swear.'

'I've heard worse.' Said Mr. Butcher mildly. I bet you have thought the agonised parent sitting opposite him. The gutter language of inner City school kids was apparent to anyone unlucky enough to be out on the streets when the home bell rang.

'What about netball practise? She's been staying behind most afternoons.'

'There is no netball practise.'

'But she told me she was on the team. I questioned her because I thought it odd, Cass not being the sporty type. Said she was first reserve.'

'Mrs. Daly,' Mr. Butcher regarded her levelly, 'the second year is fielding the only team in Brackendale High at moment.'

Lyndsey felt very stupid. And very afraid. It must have shown in her face, for the teacher said gently, 'Seems the youngster has been running rings around us all. Going back to the timetables, look at the column under music showing a healthy line of ticks. As you can see, Cassandra hasn't missed a single lesson, so we can deduce it is a subject she enjoys and therefore attends. A reasonable supposition therefore is that we'll nab the miscreant entering the Music Room for her next lesson in..... 'he checked his watch, 'roughly twenty minutes.'

Lyndsey felt hot. Her sweater was glued to her chest, and sweat pooled in the cleavage of the new bra. It wasn't entirely due to the Turkish Bath atmosphere in the stuffy wood panelled room, for she felt skewered by twin prongs of guilt and worry about her only child. And the first stirrings of anger. What the hell was Cass playing at? The little madam was going to have to answer some pretty pertinent questions when I get hold of her, she thought. The form tutor was obviously feeling the heat too, for he'd removed his jacket and flung it over the chair. Lyndsey could see twin patches of sweat staining the underarms of his blue shirt, and a faint miasma of body odour permeated the study, whilst his florid face glistened with perspiration. He was a kind man though, acknowledged Lyndsey to herself, exuding not only a warmth of temperature, but a warmth of personality too. The best kind of teacher. One who not only cared about the subjects he taught, but the subjects that received the teaching. His pupils.

'I'm trying to pinpoint when this problem with Cassandra first arose. It seems to stem from the incident with the dog.'

'The dog?' Lyndsey's voice showed her bewilderment.

'A stray in the school playing fields. Mangy beast if you ask me. Your daughter seemed to have befriended it, and when I ordered her back to the school building, she showed the first spark of contention. Quite frankly Mrs Daly, I was surprised. She was normally such a meek, quiet child, but on this particular occasion, she showed a stubborn streak quite unlike what I'd come to expect from such an erstwhile model pupil.'

Lyndsey frowned. The mention of a dog had rung some far oft bell in her head. Something tugged at her memory. Something Cass had asked her to buy, which had puzzled her at the time. Then she remembered what it had been. Dog Food.... Yes, that was it..... dog food.....

Chapter Twenty Four

CASSIE WAS INORDINATELY pleased with Mozart's progress. He was quick to learn, and, she thought with a warm glow of accomplishment, anxious to please. No-one had ever been much concerned with pleasing Cass before, and the mere fact that the dog almost fell over in his rush to her bidding, made her swell with pride. Not to mention self-satisfaction. In the stolen hours she'd just spent with him, they'd perfected the 'Play Dead' technique. At a silent command, the German Shepherd was now able to drop to the ground, and lay motionless, eyes closed, in the grim parody of sudden death. Scaling the stairs leading to the Music Room, Cassandra counted the number of tricks she'd now taught the huge animal. He could sit, beg, roll over, stay, growl, circle, attack, and even do a few steps of a doggy type waltz. Knowing that such a potentially dangerous beast was mere putty in her tiny hands, gave Cass an enormous feeling of power. She might be small, she thought, joining the throng of pupils in the corridor, she might be insignificant to her peers, but she had something none of them had. She smirked at the backs of strutting fellow classmates, knowing that she had the capability to unleash a deadly jaw snapping power against them. It was a delicious secret. When she was alone with her canine companion, Cassie felt as if she were Clark Kent in a phone booth metamorphosing into his alter ego, 'Superman'. She became 'SuperCassie', invincible, unstoppable. Mozart and her coat had become cloaks of power. Cassandra Daly, the Caped Crusader of Brackendale High. It was hot, and she was sweltering inside her padded Eskimo jacket, but Cass didn't care. Her coat was her Lion Tamer's uniform, and Mozart was the Lion. She knew the kids in the corridor were sniggering at the sight of her, and knew also the bizarre picture she must present. A small matchstick figure with spindly legs hidden in a voluminous coat, face concealed in the hood. She loved the hood. It enabled her to look out upon the world as a silent surveyor of its many foibles, reaching her own, often erroneous conclusions about what she saw. Yet no-one could see her. She could be the watcher yet not watched. If anyone had lifted the fur lined brim and looked inside, they would have been startled to see a pair of unblinking slate eyes, which photographed information ready for a sharp brain to assimilate.

Now those eyes saw something they did not want to see. Did not expect to see. Mr. Butcher standing by the Music Room door, and with him the unmistakeable angular form of her mother. Cassie stopped, feet refusing to move. She caused a log jam in the flow of pupils, and several, not watching where they were going and too busy bantering with classmates, cannoned into the back of her. The breath was knocked from Cassie's body in a whoosh.

''Wotcha doin' Daly, you prat.' Somebody said from behind. It was the voice of adolescent youth on the verge of breaking, a disparate combination of high pitched and gruff. She recognised that voice. It was Andy Collinson, the bully boy of the class.

'Fuckin ejit.' Came another.

Cassandra ignored them, looking wildly around for a means of escape, for she knew Mr. Butcher had seen her. She was instantly recognisable by her coat, and for the first time wished she wasn't wearing it. He was tapping her mother on the shoulder and pointing across the sea of heads in Cassie's direction. Should she brazen it out, thought Cass, in an agony of indecision, guessing why they were there. Sooner or later her absences from certain classes would be noticed, yet she had somehow banished this prospect from her mind. Foolishly so, she now realised.

Mozart. She must get to him, hide him, before they found out about the presence of her dog. They couldn't hurt her once she was reunited with her protégé for together they were invincible. Supergirl and Superdog. He was her refuge, and she was his protector. Cassie's mouth set in a militant line.

'Hey babe,' Someone put a hand on her arm, 'Wassup?' Cassie stared into the grinning black face of Olu. The pupil with the dreadlocks had befriended her since the start of the Spring Term, and the smaller girl could see the concern in other's eyes. Momentarily Cass faltered. Should she tell Olu about Mozart? It would be comforting to have someone on her side, but immediately she discounted the idea. The dog was her secret and must remain so.

'Cover for me,' Cassandra pleaded.

She spun around, and head bent, shoulders squared like a rugby player in a scrum, bulldozed a path through a forest of milling bodies. They were cries of 'Ouch', and 'look out', and 'Hey, careful' as she trod on toes, and knocked elbows, but Cassandra was oblivious to the protestations. She had one thought and one thought alone. To get to her dog before they did. They were the enemy. Her mother and Mr. Butcher.

Another class were mounting the stairs. Year 11's, thought the fleeing child, judging by their size. It was like trying to descend on an upwards moving escalator, thought Cass, legs flailing, feet racing, but progress was minimal. She was buffeted this way and that on the staircase, sometimes knocked backwards, and all the time conscious of her form tutor and parent in unrelenting pursuit. Cassie felt she was trapped in a nightmare, where she was running from a nameless terror and found herself in a desert of quicksand which sucked and dragged at her legs. Somehow, battered and bruised, she reached the bottom stair. Her tiny chest was heaving, and her heart felt as though it was about to make a bid for freedom through the prison bars of her rib cage.

'Cassandra. Cassandra Daly' She heard someone call. She recognised Mr. Butcher's voice, and then her mother's, 'Cassie, come back.'

Heedless, she took flight, twisting and turning through the maze of corridors which made up the ground floor of Brackendale High. The exit leading to the Sports Field was blocked by a group of teachers, so she fled through the rarefied atmosphere of the main reception area, and out of the revolving entrance doors. The surge of adrenaline coursing through her minute frame was giving Cassandra an unbelievable high. She felt as though she were flying. In the acid sunshine of the dying afternoon, she became a winged charioteer raising a whip to the imaginary Pegasus that pulled her away.

It took Cassie just three minutes to traverse the broad expanse of the playing field. The muddy green of the grass hurt her eyes, but she ploughed doggedly on. Skirting the row of tennis courts, she took her well-worn path across the white painted lines of the football pitch, oblivious to everything except her destination. She could see it now. A line of ramshackle groundsmens' sheds which housed a motley collection of Sports equipment and gardening tools. All had padlocked doors, the keys in possession of the Head

Groundsman and PE staff only, excepting one at the end of the row; a sad looking hut with sagging roof, its door hanging awkwardly on a single rusting hinge. When she'd first discovered it, Cassie found it contained broken tennis rackets, a balding broom, and a holed goalkeeper's net, all swathed in a canopy of cobwebs. Quelling her fear of spiders, she'd set to work creating a makeshift kennel. The dilapidated equipment had been stacked neatly in one corner, the floor brushed clean of dirt. She was pleased to discover, that despite its shabby appearance, the shed was relatively dry and draught free. Over the successive weeks, Cassie had secretly stowed away a treasure trove of canine goodies for the occupant. There was a padded dog bed (extra large size) bought out of saved pocket money, together with stainless steel feed bowls. Scattered on the floor were a variety of dog toys and treats. Rubber bones, cowhide chews, playballs of differing sizes, and pile of sticks. She had constructed a table out of a rotting plank and some old bricks found outside the potting shed, on which resided a lavish supply of tinned dog food, meal, mixer and biscuits. When she'd first found Mozart he'd been thin and unkempt and Cassie had determined to fatten him up, and return him to peak condition.

In this she'd succeeded. As she pushed open the door of the shed, secured with a piece of baling twine looped around a nail, a magnificent German Shepherd rose on his hind legs to greet her. His shaggy black coat shone, and yellow eyes were bright and clear. The animal seemed to exude a vitality and exuberance for life which intoxicated Cassie. She dropped down to her knees, and put her skinny arms, encased in the voluminous folds of her coat, around the huge head. Mozart licked her face enthusiastically. To have his mistress return so quickly after leaving him was an altogether new and exciting development, and he could hardly contain himself. Usually when she left, many hours would pass until the return of the tiny figure that he had grown to love. Cassandra had taught Mozart well for he knew he must lie quietly and await her return. There was to be no whining or scratching at the door, and barking was forbidden, and some instinctive sense told the dog that to keep safe he must not make a sound. So in the long hours when his little mistress was missing, he would snack on biscuits, chew his rubber bone, chase the ball around the confines of the shed, or simply doze and dream. Thus, no-one had discovered his existence. At weekends, when the school was closed, his mistress still managed to sneak away from home on the pretext of library visits, or meeting up with non-existent friends, or wandering the town centre – she would slip through a gap in the school's perimeter fence and make her way to the hut housing her beloved charge. A charge that was now dancing in paroxysm of delight around her.

'Down boy, there's a good, Mozart'. Cassie snapped the lead onto the thick studded collar. This had cost her ten pounds, which she'd managed to purloin from her grandmother for a mythical school trip. She'd also been getting extra money out of her mum using a variety of deceptions, to buy accoutrements for her dog, but there was a limit, Cassandra knew, on how much she could get away with without raising suspicion. On these occasions, she stole to fund her habit, and feed her obsession. The obsession which was Mozart.

She led him out into the bright light. The dog blinked, unaccustomed to the sunshine after the gloomy interior of his shed. Cassie had no clear idea where she was going with her charge. She only knew that she had to get off the school premises, and pronto, to a place where Mr. Butcher and her mother would not be able to find her. The dog cocked his leg up against the exterior wall of the shed, while Cassandra waited with growing impatience as a dark pool of urine spread underneath him.

'Hurry up, boy.' She pleaded.

But the animal was not to be hurried, and after what seemed an aeon to Cassie, he was ready to move on. She broke into a jog trot, the huge dog lolloping along beside her. The size of a Shetland Pony, he dwarfed her tiny figure, but it was obvious to even the most casual observer who was in control. The girl in the hooded coat.

Robbie was following at a safe distance. He'd witnessed her flight through the reception area, and identified Cassie immediately by her distinctive coat. The same coat the child proudly showed him the day he came to set up the video camera in Lyndsey's lounge, after they'd 'hit' their reluctant TV star in the library where she worked.

He didn't want to frighten the fleeing schoolgirl by grabbing that bobbing Eskimo hood. He knew she was panic stricken by the way she zig zagged across the playing field instead of taking a straight line. Her flight reminded Robbie of a trapped insect in an upturned glass, bashing itself against the walls in a vain bid to escape. Cassandra Daly was evidently trying to escape from something herself, he thought ducking down beside a car in the staff parking lot, as the child turned her head. Although the schoolgirl was some distance away, Robbie didn't want those clear grey eyes to recognise him.

He looked back at the building with its serried rows of windows, and the thought occurred of how often schools resembled prisons in their design and construction. Especially these vast soulless inner city secondary's where classrooms became cells and the pupil's reluctant inmates. Robert McCrae paused unsure of what to do next. Should he go back inside the building and alert Lyndsey to her daughter's escape? If he did that though he might lose the child, and who knew what might happen to that innocent abroad on the City streets. Reaching a decision, Robbie began to run, long legs covering the ground in easy strides, keeping the distant speck in sight. That same speck was heading towards the tennis courts, and he calculated he could skirt them and meet the runaway head on. He sped around the main School building, keeping to the verge where the ground was softer. A row of demountables had been erected no doubt to take an overspill of pupils that the original building could no longer accommodate. He could see faces peering at him through the windows, and pupils were yelling in his direction beyond the glass, but Robbie was not to be deflected from his purpose. They were probably pondering the identity of this Marathon man on their hallowed turf, he thought. Robbie slipped down a gap in the two furthermost temporary classrooms, and came out opposite a collection of huts situated at the far side of the football pitch. Robbie narrowed his eyes, trying to focus. The distant sheds reminded him of a shanty town settlement, the type often seen on news reports, housing desperate refugees. Where was the figure in the voluminous coat?

Then he saw Cassandra, in the midst of the shanty town, still running at a frantic pace. To Robbie, events were beginning to take on a surreal feel. It was as though he were on the set of the film 'Don't Look Now' but instead of catching tantalising glimpses of a dwarf in a red cape as Julie Christie and Donald Sutherland had done, he, Robert McCrae, was pursuing a pixie in blue.

'She's in the park,' said the caller, 'by the swings. Tell Mrs. Daly.

The School Secretary put down the phone and hurried into the staff room, where teachers not currently involved in lessons had gathered. Word had soon spread through the school about a missing child. Cassandra Daly, a Year 8 pupil in Mr Butcher's class. The Secretary had been alerted to the fact by the Head Teacher, who'd come into the office asking for the child's home address and the phone number of the local police. In the staffroom, Mr. Butcher stood with his hand on the shoulder of a white faced woman who sat rigidly on one of the easy chairs. On seeing the Head's P.A. enter, gesticulating wildly, he left the woman's side. Returning he said, 'They've just taken a call on the main switchboard. From a mobile. Somebody called Robbie. He says young Cassandra is in Brackendale Park with a Hound of the Baskerville's lookalike.'

Lyndsey, on hearing the mention of her daughter's name, jumped to her feet. As she made to hurry out of the room, Mr. Butcher put a hand out to stop her.

'Wait for me.' He said, 'Please....' There was such a genuine note of appeal in his voice that Lyndsey nodded. She knew he cared as much about Cassandra in particular, as he did the rest of his pupils in general.

Cassie sat on the swing, arms hanging limp around the chains. She was rocking herself back and forth, crooning softly to the Alsatian who lay at her feet,

> 'nick knack paddy whack
> Give a dog a bone
> This old man came rolling home...

The bright afternoon had darkened, and the air felt thunderous and heavy. Livid purple streaks etched the sky. Cassie tilted her head and stared up, watching a dizzying tableau of racing clouds. Apart from a jogger circuiting the park she was alone in the children's playground, and it wasn't entirely due to the weather. Mothers with toddlers were alarmed by the fierce looking hound, and the small girl that had him on a lead. She looked hardly able to control the beast and they objected to the way it growled when anyone ventured near. Accordingly, they'd gathered up their charges, strapped them in buggies, and marched off in high dudgeon complaining about 'dogs in public places without muzzles.'

Cassandra hadn't noticed that her beloved Mozart was responsible for this mass exodus, being too immersed in her own misery. She knew that trouble was brewing. There was going to be an awful lot of explaining to do, she thought with a sigh; to the school, Mr. Butcher, her mother, her dad. Her father. It would be distinctly terrible if he found out she had missed school to take care of a stray dog. Mum she might be able to get round, but not the other parent. His dislike of animals was well known, and his dislike of shirkers legendary. Cassie shuddered. She knew he would consider her missing important lessons shirking of the highest category and shirking because of a dog was likely to send him into orbit.

Mozart stretched out underneath the swing, his huge body spanning its width, while above him the small girl swung back and forth, lost in thought. The dog meant everything to her. By sheer dint of determination, she had managed to care for him in secret for all these weeks, managing to block from her mind the awful possibility that he would be discovered and taken away from her. Cassie didn't think she could bear this for Mozart had become her reason for living. To stop her mother suspecting the existence of the shaggy beast, she had resorted to subterfuge and deceit. At weekends, she slipped out of the house on the pretext of going to Mr Roshi's corner shop to look at teen magazines, only to double back across Brackendale Park and into the school playing fields through a gap in the perimeter fencing. Once there she would let Mozart out of the shed for a run, re-fill his water bowl from the groundsman's hose and open a fresh tin of food. She would stay with him as long as she dared, constantly checking her watch. Realistically she had a leeway of forty minutes or so, before her mum would start to worry, and come looking for her. So Cass would time her visits to Mozart with military precision.

There were other ways she'd deceived her mother. Not only by secreting away school dinner money to feed her charge, nor claiming to attend fictional netball practises so she could spend extra time with him, but also by feigning interest in the 'Turnaround' programme. Asking her mother to get autographed photos of the presenters to show pals in her class was a clever ruse, Cassandra thought. It made her mother believe, quite wrongly, that she had settled in at school and made friends. It also camouflaged the fact the she had been ducking lessons.

Rain began to fall, heavy drops that made a plopping sound as they hit the ground. Her face still held to the sky, the schoolgirl in the bright blue Eskimo coat let them cool her cheeks. Thunder rumbled. She closed her eyes, feeling the rain splash her lids, and sang softly to herself,

> 'this old man,
> he played two,
> he played nick knack on my shoe,
> with a nick knack paddy whack,
> give the dog a bone –'

Too late, Cassie became aware that Mozart was growling. It was a menacing sound of warning that she'd almost mistaken for thunder. Startled, she opened her eyes, blinking away the pooling rainwater.

Her mother stood in front of the swing and she wasn't alone. The man from the TV programme was with her – what was his name? Robbie something. Mr. Butcher was there too. Beyond them a white van had driven into the playground entrance, and two men got out. They were dressed like traffic wardens, in peaked caps with fluorescent jerkins, and were pulling on gauntlet gloves. Two words were painted on the side of the van in black, underneath the logo of the Borough Council. Cassie focussed watery eyes on the writing, and her heart plummeted inside her chest like a lift whose suspension wires had frayed. 'Dog Wardens.'

Chapter Twenty Five

THE GLASS EDIFICE of the Lakewater Shopping Complex glittered in the early morning sun, resembling the dome of St. Paul's Cathedral. Lyndsey could see the connection, for the former was a place of religious worship; the latter where worship of the great god consumerism was undertaken. She had read recently (was it in Raymond's Guardian?) the dispiriting fact that more modern day Britons frequented shopping malls on Sundays than churches, and, judging by the stream of traffic feeding into the car park, such a claim appeared true. Squashed in the back seat of Channel 7's People Carrier, between Savannah, Thalia, and Sidonie, Lyndsey had found the journey from North London an interminably cramped one. Robbie had arrived at 7.30am that morning, tooting the horn as he parked the cumbersome vehicle at her front gate. Hurrying down the path, Lyndsey couldn't identify any further occupants through its blacked out windows.

So it was a revelation to discover the vehicle housed not only the camera crew, sound recordist and technicians, but also Gaynor, the make-up artiste, and last, but certainly not least, the two infamous presenters. All looked faintly rattled. On the roof, battened down with webbing straps, was a pyramid of filming equipment. Lyndsey clambered on board, Robbie slipped into first gear, and the minibus pulled smoothly away from the kerb.

'Sit here precious'; Thalia patted a spare wedge on the rear seat. Lyndsey saw that her dark geometric bob sported maroon highlights, and she was wearing a chunky knit suit of caramel wool. Her co-star, Savannah, had blonde hair twisted into a French knot, and was dressed in a stunning ensemble of leather trousers and Gillet in a tortoiseshell print. Both women looked effortlessly stylish. Lyndsey knew she could never emulate them, much less match them. They had the head start on her when it came to fashion know how, but with their help she was learning the tricks of the stylish dressing trade. Buckling the seatbelt, she settled back to enjoy the journey.

Ninety minutes later, the minibus was exiting the M25 at Junction 31. Ahead the stupendous structure of the Queen Elizabeth II Bridge which spanned the Thames at Dartford, rose into the sky like some space age rocket launcher.

'Pretty impressive piece of engineering,' commented Vince Levene, the producer, peering out of the passenger window. He was sitting beside Robbie, and Lyndsey saw the familiar head with its thatched hair nod in agreement.

'It's only a fucking bridge, for God's sake,' said Thalia with some asperity. It was hot and uncomfortable in the minibus and tempers were frazzled.

Lyndsey stretched cramped limbs. She'd dressed for comfort in navy deck shoes, white cotton trousers, and a blue and white striped fleece.

'Very nautical,' commented Savannah giving the quick up and down look for which she was famous, 'where's the boat darling?' Ignoring the remark, the land locked mariner watched Robbie expertly negotiate the barrier which fronted the retail sprawl.

Welcome to Lakewater' proclaimed a billboard. It depicted an expanse of impossibly blue water on which swans floated.

Robbie reversed into a space by the entrance to Alders, and cut the engine, to impromptu applause from the weary passengers.

As the entourage assembled on the tarmac, Gaynor advanced with her clipboard, 'Quiet please people. Just give me a minute to go over the itinerary.'

There was a collective groan which the frizzy haired researcher ignored. She was dressed in a curious outfit of banana yellow dungarees, and the matching bandana failed to tame her wayward curls. Lyndsey thought she resembled a particularly manic canary, as she twittered, 'First stop is Oasis, followed by Monsoon, Kookai, and River Island. All the store managers have agreed to let us film Lyndsey shopping. That should take care of the clothes side, then we'll need to set aside an hour for accessories.'

'Is there an Accessorize branch here?' asked Thalia.

Gaynor nodded. 'All set up, including a place called 'Sardar Leather' which apparently stocks super belts.'

'Lyndsey's spent half the allocated budget so there's a couple of grand left.' Savannah gave Lyndsey a nudge.' No crap purchases today, darling. Remember, we'll be watching you.'

Gaynor consulted her sheath of papers, and continued, 'We'll aim to break for lunch at 1pm. Everyone make sure their mobiles are switched off during filming. Any questions?'

Savannah said, 'what about this poor girl's hair?' she flipped a lock of Lindsey's lank blonde locks, and grimaced.

'Appointment booked in the House of Fraser beauty salon, with their top stylist at 4pm. Cut, colour, condition, blow dry, followed by a total make up with Sidonie, and a manicure. We should leave Lakewater by six.'

The camera crew proceeded to unload and assemble the equipment onto a train of wheeled trolleys. Twenty minutes later, fronted by Lyndsey, the 'Turnaround' team entered the shopping mall and made their way to Level 1. As in her trip to London, shoppers stopped to stare at the contributor who headed such a posse of people.

Lakewater proved to be an elegant shopping complex, constructed of glass, chrome, and faux marble. The walkways were well lit, and potted palms placed next to strategic seating areas, enhanced the conservatory feel. Soft background music beguiled shoppers, whilst the strolling uniformed security guards gave a sense of protection from the retailers' scourge of pickpockets and shoplifters. The Oasis Fashion store was in a parade dominated in a pincer movement by BHS and WHSmith, and adjoined by a shoe shop with a window display of stiletto heeled boots. The crew were greeted at the door by the Oasis spokeswoman, who introduced both herself and the sales team. One in particular seemed in awe of Savannah and Thalia, noticed Lyndsey, realising that the fame of presenters had spread far and wide.

'We're all fans of 'Turnaround'' The 'Oasis' lady was saying to Lyndsey, 'It's compulsive viewing for all ages. Men are hooked too. My boyfriend never misses an episode, and simply adores Savannah and Thalia. He thinks they're the best TV double act since Morecombe & Wise.'

This last remark was greeted with awkward silence from the assembled company. Channel 7's flagship fashion programme was not intended as a comediac fest.

Lyndsey felt the sales lady's eyes upon her.

'You lucky thing, getting all this freebie gear.'

'Yes, aren't I.'

'Who nominated you?' The Manageress probed.

'Two friends submitted my pic to the research team, and it snowballed.'

'Were you mad with them?'

'At first,' Lyndsey said with feeling, 'it was a bit of a shock. Now I've got used to the idea, I'm beginning to enjoy it. Getting some pampering and being in the spotlight, does wonders for one's self esteem.'

'On behalf of the management of Oasis, I hope your experience in our store will do similar wonders for your new look.'

Lyndsey smiled her thanks, and, at a signal from Vince Levene, began to move along the hanging rails as the cameras rolled. She had been well briefed on procedure. Savannah and Thalia would view her every move on video link, and should she choose clothes contrary to their 'rules', the doyens of fashion would stage a confrontation. The ladies in question had been removed to a temporary camp opposite BHS store with half the crew. The rest were assigned to Lyndsey.

Now, she began to sift through the racks of clothes, keeping the 'Turnaround' fashion guidelines firmly in mind. Savannah and Thalia had identified her figure as 'no tits, no waist, long legs, long neck, flabby tummy (it had never quite recovered its former concavity after the birth of Cassandra) thick ankles and calves...'

The first item on her list was an ensemble practical enough for a stint in the library, but which could double as evening wear. She flicked through pencil skirts (wrong shape) knowing these would draw attention to her chunky ankles, and selected a perfect 'A' line skirt in charcoal mock suede, which she knew would bring out the colour of her eyes.

'This skirt is right for me,' she said to the camera. 'Right size, shape, colour and style. If I can find a matching jacket, it would make a terrific suit for work. Practical yet classy.'

There were no jackets that matched but she found one in a complimentary shade of soft peach which had grey flecks in the material. In the blouse section, Lyndsey pounced on a sleeveless top with a froth of frills down the front panel, in a delicious apricot silk. Thalia and Savannah had pointed out the wisdom of such a style - ruffled fronts disguised a flat chest. She took the items into the changing room, together with a pair of palazzo trousers in taupe jersey and a matching boob tube in a swirling taupe and aubergine print. The latter choice caused a momentary hesitation. Boob tubes were a definite no no unless one possessed an ample pair of breasts, Thalia had warned her, and Savannah had commented that they made skinny girls look like their top half were wrapped in a bandage.

In the pier mirror Lyndsey frowned at her reflection. Her eyes were faintly red from the tears she'd shed in the night, and her face was so deathly white it might have been chiselled out of chalk. It was difficult not to think about Cassie. Lyndsey's mind kept pulling her back to the vision of her small daughter hysterically hanging on to the dog as the wardens tried to wrest it away. The animal had gone berserk and bitten into the gauntlet glove of one, until they managed to net its head. As the Alsatian was driven away to be impounded whilst an attempt was made to trace its owners, Lyndsey, Robbie and Mr. Butcher had been left to calm a distraught youngster in an Eskimo coat.

Once back inside the perimeter fence of Brackendale High, Cassandra had managed to struggle free.

'You best take her home, Mrs. Daly.' Mr. Butcher had suggested, his bearded face red from exertion over the afternoon's events. Lyndsey concurred and, with Robbie's help, managed to frogmarch Cassandra to the car, and strap her in. The remainder of the day descended into a nightmare.

The schoolgirl suffered such a violent reaction to the loss of the dog, that, panic stricken, Lyndsey called a doctor. She honestly thought her child might have a heart attack brought on by grief. Whilst Robbie and Lyndsey waited for the GP, Cassie had screamed to her mother, 'I hate you - It's your fault they took Mozart' before throwing herself to the lounge floor and lying prostrate.

'Come on wee lassie,' Robbie had said in his gentle voice, 'don't take on so. It's not your mam's doing. The school called the wardens because they were worried the dog might cause harm.'

'He'd NEVER hurt me,' came a strangled sob, 'he was my friend.'

'Animals are unpredictable, hen.'

'Not Mozart.'

'Darling,' Lyndsey had said, stung by the display of antagonism from her child, 'The wardens have promised we can visit if the dog's rightful owners cannot be traced.'

'They'll collect Mozart, and I'll never see him again.' Wailed Lyndsey's daughter, heart shaped face ravaged with tears. There was to be no consoling her. When the doctor came he administered a mild sedative, and suggested the patient remain off school for the rest of the week. At this Lyndsey demurred, deciding to keep Cass under lock and key. She was harbouring the secret dread that the child might wander the streets calling pitifully for a dog that could no longer hear.

'The only way I can do Lakewater tomorrow is to know that Cass is safe with mum. Otherwise I shall simply cancel. My child is more important than any TV programme.' She told Robbie after the GP had gone. He had to agree. Accordingly, they wrapped the drowsy child in a blanket and drove the ten miles to her grandmother's. Renee was the model of calm efficiency when she opened the door. One glance at the tortured form of her grand-daughter told her all she needed to know, but Lyndsey filled in the blanks. She finished by saying, 'Keep her in bed tomorrow mum, and lock the windows and doors. I'll ring the school and tell them she won't be back til Monday. There's a lot to be sorted out regarding this little minx, but now is not the time. Missed lessons, bridges to mend with Brackendale High – and a mode of punishment that will convince her what she did was wrong.'

Cassie was put to bed with a mug of warm milk, and although the sedative had taken effect, she was fighting sleep with belligerence, refusing to give her mother a goodnight kiss, turning away so that Lyndsey's lips smacked the air. Renee made a pot of tea and Welsh rarebit for the three adults, and they ate in distracted silence. When her mother got up to stack the dishes in the sink, Renee's skirt rode up, and Lyndsey frowned but forbade comment. It was a good two inches shorter than her mother usually wore, and was it Lyndsey's imagination, or did Renee's customary court shoes sport a higher heel than usual. She wondered whether the older woman was interpreting rules applying to stylish dressing for the 'mature lady' in her "Turnaround Tips" bible, too loosely. The phrase 'mutton dressed as lamb' leaped alarmingly into Lyndsey head, but she quashed it, feeling both guilty and disloyal at entertaining such a thought in regard to her own mother.

All three sat in the kitchen talking worriedly until midnight, when Robbie yawned, giving Lyndsey a nudge, 'best make a move. Another early start tomorrow and I've got to get the car back, and pick up the RCU from the studio compound.'

'RCU?'

In answer to Renee's query he said, 'Roving Camera Unit. Fancy term for a minibus.'

On the drive back to Shenlagh Gardens, Lyndsey said, 'Robbie, promise me something.'

'Anything lassie.'

'Don't tell anyone on 'Turnaround' what's happened. Savannah and Thalia might mention it on air to spice up the human interest element... contributor's daughter bunks off school with stray dog, etcetera, etcetera.'

'You sound like Yul Bryner in the King and I'

'How do you mean?'

'Etcetera, etcetera, etcetera....' Robbie intoned, eyes firmly fixed on the road ahead. The night was black and oncoming headlights rushed at them, illuminating the interior of the car with a yellowy glare. Lyndsey tensed. The events of the last few hours had drained her, and she was in no mood for someone acting obtusely.

'Keep stum about Cass.' She said sharply.

Robbie regarded her in the interior mirror, eyebrows raised in mock surprise, 'Okay, bonnie lass, you have my word.'

'I shall pull the plug on the programme if this gets out, I swear. Channel 7 can jolly well sue for breach of contract if that happens, because my daughter comes first, and my private life is private.'

'It's going to be hard enough getting through tomorrow's filming knowing Cassie's trauma - having to leave her for the sake of a blasted telly show when as her mother, I ought be there.'

'Hey - stop beating yourself up Lyndsey Daly. From where I'm standing you're a pretty good mother, and none of this was your fault. In fact, if anyone is to blame it's your old man. He made it so impossible for the kid to have a pet she had to resort to befriending a stray.'

They completed the journey in reflective silence. Robbie accompanied her to the front door. 'Be ready at 7.30 in the morning.' He seemed to Lyndsey to be hesitating, tapping his heel on the step. She put her key in the lock and just as she turned it, she felt his hand on her shoulder.

'Lyn' His voice had a husky edge. As she turned, he bent his head and kissed her very softly, very gently, on the lips.

Looking at herself now in the mirror of the changing rooms in Oasis, Lyndsey could almost feel his mouth on hers. The memory of the warm tingle that coursed down her back as he held her close, pinked her cheeks. She slipped into the peach and grey ensemble, loosing her hair from its knot as she did so. It fell lank and straight to her shoulders, the colour and texture she thought, of dirty string.

Gaynor swished open the curtain,

'Put a spurt on, the camera crew are getting arsey.'

However, despite the researcher's dire warning, the production team thought the outfit worth the wait. After filming their contributor walking the entire length of the store, there were thumbs up all round from the men with the tripods and microphones.

The trouble came when Lyndsey donned the palazzo pants and matching top. As she began her second circuit of the shop floor, cameras rolling, the door burst open to admit Savannah and Thalia. Nostrils flaring, the two presenters screeched in simulated chagrin.

'Lyndsey Daly, what are you wearing?' Raged the former.

'Get that hideous abomination off.' Ordered the latter. The pair of them began to tug at the boob tube, so that Lyndsey had to hang on to it to protect her modesty.

'But it's beautiful,' she protested, 'the cut and colour, and just feel this material.'

'We agree it is a sensational piece of clothing,' said Thalia.

'On someone with a ripe pair of melons.' Said Savannah.

'Not on you darling.'

'Draws attention to your tiny tits.'

'Looks like you've crawled into an empty piece of piping.'

'A main drain in those colours.'

'Or a sewer.'

Lyndsey could take no more, 'Ladies stop. You've made your point. Anyone would think I've committed a cardinal sin..'

'You have,' came the joint response.

Vince Levene beamed 'terrific scene,' he said, 'let's cut this one, crew.'

'I know what I'd like to cut', muttered Lyndsey to herself as she returned to the changing room to dispense with the offending top. 'Savannah and Thalia's bloody heads off..'

Chapter Twenty Six

LYNDSEY INVITED ROBBIE in for a nightcap. He accepted with alacrity, and she was careful not to show the smile of triumph that hovered on her lips. The atmosphere between them had been strained throughout the day in Lakewater, and whilst Lyndsey was sure it was not evident to the rest of the Production Team, she guessed Robbie was aware and couldn't bear the thought of him going home without an opportunity to clear the air. He was embarrassed about kissing her the previous night, and Lyndsey knew she had to allay any fears that this may have created a chasm between them. An unspoken bond had grown between herself and Robbie in the short time she'd known him and now it was as if they were soul mates operating on some subconscious level where each seemed to know what the other was thinking. This moulding of human psychology was a novel experience for Lyndsey. In all her time with Ray, his thoughts and feelings had been an anathema to her – a puzzle in which she never quite found the missing piece. This crossing of personality wires had fused into an explosive relationship, where neither husband nor wife could predict the mood of the other. She often felt her marriage was a badly dubbed film, where the mouths of the actors moved out of sync with the words spoken. Ray grated against her in so many ways. Physically, emotionally and spiritually. Especially physically, she thought with a shudder, remembering the last time husband and wife had made love, when his penis has jabbed at the tender muscle walls of her vagina. It was symbolic of everything that was wrong with their marriage, she thought, that even in the act of penetration, he never managed to get the angle right. His body jarred her intimate places, just as his words jarred her intimate thoughts. He was the cheese grater, she was the cheese. He was the sandpaper, she was the stone worn down to a pebble. She shook her head to clear this uncomfortable picture from her mind, momentarily dissembled by the lack of hair flying around her face. Raising a tentative hand, it felt strange to encounter hedgehog spikes.

'Do you like your new style?' Robbie asked. 'It's taken ten years off you. You look like a teenager...' He'd followed her into the dining room at Shenlagh Gardens, laden down with carrier bags. They contained her day's purchases from Lakewater, and sported all the differing store names she'd visited on the spending spree courtesy of Channel 7.

'Thanks' Lyndsey said, 'How old are you Rob? You've never said.'

'How old do I look?'

'Oh please, don't let's play that game.'

They both laughed as she opened the drinks cabinet. She already knew his favourite tipple, as he'd asked for it the night before at her mother's. Malt whisky with a dash of ginger. Typical of a Scotsman, she thought.

'I'm thirty two.'

'You look younger.'

'Aye, everybody tells me that. Mam's seventy, yet walks three miles to the shops every day, and does all her own laundry in the bath.'

'Scrubbing the McCrae tartan?'

'Something like that.'

Lyndsey poured herself a vodka, and added some lime cordial. In the glass front of the drinks cabinet, she viewed her reflection. The short zippy style suited her urchin features she thought. It had been razor cut all around her head, yet left long at the back, the colour enhanced with golden tints. The hairdresser had also added some spikes of red, so that the overall effect was a subtle strawberry blonde, which an intensive conditioning masque had given a mirror like gloss.

'You look very pretty.' Robbie said admiringly, 'but then you know that don't you?'

Lyndsey passed him the tumbler of whisky, and sipped at her drink. It stung her tongue with a delicious mix of sweetness and sour, and she kicked off her shoes, and padded barefoot to the table and pulled out a chair. Sinking down, she put feet up to rest on the polished wood surface, thankful that Ray wasn't there to witness such insurrection. She pulled out another chair and indicated to Robbie to join her.

The room was dark, the only light spilling in from the hallway through the opened door. It had been another marathon day, and, much to Gaynor's consternation, filming had over-run by an hour and it was gone seven when they'd loaded up the minibus and left Lakewater to join the throng of traffic on the motorway. No-one had felt inclined to talk, so the journey back to London was accompanied by the rustle of magazines and snores. Robbie had somehow manoeuvred to drop off everyone else off at their various homes and hotels, leaving Lyndsey until last. She wondered whether it was by accident or design. The memory of his kiss still lingered.

He must have read her thoughts, for he said, 'did you mind me snogging you yesterday?'

Lyndsey hated the use of that slang word, but somehow, coming from Robbie in his lilting Scottish brogue it sounded almost sensual.

Deciding to dissemble, she took another swig of vodka, and shook her head. 'No. Should I?'

He shrugged. 'I don't make a habit of kissing ladies who appear on 'Turnaround' but you are the exception that has broken that rule, Lyndsey Daly. Might as well come clean. Do you remember the day I was secretly filming you in the Sports Club.'

Lyndsey did. She could picture Robbie sitting at the next table in the restaurant at the Pomegranate Health Suite with such an earnest expression on his face that her heart had melted, thinking that he'd been stood up by a date. Somehow he'd looked little boy lost. The gay waiter had certainly thought so, because he'd spent an inordinate amount of time fussing at the Scottish guy's table, smoothing tablecloths and refolding napkins.

'You looked across and briefly met my eyes. I had to turn away fearful you might recognise me from tailing you in the streets, and blowing the cover of the programme as a result. Do you believe in love at first sight?'

Lyndsey didn't answer. She wondered if she were hearing right. Tiredness was stealing over her, seeping into her veins, and the alcohol was blurring the edges of the day. Robbie's words seemed couched in a foreign language, and she struggled to understand them.

'Call me old cynic, bonnie lass, but I've always thought it a load of tosh thought up by the sentimental claptrap brigade. Crazy notion that you can catch a glance from someone, and know in that instance that you want to spend the rest of your life with them. Except that it isn't crazy, Lyndsey. It happened to me right there in that noisy café smelling of chlorine, staring at a girl who resembled the frightened deer who roamed the Highlands where I grew up as a boy. Obviously Coral and Dee told us your history, so we already knew, in the Turnaround studio, that your marriage was falling apart, and the type of guy your husband was. Always putting you down, they said. Boy did it show, hen. I've never seen a women so crushed, so defeated. Fragile too, as though a gust of wind might knock you sideways. It took all the willpower I could muster not to scoop you into my arms right there and then. There sits a lass, I thought, who is crying out for love and affection, and I wanted to give it to you in spades. I still do....'

Lyndsey swung her legs off the table, and stood up so abruptly that she got a blood rush to the head.

'Got to ring Mum.' She mumbled, 'find out how Cass is.'

Robbie raised his tumbler in a gesture that said 'go ahead', and she fled the room. In the hall, Lyndsey dialled Renee's number with shaking hands trying not to dwell on the declaration of love she'd just heard. On the fourth ring, a familiar voice said, 'hello.'

'Sorry its so late, Mum. Only been home ten minutes, it took ages to get home because we hit traffic and it was stop start all the way back to London.'

'Never mind darling. Did you have a good day?'

'OK, I guess. Glad that the filming is almost over. Only one more day to do in the studio next week, when Savannah and Thalia comment on my new look and I parade around in five grand's worth of clothes. Then my brief career as a TV star is over, thank God.'

'Not until the programme is aired in Autumn. How have they done your hair?'

'Bit like it was in my punk era, except its not black and white stripes as it was then.'

Renee said, 'heaven's that's a relief. I used to be embarrassed to be seen with you. Is that zebra really your daughter, people used to say.'

'Aw mum,' Lyndsey said with a wry smile. Although she couldn't see Renee, she knew that her parent wore a similar expression of fond amusement at the memory.

'Ray rang from Manhattan to speak to Cass, but I told him she was in the bath. Thought it best that he doesn't know about the business with the dog until he's back from the US. He's flying home tomorrow evening, landing at Heathrow at ten, and wants you to pick him up. Please go Lyndsey. It will be a good opportunity for you to tell him what's been going on with Cassandra during the car journey back; give him a chance to calm down before he sees her. I don't want the kiddie any more upset than she is already.'

'OK' said Lyndsey distractedly, but she'd already made a mental note not to tell Raymond about Cassie and the stray alsatian. It would simply inflame him unnecessarily, 'I'm leaving Shenlagh Gardens now to bring the little absconder home.'

In the lounge, she could hear a sloshing sound and guessed Robbie was topping up his tumbler with more whisky. If he drank too much, she would have to offer him the spare bed rather than risk letting him drive whilst under the influence. Lyndsey frowned. Whilst the wild side of her stirred at the prospect, her sensible side baulked at the idea of Cassandra coming home to find Robert McCrae in situ, especially in the light of recent events. She felt she needed time with her child alone.

However, Renee's next words clarified the situation,

'Leave it tonight please Lyndsey. Cassie is already in bed, fast asleep. She's been dozy all day, from the tablet the doctor gave her. Anyway, you sound like you've had a drink.'

'In bed?' echoed Lyndsey, 'but it's only...' she lifted her watch to the light, 'eight thirty..'

'Emotional upset is very exhausting darling, as you well know. The kiddie is wiped out, and if you come for her now, she'll only be unsettled further. Besides which....'

There was an awkward pause before the voice continued, '.. she blames you Lyn for having the dog taken away. I've tried to talk to her, reason it out, but Cassandra is not being terribly rational at the moment. Let her sleep on it. Things always look better in the light of morning.'

With that, Lyndsey had to be content.

She returned to the lounge, deeply troubled. The rift that had developed between herself and her beloved child seemed to be widening, and she was at a loss how to bridge it. Cassie's life had been upturned during the last year, like a shakened snow globe, and the flakes were yet to settle. The onset of adolescence, the giant step into secondary school, and the crumbling of her parent's marriage, had made the child insecure and it was easy to deduce that Mozart had imparted a sense of belonging that she so desperately craved. A four legged canine had provided what her own mother had patently failed to provide, despite Lyndsey's best efforts to plug the gaps in Cassandra's life as comforter, supporter, and a friend. There was a time when she was all those things and more to her daughter, and as she refreshed her drink with a generous slug of vodka, she reflected on the poignancy of the human condition in all its stages of development. There came a time when one's offspring were no longer dependent on the parent for emotional sustenance, and often actively spurned it. She remembered her own teenage self coming to the realisation (as a possible reaction to the untimely death of her father} that to love her mother was seriously 'uncool'. Thereafter followed years of rebellion against Renee's values, starting with Lyndsey shaving her head at sixteen and wearing a safety pin through one ear. Gradually though, as the years passed, she came back to her mother, and it was like being a storm wrecked sailor guided to shore by the comforting beam of a lighthouse. Now she knew that the one constant in her life was Renee, always at the other end of the phone or a short drive away, always ready to dispense a soothing word that came with the wisdom of years. Her mother would never let her down. Never betray or reject the fruit of the womb. Of that Lyndsey was sure.

'This is my third.' Robbie said, interrupted her thoughts. 'Hope you don't mind.'

He held up the bottle of scotch which she was alarmed to see half empty.

'Oh,' said Lyndsey inadequately, 'Shit, who cares? I'm getting pissed myself. Might as well since I won't be fetching Cass til the morning.'

'In that case.....'

'Yes?'

'Can I stay over?'

'Yes'

'With you?'

'Yes.'

Lyndsey clapped a hand over her mouth. Too late she realised what she'd said. Robbie got up and walked across to her. He prised her fingers away from her lips, and bent and kissed her. Then his arms encircled her body in a powerful embrace. Seconds turned into minutes, as they stood fused together, neither one seeming able to move. Lyndsey felt her head swim, and the room seemed to tilt dizzily beneath her bare feet. Gasping for breath, she pushed Robbie away, the edge of the lowered shelf in the cocktail cabinet cutting into her back.

He regarded her quizzically. She saw that underneath his tan, his face was lined with fatigue, and designer stubble was already darkening his neck after the day's growth. 'Is that a yes, or a no?' he asked.

'Oh fuck, let's do it.' Said Lyndsey boldly. A delicious feeling of wild abandon was flooding her body, and for only the second time in many months she felt stirrings of sexual desire emanate from between her legs, both as a result of talking to Robbie. 'Perhaps I'd better re-phrase that. Oh do it, let's fuck.' She giggled, aware that the double vodkas she'd just consumed had dulled her sense of responsibility. Robbie rested both hands heavily on her shoulders. She could hear his laboured breathing, and his fingers seared hotly through the thin cotton of her T'shirt, making her shoulders feel as if burnt by a noonday sun.

'Lyndsey Daly, look at me,' he commanded. She raised her head, and met his blue eyes that seemed to now burn with a fierce brilliance. The pupils were small black dots which danced before her gaze. Again it struck her how much he resembled the pop singer, Sting.

'I'm looking'.

'We've both been drinking. We're both on an emotional high after the day's filming, and we're both tired.'

'Your point being?'

'I don't want you to regret this. Promise you won't wake up in the morning with a feeling of dread, and wish we'd never ended up in bed. If you've got the slightest doubts, I'd rather laugh it off now and kip on the sofa.'

'Would you really?' Lyndsey said, 'rather kip on the sofa I mean?'

He shook his head and Lyndsey saw that it was done with such vehemence that the shaggy fringe masked his eyes.

'Then you needn't worry. I won't regret it. Life is too short to waste on that load of balls, and beside which, no-one need know. It can be our secret. We're alone in the house. Cassie is with her grandma, Ray is across the Atlantic, and I'm sick of being lonely. For one night – one long delicious night I want a man's body beside me, hot and naked, and.....'

'And what...?'

'Ready to do my bidding.'

'I'm your man, Lyndsey Daly. But...'

'But what..?'

'I don't want this to be a one off. Don't think my heart could stand it, and I mean in an emotional sense not because of physical exertion. I'm crazy about you woman.'

'Prove it, Robert McCrae.'

They were kissing again, and this time, she felt his hands slide from her shoulders and move down over her breasts, rubbing erect nipples through the flimsy T shirt, and onwards to her waist. He lifted the material and bent his head, and began searing her stomach with hot dry lips that moved in a deliciously erotic circle. She dug her fingers in his thick thatch of hair, and shivered slightly as his head moved lower.

Then he was fumbling with the button of her canvas jeans, tugging at the zip, until they fell to her ankles, exposing her long bare legs and lower body encased in white panties edged with lace, courtesy of the lingerie shop.

Lyndsey struggled to step out of them, almost falling over, but Robbie came to the rescue. He lifted her up from the hips enabling legs to be kicked free, and began walking backwards towards the open door pulling her with him. 'Where?' he asked, and his voice sounded ragged, gasping, strange to her ears.

Lyndsey said wildly, 'not the marital bed, I couldn't bear to think of Ray... not Cass's room, that's sacrosanct, not the guest room – my mum sleeps in there, not the lounge the sofa's show every mark…'

He bent his head and kissed her hungrily. '..the kitchen sink? It worked for Glenn Close and Michael Douglas in Fatal Attraction.'

She punched him playfully on the shoulder at this suggestion, then caught sight of the imposing dining table. It symbolised everything that was wrong in her marriage. A huge baronial affair, that seated twelve in formal splendour, it had been Ray's choice, bought not for practicality but as a statement of lifestyle. Her husband had laid down a set of laws for its use, that she dare not transgress; the use of heat resistant tablemats was mandatory, only proper beeswax was allowed when she polished its gleaming top, and any candles used in the central candlebra had to be of the non-drip kind. It was an altar to Ray's petulance, and one she had a sudden urge to desecrate.

Unbidden, she had a memory of him lecturing her the day she'd successfully completed her trial period at the library, 'So Dee and Coral came round and you cooked them lunch. Did you have the gall to use my dining room to entertain that pair of trollops? I've found a wet sticky mark on the table top Lyn. Get a cloth and clean it pronto, and woe betide if it has dulled the varnish.'

A feeling of devilment swept through her, so alien to her nature, that it left her momentarily breathless.

'On the table.' She said to Robbie. Breaking free from his embrace, she whipped the T shirt over her head, followed by the bra and panties. Naked she stood before him, gripped with a wild abandon that felt quite alien. She scrambled onto the baronial monstrosity, her bare bottom sliding on its polished surface so that she thought she must resemble a skater who'd taken a tumble. Then she was laughing, a feral laugh, which held an edge of hysteria.

'Come on. What you waiting for?'

Taking his cue, Robbie undressed, scattering his clothes over the pristine room with careless haste. Lyndsey's eyes widened at the sight of his nude body, the muscles gleaming palely in the darkness, noticing the smooth marbled surface of his chest, the taut thighs, and proudly erect penis. Clambering up beside her, they both lay together, laughing and kissing in turn. Then his hands began to move. They cupped one tiny breast in turn, kneading each nipple with an insistent gentleness, before one hand broke away and began to travel down her writhing body. The fine curls between her legs barely hid the pink gash of her flesh, and his finger probed into the moist crevice beneath, sending her into paroxysms of delight. Slowly he began to rub, side to side, keeping up a steady light pressure against her clitoris until Lyndsey felt her back arch upwards from the table in an involuntary movement. Robbie was kissing her neck, whispering words in her ear, Scottish words that she couldn't understand yet knew instinctively were endearments, as he raised his body above hers ready for the moment of penetration. His fingers continued to explore her, spreading aside the dampened lips of her vagina, and opening up the entrance to her inner secret world. Then he was inside her, his penis buried up to the hilt, like a sheathed sword, his movements gathering in momentum as the urgency of desire built.

Lyndsey felt herself losing control, not only of her body, but of her mind. Delicious tremors were running up and down her back, and her entire lower half seemed to be on fire. Every nerve ending was tingling, and there was a strange buzzing in her ears as she reached a crescendo of sensation.

She climaxed in a drenching gush, her intimate muscles contracting and expanding around the shaft of Robbie's penis, so that he too, was brought to a powerful orgasm.

He slithered out of her, and lay, panting across her chest, while she stroked his hair and tried to still the wild thumping of her own heart. A puddle of sticky wetness pooled around her bottom, and she wondered how Ray would react if he were to walk in the room at that moment. Less upset at catching his wife naked in another's arms, she thought, than the milky patch dulling the surface of his precious table.

She shuddered at the picture of her husband rushing into the room, cloth in hand, lifting both her legs to wipe the offending spillage, as if he were changing a baby's nappy. Robbie hugged her tighter, perhaps sensing her need for reassurance. How long they remained in that frozen embrace, Lyndsey did not know. An hour might have passed, or perhaps it was only ten minutes. Eventually their breathing became shallower and more even.

She thought that Robbie had fallen asleep, despite the hard surface of the table, exhausted by the frenzy of the moment, but then she knew different. Without raising his head where it nestled comfortably between her breasts, he uttered just one word.

'Wow.'

That, thought Lyndsey, said it all.

Chapter Twenty Seven

LYNDSEY RECEIVED A surprise phone call. The caller needed no introduction. She immediately recognised the high pitched tones, and almost breathless way of speaking,

'Hi Lyn, Guess who?'

'Hello Gaynor.'

The 'Turnaround' researcher, ever true to form, wasted no time on preamble. Lyndsey had to smile as she launched right in, 'the programme's being aired tomorrow, 9pm Channel 7'.

'tomorrow...' Lyndsey found herself echoing. Weeks had passed since her filming stint with the 'Turnaround' crew had finished, and it was now well into Spring. Outside in the garden the snows and bitter frosts of February had melted, and daffodils made a sea of yellow. It was early Saturday morning and she was still in her nightdress. At this unexpected news, she sat down so hard on the telephone seat it jarred her back. A stab of pain shot up her spine, but it was nothing compared to the stab of trepidation that seized her at the thought of appearing on TV so soon. She had been told that her debut as a television performer would not be until September and this had given a modicum of serenity. It was the feeling one got before exams, she thought remembering back to the dreaded time of 'o' levels at school – the calm before the storm. That blessed period when it was rather too soon to revise, and rather too late to worry.

'But I was told the autumn' She found herself protesting into the receiver. Oh God, she thought. I sound like a gibbering wreck.

'Oh sure,' came back the airy response, 'but this slot came up unexpectedly and was offered to our team. A new reality TV show was scheduled but it has been pulled at the eleventh hour due to some technical glitch. 'Turnaround' is stepping into the breach - going out as a surprise Mother's Day weekend Special.'

'Mother's Day?'

'Yeah, indirectly. I mean you are a mum aren't you? And mother's day is all about the nation's mums' being treated to the works by their offspring – you know, meals out, perfume, perhaps a nice new outfit. Turnaround will fit neatly into the concept that it is a weekend specifically set aside for the family matriarch. Not only that but the clocks are going forward tonight for the official start of Spring, which is traditionally the time for regeneration. New born lambs frolicking in pastures and all that crap. Spring Fever and Spring Cleaning. Turfing out the old, and bringing on the new. Don't you see the connection with your appearance on the prog, Lyn?'

Before Lyndsey could answer, Gaynor rattled on, 'a born again librarian.'

'Shit.'

'Sorry?'

'It's just that I'm not prepared.'

'How prepared do you need to be?' Came the brisk response. Lyndsey could picture Gaynor on the other end of the phone, clipboard in one hand, pen in the other, her python coils waving in the static air of the studio. Already she could detect the customary hint of impatience in the researcher's voice.

'Couldn't you show someone else? Another contributor to the new series...'

''fraid not. Vince has decided that the edition of 'Turnaround' featuring you is the strongest of the whole ten week run. The ace card in our pack, so to speak. This is a terrific slot to be given and he is predicting high ratings. It's been chucking it down all week, and the forecast is more rain, so hopefully people will elect to stay home and watch TV.'

'Oh' said Lyndsey, and immediately wondered whether Gaynor could hear the inflection of dismay tinged with panic in that single utterance. If she did, the researcher made no immediate comment. Instead she said, her tone bristling, 'you should be flattered we've selected you to appear in this juicy slice of primetime TV which has been handed to us on a plate. Other programme producers would kill for this slot...'

'..the point is Lyndsey, that pre-view tapes are not available, and at this short notice, we couldn't get them to you anyway. So you won't have a chance to see yourself on the box in advance. You'll be watching the prog along with the great unwashed.'

'Out of common courtesy, Vince Levene wanted me to ring and acquaint you of this change in scheduling in case you'd booked an evening out, and missed it. At least now, if you have other plans, you can set up the TiVo box.'

Lyndsey didn't reply to this. She did indeed have other plans and they involved Robbie McCrae. He was coming over, as he did every Saturday, to take her to dinner at a local Greek taverna they'd discovered tucked away in a side street in Bounds Green. It had become their favourite eating place over the past few weeks, with its authentic menu, jovial waiting staff, and Mediterranean style décor. No-one on the Turnaround team knew that her relationship with the gentle Scot had progressed from a purely professional to an intimate one, and that was the way they both wanted it. Lyndsey felt slightly shameful that they had become lovers, and whilst Robbie confessed that he wanted to 'shout it from the rooftops' he was mindful of her wish to keep it secret from everyone but themselves. He made it clear he did not want to offend the sensibilities of her mother, Renee, nor add to the insecurities of Cassandra. There was also the fear that latter might unwittingly let slip the news to her father, even if sworn to secrecy, and the prospect of Ray finding out was enough to keep both Lyndsey and Robbie silent in mutual complicity. He also admitted that it wouldn't do his career any favours with the hierarchy of Channel 7 if it became common knowledge that he was sleeping with a contributor to one of their shows, even though he had been seconded from the Turnaround team and was now working on a series featuring cowboy builders.

'they'll consider I've breached some unwritten moral code. Used my position as a TV exec to hoodwink a vulnerable member of the public into sharing my bed. The old casting couch syndrome...' He'd said to her on their first proper night together. Lyndsey, snuggled up with him under the duvet had delivered a playful punch, 'except that I seduced you, not vice versa, and we're sharing my bed not yours..'

'and what a bed it is.' He'd let out a long low whistle, and run a finger suggestively down the nearest carved post of the four poster. Lyndsey loved the way he said 'bed' pronouncing it 'baid'. It made her shiver with delight just to hear him speak.

There was no such shiver of delight as she listened to Gaynor speak however. Rather a shiver of apprehension at the prospect of appearing on national TV in just a few hours' time.

A rumble of thunder shook the house. The hall was gloomy as the sky outside the front door darkened, and a draught swept around Lyndsey's bare ankles forcing her to hop from one foot to the other in an effort to keep the circulation going.

'Are you still there?' demanded Gaynor, 'what's that funny noise.'

'Only my teeth chattering.'

'Yes, the weather is pretty shitty.' Gaynor conceded, 'which is all the better for the ratings. People will be glued to the box instead of braving the downpours, and seeing you in gorgeous new Spring season fashions will make them believe they're on holiday. A kind of vacation by proxy.'Oh hell, thought Lyndsey in dismay. She didn't want to consider the possibility of vast numbers of strangers viewing her trial by the fashion police, Savannah Hooper-Greenhill and Thalia Emmerson.

Gaynor was saying, 'One more thing, Lyndsey. Savvy and Thals have invited you to attend their book launch for "Turnaround Tips Two". The 'publication' party is being held in a scrummy club in the West End, and all the celebs will be there. You can bring a guest, and I'll be popping an invite in the post. It's not yet awhile, so you'll have plenty of time to decide who to bring.'

'Brilliant', said Lyndsey with genuine delight, making a mental note to invite Renee. Trying to choose between Dee and Coral would be too problematic. Whoever drew the short straw was bound to feel slighted, and Lyndsey did not want to risk offending either one of her fairy godmothers.

'It's been a bugger to arrange,' breezed Gaynor, 'As my swansong for Channel 7, I've had to work in conjunction with the publisher to draw up guest lists and menus.'

'You're not leaving?'

'Yes, indeedy. I'm moving over to the Beeb as a researcher on a current affairs programme. Course I shall be sorry to say goodbye to the 'Turnaround' team, but I need to be on the cutting edge of national news.'

Lyndsey nodded to herself but said nothing. She knew such a programme would appeal to Gaynor's serious side.

'When are you going?'

'End of the month,' came the clipped reply, 'Oh, and don't forget to check the TV Reviews in the Sundays tomorrow Lyn, to see if you get a mention.'

The line went dead. Lyndsey walked into the kitchen, switching on the kettle for her customary wake up cuppa. A thump sounded on the floorboards above her head. Cassandra was up. As the kettle boiled, she heard the dread sound of footsteps beginning their customary circuit of the bedroom. Round and round they went, and Lyndsey could picture her daughter, a hunched pixie in doggy print pyjamas, walking with eyes fixedly anchored on her slippered feet. This manic behaviour in her eleven year old had been going on since that dreadful day in the park when the wardens came and took away the Alsatian. The memory of the slavering beast trying to escape the nets, and Cassie's hysterical intervention still haunted Lyndsey. Mechanically, she brewed tea, knowing that it haunted the child even more. Despite a series of consultations with a Child Behavioural Specialist recommended by the GP, Cassandra still continued to display evidence of deep emotional disturbance. The constant circling of her bedroom had worn a path in the carpet, yet nothing would divert her from the need to keep walking. Lyndsey had tried everything, even resorting to physically restraining the child on the bed. Cassie had merely lain there, supine and unresisting under her mother's grasp, staring unseeing at the ceiling, only to resume the perimeter walk the moment Lyndsey let go. It was dark in the kitchen, and she had to turn on the light to see to pour tea into two matching mugs. Outside the window the sky was leaden, and the heavy air seemed to reverberate with an almost unseen threat. There was going to be another storm, thought Lyndsey.

She took the tea upstairs, adding a couple of high energy biscuits to the tray. These had been prescribed for Cassie by the doctor, and contained essential nutrients. The child ate so little these days that getting her to consume anything was a bonus, and luckily she liked the taste of the 'Vita-Bars' enough to munch through two with her morning tea. It was ironic thought Lyndsey, pausing at the closed bedroom door which bore a sign childishly scrawled on a piece of paper in red felt pen 'Keep Out – Private – Knock before entering.'. Ironic how her own weight had risen, as her daughter's had fallen. Her affair with Robbie, coupled with the reduction in stress which accompanied Ray's departure, had given her back an appetite not only for life but for food. She was eating better and with more enthusiasm. There was another reason too, she felt, for the firm covering of flesh that was beginning to mask the bony contours of her body and give her a semblance of womanly curves. It was a need to stay strong for her daughter. She knew that Cassandra was on a dangerous edge, and that the only way to help her was to keep her own self healthy. She needed to be fit and vigorous to deal with the current traumas, and any that might lie ahead. Subconsciously she guessed that her mind had prepared her body for fight not flight.

There was no point on knocking on her daughter's door. Lyndsey knew from past experience, that it would be ignored. Either the child genuinely didn't hear or was too absorbed in her own misery to react to this polite advertising of someone's presence. Balancing the tea tray on one hand, she pushed it open with the other.

Cassandra didn't look up. There was no acknowledgement in either her eyes or body language of her mother's appearance in the room. She continued to walk around in a circle, humming quietly to herself. Lyndsey placed the tray on the bedside table, and settled down on the 'My Little Pony' duvet cover, a legacy of Cassandra's younger self. Surely the child must get dizzy, she thought, watching the familiar depressing tableau. Her heart felt as heavy as the sky outside the window with its view of the street beyond, and houses where children lived who did normal childlike things such as playing, running and laughing.

Lyndsey looked at the fraught little figure of her daughter, and sighed inwardly. It was so long since Cassandra had done any of these things, she thought.

'The child is suffering from acute anxiety,' the consultant had told her at the last appointment, 'brought about by too many changes happening in her life to be adequately assimilated by her brain. The loss of the dog I'm afraid, proved to be the catalyst for disturbing behaviour we see before us.' The nurse had taken the patient away to be weighed, so Lyndsey was left alone in the office with the Behaviourist. He was a portly man, with piercing eyes, who had the disconcerting habit of rocking backwards and forwards as he talked.

'What can I do?'

'Nothing Mrs Daly beyond what we have already discussed in previous sessions. Provide her with stability. Make sure she gets enough sleep, and is kept free from stimulus and excitement.'

'Will she get better?'

'Of course. It will be a gradual process. Just as the deterioration happened slowly, so will any improvement. It will come though. Just be patient, and try not to lose your temper. Knowing the distress that the constant circling of her room causes you, is a goad to her need to mete out parental punishment, so try not to react. In the one to one sessions I've had with your daughter no secret has been made of the fact that she holds you accountable for her daddy leaving, and the dog being taken away – don't give her any more reason to heap blame at your door.'

'I am remaining calm, doctor. It is not easy, but I'm following your recommendations on how to behave around her. As though nothing untoward has happened.'

'Good. As I have said before, Cassandra needs the routine of normality in her domestic life. She is continuing to attend school?'

'Yes. It was touch and go at first, after the dog was taken away, but the form teacher is keeping a constant eye on her, and two pupils have been assigned as mentors.'

'Ah yes...the dog.' He consulted a sheaf of notes, rocking ever faster so that Lyndsey could hear the high backed chair squeak in protest. 'Mozart wasn't it?'

'That was name Cass gave him. His real name is Bart.'

Bartholomew Scout Venturer, to be precise thought Lyndsey. The dog wardens had sedated the animal back at the sanctuary and discovered the presence of an identity microchip inserted into thick muscled neck.

'We have traced the real owners of your daughter's stray, Mrs. Daly' She'd been told when Lyndsey had rang the day after the dreadful episode in the park to check Mozart's progress, 'a family from a village called Stansted Mountfichet in Essex.'

'Stansted Mountfichet., Lyndsey found herself repeating, almost stupidly, 'a village.....'

The bizarre sounding name had added, in her view, to the surreal string of events relating to the dog.

'They were en-route home from a camping holiday, and stopped at a garage in North London to re-fuel. Apparently the beast jumped out of their car and legged it down some side streets. Despite thorough searches of the area undertaken over the following days, which also involved them notifying the relevant authorities and posting 'Missing' notices, he was never found. When he came to your daughter's attention he'd been 'on the run' so to speak for several weeks. The family had quite given him up for lost, and are mightily relieved to be getting him back.'

So that was that, Lyndsey had thought. When she'd relayed this news to Cassandra thinking that the child would be mollified to know her beloved German Shepherd had been re-claimed by his rightful owners and would be re-instated in a loving home, the despairing reaction that followed made her quickly realise that she'd committed a faux pas. It would have been better to let Cass continue to believe that she might one day get the dog back, instead of which she'd unknowingly pricked the last remaining balloon of hope, on whose string her child had clung.

She handed the small figure a mug of tea, knowing from past experience that it wouldn't induce her to cease the constant circling, or even break stride. It didn't. Cassie took the drink, and sipped it mechanically as she walked. On the eighth circuit, she handed back an empty mug to her mother, who exchanged it for the first of the unwrapped breakfast vitamin bars.

'Darling, you know you were going to Nana's this evening, while mummy has to go out?'

There was no response, but Lyndsey didn't expect there to be. She carried on, smoothing the quilt cover with an air of carefully assumed nonchalance,

'the arrangement has changed. That phone call just now was Channel 7 informing that I'm going to be on telly tonight. Just think of it, Cass. Your very own mum on the box at nine.'

Was it her imagination thought Lyndsey, or was there a momentary falter in the child's step at this news.

'I thought it might be nice,' she continued, 'if you and I watch it together, curled up on the sofa.' Thinking ahead, Lyndsey had decided to put Robbie off for the evening, knowing that he would understand.

'I still wanna go Nana's' came the dull response.

'Darling, can't we just...'

'I WANT to go to Nana's' the child's voice went up an octave. Lyndsey found herself bunching up the quilt cover in a taut fist, all outward appearance of calm gone. She wanted to scream and shout, throw herself on the carpet at her daughter's feet, break a window, upturn the bed, anything in fact to break the cycle of that frantic pacing. Her mind went back to the words of the stout behaviourist at the end of their first session together, 'I've talked with your daughter,' he'd said, 'and it seems the one place that gives her a much needed sense of stability is staying at her grandmother's. She adores 'Nana Reen' as she calls her, and not only feels safe and serene in her presence, but finds her grandmother's home an unthreatening environment. I suggest you let her stay there as frequently as can be arranged in order to speed up the process of emotional healing.'

The first biscuit was eaten. Lyndsey unwrapped the second, and waited for Cassie to skirt the bed for the umpteenth time before handing it over. Her child's mechanical munching made her think of a cow's consumption of hay when tied up in a stall for milking. That same placid bovine moving of jaws and fixed expression on the wall opposite.

Lyndsey adopted a conciliatory tone, 'Okay, you can go to Nana's as arranged and watch the programme with her.'

A flash of lightening lit up the room, giving her daughter's face a ghastly pallor.

'She's wearing a mask', thought Lyndsey in despair, 'and I no longer know what lies beneath.'

Dropping the quilt, she moved a hand up to her own face and stroked the fierce point of her chin. An awful truth had hit home.

She was wearing one too.

Chapter Twenty Eight

CASSIE SAT IN the passenger seat, clutching her overnight bag fiercely to her chest. She was aware of her mother's eyes upon her, constantly flicking from the road to the back of Cassie's head. Her heart was thudding. The short journey to her grandmother's home could be a nerve wracking one. At any given moment, the driver was apt to slam on brakes and turn the hatchback around in the direction of Shenlagh Gardens. The victory of persuading the reluctant parent to let her spend the evening with Nana Reen as arranged, had been a hard won one. Especially in the light of the other's scheduled TV debut. Cassandra knew, from past experience, how easily such a victory could be snatched from her, by a mother who thought she knew best. A mother, whom the eleven year old was perceptive enough to know, was consumed by guilt at considered shortcomings in her parental skills. Cassie didn't consider being abandoned emotionally a shortcoming at all. Rather she welcomed such treatment. She wanted to be left alone, and conveyed this to her mother by being resolutely non-communicative. 'When I have kids,' she thought clutching the handle of the bag even tighter,' I shall definitely not be on their case the whole time.'

The car slowed as the driver negotiated the roundabout at the far end of Southgate High Street. Knowing that her mother was concentrating on avoiding the stream of traffic coming from all directions, Cassie shot her a quick nervous glance.

Lyndsey was biting her lower lip. Was it in concentration, or was she building up to say something? Her daughter fervently prayed it was the former.

'That's it Cass, I've changed my mind. You're not going to Nana's after all. Let's go home instead so that you can spend some time with mummy and maybe talk, darling, like we used to.'

She could almost hear the words being spoken, and they filled her with dread. How to stop her mother saying them?

Cassandra sat rigidly on the sweaty vinyl upholstery, staring out of the side window. She knew, from past experience, that if she gave her mother eye contact, or uttered a comment of any kind, it would be seized upon by the other as chink appearing in that carefully assumed armour.

'When are you going to lower your dammed drawbridge, sweetheart,' her mother had said in exasperation when she'd sat on the bed earlier. For an hour she'd watched as Cassie completed her morning circuitry of the bedroom.

'Never' thought Cass determinedly but would not give her mother the satisfaction of hearing her speak the thought aloud. The short time at Brackendale High had taught her well. Keep your head down, say nothing, stay out of trouble. It had worked at school. The bullies, bored by her mute indifference when provoked, had moved on to more reactionary victims. She hoped, that if she applied similar tactics at home, her mother would eventually give up too.

The same mother who now slammed on brakes to avoid a cyclist straying into the centre lane. Tyres hissed on the wet tarmac. Cassie looked out at the sodden streets, counting how many people had umbrellas. Rain had fallen steadily all day. Cold, slanting rain, that gushed along the gutter above her bedroom window, and smeared the glass so that the garden beyond had looked like a painting she'd once done at primary school when another pupil had accidentally knocked the jam jar of water over it.

She felt hot and sticky in the car, but didn't want to open the window. Such an action, she knew, would precipitate a host of questions.

'Are you too hot, darling?'

'Why don't you take that coat off'

'Shall I open my window too?'

'Shall I put the blower on?'

Or even worse, 'You're not feeling ill, are you? Running a temperature? Oh dear, perhaps we'd better go back and I'll call the doctor.'

She was careful to keep very still. Any shuffling would be perceived by her mother as a manifestation of discomfort, or boredom, or irritation, and indeed might trigger the very action Cassie was so desperate to avoid. A return to Shenlagh Gardens. They were nearly at her grandmother's. Keep counting, Cass told herself, trying not to be lulled by the soporific whirring of the windscreen wipers. She mustn't lower her guard. The next ten minutes would be crucial.

Twenty eight, twenty nine, thirty, thirty one....

She froze. The man carrying umbrella, a huge striped affair of the type her daddy would be using on his fishing trip today, had a dog on a lead. Not just any sort of dog either. It was a Mozart look-alike. A shaggy black and tan German Shepherd, who lolloped along at his side, paws creating mini tidal waves in the puddles.

Cassie sat transfixed. It could almost be her own dog except that the coat was slightly lighter around the tail and legs. A single hot tear plopped out of her eye and burnt a path down her cheek. She allowed it to drip onto the cuff of her Eskimo coat. To have wiped it away would have alerted her mother to the fact she was crying.

Since her dog had gone, she had seen doubles of him everywhere. Alsatians seemed to proliferate. On adverts, on the streets, in magazines, and newspapers. Only the day before, her mother's Daily Mail had sported a picture of a police dog that had won an award for bravery. Cassandra had sneaked it into her bedroom and read avidly, sitting with her back to the door so that she could bar any unwelcome intrusion. His name was Gymcrack and he had saved his handler's life from a vicious armed robber. She'd swelled with pride on reading the article. In similar circumstances, Mozart would save her life, that she knew. He'd given her complete loyalty, and how had she repaid him? By allowing him to be taken away by those horrible men with their nets.

Except she'd been powerless to stop them that dreadful day in the park. Her mother had physically restrained her, and despite kicking and biting and screaming, Cassandra had been unable to prise herself free. She hadn't managed to save her faithful canine companion, and the guilt was a constant torment and torture to her eleven year old soul.

A fierce hatred burned in that soul. Hatred towards her mother. As the car slowed to turn into her grandmother's road, Cassandra felt it surge through her, almost tearing her insides apart. She felt like the man she'd seen in a film once called The Incredible Hulk who when angry turned bright green and burst out of his clothes. For one terrible moment, Cassie thought she was about to do the same. Everything seemed swelling up inside her coat, until her body threatened to snap the buttons and rip apart the zip.

Nana Reen had been very understanding. She'd tried to explain to Cass that it hadn't been her mother's fault the dog had gone. The school had called the Dog Wardens as a safety measure in case the animal might pose a danger, not only to their pupil, but innocent bystanders in the park. Cassandra had not been convinced by this argument, but indicated to her grandmother that she had. She knew, from past experience, that Nana Reen couldn't be trusted upon to be impartial where Lyndsey was concerned, and Cass had overheard more than one conversation between her father and grandmother of late, where Nana stoutly stuck up for the errant Mrs. Daly in the face of Mr. Daly's denigrations.

The car pulled up at the kerb, and before her mother even had a chance to engage the hand brake, Cass had unclasped her seat belt and had one foot out of the door. She wasn't going to linger in the confined space with her mother a moment longer than necessary. It would only tempt fate and her mum to start questioning, thought Cass with a firm line to her mouth, and no matter how gentle those same questions were put, there was always a determined edge to them.

Nor was her mother's offer to buy a puppy a palliative for the loss of Mozart. She didn't want another dog, no matter how cute. She wanted him. No other animal would suffice, in Cassie's book. No other dog could be as clever, as attentive, as loyal, as adoring of her diminutive eleven year old frame. Besides which, her mother had offered a little dog. A poodle, or a terrier, or a miniature, she'd suggested. At this Cassie had been outraged. Small dogs, she'd shouted at her mother, were suited to big people in little houses. She was a little person in a big house. Ergo a large breed was the only one Cassandra would consider. A large breed that would protect her from the encroachment of people, and keep potential threats at bay. Not just any large breed either. It had to be a

St. Bernard like one of the film 'Beethoven' fame, or a German Shepherd, like her beloved 'Mozart.' Mother had shaken her head at this, and said that it just wasn't practicable for their lifestyle, and besides which, there was her father's dislike of pets to consider.

'Don't bring daddy into this,' Cass had screamed, 'he doesn't even live here, remember...!'

Her father. That was another reason to hate her mother. She'd got rid of daddy, just in the same way she'd got rid of Mozart. It seemed to Cassandra that the loss of them both could be directly attributed to the tall, unhappy looking woman who was, at that very moment, locking the car. She strode purposefully up the path, the overnight bag banging painfully against her ankles in their thin white socks. She refused to look back. Refused even to acknowledge her mother's footsteps shadowing her to the front door.

Her heart swelled as she stood on the step, reaching up to ring the doorbell. She loved Nana Renee's maisonette. It felt more like home to her than Shenlagh Gardens. Especially since daddy now lived there too.

An excruciating interval passed before the door opened. It could only have been a few seconds, but to Cassandra, sharing the territory of the rectangular concrete step with her mother was even worse than having her bedroom invaded. The close proximity of the other was bad enough without the knowledge that her boundary was being compromised. She felt like she did at school, when Olu leaned across her side of the desk. As though she were being encroached upon without her permission. She wanted to shrivel up inside herself the way snails did when kids in the playground put salt on them for a joke.

Cassie pulled the hood of her coat down towards her forehead, and kept her eyes fixed on her new ankle boots.

Another gift from her mother. Another attempt, she thought, with the maturing insight of a child on the borderline of adolescence, to buy her off. The rain pattered on the hood of her coat, sounding as though she were camping in a waterlogged tent. Or in a caravan. She remembered holidaying in one on a site in Devon. She'd only been about six at the time, and it had rained solidly for two weeks. Her parents had tried to make light of it, and give her a good time, but by about the third day she sensed their growing disappointment with both the weather and each other.

'Hello Hedgehog.' Nana Reen had opened the door, and stood illuminated in a flood of light from the hallway. She had tipped back the concealing hood, and given her grand-daughter a light kiss on top of the head. Cassie hoped she wouldn't pass further comment about her hair. It had been short for a week. In a fit of pique against her mother, Mr. Butcher, the dog wardens, school bullies, and everyone else who had ever upset her, Cassie had loped off her mousy locks with pinking shears. She'd meant to do it with scissors but couldn't find any. The result had been a haphazard concoction of long and short bits that stuck out every which way from her head like Shock Headed Peter – the character in a storybook Nana Reen read her when she was little. Horrified, her mother had rushed her to the local hairdressers to try and rectify the damage. Or at least minimalise it. After a brief consultation with the other stylists on duty, the one assigned to work a miracle had been forced to cut it half an inch all over. Cassie was dismayed to find the impish style made her look even more childlike, when she actually harboured delusions of looking more grown up. Now, she was disconcerted by the thought that she resembled a scaled down version of her mother.

Gladdened by the sight of her grandmother, she returned the hug, and ducked past into the hallway. In the guest room, she stowed the overnight bag containing a nightie, clean knickers and toothbrush underneath the bed occupied by her father. It smelt faintly of him, a masculine odour of sweat and aftershave, and Cassie wished he were there instead of off on one of his weekend fishing expeditions. She stretched out on the counterpane wrinkling her nose appreciatively, and thinking, catching sight of herself in the dressing table mirror, that she resembled a squirrel. Or perhaps a rabbit. Mrs. Twitchit in Beatrix Potter.

Through the opened door, she could hear her mother and grandmother involved in a whispered conversation in the hall. Cassie guessed they were talking about her.

More whispers. Then she heard the former say, this time in normal tones, 'I'd stay and watch it with you, but Dee rang just as I was leaving. Coral had seen a trailer advertising the show with a clip of me, would you believe. They're on their way over to Shenlagh Gardens as we speak, armed with wine and nibbles, absolutely adamant that we see it together.'

Cass heard her grandmother reply, in that light cool voice that she loved, 'Naturally they want to share your moment of glory. After all, it was their machinations behind the scenes that got you on the programme in the first place. Tonight at nine, you say. Only half an hour to go. Must make sure I don't miss it. Simply cannot wait to see my beautiful daughter on prime time television, and I'll record it on dvd so we can all watch together another time.'

Cassie, perched on the edge of the bed, heard the sound of receding footsteps and guessed the duo had gone into the kitchen. This was followed by the distant hiss of water issuing from a tap.

'Oh no Nana,' She thought in sudden alarm, 'please don't make her a cup of tea. She'll only come and hassle me while it brews...'

Anxious to erect a temporary barrier which might serve to deflect her mother from any such 'hassling', Cassie slipped off the bed and hurried into the dim light of the lounge. Pretended absorption in some pastime might, she hoped, present a wearisome rock face to navigate for a parent who was, by tacit admission, in a hurry to get home for the arrival of pals with pathetic bottles of plonk. There was nothing immediately to hand. Her eyes scanned the room hoping to alight on an incomplete jigsaw puzzle, or piece of abandoned embroidery, but there were no accoutrements for a display of faked purposefulness.

There was only the TV. Cassandra pressed the 'on' switch, and located the remote control in its usual position on her grandmother's coffee table. Pressing buttons, she paused at a channel showing one of her favourite programmes. Called 'Going Public', it consisted of clips of home videos sent in from viewers where people had accidents with washing lines and sailing boats, or did silly things like running a food blender without its lid, or cleaning a hamster cage and then losing the hamster.

The presenter, a plump jolly man wearing a ginger wig, was saying, 'isn't it terrible when family celebrations are ruined by uninvited guests. We just want them to take flight...' Cue audience laughter, 'In this selection the gate crashers well and truly have wings. A case of the party going with a sting...' More audience laughter.

Cassie hugged her knees under the coat, and rocked as she watched. Delicious scenes unfolded of wasps invading a garden barbecue, causing the partakers to flee, abandoning sausages and kebabs in their wake. One man even fell in a fishpond as he tried to prevent a striped marauder from landing on his beef burger. What fun, thought Cassandra, unable to stop herself from giggling aloud.

'Something's tickled your funny bone, darling.' She hadn't heard her mother come in the room, and kept her eyes fixed on the television screen as that familiar head bent to kiss her cheek. Cassandra resisted the urge to swat her parent away, just as the people on the television were doing with the wasps.

'I'm going now, sweetheart. Nana's knows you've had supper, but is in the kitchen pouring you one of her special milky teas. I'd love to stay for one but the girls will be on the doorstep if I don't get my skates on...'

Feigning boredom at this conversation, Cassandra let out an exaggerated yawn. Her mother's next words, made her immediately regret this action.

'Nana is making sure you get to bed as soon as 'Turnaround' finishes. I've told her what a sleepyhead you are these days.'

'I'm not tired.'

'Cass, don't be difficult. You have blue shadows underneath your eyes, and have been impossible to get up in the mornings for school.'

'That's cos I hate the place'

'Whatever the reason, you need a good night's sleep.'

How do you know what I need, Cassandra wanted to shout. I need my dog, I need my daddy, I need you to leave...' She clamped her jaw together in an effort to prevent these words escaping. With superhuman effort she managed to say instead, 'OK mummy, whatever..... Hurry up and get home, or you're miss yourself on telly.'

Another light kiss was planted on her cheek. She tried not to flinch. To remain impassive whilst her mother hovered, an irritating presence above her head like the insect contributors to 'Going Public.'

The presenter was screeching with laughter along with the studio audience. As the selection of home videos came to an end, he turned to the camera and said, 'A case of party invaders being told to buzz off.....'

As her mother left the room, Cassandra mouthed after the departing figure, 'you can buzz off too.'

Chapter Twenty Nine

CORAL AND DEE beat Lyndsey to Shenlagh Gardens. As she pulled up outside, they were in the process of lifting the latch on her front gate. At the sound of the engine, Coral turned, and, seeing the identity of the driver, raised the carrier bag she was holding and made a performance of pointing at the contents and miming someone drunk. Lyndsey laughed. She guessed the bag contained several bottles of Hungarian Red, Coral's favourite wine. It had a rich full-blooded taste and perfectly suited her friend's overblown personality. Dee, the more unassuming of the two, shook a large bag of tortilla chips in an almost embarrassed manner, and a tub of something green, which Lyndsey guessed, was some of her famous homemade avocado dip. The guests had come well prepared for the delectation of seeing her on telly, thought the hostess, getting out of the car. As she picked up her handbag from the passenger seat, her mobile bleeped from within its depths, signalling the arrival of a text message. Correctly guessing whom it was from, Lyndsey hovered by the driver's door, unwilling to let her pals see she had received a message, and even more unwilling to reveal the identity of the sender. Robbie was a secret not only from her family, but from her friends too. Hurriedly she pressed buttons. It was still raining, and Coral and Dee were bound to wonder why she tarried by the car getting wet. The miniature screen of the phone lit up, and a string of words appeared.

Imagine you are standing on the edge of a swimming pool hen, it read, *hold your nose, take a deep breath and dive in. At first you will feel you are drowning but as you come up for air and start splashing about, it will become fun. In the end, it will be difficult to persuade you to leave the water.....You'll be fine. I've seen the stills, and you look terrific. A TV star in the making,'*

Lyndsey smiled. Typical of Robbie she thought, to give words of encouragement in such an oblique way. All that about splashing around in swimming pools. He really was a dear.

Earlier she had rang him on his mobile, 'Rob, you'll never guess what.'

'I think I can Lassie. Just got a text from Gaynor.'

'Oh, so you know.' She felt mildly deflated, and couldn't work out why.

'About the surprise scheduling of 'Turnaround' tonight, and you being the featured contributor – Aye. Be careful who gets hold of your signature from now on, mind – autographs of celebrities can fetch a fortune on the internet.'

He was teasing her in his usual gentle way. She blurted out, 'Robbie, I'm scared stiff. This is the moment I've been dreading. Supposing I've made a complete arse of myself on camera, and end up being the laughing stock of North London.'

'Well, I've seen your bum, and it is the most complete arse in the Universe – I can vouch for that.'

'Oh stop. You know what I mean.'

'Aye, you've got stage fright my darling. What we call in the business, FFN – aka first night nerves. You were a huge success with Thalia, Savannah, and the rest of the 'Turnaround' team when we filmed you for the show. An even bigger hit with yours truly, who is winding up from a day spent secretly trailing a firm of cowboy roofers around Middlesex.' Lyndsey had wondered whether Robbie minded being temporarily seconded from the crew of the make-over programme to work on this fly on the wall expose of dodgy building practises, but he'd assured her that it was a common occurrence in the film crew game. Cameramen, he'd said, were like roving reporters.

'Should be at yours shortly. We'll give the Greek Taverna a miss, and order take away instead, then I shall chain you to the sofa at 9pm and force you to watch Channel 7 featuring a newly fledged TV star called Lyndsey Daly.'

'That's just it, Rob. You can't come after all. That's why I'm ringing.'

There was a slight pause on the other end of the phone, then she heard him say, 'Tsk, tsk, blowing me out at the eleventh hour. Who's going to be sharing the couch with you instead? Hope it's only Cassandra, otherwise I shall I get jealous.'

'Spot on, Robbie. I thought watching the programme together would present the perfect opportunity for some mother and child bonding. A forlorn hope though, as it turns out. Renee was going to mind her while we went out to dinner, and Cass insists on still going to her grandma's as planned.' Lyndsey was unable to keep the catch out of her voice. She wondered if Robbie had noticed. His next words confirmed he had.

'Ssh, hen, don't take on so. She'll come round. Just give her time.'

As always his gentle, conciliatory tone made her want to cry. Rallying she said, 'Anyway, Coral and Dee want to come over instead. They kinda invited themselves, and it was difficult for me to wriggle out without alerting their suspicions as to my other plans. Which included you, the sofa, the programme, the chilled Chardonnay, the four poster bed...'

'Especially the bed...' he'd said, in that slow sexy way he had of talking.

Lyndsey smiled at the recollection. A secretive smile. A guilty smile. The type of smile shared by two people in love, which somehow managed to block the rest of the World.

Using her handbag as a makeshift umbrella, she ran up the pathway. Breathless, she joined Dee and Coral on the front step, fished the door key out of her pocket, and let the dripping duo into the house. They shook themselves like wet dogs, kicked off shoes, then hurried into the lounge. The programme was about to start.

Lyndsey switched on the TV, located Channel 7 and muted the sound. She hated the sound of her own voice, finding it high pitched and little girlish, and didn't want to hear it blaring around the living room. Dimming the lights helped to bathe the room in a rosy glow, and drawing the curtains cut out the glare from streetlamps through the murky dark.

Her friends had made themselves at home. Dee was tearing open a bumper bag of peanuts with her teeth, whilst Coral was beginning the customary hunt in every pocket for spectacles. As Lyndsey departed into the kitchen to load a tray with plates, wine glasses, serviettes and bottle opener she couldn't resist a wry smile to herself. Her two friends had put her forward for the programme they were all about to watch because they felt her sense of style had flown out the window, yet their choice of dress was hardly an advert for taste and elegance. Coral, living up to Ray's cruel labelling as the 'Oxfam Queen', was wearing an eclectic mix of brightly coloured scarves, embroidered peasant blouse, and gypsy skirt. Her wild perm, which could rival Gaynor's in terms of tangled frizz, thought Lyndsey, was pinned behind her ears in a haphazard fashion, revealing lobes stretched by the weight of hoops that wouldn't have looked out of place through the nose of a bull.

Feisty Dee, meanwhile, had garbed herself in a tight tunic dress of tomato red, which clashed with her orange streaked hair. Her long muscular legs, which Lyndsey noted could do with a shave, were stretched out across the coffee table, supported under the ankles with a strategically placed cushion. The programme had started. As the signature theme played and the opening credits rolled, Lyndsey squashed in between her two friends on the sofa, and slid the tray onto the remaining table space.

She hurriedly de-corked the wine, and poured them all a hefty measure. Drink blurred the edges of humiliation and dulled the sense of reality, and Lyndsey felt she needed both. Emptying the glass in one gulp, she sloshed in another generous slug of the warm Hungarian red.

'There you are,' screeched Dee suddenly, pointing at the TV screen. She rocked forward excitedly, causing Lyndsey to almost spill the wine. Coral began to wriggle about on the sofa, as though she were sitting on a bed of ball bearings. It was like sitting between two particularly excitable children, thought Lyndsey, as her friends started whooping with delight.

Savannah Hooper-Greenhill, her cream dress and fringed leather beat setting off the curtain of gold blonde hair and tanned skin to perfection, was saying, 'Today we are joined on the sofa by Lyndsey Daly from North London.'

Coral clapped. Dee almost choked on a mouthful of peanuts.

'You look bloody terrible Lyn.' Said the former.

'in dire need of their make-over' echoed the latter. Lyndsey had to agree. Her friends were right she thought. Sitting between the two glossy presenters on the TV screen, the camera lens zoomed in on her pallid face crowned by its spiky mane of grease. Her eyes looked huge; the circles underneath them even bigger.

Thalia Emmerson was saying, 'So Lyndsey how are you feeling at this very moment?'

She heard her screen self reply, 'I'm having kittens. A whole litter of them. This has got to be the most nerve wracking experience of my life.'

Lyndsey topped up her wine. 'How wrong could I have been' she thought, gamely hanging on to the stem of the glass as on either side, her two friends shoved and nudged in rapturous delight, 'being filmed wasn't the worst experience of my life. This is.'

Dee said, 'When this has finished Lyn, you're going to parade the entire new wardrobe so me and Coral can give the chosen togs our seal of approval.'

Coral raised her glass in a parody of salute, 'hear, hear. We can have a girl's dressing up session.'

Lyndsey opened her mouth to protest. Not only would the virgin clothes not fit her more amply proportioned friends, but she had also been prevailed upon by 'Turnaround's production team to keep them under cellophane wrap until the programme had been aired.

'It's essential you retain the garments in pristine condition,' she'd been told, 'until the day after the show is broadcast.'

When Lyndsey had ventured to ask why, the reply, from Gaynor, had been no-nonsense, 'because if Joe Public recognises you out on the streets, you need to be looking your best. Clothes, hair and make-up immaculate. Savvy and Thals have a reputation to uphold, don't forget.'

'As if I could,' Lyndsey thought glumly, watching as her baptism of fire by television unfolded on the screen. She stole a glance at Coral and Dee. They were transfixed.

Chapter Thirty

TWO ADULTS AND a child sat grouped around the television in the cosy sitting room of a ground floor maisonette. Renee Fairbrother got briskly to her feet and switched off the set. The closing theme of 'Turnaround' abruptly ceased its tuneful renderings. An awkward silence filled the room.

Ray said, with feeling, 'bloody bitch. She promised she wouldn't mention our marriage, and there she was on telly, blabbing about it to the nation.'

'Raymond, language please,' Renee was moved to protest, 'not in front of Cassie.' She didn't want the child to hear any denigration against her mother, particularly not from her father.

'Well, its true,' Ray sounded sulky, 'don't forget I have a job to do Reen. A very important, and respected job. People in the office now know the most intimate details of my private life. Even those that had the sense not to waste half an hour watching the salacious tripe we've just been forced to endure, will soon be au fait with the content. Gossip spreads like wildfire on the computer floor, both by mouth and Email. I'll be the laughing stock.'

'Don't exaggerate,' said Renee firmly, 'Lyn said nothing detrimental. All she mentioned was that the marriage was in difficulties and you were living apart.'

'Bah!' He almost spat the word, and both grandmother and grandchild flinched, 'why the need to open her stupid mouth at all. She should have told those bloody women to mind their own.'

Renee put a hand to her forehead, and rubbed distractedly. She could feel one of her migraines coming on.' I think the presenters are famed for being pretty forceful.' Turning to Cassandra, she said, with a brightness in her voice she didn't feel, 'How did you like Mummy on TV darling?'

'I think she's a prat.' Came the reply, spoken so quietly that for a moment Renee thought she hadn't heard right. To hear such a profanity issued from the lips of her waif like grand-daughter filled her with a disturbing sense of unease. And foreboding. As though the child's innocence was being sullied by a creeping disillusionment with life.

'I rest my case', said her son in law, with a note of triumph, 'even the kid sees her mother for what she is.'

Renee had had enough. Privately she thought her daughter had acquitted herself well on television, accepting the criticisms of her dress sense with good grace, and entering into the spirit of the programme. True, there were a few sticky moments, but then Lyndsey was not a natural TV performer and had been putty in the hands of seasoned pros like Hooper-Greenhill and Emmerson.

'For now I think we should let the subject rest. There's always tomorrow to talk about 'Turnaround' in more depth.' She said, refusing to meet her son in law's eyes, 'Come on Cassandra. Time for bed my dear. I hope it is simply a case of being overtired which made you say such a horrible thing about mummy,'

For once there was no wail of protest from the eleven year old about the prospect of an early night. She slid off the sofa, gave her father a good night kiss, and followed her grandmother meekly into the bathroom.

'Clean your teeth, and wash your face, sweetheart. Nana has put your nightie on the bed ready. Do you want a milky drink?'

This was answered by a mute shake of the head. Renee sighed. What ails the child so, she wondered. Surely it couldn't still be the loss of the dog, and she seemed to now accept her parent's separation with equanimity. Why the lack of enthusiasm about seeing her mother on television, and why such a negative response to the programme after it had been aired?

'What's going on in that funny little head of yours, hedgehog?' She asked kindly, handing Cassandra the toothpaste. Renee regarded the impish face in the bathroom mirror, saddened to see the grave expression which clouded the pert features.

'Nothing.' Said her grandchild, then, 'I love you Nana.'

Left alone in his mother-in-law's lounge, Raymond Daly sat and brooded. The weekend had got off to an inauspicious start. Torrential rain had caused the riverbank to collapse, and the fish not to bite, so he'd decided to throw in the rod and come home early leaving his fellow anglers to a damp night under canvas. His arrival at his mother-in-law's, wet and dispirited, had been tempered by the joy of finding Cassie in situ. That joy was quickly dissipated by the announcement, from Renee, that in ten minutes exactly, his wife was due to appear on television. Determined to dissect every nuance of the programme, he'd showered and changed in record time and had settled himself on the sofa next to Cassie as the opening credits for "Turnaround" rolled.

Now his mood was sour. His wife had made an abject fool of herself, and in so doing, had made a fool of him too. This was something Ray did not take lightly. He had an inflated sense of his own importance, which, married to a colossal ego, made him a force to be reckoned with when crossed. He felt Lyndsey had crossed him and he was angry. Very angry.

She'd looked pretty on the programme though, he had to admit that. Especially at the end of the show, when they'd filmed her professionally made up with an urchin haircut that he loved. Too skinny, sure, and her flat chest didn't help the clothes to hang right, but the makeover team had transformed her from the ugliest of ducklings into the most graceful of swans. He'd seen a glimpse of the woman he had courted, and fallen in love with. She was no longer the grey fluttering moth that he so despised, but had emerged from her chrysalis into a vibrantly beautifully butterfly. This fact only served to make him feel more pissed off than ever. She hadn't changed for him in all the years he'd wanted her to become something different, but had willingly undergone a metamorphosis for two plummy voiced TV presenters with whom she merely held a fleeting acquaintance. There was something very contemptuous about a wife who was prepared to change for strangers but not for her own husband. Something akin to rage at this breach of marital fidelity, began to boil within him.

He felt hot, as though he couldn't breathe. Ray got up and strode across to the window. He flung open the catch and leaned out, letting the heavy rain rinse his hair and neck. Steam rose from his skin in the muggy night air.

That week at work he'd been offered a temporary secondment to New York. The firm leased a suite of offices in downtown Manhattan, and wanted an IT expert to oversee the installation of a highly technical new computer system to replace the old one which continually crashed. Ray had been told he was the man they wanted. He'd already made a flying visit as trouble-shooter, but now they wanted him on a more permanent basis. The Company were prepared to pay him handsomely for such a move, and had promised to provide luxury accommodation and an executive car during his stay. His initial response had been negative. Whilst he was more than happy to leave his wife in Old Blighty indefinitely, he was not prepared to leave his daughter. Or his mother in law, and her ample blue veined breasts.

'Take a couple of days to think it over,' The Head of Department had said, 'it's a brilliant opportunity, and one a man of your calibre would be unwise to turn down.'

The Big Apple, Ray muttered to himself, head hanging out of the window. Was it more of a lure than Renee with her big tits?

The thought of them made his penis stiffen, as it always did, when he pictured her soaping them, the sponge moving methodically around those flat brown nipples until they became erect like twin pencil rubbers.

He dropped his hand to his trousers, and began to massage the rapidly swelling member that strained against the fly zip. He felt incredibly horny. The anger towards his wife over her appearance on 'Turnaround', the lust he felt for his mother in law, and the steamy damp of the evening, made a combustible cocktail of sexual desire within him. Cautiously he shut the window, and let the curtains fall back into place. Creeping to the door of the lounge he could hear muffled voices as Renee put Cassandra to bed. His need was now urgent. He knew he couldn't have her tonight with his daughter ensconced in the spare bedroom. When Cass stayed over, Ray was happy to kip down on the sofa which his mother in law always made into a comfortable makeshift bed for him. It was an arrangement that worked. Until tonight.

Tonight when his wife had betrayed him on prime time TV in front of the entire nation.

His cock felt huge. With thumb and forefinger he rubbed the shaft through the material of his casual trousers, feeling the muscles of his bottom contract deliciously with the sensation. Renee came out of the guest room and closed the door gently behind her. She traversed the tiny hallway into the bathroom, frowning as if deep in thought, unaware it seemed of her son in law watching from behind the door to her sitting room.

Ray seized his chance. For such a large man, he could move remarkably silently when so driven, and was already leaning against the shower cubicle before Renee saw him in the mirror and spun round. She had been replacing the lid on the toothpaste, and wiping the sink free of soap scum after her grand-daughter's bedtime ablutions.

With the speed and agility of an athlete he had pulled the door shut and slid the lock. Before his mother in law could protest, large male hands with their covering of red hair were pulling at the buttons of her blouse.

Oh God, thought Renee, throwing back her head in ecstasy, 'this is what I so badly needed. I want to be swept away. Swept away by a passion so intense that nothing else matters. Not Turnaround, nor Lyndsey, nor poor little Cass...' She felt overwhelmed by the sadnesses of those she loved the most, and needed a respite, however temporary. Passion made her forget her headache, forget the Ali Baba filled to overflowing with dirty washing, forget the fact that the one mauling her responsive body was the one person to whom such an action should be taboo. Her son in law.

His hands moved roughly over breasts freed from the confines of blouse and brassiere, his fingers kneading the cool orbs until they ached with pleasure. His groans were getting louder.

'Hush Raymond,' Renee pleaded, 'Cass might hear...' but her next words were sucked away by a spasm of delight as he fastened wet lips around her left nipple and began to suckle like a baby. When this happened, the years fell away from Renee in a rushing of blood through her ears, and she was young once again with an infant Lyndsey latched on her body. It was that wonderful time in her life when motherhood blotted out every other concern; where each day was spent in a blissful cocoon with her newborn.

She could hear his breathing becoming ragged, more gasping, and knew what was about to happen. It was now the predictable pattern of their lovemaking. No penetration was involved; no touching of each other's genitals. Just the frantic exploration of her bosom by the other's mouth, as he brought himself to climax with both hands. Semen spurted over the naked top half of her body, the heat of it scorching her skin.

'Mummy's milk' Raymond said, in a little boy voice, his tongue snuffling at the sticky white liquid until, within minutes, he had licked her dry.

Chapter Thirty One

CASSIE LAY ON top of the bed staring at the ceiling. It was too hot to get under the covers, the air in the room stifling. She'd asked to open the window, but Nana Reen wouldn't allow it.

'you never know who might be prowling about outside,' was the response in a firm voice that Cassie recognised brooked no argument. She stretched out on the bed and sighed, feeling wide awake and not a little petulant at her grandmother's insistence on an early night, when she wasn't in the slightest bit tired. Often when she stayed, Nana would get out an interesting tower of board games, and set up Scrabble, Monopoly, or Cluedo on the coffee table. Sometimes, this routine was varied with card games. Happy Families, Snap, Gin Rummy. Daddy would pour himself a brandy, Nana a sherry, and Cassie a bitter lemon as a special treat. They would play until late, keeping tally on a running score card, dipping into the bowl of assorted toffees her grandmother always put on the table. These cosy evenings together, in the soft lamplight, were the highlight of Cassandra's visits to the maisonette in Arnos Grove, and something she looked forward to all day. To have them curtailed by being packed off to bed early evoked within her a huge sense of disappointment. She slithered on the satin counterpane like a restless snake, and sighed once again. It was a sigh of a child expecting a huge gift on Christmas morning, and waking to find the tree bare of presents.

She knew she'd upset her grandmother. Knew that was why she'd been ordered so summarily to bed. Nana Reen made her disapproval clear if she said something bad about mummy. Tonight she'd said something very bad indeed. She'd called her mother a prat.

Nana Reen had been saddened by this. Cassie could tell, and she now wished she hadn't opened her mouth. Not because of any loyalty to her mother, but because she hated upsetting her Nana.

Mummy had been a prat though. Parading around on that silly TV programme as though she were a model, and squawking like a daft teenager in the changing rooms of all those posh shops. Fancy letting them film her in her underwear too. Cassie blushed scarlet at the memory of her own mother standing in front of the camera clad only in a white bra and pound shop knickers. She could imagine the reaction from classmates in school the coming Monday, and decided that she would wrangle a day off. She simply wouldn't be able to face the jeers, catcalls, and snide comments that Cass felt sure would inevitably be the result of Mrs. Daly appearing on national television in a programme such as 'Turnaround' where everybody made fun of how you looked.

At least that was how her eleven year old mind saw it. She had little conception of the adult nature of the show, and its role in helping people change their appearance for the better. To Cassie's way of thinking, her mother had set her own self up as an object of ridicule, and, by association, her daughter too.

Lying supine on the bed, she wished for a reason to seek out her grandma. What excuse could she give, for wheedling an extra half hour or so out of the day, and maybe inveigling her father in a game of Draughts? She couldn't plead the need for the toilet, since Nana Ren ensured she'd emptied her bladder, washed her hands and face, and cleaned her teeth before bed. Nor could she rely on the age old standby of a glass of water, since by the bed was a jug of it with a glass put there by her grandmother in case she got thirsty in the night.

Cassandra did a few experimental somersaults on the bed. The discovery was quickly made that this required too much energy, and the exertion left her limp and breathless. She did a headstand on the pillow, walking her bare feet slowly up the flock wallpaper until they were outstretched enough to support her weight. For several minutes she remained thus, until a rush of dizzying blood to the head caused her to flop back on the counterpane.

She stared up the ceiling counting the decorative swirls in the plaster, wondering as she did so, why everything was so quiet. There were no muted sounds of the television, or Radio 4 which her grandmother and father often listened to late at night. She couldn't hear the clink of cutlery from the kitchen, nor crockery being put away. There was no murmur of voices, and Cass wondered if Nana Reen was upset with daddy as well as herself for his nasty comments about mummy's performance on TV. In the clammy dark of the bedroom, all was silent.

Cassandra reached out and switched on the bedside light. She poured herself a tumbler of water, and sipped reflectively. Then she heard something. It sounded like groaning. As though someone had toothache, or tummy upset. She remembered groaning like that when she'd been hit full in the stomach by a ball when watching boys play footie in the park. As if all the wind had been knocked out of her body, gasping as the fish did when daddy reeled them out the water during their shared fishing expeditions. The sound was coming from the bathroom.

Tentatively she slipped off the bed, and put her ear to the wall. There it was again, louder this time, the unmistakeable noise of someone in agony. It seemed to be coming from somewhere higher up. Was someone ill in the flat above?

Cass pulled across the bedside chair, discarding the neat pile of clothing on top in her rush to clamber onto the seat. She straightened up, and found herself staring at a picture on the wall of the family's day out to Alton Towers photographed the year before. Nana Reen had snapped Cassandra and her parents exiting the Log Flume. They were laughing with exhilaration, soaking wet from the water splash finale. It had been a happy day. The last truly happy one Cassandra could remember with her mother and father.

She took the picture off the wall, and regarded it with studied concentration. Was there a glimmer of something in those adult faces that she hadn't seen at the time? A foreshadowing of the unhappiness to come? Did Mrs. Daly know on that bright summer day's outing to the theme park, that she no longer wanted to be part of Mr. Daly's life?

A cry made her almost drop the picture. Startled she turned. This was a new sound, altogether different from the groaning. As though someone were strangling a cat in the bathroom next door. Then Cass saw it. In the middle of the wall where the picture had hung was a magnified spy glass. She knew what it was because they had one on the front door at Shenlagh Gardens, and her mother always peered through it to check the identity of any caller before unlatching the chain. Standing on tiptoe, Cassandra put her eye to the hole.

Renee said, 'Raymond, this can't go on.' Even to her own ears, her voice sounded as though it were coming from a long way off.

'Why?'

Her son in law was still nestled between her naked breasts. She dug her fingers into the tousled red hair and yanked his head up. Levelly she met his eyes, reading a mixture of pain and pleasure mirrored in their depths.

'It is so wrong of us. Surely you know that?'

'Come off it Reen. You enjoy it as much as I do.'

'That's not the point.'

'Tell me what is then. If you didn't want any of this to happen, why did you let me touch you in the first place. You didn't put up much of a fight that first night if I remember.'

The dancing seahorses on the patterned bathroom tiles seemed to be watching her; mocking her. She sank down, and perched herself uncomfortably on the edge of the bath. Even through the material of her skirt, the rim felt cold against her bottom. Her son in law had slid down with her, and now knelt at her feet, looking faintly ridiculous she thought, with his trousers and underpants around ankles clad in socks.

'No I didn't' she agreed before taking a deep breath and continuing, 'I can't pretend I didn't enjoy the intimacy and physical contact with a man after being alone all these years. Even though that man was married to my only child. Such a relationship to my daughter should have precluded any such liaison, I know, but…..'

'But what?'

'I can't pretend I didn't find you attractive Raymond. Still do. You are a very masculine man, quite unlike my poor Doug, God Rest his Soul. The obvious delight you gained from my body was flattering, I admit it, especially to a woman of my age. One begins to doubt one's sexual allure as the years roll by. To have such a fine specimen of manhood, in his undoubted prime, wanting and needing to undress me, caress my naked flesh…'

'Careful mother in law dearest. You'll be giving me another hard on.'

'Don't make light of this Ray. It is difficult enough for me to say as it is. Aside from my own feelings of passion, there was another reason why I welcomed your advances.'

His hands had moved up to her breasts once more, and were stroking them gently.

'Don't.' Her tone was sharp. Renee prised his fingers off her skin, and clutched them tightly, 'the reason concerned Lyndsey.'

She guessed the mention of her daughter's name would stop him in his tracks, and it did.

'What about Lyndsey?' He said in a voice that sounded suddenly sulky, like a fractious child.

Gazing into his eyes, with their fringe of sandy lashes, Renee pressed on. She had to take advantage of his full attention.

'I thought it would save your marriage. If I allowed you to use me as a release for your sexual tension. When you first moved in here Raymond, I knew you were a volcano about to erupt. There were all these emotions and desires bubbling away within you, not to mention feelings of hurt, and I desperately wanted to stop you punishing Lyndsey for consulting a solicitor behind your back. The day you moved in, I started to unpack your suitcase; make you feel at home. There was a magazine underneath your shirts. I'm sure you know which one I'm referring to. I think they are politely called 'top shelf' reading material, and the cover alone was deeply shocking, featuring as it did a nude woman massaging her own breasts.'

Her son in law had sat back on his haunches at these words, his face flushed an angry brick red. Renee noticed that his penis was hanging limp and spent over the bathroom carpet. She wished he'd put it away.

Averting her eyes, she hurriedly continued, 'my concern was that your level of sexual frustration would drive you into the arms of another woman. An affair would surely have wrecked any vestige of hope that the marriage might be saved, especially if Lyndsey had found out, which I was terrified she would. So I thought, why not me? Why don't I let him use me as a release for his passions? At least that way, I reasoned I could exert a modicum of control over the situation; stop things spiralling out of hand. As long as I could keep it secret from my daughter, I felt it was an arrangement that might work. Your libido would get satisfied without the need for a potentially dangerous fling with a woman who might, out of spite, spill the beans to your wife.'

'I could have gone to a prostitute. Sex without commitment.'

'That would have been worse. You might have picked up a disease, or heaven forbid, contracted Aids. Where would my daughter be then?'

Renee was relieved when her son in law got to his feet. He pulled up pants, and trousers, and zipped up the fly.

'So let me get this right, mother in law.' He sneered down at her, 'you let me get my rocks off with you to protect your daughter. Oh, that's rich.'

She winced at the sound of his laughter, for it was a mocking laugh quite devoid of any humour.

'Don't worry. I won't touch you again if you don't want it.' He said, turning for the door. Hand on handle he paused. Renee gulped. Tears seemed perilously close. She couldn't bear to hear any more.

'I've been offered a job in our New York office. Turned it down mainly because I didn't want to leave you. What a fool I was.'

'New York...' Renee found herself echoing faintly, 'what about Lyndsey? Cassandra?'

'Do you think I still care for Lyn? Not after tonight I don't. Not after watching her expose on national television, deriding herself in front of the great unwashed. No Reen dearest, the only thing stopping me now from jumping on the first plane out to JFK is my kid. Somehow I've got to stop Cassandra turning out a carbon copy of her mother and evil bitch grandmother.'

Renee felt faint. She clutched at the towel rail for support. Her son-in- law looked her full in the face, and something unfathomable glittered in the depth of his eyes. Then she knew what it was. Contempt.

He opened the door and smiled in a patronising way, revealing a wolfish row of teeth,

'You can put your tits away.'

Cassandra ran across the moonlit lawn that ringed the block of maisonettes, her fleeing form throwing a gigantic shadow across the grass. It was a strange shadow she thought, in an almost detached way, watching as it kept apace with her. In the hooded coat, Wellingtons and bag on her back, she looked like a wicked troll in a fairy tale, or perhaps the Hunchback of Notre Dame. She galloped in a frenzied manner, her feet beating the turf. Unsure of where she was headed, only knowing that she had to put the greatest distance between herself and that dreadful scene witnessed in the bathroom whilst her courage held. At the perimeter wall she clambered over, skinning bare knees on the rough edged bricks, before dropping down to the other side. Stumbling, Cassie picked herself up and ran on, narrowly avoiding a collision with a row of parked wheelie bins which loomed up out of the dark like a row of soldiers on sentry duty. The handbag, strung over her back with its shoulder strap, beat a painful rhythm against her thin shoulder blades, but still her legs continued to pound, covering the ground in reckless haste. Ahead lay an alleyway which she knew came out onto the main road. It would only take her a few short minutes to get from there to Arnos Grove tube station. She careered down it, her thick rubber soles crunching on gravel and broken grass. The rain had abated, but she kept up the hood of the Eskimo coat which acted like blinkers on a horse, keeping her eyes focussed firmly in front. Halfway down the alley, she disturbed a pair of mating cats. They screeched angrily in protest, eyes slits of luminosity in the dark, and she felt a paw reach out to scratch her leg. The sound they made reminded her of..... No, No, she told herself frantically. She mustn't think of that. Not now. Later maybe, when she had successfully gotten away.

At the end of the passageway, a man was smoking a cigarette. He was leaning against the brickwork, taking deep puffs. His figure threw a looming shadow on the wall. Cassandra faltered. Might he steal the handbag and try to pull off her coat? At this thought, her resolve stiffened. She was WonderCassie, with invincible powers. Not the caped crusader, but a hooded one. A superhero in an Eskimo jacket. If the man with the cigarette tried to grab her, she would disable him with a single kick from her red Wellingtons.

Cassandra concentrated on their glossy tips, leaving the alleyway and the smoker behind. Streetlights on the main thoroughfare were reflected in her boots, and she began a staccato chant to keep pace with her legs, 'salt, mustard, vinegar, pepper....' Over and over again she repeated the mantra, until she caught sight of the familiar tube sign ahead. Her mother always told her the Underground symbol was like a raspberry pie with a blackcurrant jam centre. There was something reassuring about the knowledge that here was the entrance to a vast underground network, in which she could easily conceal herself from discovery. Cassie felt like a rabbit, being pursued by a farmer with a gun, disappearing into the safety of its warren. She started singing, *'run rabbit, run rabbit, run, run, run, don't give the farmer his fun fun fun, he'll get by without his rabbit pie, so run rabbit run rabbit, run run run....* At the tube station, she paused, clutching at the roadside railings, her breath coming in ragged gasps. It was necessary to compose herself, that much she knew. Someone who looked as though they had been running was liable to draw attention and the last thing she wanted was attract the glances of the curious. Scrabbling in her grandmother's handbag, taken from the telephone table as she made her getaway from the maisonette, Cassandra located some coins and fed the ticket machine. Then she was through the automated barrier, and hurrying down to the depths below. The Southbound platform of the Piccadilly line was virtually deserted, save for a man reading a newspaper at the far end, and two swarthy foreign looking women consulting a tourist guide. Cassie sat down on a bench, pulling her coat down over her knees so only the frill of her nightdress protruded. The hood concealed her pinched white face, and wild staring eyes. In her panic to escape the horrifying scene she had witnessed between her grandmother and father, she hadn't thought to dress, merely donning the coat over her night attire, and pausing at the front door to slip on the spare pair of Wellingtons that were always kept by the porch in case she stayed over during wet weather. As she began to recover from her frantic flight, the realisation dawned that she wasn't wearing any knickers. A warm gritty gust of wind issuing from the tunnel signalled the imminent arrival of the train, and lifted the hem of her nightie. She felt terribly self-conscious and exposed. As though everyone could see her bare bum. Suddenly she could see her own father's naked bottom through the spyhole again, its deep ginger cleft shuddering. Could see the muscles clenching and relaxing as he slobbered over her grandmother's titties. They had been bare too. Cassie squeezed her eyes shut, trying to force away the picture of those giant blobs with their bulls eye centres, and her father's hands kneading them as though he were a baker getting bread ready for the oven. As the train rattled into the platform, she was violently sick over the sleeve of her coat at the memory. Shakily, Cassandra got to her feet, the Wellingtons squeaking in protest. Her hand went to the pocket, where the reassuring feel of the slip of paper made her feel marginally better. She knew what was written on the paper. A place name she had read and re-read what seemed like a million times. Her mind went swiftly back to the day when she had hidden at the top of the stairs eavesdropping whilst her mother spoke to the animal sanctuary about Mozart. She heard where his owners lived. Where they were taking her beloved Alsatian. The place where she was now headed. The place carefully written in her childish hand on a piece of paper, and kept ever since that day in the safe environs of her coat pocket.

Stansted Mountfichet.

Chapter Thirty Two

LATE THE NEXT morning, Lyndsey was awoken by a persistent ring on the doorbell. She groaned and sat up in bed, holding a clenched fist to her temple. A throbbing headache gripped her in a painful vice, and she yelped loudly. God, how much did I drink last night, she thought, having a vague recollection of a row of empty wine bottles on the table, and herself, Dee and Coral talking incomprehensible nonsense. Their 'girls' night in' had degenerated into a drunken series of reminiscences into the early hours. At one point, she could remember Dee (or was it Coral?) announcing, to no-one in particular, 'I'm nissed as a picket.', and laughing like a hyena at this spoonerism. Beginning to get maudlin, they'd moved onto the drinks cabinet, swilling down gin and vodka with a variety of mixers. Lime, Orange, and even Pineapple juice. Wincing at both the memory, and her raging head, Lyndsey peeled back the crumpled bedcovers and slowly and unsteadily got to her feet. Whoever was at the door had given up ringing and was now banging it so forcefully, Lyndsey felt sure the glass fanlight would shatter. The whole house seemed to reverberate, and her head most of all. 'All right, all right, I'm coming,' she muttered, trying to focus bleary eyes on the bedside clock. The illuminated numbers swam alarmingly into her line of vision before settling into discernible digits. 10.05am. Managing to locate only one slipper, she hobbled across the floor and out onto the landing, draping a dressing gown over her shoulders as she went. She guessed it was Dee back to collect her car. Her friend had been in no fit state to drive herself and Coral home the night before, so Lyndsey insisted on calling a taxi. When Dee had drunkenly protested, claiming that she was 'perfeckly fit to drife...' Lyndsey had snatched the car keys and hidden them behind the hall radiator. Making her way downstairs to answer the door, she reflected on the programme the night before. Her performance on 'Turnaround' had not been nearly so bad as imagined, and she felt, as the final credits rolled, that she had acquitted herself well. Coral and Dee had been fulsome in their praise, 'Lyn, you were ace,' said the former, 'kept your cool throughout, and looked absolutely stunning at the end.'

'Hear, hear', agreed the latter, 'We're so proud. You didn't let us down for getting you on the show, and didn't let yourself down either. Even Savannah and Thalia were speechless with shock when they saw your final transformation. They were grinning like Cheshire cats...'

At the bottom of the stairs, she caught sight of her reflection in the hall mirror. Her hair was standing on end as though she'd put a finger in a plug socket, and her skin had a yellow liverish look from a surfeit of alcohol, 'God, I look wrecked..' she thought, 'if only Savvy and Thals could see me now.' Through the frosted glass pane of the door, she could see the outline of two heads. Puzzled at first, she quickly realised that it must be Dee and her husband. Obviously he would have driven her over to pick up her own car. She unhooked the chain and slid the bolt. On the doorstep stood her mother and estranged husband. They were white faced, and trembling. Taken aback, Lyndsey said, 'Mum.... Ray... whatever's wrong?'

Ray pushed past her into the house. Renee followed. The trio stood illuminated in the morning sunshine that pooled through the door. After the preceding rain sodden week, the weather had miraculously cleared. Lyndsey blinked. The harsh sunlight hurt her eyes and made her head ache worse, but that was not the reason for her gripping the newel post as though it were a rock in a tidal wave. She felt suddenly very frightened by the ghastly expressions on the two faces that confronted her. Ray said, and his voice sounded hoarse, 'Cassie. Is she here?'

'No, of course not. Why should she be? She's staying over at Mums, and you're supposed to be away with the weekend anglers.'

There was a hideous silence. Fear clutched at Lyndsey heart.

'She's gone'

'Gone.' Stupidly Lyndsey found herself repeating the word.

She grasped Renee by the arm and shook her frantically, 'Mum, what's going on?'

'Darling, I'm so sorry.' Abruptly her mother sat down on the bottom stair, and buried her face in her hands. A strangled sob issued from between her clenched fingers. She said, in a voice that sounded ragged, as though the words hurt to speak them, 'I checked her last night. She was fast asleep. Then I took her in her early morning cuppa, and went to shake her gently by the shoulder....and....'

'And what?'

'She wasn't there. Just a mound of pillows, strategically placed to look as though someone were in bed.'

'Oh my God.' Lyndsey slid to the floor and clutched her mother's skirt.

'We'd better ring the Police.' Ray was already picking up the phone and dialling 999. As he waited for it connect, Lyndsey heard him say,

'this is all your fault Lyn.'

'My fault....?'

'Yes. If anything has happened to our child, I will hold you fully responsible. Some kind of mother huh! She was so upset seeing you make such a ridiculous spectacle of yourself on TV last night, that she's obviously run away. Can't face her schoolmates, and who can blame her? For two pins, I'd sod off too if it meant I didn't have to deal with the tittle tattle in the office tomorrow.' He mimicked the high pitched voice of a woman, 'Oh Mr. Daly, was that YOUR wife we all saw on telly Saturday?'

In the shocked silence that followed this accusation, the metallic voice of an operator could be heard, 'emergency services.'

'Police please.' said Ray, and then, 'I wish to report a missing child. My eleven year old daughter.'

'Where can she have gone.' Renee began to wail, and Lyndsey, used to her mother being cool in a crisis, was doubly frightened by this apparent loss of control, 'we felt sure she would have come home.'

'Has she got any money?'

'Yes. Darling, she took my bag. There was fifty pounds in it.'

'The Police want a description of what she might be wearing.' Ray interrupted them.

Ignoring Lyndsey, he directed the question at his mother in law who babbled, 'A nightdress with a doggie print, the blue puffa coat, and a pair of red wellies.'

Ray relayed this information, before giving out Cassandra's full name, address and date of birth.

'They're putting out a bulletin, and emergency call to all units.' He said, hanging up the receiver, 'a pair of coppers are on their way over to take a statement.'

This is a nightmare, thought Lyndsey. Surely she would wake up in a minute and find herself lying in bed, free from a hangover, and free from this paralysing terror. She imagined her precious child lost and frightened in the night, she imagined her lying injured in a ditch, she imagined something much much worse...

'Talk to me, Mum, or I'll scream. Tell me Ray's wrong. Cass can't have run off because of 'Turnaround'.'

'She did seem upset by the programme darling.'

'Upset enough to go off into the dark, without even stopping to dress first?'

'Oh Lyn, you know how disturbed she has been lately, what with problems settling at secondary school, and you and Raymond splitting. Maybe seeing you on tv just tipped her over the edge.'

Although grateful to her mother for avoiding mention of the Alsatian whose brief foray into his daughter's life Raymond was still unaware, Lyndsey still fought back an urge to scream. She shoved a fist in her mouth to stop herself succumbing to hysteria, and bit hard on the knuckles. Needles of pain shot through her hand, but it was nothing compared to the pain that seemed to be piercing a bloody hole in the centre of her being.

'All of which can be laid at your door, my darling wife.' Said Ray from somewhere above her head, and was it her imagination, or could Lyndsey detect a note of triumph in his voice?

The phone rang. Startled all three seemed frozen to the spot, unable to move. Was it Cassie? Ringing from some lonely phone box for someone to come and collect her?

Lyndsey sprang into action, momentarily ahead of her mother and husband. She slammed the receiver to her ear, 'Darling, is it you..?'

'Aye hen. Just ringing to say congratulations on your TV performance.'

Disappointment and despair flooded her at the sound of Robbie's voice. Normally she would be overjoyed to receive his call, but at this moment he was the last person on earth she wanted to talk to. Guilt hammered her heart as she thought of the times she had lain in his arms, whilst Cassie had been at school, or packed off to her grandma. Time spent with him should have been time spent with her precious child. A child that was missing.

'I can't talk now,' she said woodenly, 'something's happened. Sorry Robbie.' The phone dropped from her hand, and clattered to the floor.

Another silence. This time an awkward and ugly one. Her mother broke it, 'I'll make us a strong pot of tea while we wait for the Police. Give me something to do. If I sit here a moment longer, I swear I'll go stark staring mad.'

Left alone with her husband in the sunny hallway, Lyndsey was unable to meet his eyes. She knew what she would see there. Hatred. Disillusionment. Maybe a thirst for vengeance.

'I'd better go and get dressed.' She mumbled, and ducked underneath his outstretched arm. Halfway up the stairs she heard his voice float up behind her,

'Who the fuck is Robbie?"

Cassie picked at the scab on her knee. Her legs felt sore, and the deep scratch, inflicted by the mating cat, itched uncontrollably. She was hungry and tired to the point of exhaustion. Sitting in the back seat of the taxi, she forced herself to stay awake by concentrating on the unfolding scenery out of the window. Planes were flying low overhead as they prepared for landing, the noise of their engines deafening that of the cab. With the insulating properties of a sleeping bag, the Eskimo coat had kept her warm all night, but now in the full glare of the morning sun, she was uncomfortably hot. Sweat trickled down from her hairline, concealed under the hood and run down her forehead, into eyes that were dilated with fatigue, the pupils enormous black dots. Cassie blinked, and wiped them with her sleeve, recoiling momentarily at the pungent aroma of dried vomit on the cuffs. In the driver's mirror, she caught sight of the man behind the wheel watching her, a puzzled expression on his face. Quickly she dropped her arm, and stared fixedly out of the window. She didn't want him to think she was crying. He might start asking awkward questions, like 'what's the matter little girl' such as the elderly couple had asked when she'd got off the tube at the main Liverpool Street concourse the night before. Except they had said, 'are you lost lovey?'

Cassie had ignored them, walking purposefully towards the departure gates for the Stansted Express, muttering loudly. Olu had once told her at school that the way to get a seat on the bus was to act like a loony. Apparently people gave a wide berth to anyone who talked to themselves. She had found this piece of advice worked like a charm. All the way on the Piccadilly Line into Holborn where she had changed onto the Central Lane, Cassie had kept up a constant monologue. Apart from a few wary and sympathetic glances shot in her direction, no one had made any approach.

The link train with the airport had taken precisely 41 minutes to reach its destination. To give herself something to do, she had timed it on her watch. The train was exactly as she had remembered from the year before, when the family had taken the rail service on their journey to Stansted to catch the flight to Spain. Her father had borrowed a private villa in a town called Benalmadena for two weeks from the Chairman of his Company. Cassie had practised the spelling of it, looking up the region of Andalucia on the Atlas in Daddy's study prior to departure. She was good at finding places on a map.

Locating Stansted Mountfichet had posed no problem. She correctly guessed that it was situated near the airport of the same name, just off a big blue road called the M11. During a Geography lesson at school, she had searched the village on the internet and discovered it dated back from Saxon times, where its name had come from 'stan' meaning a stone, and 'sted' meaning a place. Not only did it possess a windmill, but also a castle dated back from the 11th century of the 'ring and bailey' type. Cassie had no idea what a ring and bailey meant, but she hoped to discover the whereabouts of Mozart nearby.

She'd spent the night at the airport, flitting from one group of waiting passengers, to the next, so as not to alert the security guards who constantly patrolled the perimeter. People looked at her curiously, but she averted her eyes, and started the muttering, relieved to find that they quickly looked away. She guessed she must present a curious picture to the holidaymakers waiting to be called for their flights, with her bare bloodied legs, nightie with trailing hem, gumboots, and hooded jacket, but did not care. As long as they left her alone, she was happy.

In the morning, she waited as long as she dared before plodding dispiritedly to the signposted taxi rank. Leaving too early might seem odd to any driver, and she didn't want to excite any nosy parkers. Her plan was to find Mozart, steal him away, and then, together with her dog, head off to the West Country. She'd always loved Cornwall, and felt, that at the tail end of England, no one would think to look for her there. How she was going to get there, and how she would live,

Cassie hadn't yet worked out. For now, all she wanted to do was reclaim ownership of the Alsatian.

Outside the window, the taxi had left the M11 motorway, and was heading deep into the countryside. The sun burned through gaps in the trees, every so often disappearing from view as they rounded a bend, as though it were involved in a game of 'catch me if you can.' In the fields that stretched out either side of the road, herds of Friesen cattle grazed, and Cassie idly counted their black and white forms.

She knew she wasn't going home. Not ever. Not back to Shenlagh Gardens and her mother, nor back to Nana Reen's with her grandmother and father. The three people she relied on most in the world had shown themselves to be cut out dolls made of paper, as unreliable and undependable as a balloon in a breeze. Her implicit trust had been broken, and in her eleven year old mind, could never be repaired.

In the heat of the taxi, tiredness overcame her, and she began to doze. Disturbing visions peppered her sleep. Devils with horns, and bare bottoms painted red. Swirls of smoke. The smoke cleared, and she was watching a TV screen.

'This is Turnaround' said a voice, 'tonight we welcome Lyndsey Daly, a librarian from North London.' Only the presenters were not the two posh women, but instead Nana Reen and her father. Nana Reen had her boobs on show, and her father was stroking them with his microphone. His trousers were down around his ankles, and Cassie could see his big white willy waving about as though it was a snake being hypnotised by a charmer. Her mother came on with Mozart on a lead. He had ribbons threaded through his fur, and was wearing a tutu skirt like a circus dog. On all four paws were red Wellingtons.

'Look what I've done to with this miserable stray,' her mother was saying, 'I've given him a makeover..'

'Stop it,' Cassie found herself shouting, 'Mummy, leave him alone. He's a dog not a birthday cake. Take off those decorations.'

'Shall I take off my panties instead, darling.' Said her grandmother. Cassie looked down in horror and realised that her own knickers had gone, and her private parts were exposed for everyone to see. One of the devils came over with a can of red paint and began sloshing it over the lower half of her body,

'Turnaround so we can do your bum.' He said.

Cassie woke up with a start. She was bathed in sweat, and her mouth felt dry and gritty as though she'd been feasting on sand.

The taxi had come to a halt, its engine idling. They were outside a Church, the spire piercing a sky of untrammelled blue.

'Welcome to St. John the Evangelist' read the sign beyond the wall.

'We've arrived in Stansted Mountfichet pet.' Said the driver, sliding across the glass partition. 'Where to now.'

Cassie picked up her grandmother's handbag, and slid her damp rear off the seat. She took out a wad of notes and thrust it through the windows, 'this is the place.'

Without waiting for change, or an answer, she opened the door and jumped out. Conscious of the driver making no attempt to move off, Cassie, delivered what she hoped was a parting shot,

'My daddy's the vicar.'

Cassandra decided to ask the Lord Jesus where to go next. Surely HE would know where Mozart lived. After all, HE was supposed to be all seeing, all knowing. The RI teacher at Brackendale High had a word for it - 'omni- something or other.'

She pushed on the heavy doors and entered the cool inner sanctum of the church. It was a blissful relief after the glare of the sun. Her footsteps sounded unnaturally loud, and they echoed around the vaulted roof, as though she were an elephant not an eleven year old who was extra small for their age. Selecting a pew, she slid across, and marked herself with the sign of the cross. Although not sure of the significance, she'd seen congregations do this on religious programmes. Importantly, she clasped her hands together and began to pray aloud,

'Dear Lord Jesus,' she said, with a confidence she did not entirely feel, 'You probably don't know me very well, but my name is Cassandra Louise Daly and I need to find my dog. Well, he's not actually my dog, not in a belonging sense of the word. I mean I don't actually own him. But I love him Lord Jesus, and he loves me. He is lonely without me like you were out in that wilderness place where the devil kept tempting you with apples. Least I think it was apples. Or was that Eve in the Garden with Adam? Anyway, he lives somewhere in this village. His real name is Bart. Can you lead me to him, kind and gentle Jesus, and I promise to go to Church every Sunday for ever and ever, Amen.'

It smelt musty and chalky in the nave, like one of the classrooms at school. Cassie would liked to have stayed a little longer, and maybe sang a verse of 'All things Bright and Beautiful' just to prove to God that she knew some of the words and was therefore deserving of some heavenly assistance, but she badly needed a wee. She hadn't been since finding the ladies toilets at Liverpool Street station.

She got up, crossed herself again, and made her way up the aisle. Someone had entered the Church, and was paused at the top of the steps looking at her. They were bathed in coloured light from the stained glass window, and for a moment Cassie thought it was an Angel sent to guide her. She went to move past, but they barred her way with outstretched arms, throwing a shadow across the polished wood floor, that to her youthful eyes, looked like Jesus on the cross. Cassandra was convinced it was the Angel Gabriel, and knelt at the figure's feet on her sore knees.

'Get up please.' The voice was gruff but kindly.

Humbly, she stood up.

'You're probably one of those feral children I read about in the newspapers. Let's see what you have hidden inside. A couple of hymn books maybe, or our pewter candlesticks.'

Was the figure accusing her of stealing? It was difficult to make out the angel's features, lit as it was from behind.

'I haven't pinched nothing.' She said stoutly, feeling the need to defend herself.

'You'd better come along with me anyway, young lady.' Still the voice was gruff. A hand landed on Cassie's shoulder.

'Are you going to help me kind Angel?' She asked, trustingly.

'I hope so, my child.'

Chapter Thirty Three

LYNDSEY WAS SITTING in a private room at the local Police station. Her face was taut with suppressed emotion.

It was now half past two in the afternoon, and no word had yet been reached of Cassandra's whereabouts. The child's description had been circularised to every force nationwide, and a unit from the metropolitan division were out combing the environs of Arnos Grove. Tracker dogs were searching the nearby woods at Enfield Chase.

On the advice of the Detective Inspector who was overseeing the hive of activity in the Incident Room, Lyndsey was diverting all incoming calls on her mobile phone onto the answerphone, unless they showed a private number. The hope was that Cassandra would ring her mother from a call box.

'I wanted to get her a mobile for her birthday.' She said in answer to the D.I.'s questioning, 'but my husband felt she might present a soft target for snatch thieves who prey on youngsters. Cass is small for her age you see, and not at all streetwise.'

Raymond and Renee had both been taken into separate rooms to give their statements. Lyndsey was interviewed by the D.I., who whilst seeming to have a sympathetic manner, was brusque and to the point.

'Did your daughter have any reason to run away?'

'Yes', she'd said dully, before going on to elaborate upon them. The minutes ticked away in the impersonal room, with its green painted walls, and rows of filing cabinets. Blinds had been drawn in an attempt to blot out the sun, yet the heat was still unbearable. A revolving fan seemed simply to move the air rather than cool it. Another call came through on her mobile. She recognised the number. Robbie McCrae. He'd rang several times since she'd hung up on him that morning. Only a few hours ago, yet already it seemed a lifetime. Her liaison with him, and her appearance on 'Turnaround' had taken on a surreal element, as though they had happened to someone else, not to her. She felt strangely detached from the Lyndsey Daly of the day before. That person hadn't lost her precious child.

This person had. She sipped at the cup of tea brought in for her by a motherly Policewoman, trying to quell mounting panic. The same lady had earlier given her two aspirins, when Lyndsey's worsening headache had threatened to blow her skull apart.

'Let's just go through it one more time, Mrs. Daly.' The D.I. said.

Cassandra had decided the figure wasn't the Angel Gabriel after all. As soon as they'd stepped out of the ethereal light cast by the gothic arched window she saw that it was just an ordinary person. There was no discernible golden aura, and certainly no evidence of a halo. Luckily the heavy oak doors had been propped open with a cast iron boot scraper, so she seized her chance and made a run for it.

The Angel imposter chased her, but Cassandra was young and nimble, and fear gave extra propulsion. She ran blindly away from the Church, her grandmother's bag bumping on the pavement behind. At the end of the road she turned left, zig zagging downhill like a skier doing a slalam course. Her bladder was now at bursting point. Skidding to a halt, Cassandra climbed over a wall into landscaped gardens, the centrepiece of which was an impressive War Memorial. Unable to wait any longer, she lifted her nightie and squatted down out of sight behind a tree. As the stream of urine petered out, she noticed a plaque which commemorated VE day at the base of the trunk. Misery engulfed her tiny form. Not only had she upset God, she thought, but she had now upset those poor dead soldiers too.

Back out on the road, she trudged onwards, pausing at the sign for Chapel Hill to remove a stone from her boot. It had cut the sole of her foot, so now she began to limp. The early Spring sun beat relentlessly on the hood of her coat, making Cass feel slightly sick, but whether it was from hunger she could not tell. Certainly her stomach was making strange grumbling noises, as though protesting at this perceived neglect. At the bottom of the hill, she turned left into Lower Street. She had no idea where she was, and experienced the beginnings of delirium from the heat and dehydration. She had thought a village meant a couple of cottages, with maybe a pub and post office, which would make finding Mozart a simple matter of elimination but Stansted Mountfichet seemed a vast place. Houses were everywhere, some old fashioned with black beams and swirly plaster, like the ones she'd seen in her father's 'Reader's Digest Guide to Britain', and some were more modern. There were tall houses and short ones, cottages and terraces, and a preponderance of pubs. She was passing one now. Cassandra looked longingly at the sign. 'The Dog and Duck'. She wished she could go in and buy a coke but knew there was no money left in her grandmother's bag. Her legs ached. She spied a gap between two houses, barely wide enough to pass through with a bicycle. It looked invitingly cool and dark, like a secret tunnel. Taking a furtive look each way up the deserted street, she limped inside.

An ant crawling across her face, woke Cassie. She felt stiff and sore. It took her several seconds to remember where she was. Getting to her feet, she swayed a little, and had to lean on the damp brickwork of the passageway. The dizziness passed, but she still felt faintly disorientated like when she'd got off the Log Flume at Alton Towers.

She staggered out into the street as though drunk. There was nobody about. Cassie guessed they were sleeping off the effects of Sunday roasts, or having high tea. The sort of teas her grandmother sometimes made, with sandwiches cut into triangles, and slabs of fruit cake. Angrily, she pinched herself on the wrist. Nana Reen, with her bare titties had to be banished from her thoughts, along with the vision of daddy and his naked posterior. She checked her watch, taking care not to falter. Six o'clock. The shadows had lengthened, but the air still felt moist and heavy as if someone were patting her head with a sponge. Like an automaton she continued to walk on jelly legs that didn't feel connected to her body. Although still fierce, the hood of her coat acted like a visor from the sun, protecting her delicate tip tilted nose from burning. There was a stale smell to the air, and a blocked drain by the roadside gave off the fetid stench of sewage. Cassie clutched at her stomach.

Somewhere in the distance she heard the siren of a police car. It set off a dog barking.

A dog… A spurt of excitement travelled through her body. There it was again, a low throaty sort of bark, just the sort of noise a big breed would make. It was near. Very near.

Cassandra broke into a trot, hardly noticing the pain from her cut foot. She passed one house, two houses, three.

'Whoa there, young lady.' A voice behind her called. She recognised the voice at once. The gruff tones of the figure in the Church, and, risking a glance over her shoulder, saw a body bearing down on her astride a pushbike. Cass tried to out-run the cyclist but the pavement became like a stretch of marshland, sucking at her Wellingtons. She began to sob with a mixture of frustration and weariness. The bicycle swerved in front of her, blocking her path.

'Here wipe your nose on this.' The tall lady said gruffly. She withdrew a voluminous handkerchief from the pocket of pleated skirt.

Too tired to protest, Cassandra took the hankie and blew her nose loudly.

'I'm Miss Pripps,' said the lady cyclist, 'Just on my way home to get ready for Evensong, and who should I spy running along the road as if the very hounds of hell were on her tail, but that strange little miss in the Church earlier. You'd better come home with me. You look like you could do with a cold drink and a good wash. My oh my, you're as grubby as a Dickensian street urchin.'

She took Cassie firmly by the hand, and began to march her along the pavement, wheeling the bike alongside. Cassie stole her a sideways glance. She was wearing a funny hat like an upturned flower pot, and a profusion of grey curls sprouted from the rim. The bike was funny too. Thin tyres on huge spiked wheels, with a proper wicker basket at the front.

The barking was getting louder.

'That's my pet.' Said Miss Pripps, 'Calling for his tea.'

They stopped at a gate bearing the sign, 'BEWARE OF THE DOG'. Underneath was a silhouette, fashioned out of black metal and hanging on a chain. The head of a German Shepherd.

Cassie raised shining eyes to her companion, 'Is this where Bart lives?'

'Bart?'

'Your dog.'

Cassandra could hardly contain herself, as she waited for the lady to fish around in the depths of the basket for the front door key. It creaked open. She followed the owner of the imposing bay fronted house down a long hallway, and out into a roomy kitchen with a flagstone floor. Sunshine slanted through the opened window throwing a lozenge of light across a black Labrador who sat hopefully by an empty food bowl.

'Meet Simba'

Cassandra felt her heart contract with disappointment.

'He's not an Alsatian.' She said sadly.

'No my dear, he certainly is not. Bit of a softie really. The sign on the gate was put there by the previous owners of house. The husband ran the local Venture Scouts, and his wife bred German Shepherds, from a pedigree stud dog and bitch. Their progeny are scattered all over this area. Was it an Alsatian you were looking for?'

'Yes.' Cassie wasn't sure what 'progeny' meant, and didn't like to ask, 'His name is Bartholomew and he lives somewhere near here.'

'Hardly near. He's the Clifford's dog. They live at the far end of the Cambridge Road, just outside the village. I know them you see. We run Obedience Classes in the Church Hall, and they attended regularly until he went missing.'

'I found him,' said Cassie proudly, 'in London.'

'Clever you,' said the lady. Cassandra felt herself being assessed from behind those pink rimmed spectacles. She was an elderly person, she thought. Not rounded like Nana Reen, but rake thin, like the Headmistress as Brackendale High. 'Of course we heard that he'd been found so far from home. The family were beside themselves with worry. They'd plastered posters all over the village in the vain hope that he might have found his way back here.'

'He was happy with me.'

'I'm sure he was. Would you like a glass of lemonade? It's homemade. There are flapjacks too, fresh from the oven. I bake them for the bell ringers on a Sunday evening.'

Simba decided to investigate the visitor. He lumbered over to Cassie who by now was perched on a stool, feasting hungrily on a flapjack. He licked her sore and blistered legs with a rough pink tongue.

'Drink up your lemonade. I've just got to make a phone call. Then perhaps we can see if the Clifford's are home.'

'We think we might have a breakthrough'

Lyndsey, Renee and Raymond jumped up in unison at this announcement. They were sitting in a private annexe outside the main interview room, on a row of hard plastic seats.

'A Warden from a Church in North Essex rang a Social Services hotline earlier to report a young girl whom she felt was suffering from neglect. Apparently she was bloodied and bruised, and seeking sanctuary inside. They telephoned the Constabulary at Bishops Stortford, who have dispatched a squad car to the locality. The description matches your daughter.'

'Oh Thank God' cried Lyndsey. She wanted to plant a kiss of gratitude on the lips of the taciturn Detective Inspector.

'North Essex?' Raymond sounded disbelieving, 'It can't be Cassandra.'

Renee had begun to weep uncontrollably, 'Please don't be so negative. We have to pray that it is indeed our precious darling.'

'Whereabouts in Essex.' Lyndsey asked, as something tugged at her brain. Some elusive memory. Recently, someone had mentioned the name of a village. It had a bizarre name. But who had told her? And in what connection? There was a nugget of information floating somewhere in her brain, but she couldn't quite access it.

'A place called Stansted Mountfichet.'

Then she remembered. Relief flooded her in such a gush that she wanted to laugh, and sing, and dance. In her ears she could hear the man from the Animal Sanctuary that day which seemed so long ago, but was probably only a matter of weeks,

'His registered name is Bartholomew Venturer Scout. The dog belongs to a family in.....'

Raymond cut into her thoughts.

'Get real, everybody,' he was shouting, 'It can't be our kid. She's never been to Essex, for God Sake, except passing through. What the hell would she be doing there.'

'You'd better sit down Ray.' said Lyndsey 'and I'll tell you.'

'We're in luck'

Lyndsey and Ray were sitting in the back seat of a police car as it sped up the M11, siren wailing. The Detective Inspector had just taken a call on his mobile, and was leaning over the passenger seat, his face wreathed with a smile,

'That same Good Samaritan has just dialled 999 to say she caught up with the child running along the road, and has taken her home for safety. A kiddie in a blue hooded coat and red Wellington boots.'

Chapter Thirty Four

'ANOTHER TEA, MRS. Fairbrother?' Asked the desk sergeant. He was a kindly man, nearing retirement age she thought, in the ilk of dear old Jack Dixon on Dock Green fame. Renee shook her head. She was awash with the stuff, and it had stopped offering the age old comfort hours ago. She was awash with prayer too. Feverish prayers, begging God to return her granddaughter home safely. Prayers of intercession and prayers of bargaining.

The Policeman patted her gently on the shoulder, and Renee realised she had been chanting aloud. Realised too that the uniformed officer had probably heard much worse from distressed citizens during his time on the force. She bet that relatives of villains held for questioning used more than colourful language.

Renee would have liked to have cursed. To have ranted and raved, and railed against a modern day society that made the fate of a missing eleven year old such a tenuous one. Child molesters and drug pushers had proliferated in the country over the last decade, if the newspaper and TV reports were to be believed. Renee had no reason to doubt them. Her silky V necked blouse, donned so hurriedly that morning, was stained with perspiration, and her nylons itched against her legs. On her feet were the impossibly high heeled stilettos that she'd purchased in a moment of madness, trying, she now knew, to hang onto the vestiges of youth and thus, subconsciously, hang onto her son in law. In the confines of her brasserie her breasts ached from his pummelling of the night before. He'd been unaccountably rough, she thought, shutting out the memory. He hated her now, of that she were sure. Any respect or affection he once felt towards Renee Fairbrother was swept away in a tidal wave of blame and recrimination. Instead of wishing her goodnight he'd stood in hallway and called her 'a filthy conniving whore.' He'd hissed the words, giving them an inflection of such loathing, that Renee had felt quite ill. Spitting venom like a puff-adder, which made her realise that her son in law might be a dangerous man to fall foul of. Was this hitherto hidden ugly side what had prompted Lyndsey to try and seek an escape route from her marriage.

Once again, she could see his face how it had been the night before as he departed the bathroom; distorted, ugly, lashing out with abuse of the most verbally destructive kind. Renee balled her fists, digging her nails into her palms, until a spot of blood appeared.

She felt no pain however, for physical discomfort was not permitted to register – her mind was now concerned solely with the fate of her missing grandchild.

She stared at the clock on the wall. A bluebottle, which had been buzzing drunkenly around the room, alighted on its face. The minute hand seemed to be crawling, along with the fly. Only half an hour since her daughter and son in law had left for Essex accompanied by that stiff necked Detective Inspector, yet it seemed an eternity.

Lyndsey had hugged her, face alive with hope, 'I'm making them take us to the village where they've had the sighting, mum. The Police are reluctant to involve us in an indefinite lead, but I've insisted. Stansted Mountfichet is where the real owners of the stray dog lived, so Cass must have been listening the day I spoke to the Animal Sanctuary on the phone.'

Renee had seen a new determination in her daughter. Gone was the passive Lyndsey of old. Instead, a toughened version had emerged. Appearing on the TV programme seemed to have changed more than her offspring's style of dress, Renee thought. It seemed to have given her renewed self-confidence and esteem.

'Wait here Mum' Lyndsey had ordered, 'we'll get the D.I. to radio through as soon as Cass is found.'

They'd hugged again, and her daughter had departed with shoulders squared, and a determined jut to the chin. Trailing behind his new dominant wife, Raymond looked almost sheepish, Renee decided.

Now she was in limbo. A kind of suspended animation. Waiting for concrete news of Cassandra was like waiting for a baby to be born, thought Renee remembering back to the day she went into labour with Lyndsey, as though normal life had been temporarily suspended, and could not resume until the birth had taken place. It was difficult to comprehend that beyond the walls of the Police Station, people were going about their everyday business in blissful ignorance of the agonies within. How could they shop, and talk, and eat, and argue, thought Renee, a hard lump welling in her throat, when all she could do was sit and wait for news of her grandchild. It took all her will power not to shout at the genial desk sergeant 'how dare you do your job as though nothing has happened, when we've lost our darling little Cassandra.'

She knew she felt the loss as keenly as Lyndsey and Raymond. They might be the child's parents she thought, but as the grandmother she had a less fraught relationship with

Cass. It wasn't her role to discipline and educate, but rather to pamper and guide. As such her guilt was stronger. The wisdom of her years and proven track record in motherhood, gave her an added sense of responsibility towards her grand-daughter. She should have understood the depth of Cassandra's distress after 'Turnaround' had been aired, instead of barracking her for calling Lyndsey 'a prat.' Renee realised that this display of cocky insouciance on the child's part, masked a misery so intense that it had prompted her to run away.

The door to the outer office opened, disturbing the bluebottle which had been resting on its handle. Hardly daring to hope, Renee allowed herself to look up. A uniformed officer had entered and was having a whispered conversation with the kindly sergeant. They both paused to look across at her. She knew they were talking about Cassie and strained to hear. The fly had flown to the window, hitting the glass and trapping itself behind the lowered venetian blind. It's ineffectual buzzing almost drowned out the talk of the other two people in the room.

'Good news, Mrs. Fairbrother.'

Renee was on her feet in an instant, teetering on her killer heels.

The man continued, 'Your grand-daughter is safe and well in the care of the village Churchwarden.'

She was too stunned with relief to react.

'Sit down Mrs. Fairbrother, you're in shock. I'll get PC Underwood here, to make you a nice hot cup of …'

'No more tea,' Renee found herself interrupting, and her voice sounded unnaturally high, as though she'd been inhaling laughing gas. Indeed, she did feel that any minute she would start giggling uncontrollably. With difficulty, she composed herself. 'Thank you but I'd rather get home, and have a brew there. Or perhaps a glass of bubbly in celebration of my grand-draughters' safe return.'

'We'll give you a lift in a panda.'

'There's no need,' Renee tried, but failed, to sound controlled. She smoothed down the creased front of her pencil skirt, 'I want to shop first for ingredients to bake Cassie's favourite chocolate cake as a welcome home treat.' Although her grand-child had purloined the handbag containing money and keys, Renee was more than ready to forgive such a theft. She always kept a twenty pound note in a vase by the front door ready to pay the window cleaner, and this she had placed in the breast pocket of her blouse, almost as an overthought, when leaving that morning in a state of panic with her son in law. The maisonette keys were no problem. A spare set were hidden underneath a loose paving slab.

With fulsome thanks for their help in locating her grandchild, Renee took her leave from the uniformed team. PC Underwood, the gentle eyed desk sergeant seemed almost as overcome with emotion as she did herself that Cassandra Louise Daly had been found.

Leaving the austere surroundings of the Police Station, Renee reflected on the expression 'on winged feet', to describe one's joy, and understood totally what it meant. Her feet really did feel as though they had wings attached, and just a single leap in the air would be enough to get them flapping.

She hurried up the High Street, anxious to catch Mr. Roshi's convenience store before it closed. The major Supermarkets were long shut, but she hoped to find Mr. Roshi eager to capitalise on any early evening trade. Apart from the usual melee of youngsters entering McDonalds, and drinkers gathered in a desultory fashion outside the pub, the normally busy thoroughfare was quiet on this Sunday evening. She caught sight of her reflection in a mirror shop front, and wondered who this woman was; devoid of make up with silver blonde hair stuck to her forehead, wearing a skirt rather too short for her age.

She managed to catch Mr. Roshi just as he was lowering the metal shutters. Recognising her, the shopkeeper ushered this much valued customer deferentially inside.

Purchases made, Renee debated whether to wait for a bus for the short journey home, and decided against it. If she walked, the eggs packed carefully in the carrier bag, would reach room temperature and be ready for immediate mixing with the flour and cocoa powder the moment she entered her kitchen.

She would take a short cut through the park.

Miss Pripps said, 'The Cliffords are not answering their phone,' She poured Cassie more lemonade. It had a nice fresh taste, the child thought, not sickly like the shop stuff, 'Perhaps they are out in the garden enjoying the sunset. Would you like to pop to their place in my car, and see if we can catch sight of Bartholomew through the fence?'

Cassie nodded vigorously

'Finish your drink and go and wash that grubby face.. I've some antiseptic for those sore knees.'

Cass did as bidden. Shown into a pretty downstairs bathroom, tiled in a soft butter yellow, she filled the basin with sudsy water and attacked the dirt of that endless day. She smiled happily at the mirror. Soon, oh so soon, she would see her faithful doggy friend. Piled neatly on the toilet seat was a pile of clothes.

'I've been collecting jumble for the Church Bazaar', the elderly lady had told Cass, 'amongst the clothes are a blouse and skirt which might fit. Better than that dirty frock anyway.'

'It's not a frock. It's a nightdress.'

'Even more reason to change. One can't be seen out in one's bedtime attire, it's simply not the done thing.'

Cassandra thought Miss Pripps had a funny way of talking. Like they did in old fashioned films on the telly. A member of the Royal Family had visited her primary school once as part of something called 'an urban renewal programme', and spoke in exactly the same way.

Ten minutes later they were wending their way through the village in a mini car which smelt of lavender. Despite the entreaties of her host, Cass had refused to remove the coat that she'd donned after washing and putting on the donated clothes. Her legs, under an alien skirt, tingled with the application of antiseptic, and a sticking plaster had been put on over her cut foot. These kindly ministrations, together with the refreshing drink and flapjacks, had restored Cassandra and lifted her flagging spirits.

Now she fidgeted on the passenger seat in a state of feverish anticipation.

Miss Pripps parked the battered hatchback with a great deal of juddering, outside a modern red brick house set back from the road. Privately Cass didn't think she was a very good driver since both wheels mounted the kerb. The tall figure got out, and led her by the hand up to the garden fence of the Clifford family home.

Miss Pripps began to call out, 'Hello, anybody home?'

There was no human answer, but there was a canine one. A scrabbling sound accompanied by scudding mud, as, around the side of the house a shaggy German Shepherd came racing, growling with implicit threat towards the interlopers. Reaching the fence, he skidded to a halt, then paused to sniff the air. Slowly at first, then with more enthusiasm, the fringed tail began to wag. Cassie put her arm through the slats, and outstretched her fingers. The dog allowed her to stroke his muzzle, his whine of delighted recognition sounding as though he were singing a greeting.

'Hello Mozart'.

Lyndsey brushed against the hanging metal sign of a silhouette of an alsatian's head that her daughter had seen an hour earlier. She headed the trio that walked up the path, to the surprise of both the Detective Inspector and her estranged husband. The former because in his chosen profession he was used to taking charge; the latter because his wife had never before taken the lead. He liked this new pro-active Lyndsey, and wondered whether this display of forcefulness would transmute to the bedroom. Briefly he pictured her throwing him onto the duvet, and riding him like a horse. With a bit of luck, she might even be persuaded to wear boots and crack a whip.

Pinned to the wisteria clad front door was a note, which by its scrawled writing, looked as though it had been written in haste.

'On a mission of mercy.' It read, 'Back soon.'

Lyndsey quelled her disappointment. She hoped the wait wouldn't be a long one. Every minute that stretched between the anticipated reunion with her precious child was agony.

'Mercy?' barked Ray, 'what the heck does that mean?'

'This is most irregular.' Said the Detective Inspector, 'the householder was instructed to wait with the youngster for our arrival.'

Lyndsey wished they'd both shut up, and use a bit of sense. It didn't take a mastermind, she thought, to conclude what the mission was.

'Mummy!' It was Cassandra's voice. She came running up the path, eyes shining with happiness. Behind her came a tall woman, with wire wool hair, dressed in ancient tweeds.

'Darling.' Lyndsey bent to scoop her daughter up into her arms. She held the frail body tightly, as though she never again wanted to let the child go. In her head, she said repeated prayers of thanksgiving.

Cassie was saying, 'I've seen Mozart. He remembers me.'

'That's wonderful.'

'Miss Pripps says she is going to ask the Clifford's to let me look after him when they next go camping.'

Lyndsey shook the tall woman's hand. She was too choked to speak, but her expression of heartfelt gratitude said more than words. This Good Samaritan had not only kept her daughter safe, but had taken her to see the animal that had so consumed the child's imagination.

'He's not been eating properly. Pining for me Miss Pripps reckons. Ever so thin', Cassie was saying.

So are you, Lyndsey thought, feeling the bones beneath the quilted coat. She placed her daughter gently on doorstep.

The Detective Inspector was smiling broadly.

'You've given us a fright, little lady' he said, before leading the Good Samaritan across the front lawn to a garden bench. Lyndsey guessed he was going to engage her daughter's saviour in a line of gentle questioning.

Left alone, parents and child seemed overcome with emotion. Eventually Raymond Daly said, 'What about daddy, sweetheart. Do I get a 'hello' kiss?'

As he reached out to touch her, Cassandra recoiled against her mother. 'Leave me alone.'

Chapter Thirty Five

SURPRISINGLY FOR SUCH a pleasant sunset and the lighter evenings, the park was sparsely populated. Renee passed an elderly couple walking a panting dachshund, and a group of teenagers sharing a joint under a tree.

She was planning her grand-daughter's homecoming. Time enough, she hoped, to bake a chocolate cake, and put together a welcome tea. In the freezer she had a batch of homemade quiches, and plenty of salad stuffs in the fridge. She would ice the cake with a smiley face, for that was exactly how she felt.

Was Cassandra now homesick? Was her grand-child at this very moment regretting whatever rash impulse had compelled her to run away, and wishing she were back in the cosy maisonette with her grandmother.

So lost was Renee in the picture of the emotional reunion that would soon be taking place, that she didn't hear footsteps behind her. Her heels clicked along the uneven path.

She was not quite sure what happened next. One minute she was hurrying along, the next, pitching forward head first onto the concrete. Desperately Renee fought to keep her balance, but the stilettos skewed to one side, and she landed with a thud on the path. The pain was intense, and a swirl of colours blurred her line of vision. The green of the grass, the darkening sky, the blood redness of the setting sun. A child's swing swam into view, upside down, the empty seat unmoving in the still air.

Renee could taste salt in her mouth, then warm blood began to trickle down her chin. Experimentally she moved her tongue, puzzled to encounter a gap where a tooth should have been. There was a confused babble of voices, and the sound of running feet.

Then everything went black.

Renee was slipping in and out of consciousness. She had a vague recollection of concerned faces floating above her, and her bloodied face being licked by a sausage dog. When she next came round, she was in an ambulance. At least it seemed to be an ambulance for she could hear the wail of a siren, and a man in green overalls was asking, 'What's your name love?' Renee tried to form the words but her mouth felt cracked and swollen. Her whole body throbbed with pain. Unable to move, she wondered why, and then realised that she was strapped to a stretcher, a wire cage protecting her chest. Closing her eyes, she drifted off once more into blissful oblivion.

When she awoke she was in a hospital bed, surrounded by screens. Tubes were attached to her body, and bandage swathed a head, which she realised, to her horror had been shaved. A nurse was taking her blood pressure. Renee moaned.

'Doctor, doctor, I think she's coming to.'

The nurse was calling someone but her voice sounded a long way off. Renee stared at the ceiling. The pattern on the tiles reminded her of a pavement stuck with chewing gum, and an overhead fan whirred. A man in a white coat moved aside the screen, and leant over her prostrate form. He was young, she thought, no older than Lyndsey, and his face was etched with concern. Another doctor joined them. An elderly black man with grizzled grey hair.

He spoke to Renee in a rich Jamaican accent,

'Evening Missy. How are we feeling?'

Her lips felt like fat slugs had been moulded to them, 'sore. Where am I?'

'Southfield General. You've had a nasty experience.'

'What happened?'

'We think you might have been mugged in the park. The Police are conducting a search of the area.'

Not police again, thought Renee, wearily. It seemed to have been a day for them. She struggled to remember what had happened, but couldn't. Her mind felt cotton wool-ish. The younger doctor asked, 'can you tell us your name, and who to contact? There was no identification on you. We believe the attacker stole your bag.'

'There was no bag.' She mumbled, 'Cassandra had it.'

'Cassandra?'

'My grand-daughter'.

'What about your husband?'

'I'm a widow.'

There was a smell in the air which reminded Renee of swimming pools. A chemical odour somewhere between bleach and antiseptic. She wrinkled her nose and immediately wished she hadn't. Twin forks of pain stabbed at her nostrils, making her eyes water.

'Don't cry, Missy. You need to conserve your energy. Help speed up the healing process, see?'

At this obvious show of compassion, real tears began to flow down her ravaged face.

'Please,' sobbed Renee, 'Call my daughter.' And she gave them the number.

Chapter Thirty Six

ENTERING THE HOUSE at Shenlagh Gardens, was like walking into a kiln thought Lyndsey. She had forgotten to switch off the central heating, and that, coupled with the sun beating on the windows all day, had compressed the warmth. Although it was early evening, the air had hardly cooled, and the thermometer on the wall above the telephone read eighty degrees Fahrenheit.

'Phew,' Ray said, 'I need a drink. Fancy one?'

'Iced tea would be nice.' Lyndsey hung her keys on the hook. The events of the day had left her drained.

He departed for the kitchen, whilst she went around opening windows letting in some cooling air, before ushering Cassie upstairs, and running her a tepid bath.

'You need a good soak, darling,' she said, 'then we'll talk.'

'What about?'

'Well, why you ran away for one thing. You gave us all quite a scare you know. Poor Nana nearly had a heart attack.'

'I wish she'd died!'

Shocked, Lyndsey sat on the edge of the bath. Cassie had eased her grubby little body into the water, wincing as it stung her skinned knees. She stared at her daughter, hardly registering that the tiny breasts were beginning to bud.

'Whatever makes you say such a terrible thing?'

Cassie was squeezing the sponge, dribbling water over her upturned face. 'I saw them.' She said in a small voice.

'Who?'

'Nana and Daddy. In the bathroom. They were kissing.'

Kissing?' Lyndsey found herself echoing. Rather stupidly, she thought.

'More like slobbering really. They way Mozart did when I opened tins of doggy chunks. At least daddy was. All over Grandma's bare titties.'

Lyndsey clapped both hands to her ears. It was a reflex action. She dropped them at once realising the futility of trying to block out words she didn't want to hear. The truth didn't become a lie just because you refused to listen to it. Somehow she knew it was the truth. What was the saying? Out of the mouth of babes.... Her daughter was too innocent, too unworldly wise to concoct such a tale from imagination. She looked into the clear grey eyes that regarded her across the bathwater, and saw within them no hint of deviousness.

Raymond had been stroking her mother's breasts. Reluctantly this was something that rang true. Her husband's obsession with female mammary glands had been well documented throughout the course of their marriage, both from his own lips, and her discovery of a further hidden cache of pornographic magazines under his side of the bed after he'd moved into the maisonette. They sported hideous photographs of women bringing men to climax between their cleavages.

Of him she could believe the worse. But her mother? Surely Renee couldn't have been a willing participant in such unpleasant sexual practises. With her own son-in-law? It was simply too preposterous to accept. As if reading her thoughts, Cassie said,

'Grandma enjoyed it. She had her head thrown back and was making a noise like owls. A sort of OOOH sound.'

Lyndsey squeezed her eyes shut until they hurt, trying to blot out this horrifying image. So her mother was complicit in this act of infidelity. A betrayal of such ugliness that she felt herself begin to shake with rage.

'Don't cry mummy.'

'I'm not,' she said in a strangulated voice. How dare they? She thought, struggling to regain control. How bloody dare they? Did they laugh at her ignorance of their affair. Poke fun at her small breasts. Did Ray say, 'she certainly doesn't take after her old mum in the tit department.'

Had Renee smiled in tacit compliance?

Anger was now boiling through her. The skin of her face flamed, and she felt quite murderous. She wanted to get a carving knife and slice off her husband's cock, quickly followed by her mother's nipples.

The slosh of water brought her sharply back. Cassie was standing up, drying herself with a towel.

'How did you see them? Through the door?' She was careful to keep her voice even, but her anger was a hot tidal flood. Were the contemptible pair so indifferent to the sensibilities of a child that they'd not troubled to shut the door on their lewd proclivities?

'No. There was a hole drilled through the wall of Nan's spare room.'

A Spyhole! The implication of this extra snippet of information invoked a fresh wave of disgust. So not only had Ray been engaged in physical molestation of a woman who by the bounds of common decency should have been barred to him, but he'd been spying on her too. In the bathroom. Naked after a shower.

'When?' She screamed, grabbing the child by her thin shoulders, 'when did this happen?'

'Last night. Nana sent me to bed after your programme 'cos I said something rude.'

Lyndsey let go of her daughter, and began to beat the sink basin with her fists. She was going to vomit. She was sure of it.

'Mummy, don't. You're scaring me.'

She stopped beating. She wanted to break something, urgently needing to release the tension within. She wrenched the toothbrush rack off the wall and hurled it at the mirror above the vanity unit. The glass cracked on impact, sending a cobweb of shards in all directions. Lyndsey regarded herself impassively. Her reflection became jagged; distorted.

She heard a choking sound. Cassie was sobbing, her matchstick frame heaving with shock at this alien display of violence. Lyndsey picked up the towel that had been discarded over the edge of the bath, and cocooned it around her daughter. She hugged the child close, burying her face in rough material.

'Darling, I'm so sorry.'

'I'm sorry too. For running away.'

'It was because of what you saw in Grandma Renee's bathroom wasn't it? Not because of me on 'Turnaround'?'

The child's expression confirmed the truth of this statement.

'Everything is going to be alright Cass. I promise.'

The sobbing had eased. Now she had hiccups. Lyndsey wiped the pale face tenderly with the edge of the towel.

'I'm so glad I got to see Mozart.'

'I know.'

'Glad I got to see you on 'Turnaround'

'Oh, sweetheart.'

'Glad too, that my famous mummy has been invited to Savannah and Thalia's book launch party.'

This was a huge concession from Cassie who had hitherto feigned boredom at any mention of the glitzy affair, and Lyndsey re-doubled her hugging. Cassandra's admiration filled her with a glow which countered the anger coursing her veins at her mother and husband's perfidy. Her child's next words made that glow burn brighter.

'I'm SO proud of you mummy.'

Listening outside the door, Raymond marvelled at how he managed to keep a steady hand and not spill the iced tea. The revelations overheard had filled him with an overwhelming sense of doom. Not to mention shame. He wanted to hang his head in disgust at inflicting the lurid sight of himself climaxing over his mother in law, in full view of an innocent child. His own innocent child. He cursed his folly at gouging out the spyhole, and acknowledged bitterly that he'd allowed the cool voice of reason to be shouted down by the strident one of lust. It was true what they said about men, he decided. His brains were certainly in his balls.

For the first time in his life he found the thought of his own genitalia loathsome. Wanted to twist the rubbery penis that drove him into reckless acts of sexual depravity into the tightest of knots.

His heart ached for Cassandra. Poor kid, he thought. No wonder she'd run away, unable to face him and her grandmother after what she'd witnessed. Standing on the landing, Raymond Daly tussled with his conscience, and as always he won. None of this was his fault he decided. He'd been driven to such acts of duplicity by the joint machinations of his wife and her mother.

Bloody Renee. This was her fault. If she'd had taken a firmer line with him none of this would have happened. Most respectable women would have repulsed such advances from their son in law, instead of encouraging them. Perhaps encouraging was too strong a word, he thought, descending the stairs. Welcoming was maybe more apt. Yes, she had definitely welcomed his hands on her breasts, filthy cow.

Lyndsey had brought him to this. Lyndsey and Renee between them. They had brought him to this degradation and shame. If Lyndsey had been a proper wife between the sheets, he wouldn't have been driven to seek sexual release elsewhere. If Renee had been a proper mother in law she wouldn't have allowed him to use and abuse her like a cheap tart.

He'd have been better off frequenting a prostitute.

In Raymond Daly's warped mind, a bizarre conclusion was beginning to ferment. The more he thought about it, the more he started to believe that Renee and Lyndsey were in it together, and had been from the beginning. His mother in law, he decided, had deliberately seduced him, on instructions from his wife. They'd colluded against him to destroy the marriage, knowing that he would have no grounds to counter claim in a divorce court once a Judge knew he'd been engaged in sexual relations with his mother in law.

The bitches. The conniving evil bitches.

They'd cooked his proverbial goose. Stitched him up like the proverbial kipper. Hoisted him by his own proverbial petard.

A numbness was creeping over his mind and body, dulling all feeling. He guessed it was a form of emotional anaesthesia, a safety valve in the brain that prevented the sufferer from going insane. Certainly he did feel that he was on the verge of madness.

He'd lost his wife, and his mother in law, but no longer cared. The loss of his only child was very different. Raymond cared deeply for his daughter, and despaired of ever winning back her affections.

Now he realised the reason for the silent treatment she'd meted out to him on the journey back from Stansted Mountfichet. There had been no conversation in the back seat of the Police car, and he'd assumed Cassandra was too fatigued to talk.

Even the Detective Inspector had not seemed unduly worried by Cassie's reluctance to speak.

'We'll come and take a statement from the kiddie tomorrow.' He'd told Ray, 'no need to disturb her any more today. See that she gets a good nights rest.'

In the kitchen at Shenlagh Gardens, Raymond Daly looked out of the window at a garden shimmering in the twilight, and reached a decision.

He was going to take the posting in New York. The firm wanted him to start sooner rather than later, and he was going to comply. Lyndsey could go ahead with her decision to divorce him. The marriage was beyond redemption and it didn't cause him more than a modicum of grief and soul searching. If the truth be told, he would be glad to get rid. Once the house was sold, there would be enough in the kitty for him to buy a bachelor pad, where he could indulge in his breast fantasies with a variety of call girls without fear of discovery.

The only way to repair his relationship with Cassandra was to give her time. He hoped that in the months to come, the memory of his bare arsed grunting would start to blur, and perhaps fade altogether. Or at least diminish into something that, years in the future, father and daughter could share an indulgent laugh about together.

He would put the ocean between them for the foreseeable future. She would come round eventually. He had to believe it.

Ray tipped the tea down the sink, and picked up his keys. The saloon was still parked in the road where he'd left it that morning. He would drive to the maisonette, pack, and be gone by the time his whore of a mother in law came home. She seemed to have gone missing, not answering the phone when Lyndsey had rang. He would park by the wheelie bins, and creep across the lawn at the back so that she wouldn't be alerted to his arrival.

A guy at work had told him about a hotel in London's Soho. It overlooked a lap dancing club where birds with big knockers gyrated around a pole. Raymond Daly would make a reservation and stay until his trip to New York could be organised. He'd met the Vice President of the American operation during a Company fishing trip to the Great Lakes. She was aggressively single with the hugest jugs he'd ever seen. They were like barrage balloons and he'd fairly ached to get his hands on them. She would present him with a challenge, he thought with glee. One his cock was already rising to meet.

The phone started ringing as he opened the front door.

He ignored it.

Chapter Thirty Seven

LYNDSEY CAUGHT UP with her husband out on the street.

'Where do you think you're going sicko?' Scorn made her voice strident. She was vibrating with fury, as though a thousand electric shocks were surging through her blood stream. He regarded her with a look of mild surprise, and Lyndsey began to shake. He was patronising her, the smug bastard she thought, fighting the urge to wipe the bland expression from his face. She needed to make him see just how much he'd damaged Cassie. Have some concept of the hurt he'd inflicted on not only their child, but Lyndsey herself.

An invisible force propelled her forward. It was as though a giant hand had reached up inside her, and was acting as puppeteer. She lunged at her husband, crying with hurt and pain like a wounded animal. Her nails scored twin grooves on each cheek, and her fists flailed at his body. He caught her wrists in an iron grasp.

An elderly couple walked down the road, with a dachshund bitch trailing on a lead. Its sagging belly sported a row of teats which almost touched the pavement. Lyndsey watched it, her breath coming in gasps. She could see, in her mind, a picture of Raymond touching her own mother's teats. Teats that she'd suckled as an infant, and the appalling vision caused her legs to buckle.

He held her up, supporting her body with strong arms. The passers-by averted their eyes, and continued walking, not wanting to get involved in a domestic disturbance in this leafy suburban neighbourhood. Lyndsey thought that perhaps, like her, they'd had a surfeit of dramas for one day.

'Feeling better?' said Ray in a deceptively silky tone.

'Bastard.' Lyndsey managed.

The scratches on his face were beading with blood. Part of her wanted to draw more; wanted to slash at him until she cut a main artery and he bled to death right there on the pavement. But another side, the stronger side, wanted to kiss them better. He was her husband, the father of her child, and once she'd loved him enough to marry. Where had it all gone so terribly wrong?

The rage was dissipating, beginning to recede like an ebb tide. Perhaps that has always been my trouble, thought Lyndsey in despair. I've never been able to stay angry enough for long enough. Long enough to make a difference. She saw, looking back down the years, that her passivity had given Raymond carte blanche to get away with behaviour that other wives would have found unacceptable. Like a child who continually pushes against the boundaries of the mores laid down for them, so he had trampled down Lyndsey's flimsily erected barriers. And she'd allowed him to.

She said sadly, 'How could you Ray? With Renee of all people.'

He shrugged. 'She was available.'

'You're surely not blaming her?'

'Ah blame, Lyndsey. An interesting word, don't you think? So let's examine the situation shall we?' His eyes surveyed her, and she quailed beneath their queer green light. 'Who is really to blame in this sorry saga? Surely not the husband, who is being unfairly divorced by his feckless wife, suggested that he leave his home, and then have his mother in law thrust herself at him.'

'How dare you imply that mum...'

'Oh I'm implying all right.' He cut in, and his grip tightened on her arms, 'every night after her shower, she'd be parading around in next to nothing, with her bathrobe gaping. What was I expected to do? Turn a blind eye? Perhaps you forget, my dear wife, that I am a man in his prime with male needs. Maybe if you'd satisfied those needs with a bit more enthusiasm over the years, we wouldn't be in this morass.'

He pushed her away from him, and walked around to the driver's door of the car, whistling in an insouciant manner. Blood was making tramlines down his face.

'Surely you're not leaving?' Lyndsey followed. She felt weak and drained, 'please Ray, we have to talk about this...'

'There is nothing more to say. I'm relocating to New York for six months, and shall appoint one of their top notch attorneys to act for me in our divorce.'

'You want it to go ahead?'

Things would be different now she told herself. Now that she was stronger her relationship with Raymond might stand another chance. Appearing on 'Turnaround' had given her a transfusion of confidence, as though lines of self-esteem had been pumped into her veins. She stared at the impassive face of her husband which showed no vestige of shame, and knew in that instant, that it was too late. Her marriage was as dead as the Winter which this sunny day had finally left behind.

He put up a hand and tentatively touched his cheek. Blood smeared his fingers, and he wiped them across his wife's face, transferring the sticky red liquid from his own countenance to hers.

'After being physically attacked by a screeching harridan? You betcha..'

She leaned against the hot metal of the car for support. 'I'm sorry', she said, and the thought occurred that in her disagreements with Raymond over the years, it had always been she who'd ended up apologising. Begging for forgiveness. Had he ever once said he was sorry?

'I just had to get it off my chest.'

He laughed at this, and it was a harsh laugh, with a mocking edge.

'Chest,' sneered Raymond Daly, 'What chest?'

Lyndsey watched him drive away. Through the car window, the top of his sandy head glowed orange as the setting sun. His shirt was soaked with sweat and clung to a pair of muscular shoulder blades. Lyndsey could imagine them with their wiry coating of ginger hair, and she sagged down on the pavement. For some time she sat on the kerb, head in hands, weeping silently.

Twilight settled on the streets of North London. The air cloaked the hunched figure of Lyndsey Daly in a warm dark quilt.

She leaned back and rested her head on the lamp-post, staring up at the velvet sky. Moths were dancing around the beam of light. Her dress, a Savannah and Thalia choice, in a pretty floaty print of sprigged flowers, stuck to her perspiring body. In the distance she could hear someone calling. Realisation hit that it was Cassandra, from the opened bedroom window.

'Coming darling.' With difficulty, she got to her feet. Dully it occurred to her that Dee's car was missing from the kerbside; obviously her friend had a spare set of keys and had collected the vehicle earlier in day.

Cassie was waiting at the door. She'd dressed herself in Scooby Doo pyjamas.

'Mum, what's happened to your face?'

'Nothing pet. A bit of dried blood. That's all.'

'Where's daddy?'

'He's gone.'

The child seemed willing to accept this lack of elaboration. 'Can I read awhile before lights out?'

The phone trilled, its sound an irritation. 'It's been ringing and ringing,' said Cassandra, pausing halfway up the stairs, 'but you tell me not to answer if I'm ever alone in the house.'

Lyndsey picked up the receiver and said, 'hello' without enthusiasm.

'Is that Mrs. Daly. Mrs. Lyndsey Daly?' Asked a voice.

'Speaking.'

'This is the Registrar of Southfield General. Your mother is here. I'm afraid she's had an accident.'

'An accident?'

'A nasty fall in the local park, sustaining cracked ribs, and a contusion of the skull.'

This news, coming swiftly on the heels of all the other shocks encountered during that endless day, left Lyndsey unable to react. All her emotional channels had shut down like a row of TV screens going blank. She said, in a monotone, 'I'm on my way.'

'There is no need Mrs. Daly. Mrs. Fairbrother has been sedated and is sleeping. She won't wake for several hours. The doctor would like to see you first thing however.'

'Of course'

Lyndsey hung up. She went upstairs to the bathroom and washed the blood off her face. Cassie was parading the landing, her newly shampooed hair standing in tufts. She was carrying a copy of Dodie Smith's '101 Dalmations.' The book was dog eared from so many readings.

'Dog Eared' thought Lyndsey, and let out a faintly hysterical giggle at this apt expression.

She joined her daughter in the master bedroom.

'Was that Nana on the phone?'

Lyndsey nodded, allowing herself the lie. She wasn't going to give the child any more grief to contend with. It could wait until the morning. In the morning the two of them would go and visit Renee. There would be no recriminations. Not until her mother was strong enough to bear them.

She would take each day as it came. Perhaps when the patient was discharged from hospital, she could lock the maisonette and move into Shenlagh Gardens to be nursed while she recuperated.

Lyndsey's mind was made up. She would persuade mother to move in with her and Cassandra. Just the three of them - all girls together. After all, thought Lyndsey, there were bridges to build. Between Cassie and her grandmother. Not to mention mother and daughter. Forgiveness towards Renee for granting sexual favours to a spouse could not be readily forthcoming, but Lyndsey resolved to try. Her relationship with her mother was too precious to permanently sacrifice on the altar of morality.

She pulled back the covers of the marital bed, and gestured to Cassie, 'You can sleep with mummy the whole night. I think we both need a cuddle.'

The youngster needed no second invitation. Cassandra Louise Daly climbed under the covers, and within minutes her eyelids began to droop.

The phone rang again. Lyndsey instinctively knew who was on the other end of the line.

Robbie McCrae.

He must be frantic with worry. He'd been leaving her messages all day. This time she would take his call.

She thought of Raymond Daly checking into a hotel somewhere as he planned his new life, and wondered if staff and clientele alike would be quietly sniggering at the post-it note Lyndsey had stuck on his back as he'd turned away from her on the kerb. A post it she always had kept handy for such an occasion. On it she'd written one word.

'Arsehole.'

Chapter Thirty Eight

THE FOLLOWING MORNING, Robbie sat with Cassandra in the "League of Friends" tea-room, whilst Lyndsey visited her mother. He'd insisted on bringing them to Southfield General on hearing the dreadful news about Renee.

Cassie sipped a banana milkshake through a straw, face concealed by the hood of her voluminous blue coat. She'd been silent on the drive to the hospital.

'Try and get her to open up,' Lyndsey had whispered to Robbie as they'd parted company outside the ward. She'd already recounted the events of the previous day, hinting at a private problem between Cassandra and her grandmother, which had culminated in the eleven year old refusing to visit Nana Reen's hospital bedside.

Robbie took a mouthful of tea and grimaced. It was weak with leaves floating on the surface. The tearoom was painted in garish orange, and a medley of Big Band tunes played in the background.

Cassandra unwrapped a chocolate wafer, and separated it into fingers.

Robbie saw the perfect opening gambit, 'Bet Mozart would like some of that.' He said, keeping his voice casual.

The voice that issued from the hood, said, 'chocolate is poisonous to dogs.'

'Och'. Robbie tried again, 'You know an awful lot, wee hen. Where did you learn so much about our four legged friends?'

'I watch films. 'Beethoven' and 'Lassie.' Read stories too.'

A small finger slid a wafer across the table at him. He recognised it for what it was. A gesture of conciliation. The child had treated Robbie with a studied indifference since he'd come into her mother's life. He'd understood why she'd frozen him out, and respected her for it, for loyalty to one's father was a commendable trait. But maybe the problem to which Lyndsey had referred, was now making the youngster question that loyalty. He knew Raymond Daly was involved, for Lyn had said darkly, 'Cass saw her dad and gran involved in something pretty unspeakable.' Whatever the reason behind the offering of the biscuit, Robbie saw it as the equivalent of a Red Indian peace pipe, and was more than prepared to puff away.

He munched reflectively, before saying,

'Mam told me a legend when I was wee. About a dog called Gelert and his master, a Prince Llewelyn.'

'A Scottish legend?' asked the voice.

'No, Welsh. The Prince went hunting and left his faithful hound Gelert in care of his baby son. The baby was in a cradle. When Llewelyn returned, he found the cradle empty and his dog covered in blood. Beside himself with grief, he slew Gelert thinking the animal had eaten the baby. Then he heard the baby cry. He found it alive and well beside the body of a wolf. The Prince realised that his brave hound had fought the wolf in order to save the infant.'

Huge grey eyes, stared into his underneath the canopy of fur. Robbie thought how much they resembled Lyndsey's.

'Poor Gelert.' said Cassie, her voice mournful, 'that Prince was SO mean.'

'Not mean. Just mistaken. Adults often act on impulse. The moral of that story is not to jump to conclusions.'

Cassandra said stoutly, 'I won't - ever.'

Robbie drained his cup. He could see a way to raise the issue that was at the forefront of his mind. How to engineer a rapprochement between the child and her grandmother.

'Your pa and grandma are suffering guilt just like Llewelyn did when he realised he'd slain Gelert. They never meant to hurt you by acting on impulse like the Prince. Grown-ups sometimes do silly things that children can't understand, but it doesn't mean they love those children any the less.'

'I hate Nana Reen.' came the stubborn reply, 'and daddy. They did something yucky.'

The volunteer manning the tea room came and wiped their table. She wore a vacant expression, and was humming along to the music. Robbie waited for her to leave, before continuing,

'Remember the Prince, Cassandra? He chanced upon a 'yucky' scene and killed his faithful hound because of it.'

Was there a breakthrough coming? Robbie watched the child intently without appearing to do so. A range of emotions were flitting across that pale heart shaped face. She stabbed the foaming remnants of the milkshake with the straw, then said, 'Do you think the ghost of that faithful hound ever forgave his master.'

'Aye, lassie.'

She swivelled on the chair, challenging him with the questing look in her eyes. Robbie played his trump card,

'He knew the Prince loved him.'

'Oh my darling,' Renee buried her face under the bed sheet, 'how can you ever forgive me? And dear little Cass too...'

'I need to hear your version of what happened. Raymond's defence was that you forced your attentions upon him.'

A nurse bustled across and took Renee's temperature. She shot Lyndsey an affronted look, 'Are you upsetting Mrs. Fairbrother? If so the Doctor will ask you to leave.'

The patient waved an ameliorating hand, 'She's my daughter. I want her to stay.'

The nurse marched away, muttering darkly about lax visiting times.

Lyndsey coolly regarded her mother. The wave of shock, sympathy, and revulsion she'd felt on first seeing the other's injuries, had been mercilessly trampled under the goad that was Renee's betrayal. She was unable to express any concern about the fall. That would have to come later.

She'd dressed carefully that morning. A Savannah and Thalia special consisting of a red satin blouse with a mandarin collar, and matching Japanese style skirt. Her hair had been gelled into a wheatfield of spikes. It gave her a perverse pleasure to know that she looked her best, whilst her mother looked her worst.

'I'm waiting mum.'

The figure under the metal cage writhed in anguish before speaking, 'It's too horrible for words. That my son in law actually bored a spyhole through the bedroom wall, and poor little Cass saw....'

'What did she see?'

'Please don't make me spell it out. Allow me to retain a shred of dignity.'

'There's nothing dignified in letting my husband wank himself off over your breasts.'

A groan of anguish issued from the bed. Hurt pride drove Lyndsey to continue, 'what an immoral pair you are. My mother and husband. Romeo and Juliet it isn't, more like the sordid liaison between Oedipus and Queen Jocasta.'

'What do you want of me, Lyn? To hang myself like she did?'

'At least Jocasta did the decent thing when she discovered she'd had sex with her own son.'

'Darling, Raymond and I didn't .....'

Lyndsey leaned both elbows on the bed, and regarded the patient fiercely, 'didn't what, mum? Indulge in a shag fest? I believe you. Penetration isn't what turns him on, you see. Never has been. Large breasts are the only things that have ever lit his fire, that, and a woman, willing or stupid enough to let him get his hands on them. So what category did you fall into? Willing, stupid, or both?'

She saw that her mother was twisting so violently that the turban of bandages was becoming unravelled.

'Both darling. I was stupid enough to believe it might have given your marriage a fighting chance if Raymond's sexual frustrations were given a release, and willing enough because.....'

'Because what?' Lyndsey prompted, and her voice was deadly quiet.

'Call me a pathetic old dame, but it was a pleasurable experience to have a man find me physically alluring after so many lonely years, albeit briefly. It was wrong, and I'd already told him our fling was over. I never meant to hurt you. Or Cassie. You both mean the World to me. If I lose my precious daughter and grand-daughter over this stupid aberration then I've lost everything that makes life worth living.'

Renee began to cry. Tortured wailing tears. Lyndsey got to her feet, and re-pinned the trailing bandage, 'hush' she said, and this time her voice was gentle. Gazing down into her mother's bruised and blackened face, she saw, as if for the first time, the deep furrows etched there. It was as though Renee Fairbrother had aged twenty years overnight.

'Don't cry mum. It will sting your poor face.'

'Pain is my punishment, Lyndsey. The fall was a form of divine retribution.'

'Stop such morbid talk. The injuries are not life threatening, and the doc says you'll be out in a month.'

Lyndsey felt the lump of undigested anger begin to shift slightly in her chest. It would take time for it to dislodge and work out of her system, but the tenuous process had started.

'You're going to move into Shenlagh Gardens, so I can nurse you back to a complete recovery.' Lyndsey kissed the scarred cheek. Renee was too precious to let slip away.

Raymond might have given her Cassie, but her mother had given her life.

At the entrance to Ward II, Robbie McCrae stood with Cassandra Louise Daly.

Lyndsey, pausing in her departure to consult the charge nurse about her mother's condition, saw the motionless pair. She joined them by the swing rubber doors.

Cassie had made the quantum leap of pushing back her hood so that whole of her face and head were exposed. Robbie was obviously a miracle worker, thought Lyndsey with undisguised admiration for the gentle Scot. No-one else could have invoked this concession towards normality from the child.

'She wants to see Nana Reen,' He said, and as Lyndsey went to take her daughter by the hand, added, almost warningly, 'alone.'

They stood and watched as the small figure in the Eskimo coat made her way to the bed that housed her grandmother. For Lyndsey, everything seemed to unfold in slow motion. It was like watching a movie where the reels of film had stuck. The babble of voices dimmed to a distant murmur. The shapes of nursing staff and patients blurred.

With tentative steps the child approached her grandmother. The latter raised outstretched arms.

Lyndsey leaned against Robbie, looping her arm through his in a gesture of gratitude. They watched the unfolding tableau in the hospital ward in benevolent silence. Renee had heaved herself up on the pillow and was giving Cassandra a cuddle.

The beginnings of a smile played around Lyndsey's lips. It was one of hope.

'My dear Mrs. Fairbrother.'

It was later that evening, and a tentative hand reached out to touch the arm dangling by the side of the metal bed. The patient regarded her latest visitor with a quizzical expression, 'How come you know I'm here?'

'The Hospital rang the station when you were admitted. They'd concluded from your injuries that you may have been the victim of a mugging, especially since the elderly couple who called the ambulance said a gang of hoodlums had been idling in the park.'

'Ah', Renee struggled to sit up, but the pain in her chest was too intense. She slumped back on the pillow, and stared at the off duty policeman who sat by her bed, proffering a bouquet of flowers. She hadn't immediately recognised him when he'd awkwardly approached for in civilian clothes he looked different. As soon as he'd spoken however, she knew him to be the friendly desk sergeant who had been so solicitous towards her during the agonising wait for news of Cassandra. Only yesterday, yet it seemed a lifetime ago.

'PC Underhay, isn't it?'

'Underwood,' came the gravelly voice, 'Maurice Underwood.' He shook Renee's hand, and she was amazed at the tenderness implicit in that handshake, 'How are you feeling?'

'Sore. My face and ribs ache like the very devil. But the doctor thinks there will be no lasting damage.

'Have they said how long you'll be here?'

'Three to four weeks, depending on the healing process.'

They settled into a silence, which seemed to Renee to be almost companionable. This amazed her since the Desk Sergeant was virtually a stranger. He was the first to break it, 'I hope Mr. Fairbrother won't object to me visiting his wife.'

'I'm a widow.'

'I'm sorry.'

'you needn't be,' she said, thinking how easy it was to talk to this guileless fellow. Must come from his police background she thought, yet Renee sensed an inherent empathy for mankind in Maurice Underwood's persona which could not have come from a training manual, 'my husband died when Lyndsey was young.'

'How is your daughter.'

'Fine,' she hedged, remembering with a shudder the confrontation that had occurred earlier, 'mightily glad to have got her kiddie back safe and sound.'

'Amen to that. What about you, Mrs. Fairbrother? Are you safe and sound?'

'You've lost me.'

'Well, the Hospital rang through to the station a second time to report that there was no crime committed. Allegedly, you'd fallen in the park.'

'That's correct.'

'So you weren't the victim of an attack?' He asked, and Renee thought she could read genuine concern in those soft brown eyes which were set into a feather bed of wrinkles. She tried to gauge his age, and decided, by the neatly brushed grey hair and weather-beaten face that he must be gone sixty.

'No,' she sighed thinking back to her ticking off from the Ward Sister 'Hurrying alongside the children's playground, I was so caught up with thoughts of my grand-daughter's homecoming that I simply didn't look where I was going. There was an uneven strip of pathway, and I'm afraid I tripped. My own fault really for choosing such ridiculous shoes for a woman of my age....' only from the vulnerability of her hospital bed could Renee make such an admission. The Ward Sister had said as much. She'd wagged a finger under the patient's nose whilst doing a blood pressure check, and said, 'tsk, tsk, Mrs. Fairbrother, I thought we were dealing with a teenager when you were brought it. All I could see was your feet dangling over the end of the trolley, encased in shoes with the most monstrous heels. It's a wonder you didn't snap an ankle, tottering along on those stilettos.'

Renee suddenly crumpled. 'I'm just a foolish old woman trying to dress like she did in her youth' Tears began to trickle down her sore and swollen face.

Maurice Underwood was on his feet in a flash, 'there, there,' he said tenderly, dabbing her cheeks with a tissue from a box brought in by Lyndsey and put on her mother's locker, 'don't cry. You're a very astute and intelligent lady by my reckoning. Not foolish at all.'

'Misguided then. Trying to stay young, appear young, dress young.... When I'm not.'

'Hush. Taking pride in one's appearance is not a crime.'

'Spoken like a true copper'

'Personally I think you are the most attractive mature lady I've seen in a long stretch.'

Another police analogy she thought, as the tears began to abate. It seemed that Maurice Underwood peppered his speech with them.

'It's very kind of you to say so,' sniffed Renee, 'but I think the Ward Sister had got it right. She told me I ought to be wearing comfy flatties on my feet and support hose, not stilettos and stockings.'

'Would you allow me to be the judge of that?'

Through the veil of drying tears, the patient looked at her visitor with new interest. Was he asking her out? She blew her nose noisily on the tissue, wincing at the pain it caused in her blackened eyes. 'I must look awful. Like a puffed up panda in a turban.'

'The fact your injuries are relatively minor is more important to me than your face appearing less glamorous. You don't mind me coming to visit you?'

'Of course not. I don't understand why, though, since there is nothing for the Police to investigate.'

Was it her imagination, thought Renee, or did he look faintly embarrassed. As though he were caught red handed in an act of charity from which he'd wished to remain anonymous. There was a lot of throat clearing, before PC Underwood replied, 'Off the record, I admit to being concerned for the wellbeing of a brave lady whom I encountered in the traumatic circumstance of a runaway child. When you sat in the Station waiting room yesterday, I thought you showed immense dignity in the face of such an agonising ordeal.'

'How kind.' Said Renee faintly. The strip light above her bed flickered, as though the tube within was about to expire. A Ward Orderly, recognisable by his green overall, bustled past and pulled down the blind behind the patient's headrest. The black night beyond the window was effectively masked. It was stultifying hot in the ward, radiators clanking under pressure from the boiler, and Renee sweated under the thin sheet. Maurice Underwood continued, 'I confess to harbouring an admiration for that elegant lady who didn't resort to weeping and wailing, but stayed composed. You are a rare breed nowadays, Mrs. Fairbrother, if I may be so presumptuous.'

'Please, call me Renee.' She found herself blushing at his impassioned speech.

'I've bought you some flowers.'

'They're lovely,' She said, thinking how inadequate the words sounded. 'There's a vase in the bedside cabinet, and the nurses' will show you where to fill it.'

Without further ado, the off duty desk sergeant pulled open the locker to remove the blue plastic vase. In so doing, he dislodged a stiletto shoe atop the pile of Renee's clothing which fell with a clatter to the floor.

'What I was wearing when they brought me in,' she explained unnecessarily. Maurice Underwood retrieved the shoe and regarded it almost lovingly. Renee had the sudden thought that he was Prince Charming handling the glass slipper, wondering at the identity of the wearer, and berated herself for such a fanciful notion. 'I must still be drugged up' she thought.

'Ah, the infamous heel.' He said, holding the shoe aloft, 'must have been a bit like wearing stilts.'

Renee saw the gentle amusement in his eyes, and laughed. He was teasing her, she thought.

'I used to wear winkle pickers and Cuban heels in my youth, but they'd play havoc nowadays with my bunions.' He was saying, and did she detect a note of regret in his voice, 'as you get older comfort becomes more important than fashion.'

Renee nodded. In a flash of self-revelation, she realised she'd been dressing younger to retain hold over her son in law, ignoring the guidelines in the book of 'Turnaround Tips' for skirt and heel lengths. It had been an almost subconscious bid to stave off the waning of her sexual allure. Well, she had learned her lesson the painful way. With cracked ribs and two ripe black eyes. From now on, Renee pledged to herself, she was going to dress more commensurate with her age.

'I'll go and get some water for these blooms.' Maurice Underwood had replaced the shoe in the locker, and stood up with the jug in one hand. He hovered by the foot of her bed before asking, 'Perhaps when you're discharged we could go for a gentle walk and maybe a pub lunch? Get you back on your feet and the circulation going.'

'Sounds wonderful, but you'd better come shopping first.'

'What for?' He was smiling at her, as if guessing her answer.

'To help me choose sensible shoes.'

Chapter Thirty Nine

THE LAUNCH PARTY was in full swing. Lyndsey stood by the laden buffet table, sipping her second flute of pink champagne, and feeling as deliciously light and airy as the bubbles. Above her head, a banner proclaimed, 'Turnaround Tips Two', and a display of the books, hot off the press, had been artfully arranged on a velvet-covered podium. Peals of laughter punctuated the air, and soft music played in the background. The food smelt appetizing, thought Lyndsey, unable to resist another glance at the array before her. Tiger prawns on a cascade of ice, assorted meats sliced wafer thin, a variety of quiches and salads, and, as the centrepiece, a formidable salmon garnished with cucumber scales. Robbie stood by her side, and together they drank in the heady atmosphere.

The Castellan Club, situated in the heart of theatre land, to the rear of Leicester Square tube was a marble and glass emporium camouflaged by a plain door leading onto the street. An hour earlier, Lyndsey had been greeted at the entrance by a liveried footman, who ticked her name off a guest list, and guided her up a gilded staircase, which made her feel more than ever like Cinderella going to the ball. The party was held in a room which seemed to occupy the entire first floor of the building, lit by crystal drop chandeliers, and serviced by waiters holding aloft trays bearing champagne and canapés. Robbie had seen her hovering uncertainly, and weaved his way through the throng. He'd been there since early afternoon, erecting a giant TV screen in one corner of the room. He kissed her lightly on the cheek, and stood back to admire her choice of dress,

'Wow Lyn, you look good enough to eat.'

'So do you', she said generously, thinking he looked slightly ill at ease in a suit and tie instead of his customary casual wear. As always, the gentle timbre of his voice made her melt.

Lyndsey had chosen a Savannah and Thalia special for the evening. A Grecian styled dress is oyster satin, the draped neckline of which cunningly concealed her flat chest. She'd slicked her hair back with gel, and ringed her eyes with kohl, which added to the faintly decadent look she were trying to achieve. That of a temptress of Ancient Rome, there, perhaps, to watch a chariot race. It was a measure of her growing self-confidence, thought Lyndsey, that not only had she travelled to the party alone, but had dressed with such style and panache. Prior to her appearance on 'Turnaround' she would never have possessed the nerve to wear such a revealing gown.

The first hour had passed in a whirlwind of introductions. Fashion aficionados mingled with executives from the publishing house, and, judging by the enthusiasm with which they greeted Lyndsey, all had admired her performance on the programme.

Amongst the throng were the Turnaround production team, and camera crew, with the notable exception of Gaynor, who had already left to take up her new post. Savannah and Thalia ambushed Lyndsey, in a bear hug of genuine affection, which she returned. They were fulsome in their praise for her appearance.

Savannah, a blonde vision, in caramel voile, said, 'Lyndsey Daly, no longer the mousy librarian of old.'

Thalia agreed, 'What a transformation. You look simply stunning sweetie.' Her dark hair gleamed under the crystal light, and her gown, studded with sequins, sparkled.

'It's all thanks to you both.'

'Nonsense,' said Savannah self-deprecatingly, 'we just bought out a beauty you already possessed, but simply had forgotten was there.'

'There's more to it than that,' said Lyndsey utterly without guile, 'my self-esteem had reached rock bottom prior to 'Turnaround'. Being chosen for the programme was the best thing that could have happened to me.'

'Aw shucks,' said Thalia, good naturedly, 'you're making us blush...'

They were interrupted by the Maître's announcing that the buffet table was officially open. Lyndsey joined the queue with Robbie, noticing some celebrities amongst their number. She saw the singer Lulu, looking sensational in a silk suit, and some cast members from her favourite soap. There was even a blonde newsreader who was making quite a name for herself as the new 'Angela Rippon', and a comedian who had her own satire show on primetime TV.

Lyndsey heaped her plate with a delicious medley of eatables, and helped herself to another champagne. After all the tension of the last few weeks, she wanted to throw caution well and truly to the winds and have a night to remember. Robbie had offered to drive her home once the party had finished, which gave her the freedom to get seriously tipsy. She knew with him she would be in safe hands.

The giant TV screen suddenly sprung into life, and her face filled it. She realised at once, that it was playing the edition of 'Turnaround' which featured herself, a clever ploy to further advertise the 'Tips Two' book to the assembled company. With the sound muted, Lyndsey watched her story unfold in a bemused wonderment. She still found it hard to believe that the wan figure in shabby togs being secretly filmed was herself. So much had changed in her life in such a short time, that she felt almost dizzy with trying to assimilate the new Lyndsey that greeted her every time she looked in the mirror.

Guests approached her, and lobbed questions.

'How did you find the filming?'

'Who put you forward?'

'Are you still friends with them?'

'What were Savannah and Thalia like to work with?'

'Did you agree with their advice?'

'Do you like your new look?'

'Do friends and family approve?'

Lyndsey answered them with truthful aplomb. Unused to such a high level of attention, especially from strangers, she became both bewildered and beguiled. Fame was addictive, she thought, realising what a delicious fillip it gave to one's self-confidence to know that people she had never met before, were interested in her life.

A selection of desserts was placed on the table. Robbie brought her a requested portion of hazelnut meringue embedded in a nest of cream. He had chosen lemon mousse.

'Enjoying yourself hen?'

'Oh, Rob, so much. It's a truly divine evening.'

The one discordant note, she thought, was the sight earlier of the actor Charles Dance amongst the partygoers. At least she supposed it to be him, and a momentary sadness constricted her heart. People had often told her how much Ray bore a resemblance to this star of stage and screen, and the thought of her husband, now residing across the Atlantic, was a subduing one. As she scooped up the last of the meringue with silver tipped spoon, Lyndsey acknowledged to herself that part of her still loved the roguish Mr. Daly, and always would.

'Good, you've finished that pud,' Robbie's voice cut into her thoughts, 'I want to whisk you around the dance floor again.'

Three breathless jives later, Lyndsey pleaded fatigue and took herself off to the Ladies to touch up her make-up. Outside, in the cool corridor, she bumped into Thalia who was conversing with a group from the Publishing House.

'Lyn, hang on a minute,' she called out as Lyndsey edged past, 'I'd like a word in private.'

The trio of executives rejoined the party in the main room, and Thalia drew Lyndsey to a quiet corner, where a Georgian sash window overlooked a darkened courtyard.

'How's your poor mum? Robbie told me and Savvy about her accident.'

'She's fine thanks. A bit shaken up and bruised.'

Gee thanks Rob, thought Lyndsey, feeling a spurt of annoyance with him for betraying news of Renee's fall. She hoped that no-one on Turnaround knew the extent of her relationship with the cameraman beyond that of a growing friendship, and Thalia's next words eased her mind,

'Don't worry, he wasn't blabbing about your private life, just putting us in the picture, so to speak.'

'I'm sorry, I don't understand...'

'Savannah and I have discussed it. We want to offer you Gaynor's job, as researcher on the 'Turnaround' team'

'Gaynor's job...?'

'Vince Levene has already had the contract drawn up. If you accept, you can sign it tonight, and officially become part of our crew.'

Thalia went on to briefly outline the terms and conditions, and the proposed salary. It was triple her library wage, and Lyndsey felt her legs buckle. A combination of the effects of champagne and shock at this unexpected offer. She propped herself on the wide ledge of the windowsill and gazed up into Thalia Emmerson's earnest face.

At that moment, Savannah Hooper Greenhill swung out of the Ladies toilet, hair immaculately brushed and lipstick newly applied.

'Hey, what are you two plotting?' She said with a smile.

'Ssh, Savvy not so loud. I'm trying to persuade Lyn to step into Gaynor's shoes.'

'Lyndsey, please join us. Thals and I have had to pull such strings behind the scenes to get you on board. You simply can't let us down, darling.'

'I don't know what to say...'

'Say yes, Lyn. It's a wonderful job, and we know you'll fit in well. Everybody on 'Turnaround' loves you, including me and Savvy, and with your librarian training, research will prove a doddle. We put forward your name to 'the-powers-that-be', but it was Robbie who sowed the seed. He said that with hubbie gone and divorce definitely on the cards, you might need the extra income.'

She couldn't be cross with him, Lyndsey thought, silently blessing Robert McCrae. He had obviously been working behind the scenes to make her need of a more lucrative job a reality. Her part time wage at the library would not stretch far, especially with Renee about to leave hospital and move in. But therein lay the problem,

'I'd love to accept, but simply cannot. Mum is going to need looking after whilst she recuperates, and there is Cass to consider.'

A group of partygoers, a little rowdy now the evening was almost over, tumbled into the corridor. Thalia waited for them to disappear into the Gents before continuing, 'Don't worry, we've taken all that on board. We can give you six months sabbatical, until work begins on series 3 of the show. Plenty of time to get mum back on her feet, and she'll be there to take care of Cassandra on the odd occasions when the team works late'.

'Besides which,' added Savannah, 'a lot of preliminary stuff can be done from home, so we can set you up with a laptop.'

Lyndsey knew she'd love the job. From almost the first time she'd met Gaynor, she'd harbored a sneaking envy about the other's mode of employment. How exciting to be working in the glamorous world of television.

'OK ladies you win,' she said, unable to prevent a grin spreading across her face, 'you've got yourselves a new researcher.'

'Great,' enthused Thalia. Savannah said, 'let's re-join the party and break the good news to the team.'

Entering the room, where coffee was now being served, Lyndsey found Robbie hovering by a marbled pillar. Seeing her with the two presenters, he put his head on one side and adopted an expression of feigned insouciance. He knows full well what we've been discussing, and is bursting to hear my decision, thought Lyndsey with a flood of warmth for the gentle Scot.

She couldn't wait to tell him.

Epilogue

'HERE WE HAVE Mozart', said Cassandra proudly, 'wearing his very own coat of many colours.'

She paraded the dog around the lounge with the serious deportment of an exhibitor at Crufts. Primed in advance by Lyndsey, the audience clapped and whistled their appreciation.

Maurice Underwood, Dee, Coral, Lyndsey and Robbie were grouped on sofas with the guest of honour occupying the single armchair. Renee had been discharged from Southfield General that afternoon. In honour of her homecoming, Lyndsey had arranged an impromptu gathering.

Cassandra made the Alsatian sit by her grandmother.

'Give Nana Reen your paw.' She instructed solemnly. The shaggy beast, ever anxious to do the bidding of his young friend, raised a heavy paw and placed it on Renee's knee. He was rewarded by a tentative pat to the head.

'He looks a picture,' Lyndsey said, and there were murmurs of agreement. The German Shepherd did indeed look a handsome specimen. Cassandra had brushed the shaggy black and tan fur until it gleamed, and the coat with matching collar and lead, fashioned out of suede patchwork and studded with fake diamonds, was the finishing touch to this canine glamour extravaganza. It had arrived that morning in a parcel from the Big Apple. Cassie had unwrapped it, eyes shining with excitement,

'Daddy is the greatest,' she'd said over the breakfast table, causing Robbie and Lyndsey to exchange a smile of relief. The frost between father and daughter was thawing rapidly, thanks to Raymond Daly's constant barrage of canine themed gifts. There'd been food bowls shaped like giant bones from Macy's, engraved grooming kits from Fifth Avenue, and any number of doggy gastronomic treats from the deli's.

Cassie read the accompanying letter aloud, stumbling a little on the difficult words through mouthfuls of toast, 'looking forward to the weekend. I'm off on a fishing trip to New England with the Vice President in her Winni – Winibeg...'

'Winnebago' Robbie finished for her, 'An American camper van.'

'Talking of camping,' said Lyndsey, stirring her porridge with a spoon (made by Robbie with extra lashings of cream) 'there's another postcard from the Cliffords in the mail.' The owners of Mozart were spending a month under canvas in the Lake District, and as promised had left the dog in Cassandra's care. Lyndsey passed the card around the table. It showed an artist's impression of the water fowl of Windermere.

Casually, she reminded, 'Nana is coming out of Hospital today. I thought we could have a homecoming celebration. Any suggestions?'

'Why not invite everyone round, Mummy. Show the video of you on 'Turnaround'. We could have a proper cinema screening like at the pictures, with popcorn and stuff.'

Now the event was fully underway. Mozart, divested of his fancy coat and collar, had padded from the room. Cassie, in charge of the dvd player, was making sure the assembled company had her full attention.

'Quiet everybody, please.' She said, importantly, 'Mummy is about to appear on television.'

As the opening credits to 'Turnaround' rolled, Lyndsey's face filled the screen.

'..today we meet part time librarian Lyndsey Daly from North London' It made the star of the show smile to think how many times she'd heard that intro over the past six weeks.'

'Soon to be ex-librarian' chortled Dee and Coral in unison, with no hint of censure in their voices. They'd been genuinely delighted for Lyndsey on news of her appointment as a Channel 7 researcher, and had brushed aside her obvious regret at leaving their workplace.

'Don't be daft Lyn', Coral had said, 'it's an opportunity in a million, and we can still get together at weekends.'

Dee had concurred, 'We'd take it like a shot if the job were offered to us.'

Renee's face beamed with pleasure. She was home amongst friends and family, and once again watching her beloved daughter's triumph on the makeover programme. The cuts had healed, the black eyes faded. Only the scars on her head remained, concealed by a fetching turban in lemon watered silk. It kept her scalp blissfully cool in the May evening warmth.

Robbie had opened a bumper bottle of Buck's Fizz and poured everyone a glass. Even Cassandra was permitted a sip. He called for silence, and raised a toast, 'Here's to Mrs. Fairbrother. Welcome home.'

'So formal dear. Call me Renee.'

'And to Lyndsey. Channel 7's newest recruit.'

This was greeted by impromptu applause.

Lyndsey said, 'I'd like to say a word of thanks to Coral and Dee. It was them that got me on the programme, and I can truly say my life has changed for the better as a result.'

Her two friends blushed.

'We mustn't forget dear Maurice,' said Renee, turning to the man who sat so protectively at her side, 'he's been an absolute brick to me.'

There was no false modesty from the genial desk sergeant, as he stood up and did a theatrical bow. Lyndsey approved of the kindly man who was so obviously smitten with her mother, and she with him. His caring solicitude was just what Renee needed to aid her recovery, both physically, and emotionally, she thought with a grateful smile towards Maurice Underwood.

Lyndsey passed around a dish of olives as Savannah Hooper Greenhill and Thalia Emmerson appeared on screen, 'there's cold roast beef and salad to follow. Then we can have Cassie's popcorn. She's made it herself in the microwave.'

The door to the lounge was pushed open, and Mozart sidled guiltily through the gap. Cassandra was sitting cross legged on a pouffe. He stretched out at her feet and gave a sigh of contentment.

Coral, her tongue oiled by her second glass of Buck's Fizz said, 'Lyndsey, you have new clothes, new hair, new look, new job. Maybe a new love to complete the set …?'

All heads swivelled to Robbie. He winked at Lyndsey. She winked back. This provoked knowing smiles from all in the room. When everyone's attention had returned to the programme, she telegraphed an unspoken message to him with her eyes. It said, 'I'm glad I met you.'

He responded with the same look.

Cassandra paused the disc and announced she needed to salt the popcorn. The dog lay on the floor, suspiciously replete. She was soon back from the kitchen,

'Mummy, I think Mozart has a confession to make'

At the mention of his name, the German Shepherd jumped up and began to spin around in circles chasing his tail. It was the newest trick he'd been taught.

'He's eaten the roast beef.'

This admission provoked peals of laughter.

'Cue for another toast,' said Robbie, removing the cork from a fresh bottle. It popped like a shotgun, 'to Mozart. The 'Turnaround' dog...'

THE END

About the Author

SANDIE TRAVELLER IS a true Essex girl having lived in the County all her life. Born into a large family, she has four siblings; two elder sisters living nearby, and a younger brother and sister living out of the area. A divorcee with two grown up children, Sandie enjoys spending time with family and friends. Her hobbies include the theatre, local history, and anything to do with the Victorian era, and she can often be found at Battlesbridge Antique Centre hunting for items of interest, which she says is 'one of my favourite pastimes.' When she needs to escape and get "far from the madding crowd", Sandie retreats to her beach hut on the Thames estuary where she reads, writes, and paints in blissful seclusion.

A creative writing tutor for many years, "Turnaround" is Sandie's first published novel. Having served her apprenticeship as a successful author of short fiction, which has seen many of her short stories appear in magazines such *Woman's Own, Bella, Take-a-Break, and Best,* she then found acclaim as finalist and first runner up in the *Woman's Own* national short story competition two years running, and has since won many other short story awards.

Sandie shares her Victorian home on the Essex coast with her daughter, dog, and collection of antique rocking horses. Of her life she says *"it's a madcap journey where no two days are ever the same"* Now, having taken early retirement from her career as Tutor and Administrator with a London Borough College, Sandie says she relishes the prospect of more free time in which to write.... and dream.....

Autumn/Winter 2014

Printed in Great Britain
by Amazon

21179580R00233